MIND
SWEEPER

— · —

MIND SWEEPER 1

AE JONES

GABBY READS PUBLISHING

MIND SWEEEPER AE JONES

Copyright © 2014 by Amy E Jones

Publisher: Gabby Reads Publishing LLC

Cover Art: http://theillustratedauthor.net/

Editor: http://www.demonfordetails.com/

PRINT

ISBN-13: 978-1-941871-00-3

Mom –

You instilled your love of reading in me. And you told me every day growing up that I could do anything I set out to do, as long as I was willing to work hard.

Know that this book and every one I write going forward will always be for you.

I miss you.

CHAPTER 1

An angel, a demon, and a vampire walked into a bar. No seriously, they did. And all hell broke loose. Then I got called in, or rather the team got called in, to handle supernatural damage control. My job was to manipulate people's memories. Don't ask me how. I was born with it, and, like someone born with double joints or the ability to flip their eyelids inside out, I just do it and hopefully not flip out too many people in the process.

On this particular night, I was destined to spend the evening in a bar with no chance of getting lucky. Dead bodies tended to put a damper on romance.

Not that I was dressed to attract men—my jeans, graphic tee and black work boots didn't exactly fit in with the skimpy dresses and three-inch heels worn by the other women in the bar. But then I had missed the class about fitting in, so this was nothing new.

I held open the door, and the muggy Cleveland night invaded the air-conditioned bar, steaming up the door window. Pasting on a flight-attendant smile, I barely restrained myself from muttering "buh-bye" as the witnesses filed out calmly. Calmly, because I had spent the past twenty minutes implanting them with new memories.

Instead of a demon and a vamp facing off, their recollections featured a brawl between a biker and a drunken fraternity boy. Crisis averted. Now the rest of the team could get to work.

Jean Luc peeled the tablecloth off the corpse he'd stuffed in the corner during my bit with the patrons. Even though moving the body had meant disturbing evidence, we couldn't very well keep a dead vamp—especially a *headless* dead vamp—lying around when minds had to be scrubbed and altered to believe nothing out of the ordinary had happened. Humans don't do well with *different*. So our team's job? Clean up the mess.

I studied our potential publicity nightmare—the headless body in a rumpled suit. Dead vamps always surprised me. Every movie I'd ever seen showed the vamp disintegrating. Stab him in the heart, instant ash cloud. Chop off his head, get out the dust vac. It wasn't until I met Jean Luc that I learned those movies were bunk. And since he'd been a vampire for the past four hundred years, he was the foremost authority in my book.

"What do you think happened?" I asked.

Jean Luc grinned slowly. "Well, Kyle, I would say he was decapitated."

I frowned at him. "Thanks, Dr. Obvious. I meant why the supernatural smackdown in the middle of the happy hour and hot-wings crowd?"

He shook his head. "Supernaturals are not normally this careless. There must be a compelling reason why this happened when it did."

"Have you ever seen an angel before?"

"Yes, but never one that revealed himself to humans this blatantly. Nicholas will be watching us closely until we figure this out."

I bristled. "Nicholas can chill. If he's worried we're not doing our jobs, he can come here and supervise us himself. Did you find the vamp's head?"

"No."

I didn't want to think about why someone would take it. "Where's Misha?"

"Talking to our supernatural witness in the back room."

Since the place had been busy, odds were good at least one supe would be in the crowd, and we had hit pay dirt. There'd been a shifter working as a bartender.

"Hopefully we can get a credible story from him."

I walked through the kitchen door. It was quarter-wing night and the sweet-smoky smell of barbeque sauce hit my nose. My stomach growled like a pissed-off Haltrap demon. Definitely a crime scene faux pas, perusing a dead body one second and drooling over mesquite the next.

I hurried through the kitchen and into the storage area. Misha glanced up when I pushed open the door and then turned back to the bartender, who was fidgeting nervously in a chair.

The pencil-thin shifter bounced his leg so hard his teeth were chattering. He pushed his dark hair off his forehead in a jerky motion which made me wonder what type of animal he could change into—a monkey? One of those yappy little Chihuahuas? Of course, having Misha breathing down his neck didn't help matters.

Six-foot-six and two hundred and fifty pounds of pure muscle, Misha looked like a Browns linebacker. With short, blond hair and ice-blue eyes, he was intimidating when he smiled and terrifying when he scowled. The little guy didn't stand a chance. I stayed close to the door, not wanting to interrupt the interrogation.

Misha's bass voice, laced with a thick Russian accent, rippled across the room. "So what happened?"

"The vampire came into the bar first and was acting weird."

"How?" Misha scrubbed his perpetual five o'clock shadow.

"You know vamps, normally nothing fazes them. This guy was actually nervous. He kept looking over his shoulder. Even asked me if there was a back way out. Then the demon came ripping through the front door, and the vamp took off at a dead run."

"What kind of demon was it?"

The shifter paused for a second before answering. "He wasn't a Shamat like you."

Misha stiffened. He did a good job of suppressing his demon side when he was out in public, but a shifter's nose could sniff out anything. "Then what kind was he?"

"I couldn't get a good whiff of him at first. It wasn't until later, when the angel got here, that he transitioned into his demon form—purple skin and yellow eyes. Then I knew he was a Pavel."

I gasped like a little girl. I couldn't help myself. Demons didn't show their true selves in public, ever. And a Pavel demon? Even by supe standards they were badasses.

Misha scowled at me before returning to his questions. "What happened before the angel arrived?"

"The demon tackled the vamp. The vamp bared his fangs and sank them into the demon's arm and the normals wigged out. After a couple more seconds, the room started to vibrate. My hair stood on end and all the humans froze. That's when the angel appeared. Then it got *really* weird."

Misha's gaze held mine for a second. His left eyebrow rose as if saying *How in the hell could it get any weirder?* He composed his face. "Go on."

"Like I said, the angel showed up, and the demon changed and stood between the angel and the vamp like he was protecting him."

Misha frowned. "So you're telling me the demon, who had just been fighting the vampire, was now protecting him from the angel?"

The shifter shrugged. "Hey, I know what it sounds like. I'm just telling you what I saw. The angel and demon circled each other. At first they seemed pretty well matched, until the angel pulled out a sword. The vamp tried to make a run for it, but before he got to the door he was dead." The shifter gulped and fidgeted in his seat again.

Misha prompted him to explain. "Who killed him?"

"The angel."

I stepped forward, interrupting. "What?!"

"You heard me." He glanced up toward the ceiling, his voice lowering to a frantic whisper. "The angel killed him."

Misha continued unperturbed. "What happened to the demon and the head?"

"The demon ran out the back door, and the angel followed him. I don't know what the hell happened to the vamp's head."

I stood still, even though my nerves were firing off warnings to find the nearest exit. An angel decapitated a vamp... What the hell was going on? Angels rarely showed themselves, and an angel killing another supe in front of witnesses was unheard of.

The shifter gaped as if seeing me for the first time. His nose wrinkled for a second as he tried to sniff out what I was. After another second, his eyes widened.

"You're that freaky human with powers. The Mind Sweeper. Kyle something...Kyle McKinley, right? You need to scrub my brain. Now!"

My fists clenched. You'd think I would have gotten used to being called a freak, but each time was like another dose of salt in a festering wound. "Why should I?"

"How long do you think I'll live after what I saw? If you scrub my brain,"—he looked up at the ceiling again—"they'll know I can't remember and leave me alone. Please."

"You don't know anything else?" Misha interrupted.

"I swear. I told you everything."

Misha nodded and I stepped forward cautiously. The shifter was skittish as a colt, so I placed my hand on his damp shoulder and pushed calming thoughts toward him. Scrubbing supes was not easy. Some didn't respond to me. I closed my eyes.

I pictured the fight he'd described and changed it in my mind. I replaced the vamp's image with a drunken fraternity boy. The glowing-eyed demon morphed into a leather-clad biker and the angel turned into a cop. Warmth prickled along my forehead and I reached mentally for his consciousness, easing the new images into his agitated kaleidoscope of a brain.

His shifter senses resisted my intrusion, so I backed off, leaving the new memories hanging in the ether between us. After a couple of seconds, his brain calmed down, and the energies swirled in a fixed pattern instead of bouncing around haphazardly. I tried merging with him again. A yellow haze burned my eyes, and for the briefest of moments I lost myself in the connection. Almost as quickly, I severed the link, my thoughts snapping back into my brain like a taut rubber band. My vision cleared and the shifter's scared expression relaxed. The transfer of new memories was complete.

Misha and I walked out of the room toward the front of the bar. Both Jean Luc and the body were gone, but I wouldn't have to worry about erasing anyone else's memories. Jean Luc would have avoided witnesses by using his vampire speed to load the body into the van. Misha strolled out the front of the bar and opened the van door. "Jean Luc's not here."

I went in search of him behind the building. Jean Luc stood in the middle of the alley with his arms outstretched and his head thrown back, concentrating. Not a muscle twitched. I held my breath, hoping my presence didn't disturb him, and watched him silently.

Normally, I wouldn't have used the word beautiful to describe a male, but in Jean Luc's case it was more than appropriate. With his dark brown eyes and long, black hair tied back with a leather strap, he reminded me of a sexy pirate with fangs. Women had a tendency to drive their cars off the road when they saw him on the sidewalk. Somehow I'd managed to avoid succumbing to his charms.

After a few moments, he dropped his arms. "I do not sense anything. They did not continue the fight here."

I rolled my eyes. "Jean Luc, you've been speaking English for over a century. Don't you think it's time to embrace contractions? What about a slang word here or there?"

His eyes narrowed. "When *you* learn the seven languages I speak, I will consider it."

I bowed. "*Touché*."

We spent a few more minutes checking the alley to make sure no evidence was left behind. I didn't expect to find the angel's bloody sword thrown in the dumpster, but it pays to be thorough. When we returned to our van, we found Misha sitting in the back scanning surveillance equipment worthy of the FBI.

"I just did a sweep. There've been no other reports in the city."

Who would have thought Cleveland, Ohio, would be a hotbed of supes? Maybe the lake attracted them, or the Rock & Roll Hall of Fame. Either way, it kept us hopping.

Jean Luc chose to drive, as always, and pulled away from the curb, or rather screeched away. He drove like a vamp possessed, but his reflexes hadn't failed him in four hundred years, which I constantly reminded myself about every time he took a corner too fast.

Misha smirked at me as if reading my thoughts. He could be a smug bastard.

Frustration bubbled to the surface and burst from my mouth. "What are you grinning about? All hell's breaking loose."

"Really, little one, you can be terribly melodramatic," Misha answered in a condescending tone, which didn't sit well with me.

"Excuse me? You don't find it somewhat ominous that an angel descended from heaven and killed a vampire in front of human witnesses?"

"You've been sucked into the hype, my dear. Angels are not babies with wings. They've been alive for millennia. For every artistic rendering of fat cherubs, there are just as many angels depicted with swords. Many are soldiers."

I needed some backup. "Jean Luc?"

"Misha is right. Angels are soldiers, and soldiers do what they are ordered to do."

My mouth opened like a fish chasing a worm. "You don't think"—I poked my finger toward the roof of the van—"*He* ordered the vamp killed?"

Jean Luc shook his head. "Not directly. Remember, heaven is a hierarchy. Someone lower probably ordered it."

"Holy crap," I responded, wiping my sweaty palms on my jeans.

"Stop worrying, *ma cherie*, we will figure it out."

I must have looked pretty close to losing it for Jean Luc to pull out the French. He thought it helped calm me down when I was about to lose it.

It wasn't working.

CHAPTER 2

Seven a.m. and I inhaled my third cup of strong black coffee, hoping the caffeine overload would keep me awake. After we left the bar, and Jean Luc had dropped me off at home, sleep had been out of the question.

I wasn't surprised when I got the call to come in ASAP for a briefing. I ran my fingers through my straight, chin-length, currently black hair and pulled on a pair of black pants, a gray short-sleeve T-shirt and a vest. I gravitated to black and gray clothes, since they matched my gray eyes and, more importantly, always went with whatever color I decided to dye my hair. Black was really beneath my creativity level, but I didn't need to call attention to myself for the time being. This case was a potential ticking time bomb. I had never even seen an angel before, let alone a sword-wielding one.

While running last night's events through my sleep-deprived brain, I tripped over Booger, my cat. I liked to believe he followed me around because of his undying love for me, but after briefly circling my legs, he proceeded to stand by his empty food dish and glare. At least I knew where I stood with him. No need to worry about an ulterior motive, anyway. Opening his food bin, I groaned out loud. It was empty. *Damn.* I rummaged through the cupboards for a substitute and pulled out two cans. I held them up in front of him.

"Tuna?"

He stared at me indignantly.

"Chicken?"

He circled my legs again and meowed, leaving a trail of hair behind. "Okay, chicken it is. I'll stop at the grocery store tonight before I come home, I promise."

He gave me the *I've-heard-that-one-before* look.

"Be good today." I maneuvered around the couch to the window and pushed it up just enough for him to get onto the fire escape. Locating my keys and phone, I locked up, ran down the stairs, opened the apartment building door, and scanned the street for my car.

I was glad to call Little Italy home, with its wonderful, close-knit neighborhood and turn-of-the-century brick buildings, but parking was impossible, especially with my odd hours. Just before I resorted to clicking my key fob like a loser to locate my car, I spotted it across the street. I jumped in and took off, grateful I at least hadn't had to spend ten minutes scraping snow off my car. The joy of August in Cleveland.

Normally, my morning routine included buying Italian pastries for Misha, but I didn't want to be late. Depending on traffic, it could take fifteen to thirty minutes to drive downtown to work. Our office was on the third floor of the Smithson Building. Our cover story was that we were a detective agency, which wasn't too far from the truth. We did investigate happenings and solve crimes; they just weren't your garden-variety adulterers or deadbeat dads. We worked for the Bureau of Supernatural Relations or BSR for short. Most of the time we were called the Supe Squad, which was a bit too Scooby Doo for my taste, but the name had stuck.

When I stepped into the office reception area, it was empty. I glanced at my watch. Dolly wouldn't be in for another half hour, which meant the coffee, if there was any, had been made by Misha, or, God forbid, Jean Luc. Why he insisted on making coffee when he couldn't drink it was beyond me.

The door to the back office sat open and I sauntered through. While the front reception area was reminiscent of a Mickey Spillane novel, with its beige walls, dark wood moldings and a beat-up wooden desk, the main back office area had been upgraded to the seventies.

There was a seating area and an almond-colored faux wood table we gathered around for meetings. At one point there had been a mustard yellow refrigerator I finally put out of commission with a fork that "accidentally" lodged itself into the back cooling unit. No one should have to store food in something the color of baby poop.

Even though the office reminded me of a bad acid flashback, it was more of a home than any I'd had growing up. Which was a pathetically sad statement, but true nonetheless.

Misha was parked on the lime green sofa eating a breakfast sandwich. Between bites he mumbled, "No cannoli?"

"Not today."

Misha was an amazing eating machine. Apparently his demon metabolism pretty much let him eat anything. And even though intimidation radiated from him, in reality he was a teddy bear. The irony was, his name in Russian actually meant "little bear." When I first started working with him, I gained fifteen pounds trying to keep up. Now I just sat back and watched him eat.

"Where's Jean Luc?"

"He'll be here in a few minutes. Get some coffee."

I hesitated. "Who made it?"

Misha grinned. "I did."

Taking my mug off the hook, I poured a cup and liberally doused it with cream, then sat down next to him. He finished the last of his sandwich, crumpling the paper wrapper.

"While we wait," he said, "have you heard anything interesting about the new TV season? What shows should I be watching?"

I rolled my eyes. Misha swore the best thing that had happened to him in his two hundred and sixty-year life was the invention of television. If it had been on TV at any time in the last fifty years, he had watched it. Hell, he had memorized it, since he had a photographic memory. This worked very well for the job, but not so well during stakeouts, especially when he quoted entire episodes of *The Brady Bunch*. All except the ones with Oliver. He hated those episodes.

"I haven't heard anything yet." I sipped the coffee, reminding myself to add cream to my grocery list. After another minute, I bounced my foot with impatience. "What is taking Jean Luc so long? I thought we had a briefing with Nicholas."

"He went to get the new guy."

I glared at him. "What new guy?" You wouldn't think it would be possible to frazzle a high-level demon, so his scared-rabbit gaze would have been amusing if I wasn't starting to see red. "What the hell are you talking about?"

"Um... Nicholas said he was assigning a new guy to the team. I thought he told you."

"Obviously not. So, what is he?"

He refused to meet my eyes. This couldn't be good. "Misha?"

"He isn't a supe."

My stomach dropped like I was on a roller coaster at Cedar Point. *No, no, no.* "Please tell me Nicholas is not assigning a normal to the team again. After what happened last time, why would he risk it?"

Our last normal teammate, Steve, had been a disaster. Soon as he realized Jean Luc was a vampire, he started wearing garlic necklaces and declared me a "traitor to humanity." I'd thought his pronouncement was over the top until he tried to stab Jean Luc with a wooden stake. Another myth. Stakes won't kill vamps, although I learned they hurt like the devil. Misha had to hold Jean Luc down while I pulled it out. Needless to say, good ol' Steve was not back the next day.

Before I could continue my trip down memory lane, the monitor beeped. Time for our briefing. Misha turned on the screen and Nicholas's face appeared. He was ridiculously handsome, which I'm sure helped him get his way in most things. He reminded me of Cary Grant from the classic movies Misha made me watch.

"Misha, Kyle, good morning. Where is Jean Luc?"

"*Apparently*, he's gone to pick up our newest team member," I answered.

Nicholas sighed. "Even from you I don't expect such hostility this early in the morning."

"Why am I the last to know about this?"

"This is not a conspiracy, Kyle. The decision was made overnight. Until we have a better idea of what's going on, it would make sense to have a human on the team to run interference."

"What am I exactly?" I asked flippantly, even though I was feeling anything but.

"I meant no disrespect. But you are not the most diplomatic person."

"That's a load of bull!"

Misha snorted next to me.

I huffed. "Point taken. So who is this guy?"

"He's a Cleveland police officer who is the department's media liaison. He should be perfect for the job."

"What happens when he sees his first demon? Or a rogue shifter tries to eviscerate him?"

"He'll do fine," Nicholas replied.

"You said the same thing about Steve, and I ended up spending an hour pulling splinters out of a very pissed-off vampire."

Nicholas smirked. "If you're so worried about it, I'll put you in charge of making sure our newest member falls in line. Do you think you can handle him?"

"Oh yeah, I can handle him."

Misha shot me a nervous glance and Nicholas got down to business. "Misha, give me your take on the scene last night and your interview with the shifter."

I sat there half listening and had the strangest thought. We were the supernatural version of Charlie's Angels. The original TV show of course, since I agreed with Misha that it was better than the movies. I was Kate Jackson's character. She was spunky and the true brains of the group. Jean Luc was definitely Farrah Fawcett, which would make Misha Jacqueline Smith. Nicholas was Charlie. God, I had really been spending too much time with Misha and his TV addiction. That or I had finally OD'd on caffeine.

Nicholas interrupted my tripped-out thoughts. "Do you have anything to add regarding the interview, Kyle?"

"No, as usual, Mr. Photographic Memory here didn't miss a beat."

"Contact me again when you have more information."

Nodding, Misha logged off. The door opened behind us and I turned. Jean Luc stepped into the room, alone.

"Where's the new guy?" I blurted.

He angled his head toward the door. "In the reception area with Dolly."

"Did you check him for wood?"

"Very funny."

"Does he know what you are?"

"No."

I smiled. "Please, let me tell him."

"I am not sure that is a good idea," Jean Luc said.

"Nicholas put me in charge of him," I countered.

Misha confirmed my statement by nodding. Jean Luc shrugged and stepped aside. I started for the door, then stopped.

Misha scowled. "What's wrong?"

"Nothing. Jean Luc, please tell him I'll be out in a bit to give him his orientation. That will give Dolly a couple of minutes to *welcome* him."

If Dolly's picture appeared in the dictionary it would be next to the words gorgeous, tall, blonde, and sleek. But beneath that beauty beat the heart of a barracuda when it came to overseeing the front desk. I had actually seen Dolly make school children peddling candy bars cry. So I was more than a little surprised when I finally opened the door and found new guy perched on her desk. Their heads were close together and she was giggling. Actually giggling like a tweener.

I took a long gander at the man. Not sure what I'd expected to see. The stereotypical cop who had eaten one too many donuts? I mean, a cop who sat behind a desk all day couldn't be in very good shape, right? Wrong.

I highly doubted his lean body had ever been exposed to processed sugar...or saturated fat, for that matter. He was wearing khakis and a blue polo shirt that accentuated his muscles. I studied his profile and decided he wasn't too bad looking. Dark brown hair and a strong nose. What exactly was the big deal?

Then he turned toward me and I knew immediately what had reduced Dolly to a pile of Jell-O. His eyes were the most gorgeous blue I had ever seen. They were almost turquoise—practically iridescent. *Good God.*

I rearranged my face into its normal petulant position. "Come with me."

He didn't flinch. "Nice to meet you, Dolly. I'll give you the recipe later."

I had already started to walk away and faltered when he spoke. His voice was a gorgeous, deep tone that vibrated down my spinal column and spilled over me like liquid sex. It was official. It had been way too long since I had been *involved* with anyone. I needed to take care of that soon. But first I had to get rid of the new guy.

I hatched my plan quickly. Scaring the crap out of him was the best way to move him along and demonstrate to Nicholas the team was fine the way it was. I was the only human needed.

I walked the new guy down the hall into my cluttered office. Paperwork was not my friend. Pointing to the visitor's chair, I plopped down in mine behind the desk.

He smiled but then his eyebrows drew together in confusion.

"Is something wrong?" I asked.

"No. Jean Luc mentioned I would be meeting with Kyle McKinley. Are you his assistant?"

Wow, in one sentence *Mr.-Blue-Eyes-Liquid-Sex* had managed to turn me off. I wasn't going to succumb to his charms after all. "I'm Kyle."

"Sorry. Honest mistake."

"Not really. While we're at it, I'm going to do you a favor. Whatever you do, don't make fun of Jean Luc's name—or Misha's, for that matter." I didn't volunteer that the only time Jean Luc had ever gotten mad at me was when we had first met and I had called him Captain Picard. I hadn't been able to help myself. I had never met a Jean Luc in real life. After I apologized and his fangs retracted, we became good friends.

"Do you have to have an unusual name to work here?"

"No."

"Good."

"So let me guess, your name is John Smith?"

He smiled at me. "Joe Dalton. You can call me Joe."

Clearing my throat, I drummed my fingers on the cool metal desk and stared at him. Where to begin? "Dalton, do you know why you've been assigned to work with us?"

"I was told by the captain your group is working on a case that could cause some bad press for the city. He didn't give me any specific details. Just said it could be volatile."

Which was an understatement. Captain Morrison was one of the few people the BSR told about the supernatural events we covered up. But there was only so much we could hide before people became suspicious, so Morrison ran interference for us when necessary.

"Yeah, I would say we have a volatile situation in the making. Do you know what our company does?"

"Only from my research online and from asking some of the other cops if they have ever worked with you before. You're a detective agency, but your site is somewhat vague about the types of cases you handle."

I'd give him a point for doing his homework. "We're very selective about our clients. We've even helped the police department on occasion."

He pulled his chair closer to the desk, scraping the wood floor. "Then why am I here, Kyle?"

"Last night, we responded to a call at the Erie Bar."

He nodded. "I review the call sheets after each shift. The report stated there was a fight at the bar, but by the time the squad car responded the bouncers had taken care of it."

"It's what we want the public to believe."

"What really happened?"

It was time to put *Operation Freak-Out* into play. "There was a murder at the bar last night."

"And who exactly was killed?"

"Not who, *what*. A vampire was decapitated."

"A vampire?" His eyes narrowed in disbelief, and I hadn't even gotten to the good stuff yet.

"Yeah. According to our witness, the vamp came running into the bar followed closely by a Pavel demon, and they started to fight."

He sat up straighter. "Let me see if I have this right. You're telling me a real vampire...and a what?"

"Pavel demon."

"A real vampire and a Pavel demon got in a fight at one of the most popular bars in the city and no one reported it?"

"That's exactly what I'm telling you."

"How is that even possible?"

I had to hand it to him; he hadn't a) called me crazy, b) run from the room, or c) wet his pants. Yet. "I know this is hard to believe, but there are really things that go bump in the night. They exist. Vampires, demons, shifters, they're all real."

He waved his hand dismissively. "No, I know about the supernatural. What I'm asking is how did you cover it up?"

I stared at him. Well, dang. Didn't that just sink my battleship? "How do you know about supes?"

"Who do you think helps Captain Morrison come up with cover stories when something supernatural occurs? After one too many incidents, I asked enough questions to make the captain nervous. He filled me in on what he knows."

I scowled. "Who else has he been talking to about us?"

"No one I know of. I know about the supes, as you call them, but he didn't tell me about your agency, or what you do. Which brings me back to the question of how you covered up the murder?"

"I'm a Mind Sweeper."

"Isn't that a game on your computer with the grid and little bombs?"

"That's Minesweeper. I'm a Min-duh Sweeper." Okay, it was a good thing he was cute, since he was not Mensa material. "I have the ability to wipe people's memories and replace them with new ones."

"Are you human?"

Wasn't that the question of the century? He didn't waste any time getting right to the point. "I'm human, but for some reason I've been given this ability."

And I waited for *the look*. The one I always got when someone realized I wasn't "normal." It was similar to the look you get from people when you have a giant pimple on your forehead and they try not to stare at it, which makes the situation even more awkward.

Surprisingly, he kept looking me straight in the eye and didn't appear fazed by my announcement. "What about your teammates. What are they?"

I released the breath I had been holding. "Jean Luc is a vampire and Misha's a Shamat demon."

He paused before continuing, "Does Dolly know about you?"

I laughed. "Oh, yeah. Dolly's a shifter. She can sniff out supernatural a mile away. That's why she works the front desk. She screens the clients and dissuades norms from trying to hire us."

"Norms?"

"Sorry, short for normals or humans."

"Well...okay." He leaned back from the desk and took a deep breath. "So you were at the bar and wiped everyone's memories so they don't remember seeing a demon kill a vampire?"

"Yep. Except it wasn't a demon that killed the vampire. It was an angel."

He stood up. "Excuse me. Did you just say an angel killed him? How?"

"He pulled out a sword and whacked his head off."

He paled, making his turquoise eyes stand out even more. I had finally gotten to him.

"What did the angel look like?" he asked.

That question threw me. "I don't know. They don't have wings, if that's what you mean."

"Didn't you say there was a witness?"

"Yes, a shifter."

"And this shifter didn't give you a description of the angel?" he pushed.

"We didn't think to ask. It's not like we can go to heaven and arrest him, now, can we?"

"We need to question this witness again."

A nervous tickle grew in my chest. "That could be a problem. I, ahhh...scrubbed his memory."

He laid his hands on the desk and leaned forward. "You what?"

His Alpha male posturing set off my temper. The nervousness I experienced moments ago coalesced into tendrils of angry heat in my chest. I shot up and did some leaning of my own. "Listen. You weren't there. He was terrified and had every right to be. Since when do angels come down and start lopping off heads? He begged me to wipe his memory, so I did. Now do yourself a favor and back the hell off."

Dalton kept his hands there for a few seconds longer, glaring at me, before he shoved away from the desk. He took a breath and ran his hands through his hair. "Sorry. I was thinking like a cop. You're right. It's not like we can go to heaven and flash around drawings, asking 'Have you seen this angel before?'"

I took a deep breath as well, trying to calm down. I wasn't sure how this guy had pushed my buttons so quickly. "We probably should have asked him to describe the angel. I can't imagine they all look the same."

"Do you think we could talk to the witness again?"

Shrugging, I stepped around my desk toward the door. "It couldn't hurt. I've never tried to reverse a mind sweep before, but there's always a first time."

CHAPTER 3

We came to a stop in front of the Erie Bar. I blew out a hard breath. What were we going to accomplish at nine in the morning when the place didn't open until lunch? But Dalton wanted to check out the alley behind the bar. I had insisted on driving, which I had expected would piss off Super Cop, but he didn't bat an eye. And I wasn't sure how I was going to shake him now, since he was already aware of the supernatural and didn't seem too alarmed about it. Of course, knowing about it was a different thing altogether from seeing it in the lumpy green flesh.

After parking and popping a few coins in the meter, we walked across the street and down the alley. It looked even more pathetic during the day. Not much to see, other than a very aromatic dumpster, random garbage strewn everywhere, and a pile of old rags heaped against the wall.

"Here we are. What do you hope to find?" I asked.

He shrugged slightly as he walked up and down the alley, peering from side to side. "You never know when you might spot something in daylight that you missed earlier. I always come back to the scene of the crime to go over the events again. Don't I, Sam?"

"Sam?" I grumbled. "Very funny, are you going to start calling me other guys' names now?"

"No, he was talking to me."

I jumped, actually did a little jig with my feet in the air, and jerked around to face the pile of rags that had now started to move. A man slowly emerged, sat up, and rubbed his face. He was ancient and wiry, but his eyes still held a spark.

Dalton walked over to him and squatted down. "How you doing, Sam?"

"Good, Joe."

"You know why I'm here?"

"Yeah. There was a ruckus last night in the Erie."

"As usual, you're on the ball."

He smiled and sat up straighter. "You know you can count on me."

"So what did you see?"

He frowned for a minute. "At first I thought I was having the DTs. But I haven't been drinking as much lately. I was behind the dumpster settling in for the night when the door slammed open and this thing came out."

"What did it look like?"

He scratched his elbow before responding. "Like a cross between the devil and Barney the dinosaur."

I chuckled to myself. The old goat had a sense of humor.

"Then what?" Dalton continued.

"A man came chasing after it."

"Did he catch him?"

Sam shook his head. "No, the purple thing disappeared into thin air."

"Can you describe the man?"

"Nah, he had dark brown hair and was medium-sized. I didn't see his face."

"What did he do?"

"He stood there for a couple of seconds mumbling to himself and then beamed up to the mother ship."

Okay, Sam was actually eighty-five percent right. I gave him props for knowing that much.

"Was either of them carrying anything?" I interjected.

"The second guy was carrying a big-ass sword."

"What else did you see?" Dalton prompted.

He pointed to me. "Later, I saw her and the vampire."

I gaped at him in surprise, and he scoffed at me and continued, "I know about the beasties you hide. I see lots of things in this town. Nobody pays me any attention."

I didn't bother to deny it. What was the point? "Is there anything else you can tell us?"

"The bartender came out and headed for home." He frowned. "But I think someone was following him."

"Did you see who it was?" I persisted.

"No, but I heard footsteps."

Dalton stood up and reached into his pocket, pulling out some bills and pushing them into Sam's hand. "Thanks for the info, Sam."

"Sorry I don't know more. You can check with Peter one alley over. He might have seen something. But have the girl approach him first, Joe. He don't like cops much."

We walked down the alley and slowly turned the corner. At first glance I didn't see anyone. Dalton stepped slightly in front of me.

"I'll lead."

"I'm a big girl. I can take care of myself. Besides, didn't Sam say Peter didn't like cops?"

"We have no idea how unstable this guy is."

Before I could argue, there was rustling from one of the doorways. Dalton tensed, laid his hand on his holster, and called out, "Peter?"

A small man darted out the door.

"Hey, hold up for a second." When the man ran, Dalton took off after him. "Stop! Police!"

I started to run, too, and was catching up with them when the telltale whiff of sulfur hit my nose. "Dalton, wait!" But he plowed ahead. The demon spun around and screeched. Dalton jerked to a stop, and before he could pull his gun I pushed him out of the way.

The demon opened his mouth and spewed slime at me, and I don't mean the cute green stuff you see on Nickelodeon. It was sticky, with chunks of *who-knows-what* in it, and God, did it stink—a combination of rotten eggs and day-old fish. I gasped for air and gagged. Luckily he missed my face, but my shirt and pants were covered. And then he took off again.

Dalton rushed toward me, but I put up my hands to stop him. There was no point in both of us wearing this gunk. I just had to remember to keep breathing through my mouth.

"Don't touch me. I'm fine."

He cringed. "Are you sure?"

"Yeah, next time I tell you to stop, listen. You spooked him."

"I spooked *him*? What the hell was that?"

"A Baltran demon."

"How many demon types are there?"

"A lot. I'll have Misha give you a Demon 101 course when we get back to the office. In the meantime, take off your shirt."

His mouth fell open.

"If you think I'm getting in my car with these clothes on, you're mistaken. I'm not shy, so I'll strip and drive naked if I have to."

When he pulled off his shirt, I almost choked on my tongue. His body was amazing. Just enough muscles, and a light dusting of hair on his chest which ran down his belly toward his... Holy crap, I needed to get a grip. We were in an alley and I was covered with slime.

"Can you hold onto it until I get my clothes off?"

Nodding, he faced away from me. I pulled my car keys and phone from my pocket, set them on the ground, then stripped off my clothes and chucked them into the dumpster. The bra was a goner too, so off it came. Undies were mercifully un-slimed, so those remained.

"Okay. I'm ready."

He dangled the shirt over his shoulder and I snatched it and pulled it on. Luckily it hit me mid-thigh, so I didn't look too skanky.

"You decent?"

"Never, but you can turn around now."

He faced me and his eyes danced. He had the nerve to smirk. "You look good in my shirt."

I swallowed the giggle threatening to erupt. Now who was acting like a tweener?

I cleared my throat. "Let's get going. I need to go home and change clothes before we find our witness."

Walking back to my car, we had the pleasure of passing a road crew patching the street. Even if I had been dressed appropriately, the catcalls would have been guaranteed. Since Dalton was bare-chested and I was wearing his shirt, there was no way they would keep their testosterone-laden mouths shut. It really wouldn't have bothered me so much if they'd at least been creative. I mean, how many men end up attracting women with "Oooo, baby," or "Can I have some of that?" When I spun around to issue my own scathing response, I was surprised to find the men regarding me sheepishly.

I couldn't figure out why the animals had done a one-eighty, until I turned to Dalton, who was glaring at the crew. His face was menacing, to say the least. It was a total *cop look*, and I found it both endearing and irritating. It was sweet he was trying to protect me, but, damn it, I could take care of myself. I shook my head to stop the ridiculous train of thought and stomped to my car, throwing open the door a little too aggressively.

As soon as I started to get in, Dalton grabbed my arm. "Stop."

"What's wrong?"

"Your seats are leather and it's probably over a hundred degrees in there." He pointed to my bare legs.

"Thanks for the save."

I opened my back door and located a newspaper. Spreading it on the front seat, I climbed in, knowing I would have newsprint on my ass by the time I got home. Better that than blisters.

"I live in Little Italy, so it'll take a while to get to my place."

He nodded. "I love going there. It reminds me of my grandmother. She used to make pasta from scratch."

"With the last name Dalton?"

"My maternal grandmother raised me. She was Italian. Came over on the boat."

"Misha loves Italian food. He goes there a lot for dinner."

"Can he do what the demon in the alley did?"

"Slime you? No, the one in the alley was a lower-level demon. It's one of his protective mechanisms. Misha doesn't need to slime anyone to get his point across."

"I thought you said demons don't show their demon side to normals. So what was the deal with the slime?"

"He had to have been plenty scared to do that. We weren't going to hurt him, so I'm not sure why he reacted that way."

"Maybe it isn't us he's scared of. Maybe he saw something last night and doesn't want to get involved."

"I don't blame him. This is getting stranger by the second."

We drove in silence for the next few minutes. I took a deep breath and got a whiff of something earthy and yummy. It was coming from Dalton's shirt and it made my toes curl a little bit. I glanced over at him and he smiled. Crap, I should have kept my slimy clothes on.

Somehow I was lucky enough to find a parking spot only a block away, but I was torn about what to do with Dalton. Part of me wanted to leave him in my car to swelter and another part wanted to bring him upstairs and jump him. The third rational, but incredibly boring, part of me won out, and I invited him up to wait in my apartment while I changed.

I unlocked the door and walked inside. Dropping my keys and phone on the table in the hallway, I faced Dalton.

He gave the living room a once-over. "You have a nice place."

"Thanks." I followed his gaze into the room. My couch was second-hand, but in great shape, as were the coffee table and comfy chair and ottoman I had over by the window. The only heirloom I had, if you could call it that, was my mother's old trunk, which sat along the wall. I wasn't much into clutter, except for piles of books stacked around the room.

"If you're hungry, there should be some bread and lunch meat in the fridge. Help yourself while I clean up."

"Want me to make a sandwich for you?"

Lord, how could I shake this guy if he was going to be Mr. Considerate? "I can't think about food until I've had a shower. I'll be out in a few."

I gathered up some clean clothes and hurried to the bathroom. Turning on the shower, I pulled off Dalton's shirt, taking one more whiff of his scent before throwing it in the laundry basket.

Once under the hot water, I scrubbed my hair and body twice before shutting it off and toweling dry.

It had been a long time since I had a man in my apartment, and now a man was in the next room shirtless and I was standing here naked. Shaking my head to clear the naughty thoughts, I finished drying off and got dressed.

All fresh and clean now, I sighed and went to the hall closet to get the man's button-down shirt I happened to have handy, and handed it to Joe. "This should do for the time being. I'll get your shirt back to you in a couple of days."

"No problem."

The shirt turned out to be too big for him, but it was better than having him sit around half naked in my kitchen. Or at least it's what I kept telling myself.

"Did you get something to eat?"

"Ah, your bread was a bit old."

I'm sure that was his nice way of saying it was moldy. "I haven't been to the store lately. I promised Booger this morning I would get him some food."

"Is he the guy who owns this shirt?"

I laughed. "No, Booger's my cat."

"Is he gray-striped?"

"Yes."

"He came through the window a couple of minutes ago and hissed at me before cramming himself under the couch. I don't think I made a friend."

"Booger doesn't like many people, especially men."

"Maybe he's jealous?"

"The only thing he worries about is having his food supply cut off."

"Where did you get him?"

"He showed up on my fire escape a couple of months ago and stared at me through the window until I let him in. He's been squatting here ever since. The only stipulation of our agreement is he has to be able to get in and out of the apartment during the day."

"What are you going to do in the winter?"

"I haven't thought that far ahead yet. Let's get going. If you like pizza, we can get a slice downstairs and then go find our witness."

"While you were in the shower, I called Misha to find out if the bartender was working today. He's going to get back to us."

For some reason, his take-charge attitude grated on my nerves. "How proactive of you."

He frowned. "I'm a cop, Kyle. I have worked a case or two before."

"Sorry. Let's get some food."

I had planned to drive and eat, but Dalton insisted we could spend five minutes finishing our food before putting the car in gear.

I clicked on my sync. "Call Misha." Man, did I love technology. The car placed the call, and he picked up on the first ring.

"Yo."

"Did you find out if our witness is working today?"

"He was supposed to, but he hasn't shown up yet. His name is Byron Matthews and I'm sending his address to your GPS as we speak."

"Thanks, you're the man."

"True dat."

I rolled my eyes. "Mish, stop trying to talk street, it doesn't work with your accent."

"Sorry, I just watched an episode of *Cops* in celebration of our newest team member. Call me with an update."

I glanced over at Dalton who tilted his head to the side. He hesitated before speaking as if choosing his next words carefully.

"Um, can I ask what the deal is with him?"

"What do you mean?"

"He seems a bit..."

"Strange? You aren't a demonist, are you?"

"What's that?"

"Similar to a racist." I glared at him. "Do you have a problem with him being a demon?"

"No, as long as he doesn't do anything illegal."

"Yeah, well, Misha is a TV junkie. Don't be surprised if he starts calling you by a nickname."

"Too late. He called me Joe Friday earlier."

I chuckled. "It doesn't take him long to make the leap."

The GPS interrupted our discussion. "Turn left at the next light."

I glanced at the address on the screen and then shut off the GPS. I knew where we were going. Ohio City was an eclectic neighborhood. Years ago it had fallen into disrepair and was now in the process of being rehabilitated. Byron lived in an area that still needed work.

It didn't take long to find his place. His apartment was in the basement of a large sandstone house that had been converted into multiple units years ago. We walked down the steps and knocked on the door.

I called out. "Byron? Are you there?"

No one answered. I bent down to pull back his door mat. It amazed me how many people still left their extra key under the mat. As I reached for it, I noticed a rust-colored stain on the door frame.

"It's blood," Dalton said calmly. He eased his gun out of its holster.

"I know what it is." I stood up and tried the knob. The door was unlocked.

Dalton stepped in front of me. "We don't have a warrant."

I glared at him. "Really. Do you think whatever might be in there is something we want the police department or the coroner to see?"

Dalton did some glaring of his own. "Stay out here until I make sure it's clear."

He walked slowly down the hall with his weapon raised while I stood by the door. He moved out of sight and I waited like an anxious schoolgirl. Since when did I let anyone tell me what to do? I took a step into the apartment just before a loud thunk startled me.

"Dalton?" I whispered.

Nothing.

"Where are you?" I hissed. I froze and waited for a response. What the hell was he doing?

After a few more seconds, I inched farther down the hallway. My heart was thudding so loudly I was afraid I'd give myself away. Steps echoed from the back of the apartment, and I was sneaking back there when movement caught my eye.

A door in the hallway opened and something barged through it. Before I could see who or what it was, a sharp pain struck my temple. Vision blurring, I staggered backward and cried out. My attacker ran out of the apartment.

I blinked hard, trying through the haze to identify who it was. Behind me, Dalton yelled, and then I was on my knees with him beside me. I gazed up into his iridescent turquoise eyes right before I passed out.

CHAPTER 4

Voices interrupted my sleep and I woke up slowly. Where the hell was I? I was in bed. No, I squeezed my eyes tight and opened them again, I was on a gurney in the ER. There was a curtain drawn around my bed and I was alone.

For a moment I flashed back to my twelfth birthday, spent sitting in the ER with a broken arm waiting for my mom to show up. The longer I had waited, the more pitying the stares from the nurses. How was I supposed to know where she was? After a while, Mom breezed into the hospital with her latest boyfriend, Chuck...or maybe it was Dan...in tow and scooped me up five minutes before social services was scheduled to arrive. All I had needed was one lousy traffic light to catch her and I would have been free.

My throbbing scalp put an end to my reminiscing. I gingerly reached up to touch it. Yowza, did it hurt. I took a deep breath and closed my eyes to keep from throwing up. Low voices rumbled through the curtain—first came Misha's thick accent followed by Dalton's response.

I cleared my throat. "Guys?"

The curtain pulled back and they both crowded in next to the bed.

Misha grinned down at her. "You okay, little one?"

"Yeah, I'll live."

Dalton attempted to smile but failed miserably. "You'll be fine, Kyle. The doctor should be back in a few minutes."

I tried to nod but thought better of it when my head pounded after I barely twitched. "What happened?"

Dalton spoke up. "You got hit on the head by our perp. I came running when I heard the struggle, but I didn't catch him."

"Byron?"

Dalton shook his head. "I found him dead in the bedroom."

"How did I get here?"

"I brought you in your car. Since we couldn't risk the police getting hold of the shifter's body, I called Misha and Jean Luc on the way."

"Mish, go help Jean Luc. I'm fine."

"Are you sure?"

"Yes."

He bent down and kissed me lightly on the top of the head. "We'll be in touch later." Misha walked toward the door. "By the way, my shirt looks good on you, Joe, even if it's a little too big. Take care of her."

Dalton eyes widened, but just as quickly he recovered and his face went back into neutral position. Was there a cop class for facial expressions? Before I could ask, the doctor bustled into the room. Even in scrubs she was striking. Scandinavian Barbie. I hated her. She walked over and smiled.

"Glad to see you're awake, Ms. McKinley. I'm Doctor Miller. How are you feeling?"

"Fine."

"Any pain, nausea, or dizziness?"

"No." In reality I was having all three, but did not want to risk being admitted.

She studied me closely. "Tell me the truth."

I sighed. "My head is throbbing a little and I felt like I was going to throw up when I first woke up, but I feel better now."

She picked up my chart and reviewed the notes. "I want to examine you for a couple of minutes if you don't mind."

She checked me over—shining a light in my eyes, asking me what day it was and listening to my heart, which made no sense since it was my head that hurt.

"Your scans came back. We saw no internal bleeds, but you may have a minor concussion. Let's have you sit up for a while and see how you do. If it goes well, I'll consider releasing you. But someone will need to stay with you overnight—"

Dalton interrupted. "I'll be with her."

I opened my mouth to protest and he held up his hands. "I'm taking the first shift, and then Misha and Jean Luc will relieve me."

I gritted my teeth. I hated having anyone take care of me, but if I argued I wouldn't be released.

An hour and a half later, Dalton helped me into my car. When he tried to put my seat belt on for me, I smacked his hand. I was not a child, for God's sake. He walked around and got in the driver's seat.

"Do you need to pick up anything on the way home?"

"Cat food. If we don't, we'll be risking our lives when we enter my apartment."

He nodded and drove to the small family market two streets over from my apartment. When I reached for the car door, Dalton laid his hand on my arm. "Don't even think about it. I'll be five minutes tops."

I was going to argue, but didn't have the energy. He jumped out of the car and walked into the store. I closed my eyes for just a minute while I waited.

"Kyle!"

I jerked awake. Dalton leaned toward me, a grocery bag in hand.

"I was just resting my eyes," I said.

"Well, the doctor said you shouldn't go to sleep for a while. Let's get some food in you and then we'll get you situated on your couch."

"Do you really have to wake me up every hour?"

"Just tonight. Doctor Miller said with the possible concussion we need to play it safe."

"Great. Have you heard from Misha or Jean Luc yet?"

"No. Misha said they would move the body to storage. What was he talking about?"

I hesitated, deciding how much to say. "We have a facility down by the river we use to store things we don't want the general public to see. We examine the bodies there."

"Who examines the bodies?"

"The *who* isn't important."

"What does that mean?" he persisted.

"It means we have other resources I don't want to tell you about right now."

I glanced at him. He clenched his jaw before responding tightly, "Let's get you home." He pulled out of the parking lot and drove to my street. Parking in a space mercifully close to my apartment building, he turned to me.

I took a deep breath. He had just driven me home from the hospital and bought Booger some food, so the least I could do was explain why I was being so closemouthed.

"Listen. It's one thing to bring you into the loop about our team and what we do. But in order to ensure we can keep the truth from humans, we have to rely on a network of people, some supernatural and some not. I'm not outing anyone till I get an okay."

"I get it. So you're telling me you have supes working throughout the city?"

"That's what I'm telling you."

"Amazing."

"What, you think the supernatural community just sits around on their butts doing nothing? Most have integrated themselves into society. They work, get married, have families."

He held his up hands in surrender. "Hold up. I didn't mean anything by it. I just didn't realize how widespread your network was."

Closing my eyes for a second, I berated myself. "Sorry. It's been a long day. I'm going to shut up now."

Dalton's hand touched my arm ever so lightly. He watched me very carefully, like I was a cornered animal.

"Let's get you upstairs."

Dalton got out, snagged the grocery bag and walked around to my side of the car. He waited patiently while I slowly worked myself to a standing position. He didn't touch me until I swayed slightly. Then he took my arm and steered me toward the building. Since he already had my keys, he unlocked the door and we stepped inside.

The stairs loomed in front of me and I squelched my whimpers. The last of my energy drained away.

He peered around the cramped lobby. "Is there an elevator?"

"No."

"Okay. Don't punch me for asking, but do you want me to carry you?"

"I'll be fine. Just hang onto me."

He wrapped his arm around my back, and we began our inchworm ascent. My neighbor Mrs. Grimaldi and her walker in 1A could move faster, but there would be no rushing. I got to the landing and took a deep breath. My vision blurred. Dalton took one look at me, dropped the bag on the floor and picked me up in his arms.

"Hey!"

"You can tell me off later, Kyle. You don't look good, and I don't have time for your pride right now."

His worried scowl stopped the protest on my lips. Laying my head against his shoulder, I sighed and relaxed in his arms. When I didn't fight him, he faltered for a second and tightened his arms around me.

"You're going to be fine, babe," his voice lowered to a soft tone. "We'll be upstairs in a minute."

Babe? Where the hell did that come from? I was not one to bat my eyelashes and act weak in the knees to get a guy's attention. Dalton definitely had a Sir Galahad complex. Though right now I wouldn't argue with him. For once it felt good to have someone take care of me.

Somehow he unlocked the door with me in his arms, and I reached to flip on the light switch. Booger was perched on the arm of the couch. When he saw us, he growled. I didn't know cats could growl. It was a scary noise, full of venom and the promise of drawing blood.

"Booger! Stop it!"

Booger jumped down and slunk to the other side of the room, never taking his eyes off of Dalton. Dalton set me on the couch carefully.

"Are you okay?"

"Yeah."

"I'll be right back."

He headed out of my apartment and within two minutes was back with the bag he had left on the landing. Booger growled again.

"Stop it. He brought your food," I scolded.

Swishing his puffed-up tail, the cat stomped into the kitchen.

"I'm going to feed him, and then I'll bring you a glass of water and some Ibuprofen."

I sat for a couple of minutes, concentrating on my breathing instead of the spinning room. Dalton was banging around the kitchen cupboards. It wasn't long before he came back with my water and medicine. I swallowed both quickly. The local anesthetic they had used when they stitched me up had worn off, and the pain in my head had graduated from a dull throb to relentless pounding.

"The doctor said I need to feed you. I should have bought some food at the market. Will you be all right for a couple more minutes while I scrounge around your kitchen?"

Before I had a chance to answer, the doorbell rang.

"Who is it?" I called out.

"Kyle, its Vinnie. Dad sent me with some food."

Dalton raised his eyebrow at me. I nodded for him to open the door. Vinnie stepped into the room. He was a skinny preteen boy with a large Adam's apple he had yet to grow into, and it bobbed up and down when he was nervous. Like now.

"It's okay, Vinnie, I'm on the couch."

Vinnie turned toward me and his eyes shot to my forehead. "Are you okay?"

"I'll be fine. As usual, your dad is a lifesaver. What is it this time?"

"Double order of gnocchi with marinara sauce."

"Tell him to put it on my tab."

"You got it." Vinnie handed the bag to Dalton, who dug into his pocket and gave him a tip before shutting the door.

"How did he know you needed food?" Dalton held the bag out in front of him suspiciously, like it might explode.

"Vinnie's dad, Tony, runs the restaurant down the street. He watches over me. Maybe he saw you helping me into my apartment." Okay, I left out some minor points in this story—mainly that Tony's grandfather was a demon and Tony had inherited his empathic ability, which he used to make his restaurant a success. He was never wrong when it came to choosing a dish for someone. As for me, he sent me food whenever he sensed something was wrong.

"I'll be right back." Dalton walked out of the room.

I pulled my phone out, punched in the number, and Misha answered immediately. Hitting the speaker button, I set the phone down next to me and leaned back against the couch.

"You home, little one?"

"Yep."

"Where's Joe?"

"He's getting me some food. What have you found out about Byron?"

"It's not pretty. He was tortured before he was killed, probably for information about the Erie events."

"But he didn't know anything. I wiped his memory," I protested.

"You and I know that, but the killer didn't."

I cleared my throat to stop the lump threatening to form. "Did you find anything else?"

"Jean Luc is going through Byron's apartment now to see if we missed anything. Do you need me to come over and give you one of my famous foot rubs?"

I chuckled. "I'm fine, Mish, honest. Do your job and I'll talk to you later."

I hung up the phone and jumped. Dalton stood in the doorway. I wasn't sure how long he had been there. He walked over and handed me a plate, then sat across from me and dug into his own food. The fragrances of basil and oregano wafted up from the steaming gnocchi on my plate and my stomach growled. Tony was never wrong.

"Thanks. Did you hear the call?"

"Most of it. Eat first and then we can talk about work."

I nodded and we both ate in silence. When I finally set down my empty plate, I didn't waste any time jumping right back into discussing the case.

"Byron was tortured for information. Wasn't it great of me to scrub his memory?"

He shook his head. "You couldn't have known this would happen, Kyle."

His reassurance did little to relieve the tightness in my chest. "If I hadn't messed with him, maybe they wouldn't have tortured him to death."

"It's more than likely they would have killed him regardless." Dalton leaned forward. "Do you remember anything about the guy who attacked you?"

"Vaguely. Everything is blurry. It was a male, I just don't know if he was a supe or not. Did you get a good look at Byron's body?"

"Why?" Dalton frowned.

"Because the way he was killed might help us determine who or what killed him."

I could tell he was going to protest, so I plowed ahead in my normal diplomatic style. "Listen, I'm a big girl. I won't fall apart when you tell me how he was killed. I could tell you stories of deaths that would make you lose the food you just ate." A slight exaggeration, but I was on a roll.

"Got it, tough girl. Byron was cut up. Whoever tortured him liked knives."

"Or maybe it was claws. We could be dealing with a shifter, or a demon. Maybe it was the demon from the bar?"

"No, that doesn't track. The demon from the bar already knew what Byron witnessed."

"So then who was it?"

"Maybe Jean Luc will be able to tell us something tomorrow. Why don't we take a break? Do you want more water or need help getting to the bathroom?"

I had reached my limit. His concerned face made my chest tighten again and I had reached pissed-off mode. "I can take care of myself." I stood on wobbly legs.

"It's okay to accept help sometimes."

"Says the big, strong, he-man," I retorted.

I headed toward the bathroom, praying I wouldn't fall flat on my face while I attempted to be indignant. He walked alongside, but had the good sense not to touch me.

"I can tell I'm not going to win this argument, but, like it or not, I'm sticking around 'til Misha gets here. Then he can take care of you. Give you one of his famous foot rubs."

I marched into the bathroom and glared at him before banging the door shut.

CHAPTER 5

It was official. Waking up every hour on the hour sucked. Before I could really relax, someone would wake me. The first couple of times, Dalton checked on me. At some point during the night, Misha replaced him.

Now someone was banging around in the kitchen, so I got up, pulled on a robe and went to investigate. Misha fumbled with the coffee pot, and a half-eaten box of fry cakes sat on the table.

"Good morning, sweet."

"Morning. Is Dalton gone?"

"He left a couple hours ago to go home and get cleaned up. He said he would be in the office later this morning."

For some strange reason it bothered me he was gone, but I wasn't going to dwell on it. "When did you get the fry cakes?"

"I stopped and picked some up before I relieved Joe. They were warm then."

The bakery downstairs was open all night long, much to the delight of Misha and various Case Western and John Carroll college students who piled into cars and came in the middle of the night to buy them.

Misha grinned. "Joe thanked me for the use of my shirt."

I shrugged. "That was nice of him."

"I think maybe he's a little jealous. You did tell him we're just friends, yes?"

"I just met the guy. I don't owe him an explanation for anything."

He clucked his tongue. "Humans. You overanalyze everything. Chemistry can be instantaneous. Ask my last three wives."

His statement was not as ironic as it seemed. Since it was difficult for Shamat females to bear children, demons did not mate for life unless they were biologically compatible. They stayed together for twenty years or so and then went their separate ways if no children were born.

Little warning bells went off in my head. I didn't like where this conversation was going. "He won't stick around for the long haul." I knew that from experience. "He can keep his distance."

The glare I gave Misha must have convinced him to let the subject drop.

"Do you feel up to going into work for a while?"

"Yeah. Let me take a shower and I'll be ready in ten."

When I stepped out of the shower, I got a good look at myself in the mirror and grimaced. The gash along my forehead had bruised and turned a lovely shade of purple. I didn't need to call attention to myself, so I pulled a pair of scissors out of the medicine cabinet and hacked off some hair in the front, creating bangs to hang over the worst of it. It was better than nothing.

Misha insisting on driving. He was still worried about me, which became even more apparent when he offered me more than one fry cake during the ride in.

Dolly cringed when she saw me walk in. So much for camouflaging my head. She was not very demonstrative, so I was touched she cared.

"Don't worry, Kyle, those bangs will grow out eventually."

I sighed and kept going. Mother Teresa she was not.

Jean Luc and Dalton were in the back room, bent over the computer monitor.

"What are you guys doing?"

Jean Luc walked over and kissed me on both cheeks. He was the only person who could get away with stuff like that.

"*Ça va?*"

"I'm fine," I answered automatically.

He stared at me for a moment. I could never lie to him. "I like your bangs, they are *tres chic*."

I smiled. "*Merci*."

"Where's Misha?" Dalton asked.

"He's parking the car."

I nodded to Jean Luc. "So what have you found, Inspector Clouseau?"

"Byron was clean. We found nothing illegal in his apartment or his background."

"Then we're pretty sure his death was related to whatever happened in the bar two nights ago." I glanced at the monitor. "Do you have pictures from the autopsy?"

Jean Luc opened the file. Gruesome to say the least. I was glad I hadn't accepted the second fry cake from Misha. I could see Dalton watching me out of the corner of my eye, so I refused to blink.

"What about these slash wounds on his chest? Do we know what made them?"

"Doc believes it was a knife, but she is not sure yet."

Dalton spoke up. "Do supes normally use weapons?"

"If they do not have a power which can inflict pain or death, then yes," Jean Luc answered. "But here is the interesting part. He did not die from the knife wounds. They would have been painful, but they were superficial."

"What did he die from, then?" I asked.

"Cause of death is still in question as well. Doc is waiting for some test results. Dalton and I have decided to check in at the storage facility in a couple of minutes."

"But he doesn't have clearance," I yelped. Couldn't seem to help myself, no sleep made Kyle a grumpy girl.

Jean Luc shook his head. "I talked to Nicholas this morning. He said Dalton is to be given full access."

Well, wasn't that special of him. "He's the boss. I'd like to tag along to hear what Doc has to say."

Dalton studied me. "Are you sure you're up for it?"

"Yes, I'm fine. Let's motor."

It was a little too cozy in the van with the four of us, since Misha had also insisted on coming along. We drove to our building in the warehouse district, a large, red brick monstrosity built in the twenties. From the outside it looked like it should be condemned, and luckily no one paid much attention to it. But that was the plan. We had also strategically placed biohazard signs throughout the property to keep squatters from taking up residence.

Jean Luc pulled the van into the back bay of the building and shut the door. The warehouse reminded me of every government conspiracy movie I had ever seen—rows and rows of shelves with evidence which would never see the light of day. Being a closet conspiracy theorist, I often wondered what else was being kept from all of us. Which in itself was hypocritical, since I was a keeper of the closet keys. At least the supernatural closet.

Dalton walked next to me as we wound our way toward the morgue. He was trying hard not to gape at the shelves containing beakers of God only knows what, but was failing miserably. We came to the door leading to our lab and small morgue. Jean Luc typed in the security code to access the room. The doors opened with a swish. Very evil la-BOR-a-tory-like.

The headless vampire lay in the middle of the room on the exam table. Doc Miller leaned over the body with her hands immersed in his chest cavity. She stood up and placed the vamp's heart in a metal dish. Stripping off her gloves and pulling down her mask she smiled. Even standing over a corpse she was beautiful, much like she had been yesterday in the ER. How could she look like a supermodel after she just extracted a bloody organ from a corpse? My little green monster reared its ugly head and I gritted my teeth.

Doc Miller laughed. "You need to dial down the animosity, McKinley. I can feel it from here. A girl can't help it if she's beautiful."

I smiled broadly. "All-knowing wench."

She frowned. "I am not all-knowing. You scared me to death at the hospital. Luckily Misha called so I could make sure to be available when you got there."

"Sorry, Doc, not my choice. If I had known you were on call, I would have asked the guy to wait until you were off shift to bean me on the head."

"Smart-ass." She walked over to me. "Nice bangs."

"Shut up."

She reached up and pushed back my hair, checking my scalp. "The stitches look fine. How are you feeling today?"

"Better."

"Why did you bother trying to lie to me yesterday about how you were feeling?"

"A girl can't help her natural inclinations."

"Enough with the girl talk. Introduce me to your newest team member. I didn't get a chance to meet him officially yesterday."

"Doctor Sabrina Miller, this is Lieutenant Joe Dalton. He's the media relations officer for the police department. Dalton, this is Doc Miller. As you already know, her full time job is as an ER doc. But she's also our part-time ME and a succubus."

He gawked at me like I'd goosed him.

"You know, she can suck your life energy when she has sex with you."

His eyes actually bugged out more.

"Don't worry, you're safe. She's reformed."

"Good to know," he croaked.

Doc Miller beamed at him. "Sorry for the playacting in the ER yesterday, Joe. But we don't acknowledge each other in public."

"Got it." Dalton stared at her like a deer in the headlights.

Okaaay... It was time to move things along. "What have you got for us, Doc?"

She walked over to the other exam table and folded back the sheet. Even though I had seen Byron's body in the earlier photos, I was not prepared for the live rendition. I stifled a gasp. Staring down at his body, I kept hearing his voice when he begged me to wipe his memory. But it hadn't been enough to save him. A lump lodged in my throat. Why did life have to suck?

Doc interrupted my thoughts. "First of all, the slices on his chest were not made by a knife as I first thought. It appears as if the skin split apart from the inside. I've never seen anything like it."

I gulped. "And that's how he died?"

"No, his heart stopped."

"He had a heart attack from the torture?" Dalton asked.

"No, a heart attack would have caused tissue scarring and there was none."

"So why would your heart just stop?" I had to ask, although I wasn't sure I wanted to know the answer.

"It wouldn't stop under normal circumstances." Doc glanced at Misha.

I glared at him. "Have you seen this before?"

"Not personally, but there have been cases of this." He hesitated. "There are demons with the ability to stop a person's heart."

"What! Why haven't you told me this before?"

"I've not heard of this in over a century, little one. I didn't see any point."

I opened my mouth to protest some more, but he continued.

"I did not see any point in telling you about these demons, since they were tales told to me as a child. Demons this powerful are no longer allowed on earth. They are too dangerous."

I blurted, "So you're telling me some rogue demon is on the loose?"

"Yes, it looks that way."

Dalton jumped in. "If something is powerful enough to stop a heart with a thought, why would he knock Kyle over the head?"

Misha pursed his lips. "I don't know."

"Maybe we are dealing with two attackers?" Jean Luc spoke up.

Great, because things weren't already complicated enough. "Why would they both go after Byron? They obviously believed he knew something important."

Dalton shook his head. "I think we're missing something here. We need to start back at the beginning. The question we should be asking ourselves is, what is so important about this vampire that a demon and an angel would fight over him?"

Doc Miller, Jean Luc and Misha nodded. *What the hell?*

"Doc, have we ID'd the vamp yet?" Dalton asked.

"I'm running his fingerprints through the database right now."

Dalton continued. "Misha, can you research demons who have the ability to stop someone's heart? Jean Luc, would you check with your other vampire contacts to see if they have heard anything about a vampire going missing?"

I interjected. "Why was the vamp's head taken?"

"Good question." Dalton addressed the group. "Would the head be a trophy?"

"Supes don't normally play the psychological games humans do," Doc Miller said. "And before you ask, they wouldn't eat it, either."

Dalton grimaced. "Thanks Doc. Can you call someone on the team as soon as you have positive ID?"

"Sure can. Misha, why don't you show Joe the storage area? There are plenty of interesting things for him to look at. I'm going to spend a couple of minutes checking Kyle over."

The guys filed out and I walked back to her. "I'm fine, I swear."

"What's the deal with you and Lieutenant Beautiful Eyes?"

"Nothing."

"I'm getting some strong vibes from him."

"I'm sure you are, Doc. I'm surprised the corpses don't sit up and ask you out on a date."

She glared at me. "I don't mean vibes toward me. I mean vibes toward you."

I shook my head a little too emphatically. "Your powers are misfiring. Nothing's going on between us."

"Why do humans overanalyze everything?"

"Have you been talking to Misha?"

"No. Why?"

Dalton poked his head back in the room. "Kyle, are you ready to go?"

Since when had Dalton become the leader of the band of merry males? *Operation Dalton Has to Go* was back in play. It was one thing to put up with an overprotective vampire and a demon, both trying to boss you around. It was another to have *Mr.-Joe-Blow-Normal* think he could step in and play leader. There were too many males in the lifeboat, and one of them needed to go over the side.

CHAPTER 6

Driving back to the office, the tires squealed as Jean Luc took the corner of Lakeside and Ontario on two wheels while Misha hollered "yee-haw," and quoted lines from *The Dukes of Hazard*.

I closed my eyes and took some deep, cleansing breaths. Soon I was on a tropical beach, the fragrance of cocoa butter wafting through the air. A tanned, swim trunk-clad waiter slowly walked toward me carrying a Mai Tai. I ran my eyes up his magnificently toned legs to his six pack abs and paused, taking in his muscles as they flexed. I continued my perusal up his strong arms and shoulders until I came face to face...with Dalton and his haunting turquoise eyes.

I jerked awake and blinked. Jean Luc screeched to a halt in the office garage. Misha glanced over from the seat beside me and smirked. "I thought I might need to carry you into the office."

From the front passenger seat, Dalton watched the two of us in the rear view mirror. His eyes narrowed slightly when Misha made his comment. Maybe Misha wasn't off base about Dalton's jealousy. A new plan to get rid of Dalton started to germinate. But I had to tread carefully.

In the reception area, Dolly sat filing her fingernails to points. I didn't bother asking her why. Dolly wasn't the sharing type. I didn't even know what animal she could shift into.

It was considered rude to ask a shifter what their animal side was, and Dolly had never opened up to me about it. I had often wondered, but eventually decided speculating about it was more fun in the long run.

Misha excused himself to run research on his computers, and Jean Luc left to place calls to his "vampire network" as I liked to call them, to see if any were missing. Which left Dalton and me alone in the back office.

I walked over to the coffee pot and poured a cup of thick-as-mud coffee—damn Jean Luc—and sat down on the couch. Awkward silence permeated the office. Dalton was the first to cave.

"Did Doc say you're okay?"

"Yeah."

"Maybe you came back too soon. You don't normally fall asleep in the car do you?"

"I *normally* don't have someone waking me up every hour on the hour. I didn't get much sleep."

He wandered over to the counter and reached for the coffee pot. I stifled the urge to warn him. If I couldn't convince him to leave, maybe Jean Luc's coffee would. Before he was able to take a sip, his cell phone rang. He checked the screen.

"It's Doc Miller."

That was fast. How in the hell did she even have his number? I blatantly listened in on the conversation. His part at least.

"Doc...great, thanks. I'll let the rest of the team know. Right." He laughed. "Thanks." He hung up the phone. "Doc ID'd the vampire. His name is Charles Hampton. I'm going to get Jean Luc and Misha and we can start digging into his past."

I nodded. "I'm going to make a fresh pot of coffee."

Ten minutes later the four of us sat around the table. Misha typed away on his laptop. Jean Luc had not recognized the vamp's name, so he must have been new to the area.

Misha leaned forward, chewing his lip intently while he hammered away on the keyboard. After a few more seconds, he clapped his hands and sat back. "Got him."

Always low on patience, I piped up. "Don't keep us in suspense, Misha."

"According to what I could find, until a few months ago Hampton was based out of Chicago. It states here he was an antiquities dealer. He supposedly imported artifacts from Africa and Asia to the States and sold them for a pretty penny."

I rolled my eyes and Dalton spoke up, "I take it you don't buy the story?"

"Do you?" I countered. "What did you find about him in our database?"

A couple of clicks later, Misha continued. He moved the laptop so we could see the picture. "He was relatively young. He was turned only fifty years ago by Sebastian."

Jean Luc tensed. Far more emotion than he normally showed. It was the equivalent of one of my temper tantrums.

Dalton asked, "Who's Sebastian?"

I glanced at Jean Luc, who motioned for me to explain. "He's a founding vampire. There are only a few vamps allowed to turn humans. Sebastian is one of them and, unfortunately, the vast majority of vamps he sires are bad news, in their human lives and their vamp lives."

Dalton spoke to Jean Luc, "What do you think Hampton was up to?"

"He could have been dealing in stolen merchandise, money laundering, or anything else illegal."

"Next steps?" Dalton asked the group.

It was amazing how quickly Dalton had taken on the de facto leader role. Why were Misha and Jean Luc not bristling? Had living for centuries lowered their testosterone levels? Well, I could take charge with the best of them.

"Misha, do you have an address for Hampton?"

"Yep, he had one of those refurbished downtown lofts."

"You stay here and keep digging into his past. In the meantime, Jean Luc and I will go check out his place."

Dalton cleared his throat. "I think I'll tag along with the two of you, if you don't mind."

I smiled. "Let's go."

Hampton's loft building was upscale. He must have been into something major to afford it. This wasn't going to be an easy break and enter.

We walked into a lobby with sleek, blue leather couches, an abstract brown and blue wool rug, and large potted plants scattered strategically around the space. Light jazz played softly from hidden speakers. The lofts were definitely out of my price range.

However, the opulence did not hide the Fort Knox vibe. A security pad next to the elevators taunted us. We had little chance of getting upstairs on our own. I pointed to the small gold sign above a door in the lobby that read Thomas White, Apartment Manager. I smirked at Jean Luc. "You ready to go upstairs to visit our friend Mr. Hampton?"

Jean Luc flashed a quick grin, his fangs just peeking out. "Ready when you are."

Dalton's eyebrows furrowed, but I wouldn't enlighten him now. He would see what was what in a minute.

I knocked on the door and an older man answered. He reminded me of an English butler with his white hair, mustache and dark suit.

"May I help you?"

I smiled at him. "Mr. White?"

"Yes."

"We're guests of Mr. Hampton. He left instructions to let us into his apartment."

The man shook his head slightly. "I haven't spoken to Mr. Hampton in a couple of days. I don't remember that."

I went to work. I created a memory, using the photo Misha had showed me of Hampton, and pictured him standing in this very doorway instructing Thomas to let us into the apartment when we arrived. Holding that image for a few moments, I waited till warmth bubbled along my forehead. It was time to insert the image into the manager's brain. His energy pattern was fluttering softly and I weaved the memories around his current thoughts.

"I'm sorry, but unless Mr. Hampton is here I can't..." The man's eyes widened and he smiled as recognition hit. "Wait, I do remember Mr. Hampton telling me you were coming. I apologize. I will escort you upstairs at once."

I wanted to watch Dalton's reaction, but I needed to concentrate until we got upstairs to make sure the memory solidified.

We headed up the elevator and were in the apartment lickety-split. When Thomas left us alone, I faced an astonished Dalton.

"How?"

"I'll explain later."

We went to work. The loft had large windows with a panoramic view of the city. The main living area was an open floor plan, kitchen, dining and living areas all in one. There was also a small office area in one corner of the room. I headed straight for that. Misha had instructed me to download as much information as I could onto the flash drives he had given me. So I went to work.

Meanwhile, Dalton and Jean Luc scoured the rest of the room, rifling through everything. I was downloading files on the first stick when a hand touched my shoulder and I jumped. "Jesus, give a girl some warning next time."

Dalton held up his hands. "Sorry. Will you be okay up here? Jean Luc and I are going to check the rest of the loft."

"As soon as my heart starts again, I should be fine."

He nodded and disappeared down the hallway.

The files continued to download, and I didn't bother taking the time to open them. Misha would sort through everything back at the office. After a couple more minutes, the flash drive registered as full and I pulled it out and put the second one into the USB port.

The longer I sat there waiting for the computer to do its thing, the more anxious I became. For a second, when the loft doorknob rattled, I thought I was imagining it. But when the door swung open, I grabbed the first flash drive and stuffed it down my shirt. I didn't have time to pull the second one out of the computer. I stood and spun around, my heart thumping like a jackhammer.

"Well, well, well. What do we have here?"

Four men crossed the threshold, three of them scowling menacingly while they cased the room. The man who had spoken stood in the middle of the group. He was smaller than the others, but they still deferred to him.

He was dressed in a ridiculously expensive gray suit and shoes. His blond hair was wavy, and he had the greenest eyes I had ever seen, eyes that would have been gorgeous if there had been even a spark of humanity in them.

This had to be Sebastian.

"Jean..." Before I could get his name out, Jean Luc appeared in a flash, standing between me and the vamps. A few seconds later, Dalton came running from the back.

Sebastian stepped forward. "Jean Luc. It has been a long time."

"Yes, it has."

"What brings you here?"

Dalton interrupted the conversation. "Who are you?"

I cringed. *Stop talking!*

Jean Luc hissed at Dalton. "Mind your tongue, boy. I keep you around for pleasure. Do not make me regret my decision."

I held my breath, praying Dalton wasn't dumb enough to talk back.

After a second, Dalton lowered his eyes. "Sorry, sir."

Sebastian laughed. "He's feisty, Jean Luc. I can see why you like him. Could I interest you in a trade?" He raised his hand and casually gestured toward his entourage.

"Thank you for the offer, but, besides his obvious attributes, his connections help with our cause."

"Yes. We mustn't let humans know too much. So why are you in Charles's apartment?"

"You are aware that he died," Jean Luc stated.

"Of course. He was relatively young, so the severing of his energy was not too hard on me."

"He was killed in a public venue."

"The Erie Bar?" Sebastian asked.

"Yes," Jean Luc answered. "Would you have any idea why he was killed?"

He shrugged. "He was a petty thief with delusions of grandeur. I warned him on multiple occasions that he needed to take things slowly. But children often have minds of their own."

I swallowed the bile in my throat. Talk about delusions of grandeur. When Sebastian turned toward me as if he could read my thoughts, I lowered my eyes. *Shit.*

"Look up at me, pet."

I raised my eyes slowly, schooling my face into an emotionless mask even though my stomach somersaulted.

"Are you the one who can erase memories?"

"Yes."

"Extraordinary." He ran his eyes over me and came to a stop on my forehead. "You have been injured recently." He closed his eyes and sniffed.

I took a step back, my feet moving before my mind could scream *stop!*

He opened his eyes and laughed deep in his throat. "I won't hurt you. You are too unique."

Jean Luc spoke up. "We would like to search the apartment for any evidence that might help us understand what happened."

Sebastian shook his head. "Unfortunately, I cannot allow you to do that. You see, I own this loft. I merely permitted Charles to live here. Therefore, this loft and everything in it are my property."

Jean Luc bowed his head slightly. "Of course. We will be on our way then."

Sebastian smiled and walked over toward me, running his eyes over the desk and laptop. "The flash drive stays here as well."

I jerked and almost clapped my hand on my chest. But his eyes were resting on the flash drive still in the USB port.

I nodded like a bobble-head doll and backed away from the desk.

"Let me know if I might be of any assistance with your case, Jean Luc."

The three of us walked out of the apartment slowly. I wanted to scream and run like a college girl in a slasher film, but I put one foot in front of the other until we had closed the door and were out in the hallway.

Jean Luc motioned for us to keep quiet, and we left the building in silence. I waited to speak until we were safely back in the van.

"God almighty, Jean Luc, he's one crazy son of a bitch."

"And very powerful." Jean Luc looked pointedly at Dalton. "I apologize for speaking to you that way. Sebastian does not place much value on humans. He will not tolerate insubordination."

"You were protecting me, and I appreciate it. Sorry about going into cop mode. I wasn't expecting it to be Sebastian."

Jean Luc frowned. "I do not like that he is involved in this. For him to come personally to Hampton's apartment means something significant is happening. I wish we could have had more time to examine his things."

"It wasn't a total loss." I reached down my shirt and pulled out the jump drive. "We need to get this to Misha."

Jean Luc smiled and this time his fangs flashed in all their glory.

CHAPTER 7

Misha practically salivated when I handed him the flash drive. Zooming back to his office, he barely managed to nod when I hollered, "Good Luck".

I rolled my eyes at Jean Luc and Dalton. "We won't see him again for a while."

Jean Luc agreed. "Go home, *ma petite*. It has been a long day."

I opened my mouth to argue and then acquiesced. There was no point sitting around waiting for info when I could do that at home. "Sure, that'll give you and Dalton some alone time together." They both gave me puzzled glances, so I enlightened them. "Well, since Jean Luc thinks you have 'obvious attributes' I thought the two of you might want some alone time."

Dalton opened his mouth and then seemed to think better of his first response. "I'm flattered, of course, but I..."

Jean Luc smirked and put up his hand to keep Dalton from stepping on his own tongue. "Please do not concern yourself over my feelings. You are not my type."

I laughed. "Now that you have straightened that out, I'll see you both tomorrow."

"Ahhh, Kyle? Didn't Misha drive you in today? How are you going to get home?" Dalton asked.

"Jean Luc?" I turned around and that chicken-shit vampire was nowhere to be found. Why couldn't I have been born with super speed? Now that was a cool power.

Dalton grinned. "I'll give you a ride home."

When we reached the parking garage, Dalton clicked his key fob and the lights blinked on a newer model silver SUV.

"Where's your cop car with fast food wrappers all over the back seat?"

"Captain thought it would be a good idea not to scream 'cop' while I was working this case, so I'm driving my own car."

While Dalton drove us toward Little Italy, I leaned back against the headrest, watching the city rush by.

"Kyle, will you tell me more about your power?"

I stared at his profile as he drove. "What do you want to know?"

"How does it work?"

I shrugged. "I'm not sure exactly. I can change people's memories."

"So, with the manager today, you planted the conversation with Hampton."

"Exactly."

"Why didn't you just tell him to take us upstairs?"

"It doesn't work that way. Except for minor suggestions, like making someone sleepy or hungry, I can't really compel people to do things. But I can insert memories to steer them in the right direction. I just can't force them to do anything against their will."

He glanced over at me for a moment. "Does it hurt you?"

I wasn't expecting that question. Few people who knew about my gift ever asked about how it affected me. They were more interested in the power itself.

"Sometimes it'll make me tired, or I'll get a headache, depending on how long I use it."

"Maybe you shouldn't use it, then."

I stared at him in shock. Not one person had ever suggested that I not use it. "I've been given this gift...power, curse, whatever you want to call it...for a reason. I'm supposed to use it."

"How long have you had it?"

"That's a longer story than this car ride."

"How about telling me over dinner, then?"

"It isn't exactly a public conversation."

He wouldn't be deterred. "Why don't we get takeout from one of the restaurants on your street and eat it in your apartment?"

My mind screamed *Danger, Will Robinson, Danger!* But he blinked his baby blues at me and I said yes without a moment's thought. *What the hell?*

I pulled out my cell and hit seven on my speed dial. "Tony, it's Kyle. I need some take-out. Yeah, two specials and some garlic bread. I'll be there in ten."

"What are the specials?" Dalton asked.

I smiled. "It varies, but I'm sure you'll love it."

He dropped me off in front of the restaurant and pulled away to look for parking.

Tony met me at the counter, smiling like a Cheshire cat. "Dinner for two?"

"Cut it out, Tony. It's not what you think."

"Well, I put something special in the order, just in case. I'll put it on your tab."

"Thanks."

I walked out of the restaurant. Dalton stood on the sidewalk waiting for me. He reached for the bag, and I handed it to him without a retort, which was very Zen of me. We were two blocks from my apartment, so it took us a couple of minutes to walk there. There were a number of people sitting at tables outside eating, while others strolled along the street like we were. The evening air was perfect, having cooled down from the earlier muggy heat.

We made it up my stairs considerably faster than the evening before, and walked into my cat-free apartment. Booger must have still been out carousing. I went into the kitchen and put plates on the table. Dalton set the bag down and opened up my silverware drawer, pulling out knives and forks, making himself right at home...in my apartment.

I pulled two glasses from the cupboard and a bottle of red wine from the pantry. Oregano permeated the kitchen. Within a couple of minutes we were eating eggplant parmesan over angel hair. After I poured us each a glass of wine, we ate in silence for a while. I swirled the pasta and sauce together on my fork and took a large bite, savoring the sweet tomatoes, but also looking forward to the surprise Tony had added—a piece of tiramisu. I had stifled a moan at the sight of it.

Dalton finally spoke. "This is some of the best eggplant I've ever had."

I nodded between mouthfuls. "Tony is a gifted chef. Wait until you have the tiramisu, it's like an orgasm on a plate." *Had I just said that out loud?*

Apparently I had, since Dalton choked on his wine.

"Are you all right?" I reached over the table and thumped his back. "Put your arms up in the air."

He cleared his throat. "I'm fine...wrong pipe."

We sat there in awkward silence for a minute, until I decided to fill the void.

"So, you asked me earlier about when I first realized I had my power."

"Yes."

"I was fifteen."

"What happened?"

"Oh, some dilhole by the name of Gerry Williams and three of his football buddies decided it would be fun to dump water down my front. It was their demented version of a wet T-shirt contest. I remember standing there dripping wet, and promising revenge on their sorry asses." Okay, that was a bit of an exaggeration. At the time, I wanted to shrivel up and die. Looking back as my adult self, I wanted to give them an ass-kicking.

"The next day the buddies sans Gerry cornered me in the hallway and told me that during lunch period they were going to tell everyone what they had done to me. I glared at the three of them and wished it had never happened, that they would just forget about it. After a couple of seconds, all three got confused looks on their faces. They walked away without saying a word."

I stopped and took a sip of wine. I hadn't thought about high school in a long time and all my teen angst rushed back uninvited.

"How did you figure out that it had actually worked?"

"I didn't go to the cafeteria—I'm not a glutton for punishment—and later one of my friends told me Gerry started blathering on about me and what he'd done. But no one would back him up. Gerry was so pissed off he punched one of his friends and got suspended from playing football for three games."

"Did Gerry come after you?"

"No. At first I thought I was losing it. I mean, how could you change something by wishing for it? But I still remembered what had happened and Gerry remembered what had happened, so he stayed away from me. He started calling me a witch behind my back. I was just happy to be done with him."

"I'm sorry you had to go through that."

I shrugged. "No big deal. High school sucks for everyone."

"Yeah, but you had to face that and your power. It had to be difficult. Did your family help?"

I stared into pity-filled eyes and my chest tightened. I was done with this conversation. I stood and cringed when the chair scraped loudly across the kitchen floor. "I didn't tell my family. Like I said, no big deal. Are you finished?"

He nodded and handed me his plate. I walked over to the counter and placed the dishes in the sink.

"Does your power work on everyone?"

I faced him and leaned against the counter. "There have only been a few humans I've been unsuccessful with. Supes are hit and miss. Some I can change their memories, others no way."

"What about Jean Luc and Misha?"

"I don't know. I've never tried."

He stared at me, his right eyebrow rising in disbelief.

"Listen, trust means a lot to me. I've never tried to use my power on either of them."

He held up his hands. "I didn't mean to offend you. I'm sorry."

I shook my head. "You didn't. To be honest, I've wondered before if I would be able to do it. My gut tells me Jean Luc is a definite no. Misha is questionable. But he's more powerful than he lets on."

At Misha's name, Dalton opened his mouth to say something, but hesitated before continuing. "How did you end up here?"

"Well, if you think high school was interesting, you should have seen me in college. Living in a dorm with thousands of eighteen-year-olds was a touch overwhelming. I lasted six months and then took off on my own."

"To do what?"

I chuckled. "Let's just say I was a bit naïve back then. I thought I'd go out and find a fulfilling, well-paid profession without any discernable skills or a college education. Eighteen months later, I was trying to cheat Vegas casinos out of money."

His eyes widened. "By yourself?"

I hesitated, choosing my words carefully. "I had some help from a friend." He didn't need to know about Jack and my naive belief that he loved me and not what my power could do for his bank account.

"Did you get caught?"

"A casino security guard figured out what was going on. He arrested me and started to interrogate me. I tried to erase his memory, but he just laughed. He was a vamp. Of course I had no idea that the supernatural even existed back then. Instead of turning me over to the police, he called Nicholas, who offered me a job using my skills for what he called 'a good cause.' At first I thought he was propositioning me, but he was serious. I've been working for the BSR ever since."

"What happened to your friend?"

"We parted company." More like he ran for it the minute I got caught.

Dalton paused for a moment as if he wanted to ask me more about Jack, and I held my breath.

"What's the deal with Nicholas? I haven't even spoken to him yet."

I started breathing again. "Before we talk about him, I'm going to make some coffee. You have to have coffee with this tiramisu."

He grinned for a moment. "If tiramisu is an orgasm, what's the coffee?"

"Foreplay."

He dropped his forehead on his palm, chuckling and shaking his head. "Jesus. You're something."

"Let's have the dessert in the living room. I'll bring in the coffee."

He collected two plates, forks and the dessert box and turned toward the living room.

"Don't start without me," I called.

He glanced back over his shoulder, his turquoise eyes locking on me. "You have nothing to worry about."

I gulped and pulled the filters and coffee out of the cupboard. *Get it in check, girl.* Had I not just been talking about snake-in-the-grass Jack, and now I was drooling over another man?

I stuffed the filter into the top of the coffee maker and dumped in two scoops. What had happened to *Operation Get Rid of Dalton* and *too many men in the lifeboat*? Carrying the carafe to the sink, I filled it with water and poured it into the coffee maker. A little bit of wine and compassionate blue eyes and I was not making sense. Deep breath in. *You are in control of the situation. Remember that.* Deep breath out.

I walked into the living room with two mugs of coffee and a new attitude, my chastity belt snapped firmly back in place, until he smiled at me. My blithering self rushed back in full force.

I set the coffee down and cleared my throat, refusing to make eye contact for a second.

"Are you okay, Kyle?"

"Yeah, I was just trying to remember what you had asked about in the kitchen."

"Nicholas?"

I took another deep breath and was able to rein in my libido. "Right. He's our boss. To be honest, I don't know much about him personally. He offered me work, and I did some minor jobs for him until he hooked me up with the team here in Cleveland, and I met Jean Luc and Misha."

"What is Nicholas?"

I thought for a second. "Honestly? I don't know. I've spent a lot of time over the years wondering about it. He has to be more than human, but I'm not sure what he is. I'm pretty sure he isn't a vamp, or Jean Luc would be able to sense that. Maybe he's a high-level demon or something off the radar screens."

"So Jean Luc and Misha don't know what he is either?"

"They both say no. If anyone might know, it would be Jean Luc, since he's been around for more than four hundred years."

Dalton leaned forward and gawked at me. "What?!"

I smiled. "Don't let Jean Luc's laid back attitude fool you. He is a very powerful vampire. The longer vamps live, the more powerful they become."

He grimaced. "Like Sebastian. You know, one thing is bothering me about our encounter with him."

"Just one thing? I felt dirtier after talking to him than when I was slimed yesterday."

"When Jean Luc talked about Hampton being killed, Sebastian mentioned the Erie Bar. How did he know about the bar? You wiped everyone's memories."

"Good question. The only people who know what happened are the team."

"You're forgetting about the demon and the angel."

"Do you think he's working with the demon?" I didn't even want to imagine that psychopath being in league with the angel. I had enough trouble sleeping at night.

"Could be. Byron said the demon tried to protect the vampire from the angel, right? So they could've been working together."

I nodded and took a sip of my coffee, then noticed the empty plates on the table. "You didn't open the dessert?"

"I said I would wait for you." He opened the box. "Besides, the way you feel about this dessert, I thought you might want to eat the whole thing."

"Nope, split it in half. I want to be fair."

He laughed. "Since when?"

He handed me the plate and a coil of heat swirled in my belly. This was ridiculous. When had I turned into Scarlett O'Hara who needed Rhett Butler to carry her up the stairs? Wait, bad analogy, since that had actually happened yesterday.

I concentrated on my dessert, savoring the first bite. Dark chocolate, coffee, and ladyfingers—the triad of all that was holy. The second bite was even better.

"Soooo...what do you think?" I asked.

His eyes bored into mine. "It's amazing."

We ate in silence, and, with each bite, the tension grew and took on a presence of its own. I chewed faster, trying to finish so that I could find a way to get him out of my apartment. When we were both done, I carried the mugs back into the kitchen. I turned and found him within touching distance, carrying the plates.

"Let me help you."

"No, I can finish this later. I'm sure you want to get going."

"I'm not in any rush." He walked up to me and reached over to place the plates in the sink, cornering me. This was definitely my fault. What sane woman talked about orgasms and foreplay with a man and didn't expect to end up in this situation?

My breathing sped up as he leaned into me and blew lightly over my neck. My entire body came to attention, goose bumps shooting up my arms. Then it happened.

My cell phone rang. *Crap.* I thought that only happened in the movies. He let out a little groan when I ducked under his arm.

The *Hawaii 5-0* theme song filled the room. "It's Misha, I better get it." I reached for my bag and pulled out the phone, flipping on the speaker.

"Hey Mish, do you have any news yet?"

"Not yet, little one. I'm calling to apologize."

"For what?"

"This morning in the car, we had talked about going to dinner tonight and I totally forgot about it. I'll make it up to you another time, yes?"

"No problem."

"I'm going to stay at the office tonight to work on the computer files. Can you bring me in something for breakfast tomorrow? You know what I like."

"Yep, I'll see you in the morning."

I hung up the phone. Dalton had retreated to the other side of the room.

"I better get going. Thanks for dinner," he said as he walked to the door.

What the hell just happened?

By the time my apartment door closed, I was wracking my overly tired brain to figure out why he had bailed. What was the one-eighty about? After I calmed down, and my hormones were no longer clouding my brain, I thought about the conversation with Misha and laughed. We had totally sounded like a couple. "Bring me breakfast, you know what I like." I couldn't have planned it better myself if I'd tried.

So without any effort on my part, the operation to oust Dalton was back in play. The only problem was, I wasn't sure I wanted to get rid of him anymore.

CHAPTER 8

My morning routine re-established, I walked into the office and plopped the pastry bag next to Misha, who sat hunched over his computer.

He lifted his face, his eyes gleaming like a small child. "What did you bring me today?"

"Biscotti."

"I should marry you."

I laughed. Misha grinned and then peered over my shoulder. "Good morning, Joe."

I cringed. It was official. The Fates did not want the two of us together. I turned and plastered a smile on my face.

"Dalton."

"Morning." He walked over to the counter, reached for the pot and stopped. He glanced questioningly back at us.

Misha piped up. "Don't worry I made it."

Dalton nodded and poured himself a cup.

"You're a quick study, Joe," Misha chuckled.

Dalton joined us at the table. "Have you found anything in the files?"

"Plenty. I have only gotten through a few of them so far. Most of the business files seem legitimate. Ledgers of items being bought and sold. But I know when I dig further into this, I'll figure out what he was hiding. I did find something interesting, Kyle. A twenty thousand dollar transaction between Hampton and Kevin Doyle several months ago. Hampton was still in Chicago then."

Before Dalton could even ask, I enlightened him, "Kevin Doyle runs a pawn shop on Chester Avenue. He's a smarmy demon who uses the shop to front his illegal import business. If Hampton was dealing with him, then it's not legit."

Dalton stood. "I think it's time to pay him a visit."

The annoying little bell rang above the door as Dalton and I entered the Wee Bit o' Ireland Pawn Shop. A voice with a lilting Irish brogue called out to us from the back of the store, "Be wit' ye in a minute."

Pawn shops always amazed me. Shelves of electronics that haven't been in vogue for decades, jewelry and whatever else could potentially bring in money, lying about in no real order. I walked toward the back counter with Dalton on my heels. I wanted to be as close as I could to the little worm in case he tried to make a break for it.

Kevin Doyle strutted out of the back and stopped abruptly when he caught sight of me. He was maybe five foot six, with buggy eyes. He also had thinning hair and a ridiculous comb over. Apparently, demon males were as vain and clueless as human males when it came to male-pattern baldness.

"What do you want, McKinley?"

"Really, Doyle, it's been too long. What happened to your lovely Irish brogue? Do you only pull it out for unsuspecting customers?"

"What do you want?"

"We need to ask you a few questions."

"About what?"

"Charles Hampton."

"Don't know him." His right eye twitched.

"Really, so the money he gave you would not show up in your books?"

He shook his head emphatically. "I deal with a lot of people. Do you think I remember everyone?"

"The ones who give you twenty grand? Yes, I do."

He growled and Dalton tensed beside me. Up to this point, he had been hanging back, letting me do all the talking. Doyle took one look at him and stopped. I couldn't see Dalton's face, but I imagined he was doing one of his classic cop faces. I really needed him to teach me how to do that.

"Are you going to cut the BS now and tell us what Hampton paid you for?"

"I'll need to check my books."

"Let me guess, they're in the back room. Don't even try to make a run for it. I'll just stake out your pawn shop until you come back."

He sighed. "Fine, Hampton wanted me to find him a straend."

I enlightened Dalton. "Straends are instruments of torture. Very effective, too. Almost all humans succumb to them, and it does a pretty good job on supes, too. Of course they've been banned for over a century."

Doyle sputtered. "He wanted them for ornamental purposes."

"Whatever helps you sleep at night. Since this transaction was a few months ago, did you send them to him in Chicago?"

"Yes."

"And he only paid twenty for them? You must be slipping. Did he have you locate anything else?"

"No. Are we done now?"

"You're awfully anxious to get rid of us."

"I have a business to run."

I glanced over my shoulder at the empty shop and then back at him. "They're lining the aisles. I'll leave you in peace if you tell me what else you're hiding."

"I'm not hiding anything." His eye twitched again.

Man, he had a ridiculous tell. I would love to fleece him at poker.

"I've got an idea. I'm going to find a woman and tweak with her memory a bit, have her remember you propositioning her. Then I'm going to send her to Coleen."

He turned an interesting shade of puce, and his eyes bugged out even more than normal.

"You wouldn't."

"Try me."

We stared at each other for a few seconds before he finally caved.

"Word on the street is they're looking for Hampton."

I shrugged. "What's the big deal about that?"

"They are specifically asking for his head and offering money for its retrieval."

"Do you know who is asking?"

"No."

Interesting. "If you hear anything else, get in touch with me ASAP, or Coleen will have a special visitor."

Dalton drove back toward the office while I sorted through everything we had learned from Doyle.

"So who is Coleen?"

I smirked. "His wife. Dalmot demons are matriarchal. The females are dominant and can be extremely powerful. You don't cheat on them, ever."

"What happens if you do?"

"They have a giant tail like a scorpion and they beat you to death with it."

"God!"

"Then they eat you."

He glared at me. "Kyle..."

"The tail is a bit of an exaggeration." I laughed. "And demons aren't into cannibalism."

"I really need to have Misha tell me more about demons."

"Might be a good idea."

"Why would Hampton risk buying a straend?" Dalton asked.

"To ensure he could extract information from someone."

"What kind of information?"

I shook my head. "Not sure, but if an angel is willing to go all warrior on someone's ass, then I think it must be pretty bad."

"What's the deal with the head?"

"That one is totally puzzling me."

"Do you think Doc Miller might have an idea?"

"It couldn't hurt. I'll see if she can meet us. Maybe Misha and Jean Luc can throw in their two cents' worth, too."

Dalton and I made it to the storage facility first. Doc Miller had just gotten off her shift at the hospital and would meet us shortly. Then we'd conference in Jean Luc and Misha once she arrived.

I walked slowly through the shelves staring at the different items we had nabbed over the years.

"Does this place creep you out?" Dalton asked.

"No. It's necessary."

"So you don't think people can handle the truth?"

"I think humans would exploit supes if they knew about them." He locked his eyes on me and I squirmed under his gaze. "What do you think?"

He thought for a moment. "Some could handle the truth, but others would treat it as an excuse for bigotry."

"What did you do when your captain told you about the supernatural world?"

He smirked. "Honestly, I thought he was losing it. I almost called in a psych eval on him."

"What stopped you?"

"I started to think about all of the bizarre cases and the excuses he has given me over the years, and I realized the existence of the supernatural made some kind of twisted sense."

"So what was the first thing you did when you realized he was telling you the truth?"

"I went on the Internet to do research."

I shook my head. "A lot of what you find out there is bull."

"I figured that out the first time Jean Luc walked outside during the day and didn't burst into flames."

"Yeah. He can't stay out too long during the day, but he won't combust. Don't try to stake him, either. It doesn't work. Although it does piss him off."

"What about garlic or crucifixes?"

"Nah."

"So what *is* the truth about vampires?"

"They drink blood and live for a really long time. They are sired by other vampires who gain strength from the connection, so only certain vampires are allowed to sire."

"Like Sebastian."

"Right." *Now* I was creeped out.

He walked down the aisle and stared at a broadsword. "What about demons?"

"Each clan is different. There are twelve modern clans I'm aware of on earth. Each has their own distinctive features and powers."

"What does Misha look like?"

"My understanding is that a Shamat has reddish-orange skin with black eyes, but I've not seen Misha's demon side. He doesn't show it in public."

"And Doc Miller?"

"I don't know if Sabrina has a demon side that is visible. A succubus's ability to siphon life force out of humans is unique."

"What else do I need to know?"

"A lot. The most important thing to remember is that supes are like humans. They're both good and bad. Vampires can be noble like Jean Luc, or power-hungry like Sebastian. For demons, the really bad ones are normally not allowed on the planet, which is a good thing."

"Too bad we can't say the same thing for humans."

"Amen, Brother Dalton, amen."

A voice interrupted my sermon. "Hello?"

I hollered, "Hey Doc, we're back in the shelves, we'll be right up."

We walked through the door. Doc stood in the morgue, dressed to kill in a short black dress with spaghetti straps and three-inch sandals. I didn't dare check out Dalton's reaction.

I glanced at the clock on the wall. "Ah, Doc, it's one o'clock in the afternoon. Where are you going dressed like that?"

"I have a date. He wants to take me to Baltimore for dinner, so we're going on his jet."

"What he wants is to take you to bed."

She grinned. "Well, duh. Now what can I do for you?"

"We need to get Misha and Jean Luc on the phone first."
I entered the number on the speaker phone and clicked on
the monitor. After a few seconds, Misha's face flashed on the
screen.

"Hey guys. Wow, Doc, you look great." Misha turned away.
"Jean Luc, hurry up so you can see Doc, she's smokin'."

Jean Luc's face appeared. "Misha is correct. You are beautiful."

Doc smiled. "Thanks. As much as I enjoy all the compliments, I have a plane to catch. What do we need to talk
about?"

I filled the group in on the conversation Dalton and I had
with Doyle. Misha almost shot coffee out of his nose when
I told him about my threat to go to Coleen if Doyle didn't
help us.

When I finished my summary, Dalton launched the first
question. "How do these straends work, exactly?"

Doc frowned. "It's a metal piece in the shape of an eight
or infinity sign. It's placed at the base of the neck. Small
tentacles extend from it, insert under the skin, and link to
nerve endings. It causes excruciating pain, especially if the
person lies."

"And why is everyone so hot to find Hampton's head?"
Dalton countered. "Can he be brought back to life?"

Jean Luc shook his head. "No. Once a vampire loses his
head, there is no reanimation."

"Then what can you do with a severed head? And why
would someone be willing to pay a large amount of money
for it?" Dalton persisted.

"Maybe they want what's in it?" Doc suggested.

"Brains?" I grimaced.

"No, memories. Hampton used straends on someone to
extract information. It makes sense, then, that Hampton

would have that information in his memory. Misha, correct me if I'm wrong on this, but I've heard stories over the years that certain demons have the ability to extract memories from other beings. True?"

Misha frowned. "I've heard rumors of pulling memories from people, yes. But from a dead vampire?"

I interrupted. "Could whatever stopped Byron's heart also be able to pull memories from a head?"

"Maybe," Misha agreed.

Dalton nodded. "So we need to find the head first."

And, I thought, we needed to find out what this vamp knew that could trigger an apocalyptic power struggle.

CHAPTER 9

Dolly handed me a message before Dalton and I made it two steps into the office. Tim Connor had called. I cringed. I had offered to help his daughter, Trina, forget a horrible experience, but he had not trusted me at the time. Now a couple of weeks had passed. Since he was calling, that meant things were not going well.

Dolly bit nervously at her lower lip. She was aware of the case, since the family were shifters.

"Where's Jean Luc?"

"He's in his office. I'll let him know that you need him to go with you." Dolly got up and walked into the back room.

"What's going on?" Dalton asked.

"I've got to handle something concerning a previous case. I need Jean Luc to come with me."

"Do you need help?"

"No, you can't help with this." I watched his jaw set and plowed on before he could argue. "It's a sensitive case, and the family doesn't trust outsiders."

"No problem. I'll stay here with Misha and help go through the computer files."

Jean Luc and I took the shoreway to the burbs. He drove past Trina's school and followed the streets she used to walk home so I could become familiar with them. After a few minutes, we pulled up in front of a two-story Tudor house with a well-kept lawn. The American dream.

We walked up to the house and, before I could ring the bell, the door opened. Tim Connor's wife, Stephanie, stood in the doorway. I bit my tongue to stop from gasping. I had met her two weeks ago, and since then she had aged ten years. Her blonde hair was pulled back in a tight ponytail, accenting her haunted green eyes.

I nodded at her. "Stephanie."

"Thank you for coming." She stepped back, inviting us into the foyer. "Tim is in his office."

We followed her through the hall to a door on the far right. Connor sat behind his desk staring out the back window. His wife walked over and rested her hand on his shoulder, practically whispering his name, as if afraid to startle him.

"Tim, they're here."

He turned toward us, looking even more worn down than his wife. "Jean Luc, Ms. McKinley."

We sat down across from his desk, while his wife remained standing behind him, her hand still resting on his shoulder. Where Stephanie was blonde and fair, Tim was dark, with brown hair and eyes.

"Thank you for coming so quickly."

I leaned forward. "How's Trina?"

He swallowed hard. "She's not well. She's haunted by the memory of that man and what he threatened to do to her."

I gritted my teeth. A poacher had grabbed Trina on the eve of her twelfth birthday, when shifters normally change into their animal forms for the first time. The scum had told her that when she changed into her animal, he was going to skin her. Virgin pelts, as the poachers called them, were worth a lot of money. Luckily the pack had found her and taken care of the poacher, pack style. I hadn't asked for the details.

"You want me to remove the memory?"

"Yes, but first, I owe you an apology."

I shook my head. "No you don't. You were trying to protect your daughter. I was a stranger who came into your home and announced I was going to mess with her memories. I can understand why you said no."

"I should have listened to my heart at the time. I..." He hesitated. His wife squeezed his shoulder supportively. "I was afraid to go against Griffin."

Jean Luc explained for my benefit. "He is their leader."

I glanced between the two men in confusion. "I thought you were the pack leader."

Tim nodded. "I am one of the pack leaders. Griffin is the leader for the entire region. I report to him, as do all the other pack leaders. When he found out what happened, he didn't want any outsiders involved. He instructed us to close ranks. Again, I'm sorry for not giving you a chance."

"Griffin has agreed to me helping you now?"

He continued to avoid eye contact. "He's overseas. I can't wait until he returns. It's been a painful two weeks for Trina."

"I understand." This Griffin sounded like a piece of work.

"Would you be willing to help our daughter?" Tim finally met my eyes.

"Of course. But you need to know this might not work."

Stephanie spoke up. "Why not?"

"Sometimes I can't change memories for a supernatural. Plus, Trina was taken two weeks ago. This means it's now a long-term memory, and those are harder to change. I don't want you to lose hope, I just want to be up front about what's possible."

Tim reached up and placed his hand over his wife's. "We want you to try. We've been telling everyone she's sick. She's hasn't left the house since that day and isn't sleeping at night." He hesitated. "And she hasn't had her first change yet."

That couldn't be good. "What happens if she doesn't change soon?"

Stephanie choked back a sob. "She might never change."

"I know this is going to be painful, but I need you to tell me exactly what happened on the day of Trina's abduction. I want to be fully prepared before I try to scrub her memory. Also, I need to see your entire house, including Trina's bedroom."

Stephanie and I walked slowly into the back sunroom, the only room I hadn't seen yet. Trina sat on the couch painting her toenails. She was small for twelve, with long brown hair held back by an orange hair band that matched her flowered sundress.

It would have been the perfect picture of childhood bliss if not for the fact that she cowered when we approached her. She watched me with terrified chocolate eyes. My chest tightened and my skin tingled as anger percolated just beneath the surface. I wanted to bring that poacher back to life so that I could kill him all over again.

Stephanie sat down and attempted to sooth her daughter in a voice tinged with desperation. "It's okay, baby, Kyle's here to help you."

Trina's eyes met mine again, appraising me with a wounded look too old for her years. *Damn.*

I pushed my emotions away and locked them in the small room in my brain I used when I needed to regain control.

Smiling, I sat down across from her and pointed to her toes. "That's a cool color. What is it?"

She picked up the bottle and read the label. "Purple Passion."

"Nice. I may have to dye my hair purple."

Trina smiled slightly, then seemed to catch herself and stopped.

"Would you paint my fingernails for me?"

Trina glanced at her mother, who nodded. I leaned forward and held my hand out to her. She eyed me warily for a moment, then pulled the brush out of the bottle and ran a single stroke over my index fingernail. I sat deathly still, afraid any movement would cause her to bolt from the room. She titled her head in concentration as she carefully ran the brush along either side of my nail.

"I need you to think about something for me, Trina." The nail brush hesitated in the air, shaking slightly. "You don't need to talk about it out loud. I just need you to think about the last time you were walking home from camp. Just for a second." Trina's breathing accelerated and I continued in what I hoped was a calm voice. "That nail looks good, keep going."

Trina's head jerked slightly in what I hoped was a nod. Shoving the brush roughly back into the bottle she pulled it out and painted my middle finger. I went to work, imagining Trina walking from camp. But in my version, instead of being grabbed by the man in the van, she made it home. She walked into the house and told her mom she wasn't feeling good.

Then I filled in memories of lying in bed for days while she recovered from the flu, her mom not far from her side. This took a little imagination on my part, since I didn't know what it was like to have your mom take care of you when you were sick. Telling her to "stop crying, you're going to wake up Momma's newest boyfriend" was not a memory I would inflict on any child.

I worked the memories slowly into her as she painstakingly painted my nails. By the time she had finished the second coat, I was done. She sat back and smiled at me.

"How are you feeling, Trina?"

She bobbed her head. "Good, I had the flu but Mom's been taking care of me. When I don't feel good she makes me cinnamon toast."

"Sounds good." The knot in my stomach loosened, but I kept the door to that room in my head closed. I glanced over at Stephanie who was fighting back tears. "Do you think she'll make us some?"

"Mom?"

"Sure, I'll be right back." Stephanie grinned and rushed out of the room.

"Sorry to hear you were sick on your birthday."

"Yeah. I wonder if Mom will let me have some friends over this weekend."

"You'll have to ask her, but I bet first she'll want to make sure you're feeling better."

"I feel much better today." Trina's smile illuminated her face. "Maybe she'll let me go to camp tomorrow."

I looked quickly at my hands, but they blurred as my eyes filled. "You did a great job on my nails."

Jean Luc and I made it back to the office in record time. He dropped me off and left to do some sort of vampirish errand after I insisted I was fine. When I stepped into the reception area, Dolly glanced up expectantly. I simply nodded and she smiled. There really wasn't anything to say. I continued to the back office. Misha and Dalton were sitting in front of laptops at the table.

"So what have you guys found?"

Misha spoke up, "Not much yet. How's Trina?"

"She's good. Is there any coffee left?"

"Yep."

Dalton stood and stretched, picked up his mug and followed me to the counter.

I reached for my mug, hip-blocking his way, and smiled. "I get the first cup."

The pain came without warning, shooting up the back of my neck into my head and back down again. I lost the grip on my mug and it fell to the ground, shattering.

Dalton gripped my arm. "Are you okay?"

"Damn it. I loved that mug."

"Kyle, what's going on?" he persisted.

"I'm getting a migraine. No big deal." I bent down to clean up the mess and my head swam.

Misha rushed over. "I've got it. Why don't you go home? You have to be exhausted."

"I'm fine."

Instead of listening to me, Dalton grabbed both of my arms and forced me to sit down.

I tried to jerk away from his grip. "I told you I'm fine. This happens sometimes."

"Your nose is bleeding."

I reached up and wiped my hand under my nose. Pulling it away, I stared at my crimson fingers, and a small trickle of fear crept up my spine. *Well, that was a new one.* Dalton handed me some paper towels.

"Lean your head forward a little and pinch your nose shut."

I sat that way for a few minutes until the bleeding stopped. In the meantime, Misha had cleaned up my mug and was hovering, while Dalton's facial expressions alternated between concern and irritation.

"I'm good."

"Are you sure?" Dalton asked.

"Positive," I replied, although I was far from it.

"Is this from using your power?"

"I think so."

He growled, "Why would you risk yourself that way?"

And right then, the fear I was suppressing changed to anger. Sir Galahad needed skewering. "Because it's part of my job and you can't stop me from doing it. You're not my boss. As a matter of fact, you aren't even a permanent team member, so your vote doesn't count around here." I stood. "I'm going home and, before you ask, I can drive myself. See you tomorrow, Mish."

After I found a fairly close parking space at home, I sat for a moment with my eyes closed. The migraine pain thrummed on my right side and nausea threatened. Nervousness tightened my chest. It had never been this bad before. A rap on my car window made me jerk in my seat. Vinnie's wide eyes stared back at me through the glass. I rolled down my window.

"Didn't mean to startle you, Kyle." He held up a bag. "Dad sent me."

I shook my head. "I can't eat anything too spicy right now."

"It's cream of wheat. Dad said put a little sugar on it. He also said to pull your curtains and block the light out of your bedroom before you lie down."

I should know better than to doubt Tony. "Thanks, Vinnie."

I ate about half the cream of wheat and then settled in my bed. I was just dozing off when my cell phone rang. Reaching for it on the bedside stand, I checked the screen. Dalton. I powered down my phone, turned over and went to sleep.

CHAPTER 10

My doorbell rang at three a.m. and I reached for Stanley—the nine millimeter I kept behind my headboard. I wasn't naïve enough to think my power could stop a killer supe before he maimed or killed me, so Stanley was my trusty sidekick whenever Jean Luc or Misha weren't within shouting distance.

I flipped off the safety and walked quietly to my front door, adrenaline kicking my nerves into hyperdrive. I eased slowly up to peer through the peephole. Misha waved at me. I took a deep breath to calm my heartbeat, put Stanley's safety back on, and yanked open the door.

He grinned and pointed to the gun resting against my leg. "What's the deal with Stanley?"

"I don't know, maybe because it's the middle of the night and you're pounding on my door?"

"We tried to call you, but your phone keeps going to voice mail. Grab some clothes; Jean Luc is double-parked out front."

"What's going on?"

"Dalton called. He needs us at the city morgue. Says it's related to our case."

"I'll be right down."

I dressed in five minutes flat and ran down the stairs. Jean Luc was parked out front as promised. Three college girls standing outside the all-night bakery were giggling and waving at him. He was an undeniable chick magnet.

He screeched away from the curb once I was inside, and I snapped on my seat belt out of sheer self-preservation.

"What do we know?" I asked.

Jean Luc started. "Dalton called. The Coast Guard pulled a body from Lake Erie tonight."

"Is it a supe?"

"Dalton is not sure, but he wants us to examine it. How are you feeling? Misha told me it was worse this time."

"I'm fine. It was a lot of memory to scrub."

Jean Luc shot me a sideways glance. I wasn't sure he bought it. We arrived at the morgue and drove around back, where I spotted Dalton's SUV. When we parked, he got out, and we all followed suit, walking over to join him.

"Thanks for coming. We're going through the back service entrance so we don't draw attention."

The morgue was never a fun place to be, and at three in the morning it was downright depressing. The interior was poorly lit and painted a dingy green, which was not a good choice for morgue-chic. We walked into the main work area. Thankfully the exam tables were empty.

Dalton went over to the counter and opened a container of menthol gel, smearing some under his nose. He held the container out to me and I smeared a glob under my nose as well. If big rough, tough cop thought he needed it, what was coming must be bad, and I wasn't about to argue. He held up the container to Misha and Jean Luc who both shook their heads. He then pulled a pair of gloves out of a box and snapped them on.

Walking over to the bank of drawers in the wall, Dalton pulled out the middle drawer. God almighty, it was disgusting. The poor guy must have been in the water for quite a while. *Just breathe in the nice menthol and concentrate on what Dalton is saying.*

"The coroner thinks he was in the water for at least a week."

Jean Luc studied him. "I do not think he is supernatural."

Dalton nodded. "I didn't think so, either. I brought you here for this."

He reached down and turned the guy slightly so we could see his back. There was a red mark on the base of his neck in the shape of an eight.

"Is it what I think it is?" Dalton asked.

Misha pulled out his phone. "I'm going to take some pictures and send them to Doc, but I'm pretty sure this guy was tortured with straends. What does your coroner think it is?"

"He doesn't know. Said it might be some sicko's idea of branding the guy."

"Do we know who he is?" I asked.

"Not yet, but the detectives are on it."

I took a shallow breath through my mouth. "If we find out who he is, maybe we can figure out why Hampton would torture him."

Dalton shut the drawer with a resounding clank. "We'd better get going. I don't want anyone to find us in here."

We slipped out, and when we reached our cars, Dalton turned to us.

"Sorry to bring you all here in the middle of the night, but it was the only time to be sure we could examine the body. I'll see you in a couple of hours."

Jean Luc drove the van back to work since there was really no point in going home. I lay down on the couch to catch a few more hours of sleep. Minutes later mumbling voices woke me. I sighed. Could they not cut me some slack and let me sleep for a little while?

I opened my eyes. A blanket covered me. *When did that happen?* I looked around. Dalton was sitting at the table working on the laptop.

He glanced over at me. "Good morning."

"Morning. What time is it?"

"Around nine-thirty."

"What?! Why didn't you wake me?" I sat up quickly.

He shrugged. "You needed the sleep. I haven't heard anything from the detectives on the John Doe they pulled from the lake, so we let you sleep."

"Where's Misha and Jean Luc?"

"Misha's out buying supplies and Jean Luc went into his office and shut the door. Said he couldn't stand your snoring."

"I don't snore."

"Sure, whatever you say. Are you ready to hit the road?"

"Where to?"

"I want to go back to the alley behind the bar and see if we can talk to Sam again."

"You think he knows something more?"

"I think we have better questions to ask now."

"Give me five minutes. I'll meet you at your car."

We walked slowly through the alley behind the bar, searching for Sam, but couldn't find him. I nodded toward the cross alley.

"Do you want to look for Peter?"

"Yeah, hopefully he will be more receptive today." Dalton stopped. "I have one of those police-issue rain ponchos in the car. Do you want to put it on first?"

I shook my head. "When did you become a comedian?"

He shrugged. "There's a lot you don't know about me."

We walked into the alley and checked the doorways, hoping to find Peter squatting in one of them. When we came to the last door, he was sitting on a wooden box snoring softly.

Great. I really did not want to startle him. Dalton and I glanced at each other and took a careful step back.

I whispered his name. "Peter?"

He slowly opened his eyes and stared up at us. I smiled at him, praying we wouldn't have a repeat performance of the other day. I held up my hands in front of me. "Peter, we are not going to hurt you. Can we talk to you for a minute?"

He looked down, shamefaced. "I'm sorry about the other day, miss. I was scared, and when he came at me"—he pointed at Dalton—"I didn't know what to think. Afterwards, Sam told me who you were."

"It's okay," I responded. "Why were you so scared?"

"The night before, I saw what happened in the alley."

"Can you tell us about it?"

"I was going over to check on Sam before I turned in for the night. Before I made it around the corner, I heard a loud bang. When I peeked around, I saw the metal door to the bar had been slammed into the wall. I was shocked to see a Pavel come storming out the door, and in his demon form."

"Did you recognize him?" I asked.

"No, but maybe if he had changed to his human form, I might have."

"Then what happened?"

"The Pavel disappeared. Then the angel came out next, carrying a sword. That shocked me more than anything else. I've never seen an angel before, but I knew what he was. He stood for a minute and then disappeared, too."

"Was either of them carrying anything else?"

"No, neither had the head."

"How..."

"Word on the street is they're looking for the vamp's head, so I put two and two together."

"Did you see anyone else?" Dalton interjected.

"I saw Sam move behind the dumpster and knew he was safe. But I didn't see anything else."

"What about later?" I asked.

"I took off then. A couple hours later, I heard Byron cut through my alley on his way home. He usually gives Sam and me leftovers, but he kept on going this time. I figured he was probably upset by what had happened."

"Was he carrying anything?"

He shook his head. "Nope."

"Was anyone following him?"

"I think so. I heard footsteps."

"Did you sense anything?"

"I think it was human, but I can't be sure."

Dalton jumped in. "Have you seen Sam lately?"

"Sam decided to move for a while. Thought it was too dangerous here right now."

We said our goodbyes and walked back to the car.

I bit my lip to stop from screaming. "Well, crap. We aren't any closer to finding out who has the head."

Dalton started the car. "At least Peter corroborated Sam's story. So the question is, if the angel, the demon, and Byron didn't take the head, then how did it disappear?"

"One of the humans?"

"You scrubbed them."

I shrugged. "I'm going to have Misha pull their names once we get back to the office."

We drove in silence for a minute until Dalton cleared his throat. "Before we get back to the office, I want to say I'm sorry about yesterday. You're right, I don't have the right to tell you what to do or how to use your gift."

My mouth dropped open in surprise.

He continued, "Misha explained to me about Trina and what you did for her."

"Sometimes my ability actually helps someone."

"I don't remember seeing an Amber Alert for Trina. Was it handled without police involvement?"

"The pack went after the poacher. You don't mess with a shifter's family. They found the guy within twenty-four hours. He had Trina locked in a shed."

"Jesus. He didn't hurt her, did he?"

I swallowed the disgust threatening to well up. "He didn't want to damage her before she shifted for the first time. Don't ask me what happened to him. You don't want to know."

He nodded.

"About yesterday. I know you were worried about me. Believe it or not, I can usually take care of myself. Even though you've seen me slimed and bleeding more than once, I'm not weak."

He stopped at a red light.

"I would never use the word weak to describe you, Kyle."

I blinked at the intensity of his stare, a tendril of warmth uncoiling in my chest. "Thank you."

"Pigheaded, impetuous, smart-mouthed. Those are the words that come to mind."

"Wow, Dalton, way to ruin a moment."

The light turned green and he drove through the intersection, laughing.

CHAPTER 11

I stood with my mouth gaping as Misha pulled a cordless drill out of his tool belt and attached a white board to the wall in the back office. I backed out of range. Whenever Misha used power tools, trouble was sure to follow.

Dalton held the board up until Misha finished drilling and attaching the screws.

After he thanked Misha, I raised my eyebrows at him, and he said, "I asked him to get a white board so we can plot out the case."

"You should never send Misha alone to the store to buy things. He always comes back with some sort of high-tech gadget."

"It's just a white board with dry erase markers. What's so high-tech about that?"

Misha smiled. "Actually, this is a special board. If you flip the switch in the corner, anything written on the board can be downloaded to a computer for storage. Here are the markers, and I have already installed the software on the computers."

I laughed. "I told you. I don't know why you fight me, Dalton. You should be bowing to my superior intelligence."

For some reason he ignored my statement and spoke to Misha instead. "Is the board ready to go?"

"Yes, ready when you are."

Dalton walked over and picked up the marker. "Then let's start with a timeline of what's happened. What should we list as the first event?"

Misha spoke up. "Fight in the bar where Hampton was decapitated."

I shook my head. "No, the first event we know about is when Hampton purchased the straends from Doyle."

The new marker squeaked across the board while Dalton took notes. "Then we have the torture and murder of our John Doe a week ago. Presumably by Hampton or someone working for Hampton. Then Hampton's death."

"Right." I agreed. "The million dollar question is the missing head. Misha, can you pull up a listing of people who were at the bar that night? If Peter's account of the event is correct, Byron, the angel, and demon didn't take the head, so we have to consider the others. Maybe one was a supe and we didn't realize it."

Jean Luc spoke from behind me and I jumped. "Other than Byron, I did not sense any supes in the bar."

I scowled back at him. "Jeez, give a girl some warning before you sneak up on her."

He bowed mockingly. "I apologize."

Dalton brought us back on topic. "Could another supe have been there and already left the building?"

"I don't think so," Misha said. "I asked Byron if there were any more supes in the bar at the time of the incident and he said no."

"What if they showed up afterwards? Maybe somebody Hampton was supposed to be meeting close by?" Dalton persisted.

"Wouldn't Byron have noticed someone coming in after the fight?" I argued.

"Not necessarily." Misha walked over to the board. "Maybe it was another demon or angel who materialized, snatched the head, and then dematerialized."

"Or maybe a vamp with super speed?" I turned to Jean Luc. "Would a vamp sense another one's death?"

"If the vampire was close by, they would more than likely experience a general loss of energy, yes. If they were from the same sire, most definitely."

Maybe we were on to something. "Sebastian knew the second he died. If Hampton was meeting Sebastian or one of his fledglings, they could have gone in and swooped up the head before we got there."

"Here's what I don't understand, Jean Luc," Dalton said. "Why wouldn't Hampton have poured on the super speed to get away from the demon?"

"He was a relatively young vampire. It can take decades before powers mature. He probably did not have the ability yet."

Dalton turned back to the board and listed the suspects who might have the head. "Okay, now let's talk about Byron. I have a theory about why the demon went after him. Normally, when an event occurs in front of humans, you erase their minds but don't erase any supe memories, correct?"

I nodded.

"So the demon went after Byron thinking he was the only one from the bar who remembered what had happened."

"It makes sense," I conceded. "But like you said before, if the demon had been in Byron's apartment when we arrived, he wouldn't have bothered hitting me over the head."

"Agreed. Peter said a human followed Byron. We need to figure out who the other perp was and why he was in the apartment while we were there. Jean Luc, did we dust for prints or pick up evidence from Byron's apartment?"

"Yes. I have a partial print I was able to extract from the statue that the guy used to attack Kyle. Since demons do not have prints while they are in their demon form, we can rule the Pavel out unless he transformed to human. I processed the prints through our database and found nothing. I am running them through human channels now."

Dalton grinned. "I won't even ask how you can access police and FBI databases. What else do we know?"

Misha spoke up. "I've been researching demons. Even though Pavels are powerful, they normally do not have the ability to stop a human heart with a thought. He would have had to call in some huge favors from the demon realm to garner that power."

"What's a demon realm?" Dalton asked.

Before Misha could answer, Dalton's phone beeped. He pulled it out and checked the screen. "It's a text from one of the detectives working the John Doe case." He clicked on the screen. "Good news. We have an ID on our Doe. His name is David Cowell. He was a former Jesuit priest. He taught religious studies at John Carroll University until a year ago."

I piped up. "Former? Did he leave or did the church kick him out?"

Dalton answered, "Only one way to find out. Let's go visit the campus. Misha, can you enlighten me later about demons and the demon realm?"

"No problem. I have a PowerPoint presentation that explains the basics. We'll go through it when you get back."

I laughed when Dalton's mouth dropped open.

Dalton and I walked around John Carroll's quad toward the administrative offices.

I pointed to the building. "The offices are over to our left."

"You're familiar with the campus?"

"Yeah. Misha, Jean Luc and I were here a few years ago. We had to cover up for a drunken freshman shifter who decided it would be hilarious to show his tail to his roommates. You would think it would be easy to scrub a drunk's mind, but it's not."

"I can imagine."

We walked up to the building and opened the door into the main area. A student sat behind the front reception desk.

"Lieutenant Dalton, Cleveland police. We need to speak to Father Brown on a police matter."

The girl's eyes widened. I wasn't sure if it was the reference to the police or because Dalton had turned his killer eyes in her direction. I had to hand it to her, the girl held it together.

"Take a seat. I'll call Father's office to see if he's available."

Within two minutes, Father Brown appeared. "Please come with me."

We walked down the hallway and around the corner into Brown's office. Large windows overlooked the quad. Since it was summer, the campus was relatively quiet.

After the door was securely shut, he gestured for us to sit. "You are here on police business. Is this about David, Lieutenant? The detectives were already here this morning."

"Yes. We need to ask you some additional questions about him. They must have told you his death is a suspected homicide?"

Father Brown nodded. "I have been thinking about it all day. I can't imagine why anyone would want to kill David."

I leaned forward. "Maybe someone was holding a grudge?"

"I don't know why they would."

Dalton continued. "David left the priesthood?"

"Yes, he was a priest for twenty years and decided he could not continue in the life."

"Did he decide, or did the church decide for him?" I asked.

Father Brown frowned. "The reason for his leaving is not what you're thinking."

"Would you enlighten us, please?" Okay, I probably needed to dial down the sarcasm.

Father Brown turned to Dalton. "Are you Catholic?" Dalton nodded.

For some reason he didn't bother asking me. "The basic teachings of Catholicism, as with most Christian doctrine, include the concept of good and evil. Humans were made in the image of God and were led astray by temptation. God sent His only Son to earth to save us from our sins. Evil and the temptation to do evil things to ourselves and others, as well as the avoidance of this path, are part of our daily challenge."

He hesitated before continuing. "Even though we speak of the devil in our teachings, we believe he works through people. David began to believe there were actual demons among us."

This was not good. "What do you mean, Father?"

"He believed there were people who had actual demons inside of them. These people looked like you and me, but could turn into demons."

My stomach twisted. "What did he do about it?"

"At first he simply told me and some of the other priests. We sent him to counseling, but he wasn't swayed from his conviction. When it started to become part of his teachings, we had no choice but to remove him from the classroom. It was one of the hardest decisions I have ever had to make."

"When did David start having these ideas?"

"About two years ago. He went on a sabbatical, and when he returned he was withdrawn and quiet. A few months later he started talking about the demons."

"Where did he take this sabbatical?"

"He spent a month in Rome and then traveled around Europe on his own for another two months. I'm not certain of all the places he went. Do you honestly think his delusions caused his death?"

"We are following every lead. If we know his frame of mind, it might help us figure out what happened to him," Dalton volunteered. "What had David been doing since leaving the priesthood?"

Father Brown shook his head. "I'm not sure. He became very closemouthed about it. Whenever I asked him, he would tell me it was safer if I did not know the details, and I didn't want to push him. I was afraid he would shut down altogether."

Dalton stood and pulled out a business card. "Thank you for your time, Father. If you think of anything else that might help us, please call me."

"Yes, I will. Thank you Lieutenant and Miss...?"

"Smith." I answered.

Father Brown stared at me for a second and nodded. He had the same look Doc Miller gave me when I lied to her.

When Dalton and I stepped outside the building, he rolled his eyes. "Smith?"

"He doesn't need to know my name."

"If you're going to lie, you could be a *little* more creative."

"It got the job done."

He frowned. "Or it made him more suspicious."

"We need to check out Cowell's place."

"Agreed, but we can't go there now. The detectives and investigative unit are probably still working the scene. We'll wait until tonight to sneak in and check it out."

I smiled. "I love being stealthy. Jean Luc will want to come too. He's the king of stealth."

CHAPTER 12

I had fallen into a rut. It was midnight, and here I was again, standing outside my apartment with a box of cream sticks, waiting for my ride. Only I could have a late-night rendezvous which included whipped cream and three beautiful males, none of whom were sleeping with me.

I shook off my pity party when Jean Luc came down Mayfield Road way too fast and screeched to a stop in front of my building, the smell of burnt rubber filling the air. The back door of the van opened and Misha held out his hands. One to help me into the van, the other to snag the pastry box.

"What have we tonight?"

"Cream sticks."

Misha sniffed. "Chocolate?"

I smiled. "Yeah, and I had them throw in some maple cream for variety."

"I don't know what I would do without you."

I sat down in the seat, catching a frown on Dalton's face which he masked quickly. I had forgotten about the whole *Misha-as-my-boyfriend* scenario I had been spinning. I would need to take care of that at a later and much more private time.

"So where are we heading?"

"Parma," Jean Luc responded.

"Pierogi," Misha mumbled.

I laughed. "Eat your pastries, Mish. There are no all-night restaurants serving pierogi in Parma."

"What are pierogi?" Dalton asked.

Misha gasped. "You can't be serious."

Dalton held up his hands. "Sorry, but I'm not originally from here. And I've only lived here the past few years."

I decided to enlighten him. "Pierogi are a Polish food. They are similar to ravioli, but the pasta is thicker, and they're stuffed with a combination of mashed potatoes and anything else you can think of—cheese, onions, and broccoli, to name just a few."

"I think I've seen them in the frozen food section. I'll have to try them."

Misha gasped again. "Don't you dare!"

"Misha, knock it off. You sound like a debutante with the vapors. What he means is, you have to have authentic pierogi. Come to Parma and find a mom and pop diner with a grandma working in the back rolling out the pierogi by hand."

"There's one Kyle and I go to quite often. You'll have to come with us next time."

Dalton's jaw tightened before he spoke. "I'll do that."

I flipped open the box lid to distract Misha from saying anything else.

"Oh. Baker's dozen. Thanks, Kyle."

Dalton turned in his seat. "That's a lot of donuts for the four of us."

"Actually, Jean Luc doesn't eat and I'm not hungry. I brought the dozen for Misha and had them throw in an extra in case you wanted one."

Dalton gawked as Misha dug into the box and pulled out a stick, taking a large bite.

I reached into the box and pulled out a maple cream, handing it to Dalton. "His demon metabolism allows him to eat anything he wants without gaining weight. If it could be bottled and sold to humans, we would make millions."

Thirty minutes later we arrived at Cowell's house. Misha had eaten half the box already.

Misha and his cream sticks would stay in the van to monitor police traffic while the rest of us searched the house. We parked on a back street and cut through the yard to get to the small bungalow. Police tape formed an 'x' across the door. Jean Luc had the door unlocked in about thirty seconds. Even Dalton was impressed.

We slid under the crime scene tape and stepped into the house. Dalton and I turned on our flashlights, but Jean Luc didn't bother since he could see in the dark. The house looked like a cyclone had hit it.

I aimed my flashlight around the room, taking in the kitchen and the mess. The cupboards were open and the contents strewn everywhere. I wrinkled my nose at the spoiled food littering the floor. "God, the police got a little carried away."

Dalton spoke up. "Cops didn't do this. Captain told me the place had been ransacked before today."

"We should split up," Jean Luc said. "I will take the front of the house. The two of you should remain in the back so your lights are not detected."

Jean Luc sped off and we went down the hall to the bedrooms. Dalton and I split up, and I took the first room on the right. All I found were a twin bed and a dresser. The drawers had been pulled out, but they were empty. The closet was bare. Shining my flashlight around the room, I noticed a box under the bed. I pulled it out and found items from Cowell's childhood, probably mementoes kept by his mother.

Next down the hall was a small bathroom. A few toiletries littered the floor. The next door led into a larger bedroom with a full bed and two dressers. Again, the room was bare, with the exception of a sixties wedding photo.

Through the last door across the hall I found another small bedroom, but this one had been used recently. Sheets and a blanket had been stripped from the mattress, and clothes were scattered around the room. Dalton was sitting at the desk in the far corner, going through the drawers.

He glanced up when I came into the room. "Did you find anything?"

"The other two bedrooms were empty. What have you found?"

"Not much. Cowell wasn't a hoarder, that's for sure."

"Well, he was a priest for twenty years, he probably wasn't too materialistic."

Dalton stood up. "There's nothing in this desk, either. Why do you think he was staying in this small room instead of the master?"

"I think this was his childhood home. Maybe he didn't think it was right to stay in his parents' bedroom."

"Well, I can't believe he wouldn't have something stashed here."

"Maybe the cops already took it as evidence?"

"No, I checked the inventory list. They took very little from here. They're as confused as we are. They did dust for prints to see if they could figure out if the killer grabbed him here."

"What do you think?" I asked.

"I think whoever tortured Cowell didn't get what they needed from him and hoped to find it here."

"Yeah, but where would it be? Wait, maybe he had a secret hiding place."

"What?"

"When you were a kid, didn't you have a secret hiding place in your bedroom? You know, somewhere you could hide your treasures?"

"Under my mattress."

I rolled my eyes, but I didn't think he could see me in the dark. "Not the most creative place, Dalton. Please tell me you didn't stick your Playboys there. Your grandma knew for sure about those."

"I didn't keep Playboys in my room."

"Of course not." I decided to let it drop. "I think the other small bedroom was his childhood room. I'm going to go check the floorboards and the heating ducts in there. You check in here."

I walked back to the first bedroom, and was crawling around knocking on the wood floor hoping for a loose floorboard when Jean Luc walked in.

"The rest of the house is pretty empty."

"I'm looking for a secret hiding place."

Jean Luc nodded and joined the hunt. I loved a male who didn't ask questions. After a few more minutes, I found a loose baseboard. "Jean Luc."

He was there in a flash, helping me pry it off. There was a space between the wall and the floor, and I reached in and touched a thin book. Pulling it out and opening it, I aimed my flashlight on the page. It was a drawing of a demon. Quickly flipping through, I found more pictures and writing.

Dalton walked into the room as Jean Luc helped me to my feet.

"I didn't find anything in the other room."

"We did. Let's get out of here before someone notices us."

As if in answer to my statement, all of our cell phones beeped. It was a text from Misha. *Cops R here.*

Jean Luc spoke first. "You hide, I will distract them."

"But, Jean—" Before I could get the rest of the words out, Jean Luc grabbed me around my middle and I was riding an invisible wave of speed. Within seconds, I came to a halt. My knees were knocking as my stomach tried to catch up to the rest of my body. My flashlight had been turned off and placed in my pocket. In an instant he was gone again. I groped around, trying to decipher where I was and touched an empty coat hanger. *A closet.*

In the next second there was a whoosh of air and Dalton was plastered against me. Jean Luc shut the door, closing us in the closet. "Be quiet. I am going to create a diversion."

I stood there in shock for several reasons. One, Jean Luc had never used his super speed on me before. Two, it was pitch dark and the cops were right outside the door. And three, I was pressed up against Dalton, and it was more than pleasant.

My heart raced and my legs were still unsteady from my *faster-than-the-speed-of-light* trip across the room. I trembled a little and gripped the book harder. Dalton reached around me, placing his hand on the small of my back to steady me. I wanted to see his face, but it was pitch dark. I took a couple of deep breaths, which in hindsight was not a good idea, since it filled my lungs with Dalton's scent and pressed my breasts up against his chest.

My earlier observation was correct. He was rock solid. Before I could embarrass myself further by rubbing against him like a cat, shouting from outside stopped me.

"Stop! Police!"

Footsteps pounded and then the police car took off after Jean Luc, sirens blaring.

Dalton and I stood there for a second longer before he spoke. "We'd better move. They'll call in backup to help with the chase and come check the house."

"Let's go, then," I replied, my voice sounding strained to my own ears.

Dalton opened the door and reached for my hand, linking our fingers. We walked through the dark house carefully, not daring to turn on our flashlights. Once out the back door, we dashed across the yard and through the trees to the next street.

Misha waited for us in the van. As we piled in, he started the engine. "Glad to see you two. We have to go meet Jean Luc a couple of streets over. He called me a minute ago." He pulled away from the curb. "This whole night reminds me of a *Mission Impossible* episode."

When Misha began to hum the theme song, my normal reaction would have been to reach up and smack the back of his head, but my hand was still warm from Dalton's touch earlier. Misha could sing all he wanted to.

Five minutes later, we pulled up in front of an all-night laundromat. Jean Luc jumped into the passenger seat, much to my surprise, and Misha's. "I want to read the book while you drive."

I handed it to him and he paged through it. After a couple of minutes, my lack of patience got the better of me. "What's in it?"

"Drawings of various demons. I recognize some of them. Misha can take a look at this back at the office. Cowell's notes are in Latin and, unfortunately, I am a bit rusty, so I will need to do some research before I can translate it for you. As far as I can tell, the main themes are heaven, hell and damnation."

Once we were back in the office, Jean Luc and Misha got to work on the book right away. Dalton volunteered to take me home.

We rode in silence, although inside my body was hopping around like a bunny rabbit on a sugar rush. I hadn't had a good adrenaline rush in a while. It still surged through me, and being this close to Dalton wasn't helping it to calm down. He, on the other hand, seemed to be cool as a cucumber. Why couldn't I control my emotions that well? As the silence continued, memories of the closet and Dalton's body pressed against mine invaded my thoughts. So much for trying to calm myself down.

Pulling in front of my building, Dalton double parked and got out, walking around to my side. He opened the door and I stepped out. Escorting me to my building, he stood there for a moment outside the door.

"You okay?" he asked.

I swallowed. "Yep, you?"

He grinned. "All in a night's work."

Before I could move, he boxed me in, arms on either side of me. He leaned forward, his face mere inches from mine. He stared at me for a second as if asking permission. I bridged the gap and our lips met. His were surprisingly soft and full against mine. I wanted to gobble him up. Trying to remain calm, I slowed down my kissing until his lips parted and his tongue slid against my lips, asking for permission to enter. I opened my mouth, moaning slightly when his tongue began to play with mine.

I leaned further into him, pressing against his chest and threading my fingers through his hair. Holy God, it was like a religious experience. Just as I settled into the kiss, he backed away. I blinked at him in confusion.

"I'm sorry, Kyle. This isn't fair to you or Misha."

What was he saying? My ears were buzzing. Hell, my whole body was buzzing. What the hell did Misha have to do with this?

"I'll see you tomorrow."

"Wait, where are you going?"

"This isn't right."

"But..."

"Don't say anything. I don't want either of us to regret this in the morning. Good night, Kyle."

He walked over to his car and got in. This was ridiculous. I hurried over to him and he rolled down the passenger window.

Before I could say a word he spoke, "Misha and I need to have a talk before this can go any further." He rolled up the window and pulled away.

I watched him drive away, my feet glued to the sidewalk. How could something backfire so horribly? Of course, I might have deserved it for trying to be conniving. I was determined, pigheaded, opinionated, yes—but conniving? I called Misha on his cell and got his voice mail. "Mish, call me as soon as you get this."

Crap.

CHAPTER 13

I jerked awake, slammed my hand down hard on my alarm clock, and cringed when the plastic knob snapped and came off in my hand. I had been dreaming, but the specifics escaped me. When I reached for the memory, dread filled me like cold fingers wrapping around my spine. I shivered. Remembering the dream was not that important.

I took my phone off the nightstand and checked to make sure the battery wasn't dead. It was fine, but Misha had still not called me back. *Great.* Dalton was too damn noble for his own good. Why did he need to talk to Misha, anyway? Even if Misha and I were seeing each other, I made my own decisions about who I got involved with.

I paused my internal soliloquy long enough to get ready. I stopped at the bakery on the way to work to buy warm apple streusel. Since it was Misha's favorite, I could hopefully butter him up...or at least apologize if he'd already had an awkward conversation with Dalton.

Running up the stairs to the office, the scent of apples and cinnamon trailing behind me, I plowed through front reception into the back room to find both Misha and Jean Luc there.

"Is Dalton here?"

Jean Luc smiled. "Good morning to you, too, Kyle. Dalton called. He has to deal with a police matter this morning. He plans to call in later so we can go over our case."

I walked over to Misha. "Have you talked to him today?"

"Not yet. What have you brought me?"

I let out the breath I had been holding. "Apple streusel."

Misha's right eyebrow shot up. "Jean Luc, I think Kyle has done something wrong."

"What're you talking about?" I sputtered, plopping the box on the table with a soft thunk.

"You only bring me streusel when you need to apologize. What's going on?"

Since when did Misha become so intuitive? "Um, you know a couple of days ago when you told me to be honest with Dalton about us?"

Jean Luc interrupted. "What exactly have I been missing?"

"Dalton thinks Misha and I are a couple."

"Oh." Jean Luc grinned.

I looked down and ran my fingers over the pockmarked table. "Yeah well, it gets worse. I didn't exactly clear up the misconception."

"Kyle..." Misha grumbled.

"Well, you didn't help matters."

"What do I have to do with it?"

"Let's see. First, you make an offhanded comment about the shirt he was wearing being yours. Then Dalton over-heard us on the phone the other day and you were all, 'Kyle, you know what I like to have for breakfast,' in your sexy Russian accent. What's a guy to think?"

"You think my accent is sexy?"

"Mishaaaaa! Stay focused," I groaned.

"Sorry, I don't understand what the problem is. I thought you wanted to brush him off."

"Yeah, well...not so much anymore."

Misha smiled like a Cheshire cat. "Then why didn't you just tell him the truth?"

"I was going to last night, and then he got all proper and told me he had to talk to you before we could go any farther. It was just a kiss, for cripes' sake."

Jean Luc laughed. I gaped at him in surprise. He was not normally much of a laugher. "*Ma petite*, you are so adorable. Why do Americans have so much trouble expressing their emotions? I shoved you both into a closet and you still are not talking to each other. I thought proximity might help matters."

"What?" I blurted.

"It is obvious you care for each other. I personally thought it was both pragmatic and imaginative of me to put you together in the closet."

Good God, I had my own supernatural matchmaker.

Misha nodded. "I told her the other day humans worry too much about such things."

I gritted my teeth. "Guys. Stop being so patronizing and help me out here."

"Did I not say this would backfire on you, little one? You should have jumped him days ago."

"You're right. Is that what you want to hear?"

"It's a start."

"Fine, I'm sorry for having dragged you into the middle of this. Now eat your damn streusel."

I stomped out of the room to my office. It wasn't very mature, but that was just tough. I plopped down to have a good old-fashioned pout, but then realized I hadn't asked Jean Luc about Cowell's journal. I walked back down the hall and slowed to a stop when Misha and Jean Luc's conversation reached my ears.

"I owe Joe twenty," Jean Luc groused.

"Quit your whining. I owe him fifty. I didn't think she'd even tell what was going on, let alone apologize."

I walked into the main area, and tried to count to ten before erupting. It didn't work. "What the hell are you two talking about?"

Misha actually had the decency to cringe. Jean Luc shrugged at me, making my blood pressure rise even faster.

"Well," Misha sputtered. "It was Joe's idea. He thought we should let you confess what you had done, instead of telling you we knew what was going on."

"Did he, now? And *when* did he come up with this glorious plan?"

"Yesterday. He asked me about our relationship. I told him the truth, and he wasn't too happy about you lying to him."

"He called you last night after he dropped me off?"

All of a sudden, Misha wouldn't meet my eyes.

"Misha?"

"We talked on the way to pick you up last night."

"The low-down dog." My face heated and I almost growled. He'd already known I wasn't involved with Misha when we were kissing.

Misha raised his hands as if to placate me. "Kyle, take it easy. Let's not make this worse."

I smiled at him, which immediately ratcheted up the tension in the room.

"Don't worry, I won't say a word about this to him. And if you ever want me to bring you pastries again, you won't say a word about this conversation, either."

Misha reached for the streusel box, probably fearful I would take it away from him now. "Fine," he replied grudgingly. "But rethink whatever you're planning."

Jean Luc shook his head. "It is no use, Misha. This reminds me of your soap operas. No one ever learns their lesson on those, either."

I was ready to launch a retort, when the intercom buzzed and Dolly's voice came over the speaker. "Joe's on the phone asking for a status update."

I tamped down my anger. This would have to wait. We had a job to do.

Jean Luc replied, "Thank you Dolly, we will pick it up here." He punched the outside line. "Joe?"

"Yeah, is everyone there?"

"Yes we're all here," I answered as sweetly as my teeth would allow me to without sprouting a cavity.

Dalton plowed ahead. "Jean Luc, what did you get out of the book?"

"Most of the drawings are of demons. Misha was able to identify their clans with the exception of two pictures he must research further. I was correct, it is written in Latin."

"But you have been able to interpret it?"

"Most of it, yes. It has specific, quite accurate descriptions of various demons and their traits. What will take me more time is the writing on the inside front flap. It appears to be a poem, or maybe a psalm, but it is in a language I have never seen before. Cowell was attempting to interpret it himself."

"What did he have so far?" Dalton asked.

"He translated some of the lines, but they are not complete. It starts with *Evil thrives amongst us.* Then the word *Angels*, then some more words which are not translated, followed by the word *battle.* The next line has the word *weapon.* Then there is another stanza not translated."

We sat silently for a minute before I spoke, "Boy, that's sure a pick-me-up."

"I will let you know if I can figure out the other lines."

Dalton continued, "Misha, have you found anything else in Hampton's computer files?"

"Nothing that looks illegal. Everything so far seems aboveboard. I was going to have Kyle help me with it today."

Oh, joy, I could hardly wait.

"I'm going to be at the police station for most of the day, but I'll follow up with you later."

"Bye. Have a nice day." I pressed the disconnect button as Misha and Jean Luc watched me warily.

I rubbed my gritty eyes and pushed away from the table. I had been sitting for too long, and the remnants of our lunch from several hours ago still lay in the open pizza box on the table. The computer files were getting us nowhere. I stood up to stretch.

"I can't find anything in these files," I whined.

Misha sighed. "I told you they were clean. I was hoping you would spot something I missed."

"But, don't you see, that's part of the problem. The books are too clean. No one can run a business without making adjustments. There are no returns or deductions for damaged items. No shipping cost issues. There is no way these can be the real thing."

Misha yawned and stretched as well. "So he cooked the books and we're looking at his clean copies."

"Yep, I should have shoved the second memory stick down my bra instead of this one."

Misha smiled. "You were lucky to have gotten this out from under Sebastian's nose."

I almost shuddered at his name. "You're right. He is one scary vampire. Speaking of vampires, where has Jean Luc run off to?"

"To follow up on the case we had with the demon twins a couple of weeks ago. He wants to make sure the parents are keeping them in line and they aren't fighting with each other in public anymore."

"That was a tough one, wiping half the soccer team's memories of the boys throwing energy balls at each other."

Misha laughed. "I think they learned their lesson."

"Did you ever do anything like that as a baby demon?"

"I got into trouble, yes. But remember, when I was a child you didn't have to worry about camera phones and YouTube."

"Which is why we need your technical expertise. I don't know what we're going to do when something big finally goes viral."

Misha shrugged. "People will think it's a hoax."

"Let's hope so." I filled the empty coffee carafe with water and brewed a new pot. Hazelnut filled the air. "Okay, what are our next steps?"

Misha went over to the white board and picked up a marker, writing "Cooked Books" next to Hampton's name. "I'm going to start working on the demons in Cowell's book I don't recognize."

"If they aren't in our database, do they exist?"

"There are many things in the supernatural world we do not have documented. Cowell's account of the other demon clans was accurate. I have listed the seven he had researched on the board. Maybe the ones I don't recognize are not allowed out of the demon realm."

"Like a demon who can stop a human heart?"

"Possibly," Misha answered. "I'm going to have to leave for a while to do the next stage of my research."

"Do you need me to tag along?" I knew damn well he was going to see his clan leader and I wouldn't be allowed to go.

"No. You can't come with me, Kyle."

"One of these days I'm going to meet your Grand Poobah."

Misha smirked. "It will be an interesting meeting, I'm sure." He walked to the door. "I won't be back until late."

"I'll see you tomorrow. Call me if you have any news."

I went back to my office and had only been sitting for a couple of minutes when footsteps sounded in the hallway.

"Misha, did you forget something?"

"It's me."

Dalton stepped into the doorway and I gawked at him. He was decked out in a charcoal gray suit with a light blue shirt and tie, and his turquoise eyes were even more vivid, if that was possible. *Stay focused! Remember, you're pissed at him.*

I nodded, since I was trying to choose my words carefully before speaking. Plus, I didn't want any drool to escape my lips. It would defeat my whole *keep-him-at-arm's-length* strategy. He took a step into the room, but then stopped, as if testing the water. It was frigid.

"So...did you find anything in Hampton's files?" he asked.

"They're too clean. He clearly wasn't running a legitimate import/export business. I don't know what else we're going to get from them."

"Where are Jean Luc and Misha?"

"Out."

He stood there staring at me and I stared right back at him. I counted to ten. I wasn't going to small talk him to make the awkwardness easier. If he had something to say, he needed to spit it out.

"Sorry I wasn't able to help today. We had a big court case, and I had to be there in case we had a media issue."

I shrugged. "We survived without you."

He took a step closer. "Kyle, what's going on?"

"What do you mean?"

"You're obviously pissed about something."

I forced my voice to remain calm. "I don't know, maybe the fact you played me last night."

His jaw tightened. "How does it feel? You've been doing it to me for days. You should have seen Misha's face when I asked him about your relationship. I felt like an idiot."

"Okay, *touché*. Glad to see I'm a joke." My stomach twisted. "Was the kiss really necessary to prove your point?"

"You are not a joke to me, Kyle. Far from it."

He leaned over the desk into my personal space. Why did he have to smell so damn good?

"And the kiss was not to prove a point. I have wanted to kiss you for days."

My breath caught for a second as I stared into his eyes. They had turned a darker shade of blue. What was it about this man? But I stopped myself from getting sucked in. I pushed my chair back hard from the desk, stood and glared at him.

"I hope the kiss was memorable, because it's the first and last one you'll get from me." I marched around him and out the door.

CHAPTER 14

Who did he think he was, anyway? I drove home very proud of myself for shooting Dalton down. We had only known each other for a short time. We were not in a committed relationship.

I sat down at my kitchen table with a bowl of cereal. As I poured the milk into the bowl, a sour odor hit me and I gagged. The milk lay in lumps on top of the cereal. At the rate I was going, I was going to poison myself some day. I crammed the mess down the disposal and sat down again in a huff, no longer hungry.

By the time I crawled into my bed alone, I was second-guessing myself over the whole Dalton thing. I mean, what did he really do that was so bad? I shook my head. Weak. I was so weak.

I shut off the light and closed my eyes. I would gather strength overnight so I could be indignant with Dalton again. Work was the only relationship I wanted with him. I kept saying it to myself over and over again, hoping to make it true. And then I went to sleep hoping I wouldn't dream about him.

The wailing wind woke me. But instead of being in bed, I was sleeping in a fetal position on damp ground. Sitting up, I tried to make out where I was, my heart thudding loudly in my chest. I blinked, wanting my eyes to adjust to the dark so I could figure out what was going on. There was a weak shaft of light high up along a wall. I stood slowly, my arms held out in front of me so I wouldn't run into anything while I moved toward the light.

I inched my way to the wall. When I placed my hands on it, the cool metal surprised me. Peeking out through the narrow opening, I saw a pole light illuminating the yard. In front of me was a tree with no leaves, its empty branches swinging in the wind. I listened, praying to hear something besides the wind and my ragged breathing. After a couple of seconds, there was a tinkling sound, of metal and glass knocking together.

I knelt down, folded in on myself, and sobbed, my cries drowned out by the howling wind.

I jerked awake and sat up in bed, instinctively reaching behind my headboard for Stanley. What the hell had that been about? I tried to catch my breath while my eyes darted around the room. I had never had such a vivid dream before. Booger sat in the doorway watching me.

"It's all right, dude, I just had a bad dream."

He swished his tail and disappeared down the hall. After I calmed down a bit, I returned Stanley to his hiding place and checked the clock. Six a.m. No point in trying to go back to sleep.

I stood in the warm shower for an extra ten minutes to wake myself up. Stepping out, I checked my forehead in the mirror. The bruise had turned into a lovely shade of egg-yolk yellow.

In the kitchen I found Booger asleep on the kitchen table—the only place he was forbidden to stand, sit or lie on. That and the kitchen counter. I shooed him off the table and plopped a can of cat food in his dish. He circled my legs and purred. I read the can and grimaced. Dalton had bought the high-end cat food.

"Don't get too attached to this, okay? Once it's gone, it's back to bargain kitty food for you."

Booger tilted his head up, and for a minute, I could've sworn he rolled his eyes. Lord, everyone was against me.

Even though I arrived at work early, all three guys were already there. Was I the only one who slept? I walked over to the full coffee pot. Misha wrinkled his nose and then shook his head slightly. *Damn.* Now I would have to wait until Jean Luc left the room before I could make a new pot.

I plopped down in the empty chair at the table. "Good morning. What do we know at this point?"

Dalton watched me warily, but said nothing.

Misha jumped in. "I was just going to show Dalton my PowerPoint presentation on demons, to bring him up to speed. Want to watch?"

I smiled. I couldn't think of a more fitting punishment for Dalton. "Go ahead and get started. I'll be back in a couple of minutes."

Misha clicked on the keypad and the first slide appeared. "There are twelve clans of demons currently living on earth. Each has its own distinct set of features and powers. I will go through each clan and describe it to you..."

I hightailed it back to my office and sat at my desk. Closing my eyes for a second, I replayed last night's dream. What the hell was it supposed to represent? I straightened my desk and drawers, throwing out broken rubber bands and twisted paper clips, before wandering back to the front area. Hopefully, Misha had finished his presentation.

No such luck. Misha's arms swayed above his head as he demonstrated some kind of dance. The PowerPoint slide reflecting on the whiteboard was titled "Haltrap Demon's Molting Schedule." To my surprise, Dalton was actually asking questions.

"So depending on the strength of a demon's powers, there are classification levels?"

"Yes. Shamats like me are pretty high in the hierarchy, but the Pavel who fought the angel at the bar is the highest level allowed on earth, and that decision has been questioned over the centuries."

"Dalmots like Kevin Doyle, our pawnbroker, are low-level?"

"The female Dalmots are more powerful than their male counterparts, but overall they are somewhat harmless. So if you add Doc, you have already met three demon types."

"Actually, I've met four. Kyle and I ran into a Baltran demon in the alley."

Oh, crap.

"Kyle didn't mention that to me." Misha turned to Jean Luc, who shook his head.

"Well, she probably wants to forget about the whole thing, since he slimed her," Dalton explained.

Misha laughed, a deep belly laugh I had experienced in the past, which would go on for days if I let it wind up too much.

I hurried over and sat down at the table. "Misha, how did your talk with your clan leader go last night?"

I glared at him. He wiped the tears out of his eyes—was it really so funny?—and answered me.

"He didn't recognize the pictures I showed him, but he's going to have the elders review them and get back to me." He turned to Dalton. "There is a hierarchy established within the clans. Each clan has a clan leader and a group of elders who advise the leader."

Dalton reviewed the white board. "So, why do you think Cowell only has seven demons identified of the twelve?"

"I'm not sure. Maybe he didn't have time to figure out the rest."

We were missing something. "What I don't understand is how he could have gathered all the information he did have on the seven clans. I can't believe he could have done it without help."

"Maybe those connections are tied to Hampton? Hampton thought Cowell knew something important enough to torture him for it," Dalton threw in.

"And since an angel and a demon were both after Hampton, they must think he was successful in extracting the information from Cowell," I added.

"Besides the leaders within the clans," Dalton asked, "do you have leaders who lead across the clans? In other words, how do you keep the peace?"

"We have the Council of Twelve. Each member represents a clan, and they meet if there is unrest. And then there is the Full Council which also includes the vampire and shifter contingencies."

"Have you ever had to go to the Full Council?"

Misha swallowed hard. "Nicholas's philosophy is the issue should never get bad enough to require involving the Council."

Before Dalton could respond, Dolly buzzed the intercom. Misha hit the button. "Yeah, Dolly?"

"Someone's on the phone. He wouldn't give his name, but he insists on talking to Kyle."

I hit the outside line. "Hello?"

"Is this McKinley?"

It took two seconds to recognize the worm. "What do you want, Doyle?"

"First, pick up the damn phone. I don't want to be on speaker."

I reached over and grabbed the handset. "Is that better?"

"Yes. I have some information for you on the matter we discussed before."

"Spill it."

"No! Not over the phone."

I rolled my eyes at the guys. "Fine, I'll meet you at your shop."

"No, I don't want anyone to see you there. Meet me behind the State Theater in an hour."

"The next words out of your mouth better not be, 'come alone.' I'm not naive. This better not be a trick, Doyle."

"No tricks, but after this we're even." He hung up.

Dalton leaned forward. "What's the deal?"

"Doyle wants to meet with us. Apparently he has more information."

"I'm coming with you."

"Misha and Jean Luc can come, too. Doyle is nervous as hell, and I'm not getting a good feeling about this."

Dalton and I went in Dalton's SUV, and Jean Luc and Misha followed separately. The plan was to have Jean Luc circle in the van while Dalton and I spoke to Doyle. Misha would stay out of sight and watch our backs.

Dalton glanced over at me a couple of times while he drove, but didn't say anything. Finally, I couldn't stand it anymore. "Spit it out, Dalton."

He sighed. "This probably isn't the best time for this, but I'm sorry about yesterday. I was pissed at you and thought you needed to be taught a lesson. I don't want you to ever think you're a joke."

I nodded and stared out the window. I had nothing pithy to say, and for once I didn't think it was warranted anyway. I took a deep breath before facing him. "I'm sorry, too. I shouldn't have let you think Misha and I are a thing."

"Why did you?"

Indeed, why did I? Did I even know? I probably needed some extensive therapy to figure out what the hell my problem was, but he was waiting for an answer. "The last human teammate we had was a disaster. I didn't want to deal with another one. So instead of giving you a chance, I tried to scare you off at first."

"I remember."

"And when that didn't work, Misha mentioned he thought you were interested in me and jealous of him, so I decided to work with that. Silly, huh?"

"Not so much. Misha was right, I am interested in you." He parked the car and gave me his full attention. "Do you know you refer to humans like you aren't one?"

I opened my mouth and closed it. Again I was at a loss for words. "I didn't realize I did that. But you have to admit, I'm not exactly normal."

"No, you're special. You just haven't figured it out yet."

Whoa—alarm bells were clanging in my head. It was time to steer this conversation out of murky waters. "So we're calling a truce?"

He grinned. "Truce."

Dalton and I got out and went down the alley behind the theater. After a few seconds, I spotted Doyle standing in a doorway. This was a little too reminiscent of my recent slime experience. Before I even got close to him, I could tell Doyle was a nervous wreck. His eyes were darting from side to side, and he let out an audible sigh when he saw us coming.

"About damn time."

I stood in the doorway with Dalton next to me. He faced sideways, watching the alley.

"What's with all the cloak and dagger stuff, Doyle?" I asked.

"You wanted to know if I heard anything else about Hampton."

"Yeah, but what is so hush-hush you couldn't tell me over the phone?"

"There has been a lot of chatter lately about Hampton's head. The price tag has gone up. They are offering three million for it."

Whoa, things were getting serious. "Who are 'they'?"

"I'm pretty sure it's coming from the demon pop. Speculation is the vamps might already have the head, but they aren't talking."

"Who is in a position to offer so much money?"

Doyle's eyes darted from side to side again before answering. "There are only a few supes I can think of with that kind of pull. I wrote them down for you." He handed me a piece of paper. "Now we're even. I don't care if you go to Coleen or not, I'm done."

"We're square, Doyle. Thanks for the info."

He stared at me for a moment, as if struggling to decide what to do next. "You need to be careful, McKinley. This information came to me too easily. I don't know if they assumed I would give it to you or not, but you need to watch your step. Take my advice and back off. I'm going on an extended holiday myself."

He scurried deeper into the alley, and then out of sight. I was sure he had a rabbit hole to slink into somewhere.

Dalton and I walked back the way we came. Misha waited at the end of the alley as we approached.

After a few steps, tires squealed behind us. Fully expecting it to be Jean Luc, I was surprised when Misha screamed, "Run!"

I looked back, wasting precious seconds, as a blue pickup truck barreled toward us. My stomach bottomed out. Dalton reacted first, grabbing my hand and dragging me away at full speed. We were still midway down the alley with nowhere to go. Misha ran toward us. *What the hell was he doing?* Before I could scream for him to turn around, Dalton shoved me hard into an alcove, slamming me against the bricks. He kept running. After a few seconds, the truck sped past me.

There was no way Dalton could outrun it.

CHAPTER 15

Tires squealed and I flinched, expecting to hear a thud when the truck smashed into Dalton, but there was nothing. Racing from the alcove, I tripped, goggling at the scene in front of me.

Dalton dangled in midair like a marionette. *What?!* Further down the alley, Misha stood with his arm raised like a puppet master. Somehow, he was holding Dalton up in the air using telekinesis.

Then the truck changed trajectory and barreled toward Misha. I screamed a warning just as the driver pointed a gun out his window. Misha made a careless, swatting motion with his other hand and the truck lurched sideways, missing him. Unfortunately, the man still managed to get off a shot before the truck careened around the corner and out of the alley.

I stumbled toward Dalton while Misha slowly lowered him to the ground. When Dalton's feet touched the pavement, I reached for him, desperate to reassure myself he was real, that what had just happened wasn't a nightmare. Only after my hand actually touched his face did the tightness in my chest ease a bit. He grabbed my shoulders and held me out in front of him, running his eyes over me quickly before yanking me hard against his chest.

"Tell me you're okay," he demanded.

"Yes," I squeaked. "You?"

"Yes." He let me go, and pulled out his gun, giving it a fast check before we joined Misha.

Smartass comments fired off in my head about Misha and his newly revealed superpowers, but my steps faltered when he hunched forward, hands on his knees.

"Mish?" I took off running, my heart thudding so hard in my throat I had trouble breathing. "Misha, what's wrong?" He stood and blood ran down his arm. "Jesus, you've been shot!"

"I'll be fine, little one. It's just a scratch."

Dalton examined Misha's shoulder and then his back. "It's more than a scratch. You took one in the shoulder, and I don't see an exit wound."

Misha pressed his hand against his shoulder, staunching the blood. "A bullet wound like this isn't serious for a demon. Doc Miller will fix me up in no time."

Tires squealed and we all tensed again.

Dalton pointed his gun down the alley, until we realized it was Jean Luc who barreled toward us. He pulled the van to a halt, barely putting it in park before he jumped out.

"What happened?"

"A truck just tried to mow us down and Misha saved our asses." I clenched my hands to stop them from shaking.

Dalton spoke up. "You guys get out of here. We don't need any more publicity. I'll stay and run interference with the cops."

I shook my head. "You can't stay here alone. It's not safe."

"I'll be fine. The guy is long gone."

Before I was able to protest, sirens wailed in the distance. "Okay, we'll take Misha to get sewed up, and then let's meet to discuss our next moves."

Misha and I climbed into the van and Jean Luc drove toward the storage facility. I pulled on a pair of gloves and opened our first aid kit, looking for something to keep Misha from bleeding all over the upholstery.

"Misha, quit squirming and let me take care of you."

"I'll be fine. It should have stopped bleeding by now. If Doc isn't available to take the bullet out, it will heal on its own."

I smiled at him. "We can't have that. You'll set off metal detectors at the airport. Jean Luc, did you get a hold of Doc?"

"Yes, fortunately she was home. She is on her way to the facility now, and will probably arrive before we do."

I sighed. I wanted Doc now, not later, so she could tell me Mish was going to be all right. I pressed more gauze on his wound. Blood was still flowing freely, though, and it didn't make sense. Usually Misha was an amazingly fast healer. But now he had even broken into a sweat.

"Misha, tell me how you're doing."

"Just a little tired. I'll be fine."

I caught Jean Luc's eyes in the rearview mirror. He sped up.

"I think you should probably stay awake. Doc is going to want to give you grief about getting yourself shot."

"Of course. I can't disappoint Doc." Misha tried to smile, but his lips didn't appear to cooperate. "I don't feel very good, Kyle."

I blinked hard a few times, suppressing the tears. "We'll be there soon. Hang in there for me."

Misha nodded.

Jean Luc made a call on his cell and spoke in rapid-fire French.

The next few minutes were a blur. I pressed gauze against Misha's shoulder and talked to keep him awake while Jean

Luc raced to the facility like a bat out of hell. I almost sobbed with relief when we pulled through the back bay door and I saw Doc's car parked inside. She ran toward us, pushing a gurney.

Jean Luc flashed out of the driver's seat and had the van door open before I even registered what was happening. He picked Misha up and put him on the gurney, and I knew Misha was in as bad shape as I'd feared when he didn't protest about Jean Luc carrying him.

We ran toward the morgue. I wanted to scream "no" when I saw where we were going, but Doc led us past the main area into a makeshift operating room.

Doc pulled the gauze away and cut off Misha's shirt, examining the wound.

I gaped at it. The hole was swollen and red...and the bleeding had increased. "It looks infected. Should it look like that already?"

"What type of gun was it, Kyle?" Doc asked.

"Just a regular automatic, maybe a .45. I'm not sure. Why isn't it healing?"

"I don't know. The bullet may be toxic. We need to get it out. Both of you wash up, I'm going to need your help."

Jean Luc flashed away. I stood for a second staring at Misha. He couldn't die.

"Kyle, go!"

I ran out of the room to the sink in the morgue. Jean Luc was just finishing up. He nodded at me slightly and then left the room. I yanked off the bloody gloves with a loud snap and scrubbed my hands quickly before running back to help.

Doc had stripped Misha and covered him with a sheet. Jean Luc set up an instrument tray and then started an IV. Doc reached for a bottle of betadine and poured it over the wound. Misha moaned.

"Sorry, big guy. I'm going to get this bullet out of you as fast as I can." She held out her hand to Jean Luc. "Forceps." She used them to dig around in the wound.

"Shouldn't we knock him out or something?" I blurted.

"No, I need him to stay awake." She pulled the forceps out. "The bullet must be further down in his shoulder. Scalpel."

Jean Luc handed her the blade and I swallowed hard as she cut open his shoulder. Misha gritted his teeth and I squeezed his other arm.

"Look at me, Mish," I said. "You're going to be fine. When we're done, you'll have a really cool scar you can show off to the ladies."

His blue eyes brimmed with pain and I smiled at him. He was going to be fine. He had to be. After a second, Doc gasped. She stumbled back a few steps and bumped into the tray, sending several instruments clattering to the floor.

Jean Luc steadied her before she hit the ground.

"Doc!" I stepped toward her, but she held up her hand.

"Stay back, Kyle." She peeled off her gloves and Jean Luc rushed her to the sink.

I stayed with Misha, who was now turning gray. After a minute, Doc and Jean Luc came back to the table.

"What's going on?" I demanded, keeping my voice as even as I could.

"The bullet broke open and has released some kind of poison that must be toxic to demons," Doc said. "We need to get it out of there and then clean the area."

"Are you okay?"

"I will be. I can't work on him anymore, though."

"Let me do it." Jean Luc volunteered.

Doc shook her head. "I suspect this might affect you, too, Jean Luc. Kyle, you'll have to do it."

The room closed in on me and I squeezed my eyes shut to stop the spinning. No way could I do this.

"Kyle. Did you hear me?"

I opened my eyes. Misha's pale face took center stage. "Yes. Tell me what to do."

"I need you to feel around for the bullet fragments in his shoulder. Using your fingers."

Jean Luc helped me slip my hands into a pair of gloves. As I walked around to the other side, Misha's eyes followed me the whole way. I took a deep breath and stuck my finger into his shoulder. Dear God, I actually had my hand inside someone else's body. I felt around slowly, hoping to find evidence of the bullet. After a couple of seconds, I bumped a hard edge.

"I found a piece."

Jean Luc handed me the forceps, and I gripped the cold metal for a second, steadying my breathing. Then I eased the forceps in and pulled out the bullet slowly. I held up the piece for Doc to see from across the room.

"It's the bottom half. You need to find the top piece, too."

Jean Luc had put a metal basin on the instrument tray next to me, and I dropped in the bullet, hearing a satisfying clink as it hit. I took a deep breath.

I spread Misha's wound with my fingers again and could feel him tense, unsuccessfully trying to stifle a moan. Pulling my hand back, I watched his face. He nodded for me to continue. After digging around for a few more seconds, this time using the forceps, I scraped against another piece of the bullet.

"Got it!" I pulled it out.

I held up the second piece for Doc to see.

"That's the other half," she said. "I think we got it all, but just to make sure, do another sweep with your fingers."

I stuck my fingers in and felt around. "I think we're good."

Doc stood next to me and smiled. "Next step. I need you to take the suction tube and remove as much of the blood from the wound as possible. There's no way to be sure how much of it has been poisoned or infected."

I did manage to keep it together while I put the suction tube in his shoulder, but flinched at the whirring sound. The blood spattered up through the clear tubing, spotting the sides. Closing my eyes for a second, I swallowed back a wave of nausea.

"You're doing great, Kyle, just hang in there."

I opened my eyes.

"Okay, that should be enough," Doc said.

I pulled the tube out of Misha's shoulder and waited for further instructions. Instead, she motioned to Jean Luc. "Hang the other bag of antibiotics on his IV. Misha, you need to change."

Misha glanced at me and shook his head.

"What's the problem?" I asked.

"Normally, Misha would be able to heal himself, even in his human form. But he's too weak right now. He needs to change to his demon form so he can heal. I don't want to sew him up. I need to make sure he actually *can* heal so I'll know the poison is completely out of his system."

"So...why doesn't he?"

No one answered me. And as I peered from face to face, I knew. He didn't want to change in front of me. And I saw red. The fear and adrenaline coursing through my veins from watching one of my best friends almost die hardened into hurt and anger, and it was ugly.

"Oh, for God's sake, Misha! I just saved your freakin' life, and I'm still not worthy to see your demon form? Fine! I'll wait out in the hallway."

I slammed through the doors, peeling off my gloves and chucking them in the biohazard bin. I rushed to the sink, and turned on the water, but as I reached for the soap, my hand trembled so hard I had to grip the sink to steady myself. After a minute, I was able to wash my hands, and was drying them when Jean Luc came up behind me.

"Kyle."

I spun around. "Is he okay? Please tell me the wound is healing."

"Yes, it is healing."

I released the breath I'd been holding. "Thank God."

"Kyle, I feel I should explain something to you."

I held up my hands. "I know. I was out of line in there. I'll apologize to him later. I know I shouldn't expect him to treat me like another supernatural. I guess, since we've worked together for years, it hurt when he shut me out."

"You misunderstand Misha's reluctance to show you his other side. It is not your worthiness which is in question. He is afraid you will think less of him when you see his demon self."

My mouth fell open. "What?"

"He does not want your friendship to change. He is afraid you would not be able to relate to him in the same way afterward."

My heart clenched. He was worried about what I would think of him? "What a lunkhead. I don't care what he looks like, demon or not. He'll always be my friend."

Jean Luc smiled. "That is what I have told him, but I think it will come best from you."

I hesitated. "He wants me to see him?"

"Yes, are you ready for it?"

I walked slowly toward the room as Jean Luc pushed open the door. Misha's now jet-black eyes settled on mine. He had grown. His skin was mottled, now mainly orange, with red splotches over his chest and face. Taking a deep breath, I stepped up to the bed. His eyes were filled with uncertainty, and I smiled as I gazed at him, awed at how important this moment was to both of us. I laid a hand on his arm, surprised to discover his skin was soft.

I shook my head at him. "You stubborn Russian. If you think a little red skin and black eyes would ever change my feelings for you, then you don't know me. I think your demon half is sexy as hell. No wonder you have no trouble finding wives."

He grinned at me and laughed, his beautiful belly laugh bouncing off the walls.

I had propped my head against the back of the couch in Doc's office when the door opened and Dalton rushed in.

"Doc just told me what happened. Sorry I wasn't here to help."

I shrugged. "None of us realized how bad it was until it was almost too late."

He sat down next to me. "Are you okay?"

"I'm fine." *Liar, liar.* "I just needed a place to chill for a couple of minutes. How did it go with the cops?"

"Well, considering the fact I couldn't give them any of the relevant data, it was pretty much a nonevent. They are chalking it up to a drunk or drug addict driving through the alley on a tear."

"Well, we need to figure out why they were after us."

"I don't think they were after us."

"How can you say that?"

"The bullet you pulled out of Misha was made specifically to kill demons. I think they were after supernaturals, and we just got in the way. Do you think Doyle set us up?"

I sat for a moment, considering it. "No, I think he was a pawn in this whole thing. I don't think he would have bothered with a warning if he'd set us up."

I reached into my pocket and pulled out the list Doyle had handed us in the alley. "We need to check out these names. Misha will be down for a few days, but I'm pretty sure Jean Luc can help with the search." I unfolded the paper and it rattled in my shaky fingers. *Damn it.*

Dalton reached for my hands and held them in his strong grip. "Misha is going to be fine. Doc says you're a natural."

I shook my head and watched his thumbs rub across the back of my hands. I was not going to cry. Dalton let go of one of my hands and placed his fingers under my chin, tipping up my face so he could look me in the eye. He went blurry, then he smiled and hugged me to his chest while I bawled. Plus alarm bells were going off in my head. I liked being in Dalton's arms way too much. After a minute, I sighed and pulled back.

Dalton's concerned look took my breath away.

"Better?"

"Yeah, thanks." The electricity between us was like late summer lightning, so I needed to ground us in reality. "Don't think this means you're getting lucky. We only called a truce earlier. No peace treaty has been signed yet."

"Trust me, I haven't forgotten." His words sounded sincere, but his eyes danced mischievously.

I didn't trust him for a second.

CHAPTER 16

I blew out a shaky breath. I had been vegetating long enough in Doc's office. Dalton had already gone down the hall to double-check some details with Doc. Running my hands through my hair, I stretched and stood slowly. I was definitely not getting enough sleep, but it would have to wait until after we figured out who shot Misha. And why.

On my way down the hall, I stopped to check on him. When I opened the door, the room was empty. My stomach sank. Controlling myself, I walked quickly to the main morgue area. Doc and Dalton stood near a lab table reading a report.

"Where's Misha?"

Doc smiled. "He's fine. I moved him to a room with an actual bed. He wasn't comfortable on the metal table."

"He's going to be okay?"

"He should be fine in a couple of days. He just needs to take it easy."

My stomach unclenched. "Where's Jean Luc?"

Dalton replied this time. "He went back to the office to run the list of names Doyle gave us."

"What's going on in here?"

"Doc was just going over the lab results on the bullet."

"What have you figured out?"

Doc set the report down. "The bullet itself was silver. It was designed to break apart like hollow-point bullets. Inside was a compound of pure iron and salt."

"Why that particular mixture?"

"I think whoever designed it thinks it's a deadly cocktail for all supes. Silver for the shifters and vamps, iron and salt for the demons."

I shook my head. "Misha eats salt all the time."

"Salt has been believed to be a weapon against demons for centuries," Doc said. "However, demons who live on earth are not susceptible to it. But pure iron would definitely hurt us."

"What about those in the demon realm?"

"Iron would affect them like the demons on earth. Salt would also hurt them. I just don't know if it would be strong enough to kill them."

"So they weren't gunning for us," I said.

"It doesn't matter." Doc scowled. "The bullet still could have killed either of you."

"I think the truck would have taken us out before the bullets. If it hadn't been for Misha's telekinesis, Dalton would be dead."

Doc took a step toward me. "What did you say?"

"Hey, I was surprised, too, to discover he could move things. He's never mentioned the power to me before, but I'm not going to complain."

Doc stared at me pointedly. "I think both you and Dalton shouldn't discuss this with anyone else until you can talk to Misha further."

"What's the big deal?"

"There's obviously a reason why Misha hasn't told you about this power before now. It's not my place to explain the ramifications."

"Fine, Cryptic-Girl, I'll ask him myself. Can I go check on him?"

"Yes. He's down the hall, third door on the right. And no badgering!"

My eyes widened in mock innocence. "I would never badger. Cut me some slack."

I glanced over at Dalton, who had the nerve to roll his eyes. *Another party heard from.* I marched down the hall and opened the door slowly, slipping into the room. Misha was back in human form. As I stepped closer to the bed, his steady breathing calmed me down. He was sound asleep. The questions Doc had triggered would have to wait.

I stood for a couple of minutes watching him sleep and then tiptoed out. As I headed back to the morgue, loud, unfamiliar voices echoed down the hallway. I jogged the rest of the way back to find Doc and Dalton standing toe to toe with three very large men.

The tallest of the three seemed to be doing all the talking, or rather commanding.

"Where is he?"

Doc answered him. "He's resting in a room down the hall."

"What's going on here?" I asked.

They turned toward me in unison, which would have been amusing if their faces hadn't all been so belligerent.

"I am here to see Misha," Mr. Master and Commander announced.

"And you are?"

His ice-blue eyes looked me over, as if gauging the necessity of explaining anything. "I am Boris Chesnokov, the Shamat clan leader, and I will be taken to Misha. *Now.*"

I perused him slowly. *Well, well, well.* I finally got to meet Grand Poobah in the flesh. He was around the same height as Misha, but with brown hair and a rugged face. He was wearing a killer suit which I'm sure cost more than my entire wardrobe. I could actually feel the power radiating from him. He clearly was used to getting his way. However, his arrogance annoyed the crap out of me.

"I don't care if you're the Tsar of Russia, you aren't getting into his room unless Doc says it's okay."

Doc nodded. "Fine, but only one of you at a time. He's still recovering."

We headed down the hallway en masse. When we reached Misha's room, I stood in front of the door for a second, blocking the way. "He was sleeping when I checked on him earlier, so take it easy when you go in."

Boris stalked into the room, shutting the door behind him. The two barbarians accompanying him stood on either side of the door, casing the hallway. Their expressions showed no emotion, reminding me of the guards at Buckingham Palace.

After a couple of minutes, Boris came out and closed the door behind him. He seemed much calmer. "Please explain what happened. I'm still unclear about the events."

Since he said "please" I decided I would enlighten him. "Misha took a bullet, saving Dalton and me from being mowed down by a truck."

"But it's not a life-threatening injury for us. Why is he still in bed?"

"The bullet contained pure iron," Doc volunteered, "which started to poison Misha's system."

"But you got it all out, yes?"

"Yes, I believe so," Doc answered.

Boris clenched his jaw. "Who would do such a thing?"

"That's what we're trying to figure out," Dalton interjected.

I butted in. "Misha came to you and asked about the drawings of demons we discovered. Have you been able to identify them?"

Boris's expression slammed shut. "I will be speaking to Nicholas today. Our clan takes care of its own."

"Are we going to start beating our fists against our chests and grunting next?"

His eyes narrowed on me. "I do not care for your tone."

"I'll drop the tone if you drop the superiority complex. We're all trying to accomplish the same thing here."

"And what would that be?"

"To figure out why an angel felt it was necessary to chop off a vamp's head in front of human witnesses. Something bad is coming, and we need to be prepared. This is not just about your clan. It's about all of us."

He grimaced. "And yet Misha was the one injured. Who will be there to protect him going forward?"

I stared deep into his eyes and did not like what I saw. "What are you really upset about? The fact Misha took a bullet, or that he took a bullet protecting humans?"

"Kyle," Doc hissed.

Boris's eyes widened in surprise. "You're Kyle? Misha has told me much about you."

"He has told me very little about you. I don't understand why your clan is so secretive."

"We do not want humans knowing about our world."

"Well, I am not like most humans."

Boris had the nerve to smirk at me. "No, you are not."

Misha's door opened, and he stepped hesitantly into the hall. He was pale and gritting his teeth. I had only seen him pissed once or twice before, and it was never pretty.

The two guards jerked to attention.

Misha glared at Boris. "Enough."

Boris responded in Russian. Misha shook his head.

"Do not insult them by speaking in Russian, Father."

My mouth fell open. "Father?"

Boris started swearing in Russian. Over the years, Misha had taught me all the juicy Russian curses, and Boris was grumbling a few choice ones.

"I need to speak privately with my father for a moment. Doc, would you please join us?"

The three of them walked back into Misha's room and shut the door.

Dalton's fingers wrapped around my arm and he dragged me down the hall, away from the guards.

I shrugged out of his grasp. "What the hell are you doing? I don't need another Neanderthal in the mix right now."

He practically growled at me. "Would you just chill for a minute?"

"What's the big deal?"

"Stop pissing the guy off, already. At the rate you're going, he's not going to want to talk to us at all."

"As far as I'm concerned, I hope we're done talking."

Dalton let out a harsh breath. "Did you get a good look at the list Doyle gave us?"

"No, why?"

"Because Boris was number two on the list of supes with enough money to buy Hampton's head."

"Great."

"Yeah, and right now he's not exactly feeling cooperative."

I stared down the hall at the closed door. "I can't believe he's Misha's father."

"Misha has never talked about him before?"

"No. I thought his father must be dead."

The door opened and Doc stepped out. She motioned to us. "Kyle, Misha wants to see you now."

I walked toward the room, Dalton close behind. Doc held out her hand and blocked his progress. "You need to stay out here with me, Joe."

"Play nice," he muttered to me.

I stepped inside. Misha was back in bed. His father was standing at the foot. I walked over to Misha's side.

"What's up, Mish?"

"I have declared you my *sestra*."

"Sounds ominous."

"It means you are Misha's sister...a member of our clan," Boris offered.

My throat tightened and I swallowed hard to clear it. "Why?"

"Misha explained you saved his life. He is beholden to you and has asked that you be adopted into our clan."

"But I'm not a demon."

"No, but we have adopted other non-demons into our clan when it is merited."

I started to protest, but Misha reached for my hand. "Please, Kyle, it would be an honor."

I met his gaze for a second. "Okay, as long as I don't have to drink demon blood or anything like that."

Misha laughed. "No, nothing like that. You just need to say 'yes,' and it's official."

I squeezed his hand. "Yes. Now, you've had enough excitement today. You need to rest a while. If you're a good little demon, I'll bring you some pastries later."

"Yes, ma'am."

I glanced over at Boris. "I'll leave you two alone now."

I stepped out into the hallway. Dalton waited for me.

"Where's Doc?"

"She went back to the morgue. She told me what was going on. So...you're a demon clan member now?"

"Yes."

"Does that mean we can ask Boris some questions?"

"We'll find out soon enough."

CHAPTER 17

Boris sat in a chair with both guards flanking him. It seemed a bit over the top. Kinda reminded me of *The Godfather*, but demon-style.

"How may I assist you?" he asked.

I glanced at Dalton who nodded for me to proceed. "When Misha was attacked, we were collecting information from a source."

"And what did this source tell you?"

"It's not a secret in the supernatural community that Hampton's head is missing, and that apparently someone is willing to pay a lot of money for it. We've compiled a list of supernatural community members who have the money and connections to offer this type of reward. You're on the list."

Boris shrugged. "It makes sense, since I do have both the money and the influence, but it is not me."

Dalton interrupted, "Why would someone want his head, anyway?"

"Misha asked me if it was possible for a demon to extract memories from a dead vampire."

"And?" I coaxed.

"And, I don't think it's beyond the realm of possibility."

I stared at him for a moment. "Are there demons on earth with this kind of power?"

"There shouldn't be, no. But that doesn't mean someone from the demon realm with that kind of power is not here right now."

"Misha also mentioned a demon might be able to harvest another demon's powers."

Boris leaned forward. "Yes, but it is not advisable. That demon would be beholden forever to the demon who lent him these powers. He would become a virtual slave."

"Have you heard anything about what Hampton might have known that would cause this much trouble?" I persisted.

"No, we have not heard anything about what specific knowledge they might wish to extract. May I ask who else is on the list?"

Since I had not had a chance to look at the list, I turned to Dalton, but he hesitated.

Boris smiled. "If you are reluctant to say, perhaps I could tell you who should be on the list and you can tell me if I am correct."

Dalton nodded.

"Besides me, the most obvious choice is Josiah Akers. He is the head of the Pavel clan. Sebastian, as a Founding Vampire, would also be high on the list. He has both the power and the money. Since Hampton was one of his, he would also have added incentive to locate him if he was involved in Hampton's dealings. Seamus Griffin is the head of a large contingent of shifters in the Midwest and East Coast. He also has the means. Was I close?"

"You got them all."

"Yes, well, there is one other who should be added to the list."

"And who would that be?" I asked.

"Why, your boss, Nicholas, of course."

I flinched slightly, which I'm sure Boris noticed. "Why would Nicholas be involved? He's the one trying to stop this."

Boris shrugged. "The one thing I have learned about Nicholas over the years is you cannot always determine his motives or predict what he will choose to do." Boris stood. "I will contact you if I hear anything that might help you. I will also have my elders work on the drawings Misha brought me."

I stood as well and walked over to him. His change of demeanor was more than unnerving. "Thank you for helping us with this. I have to ask though, why the turnaround?"

"You saved my son's life and he has declared you his *sestra*. So you are now my daughter."

"And it's as simple as that?"

He grinned, reminding me of Misha. "Yes. I will contact you with any information I find."

"Thank you."

I watched the three of them walk out. Dalton chuckled beside me.

"What?"

"You are blessed, woman. How you can go from pissing off the head of a demon clan one minute, to having him wrapped around your little finger the next is beyond me."

"I am a master of diplomacy."

"Well, Miz Diplomat, I think we need to talk to a few more people on this list."

I smiled. "Ready when you are."

Dalton drove back to the office. He took a corner a little too fast, as evidenced by the squealing tires. "Sorry about that."

I shrugged. "No problem. Compared to Jean Luc you drive like an eighty-year-old grandma."

"Thanks, I think. So what did you think of Boris's story?"

"Since we don't know why everyone wants the head, I can't rule him out completely, but I just don't feel he's in on this."

"What about Boris's suggestion to add Nicholas to the list?"

"Nicholas would have the power and the means to pay for the head. I hate to sound like a broken record, but until we know what's locked inside Hampton's skull, we can't rule anyone out."

"I agree. I think it's time for me to get to know Nicholas," Dalton murmured.

Fifteen minutes later we parked and trudged up the stairs to the office. When I opened the door, Dolly popped up.

"How's Misha?" she asked.

"He's doing fine. Doc wants him to rest for the time being. Didn't Jean Luc tell you how he was?"

"Yeah, but you know vamps, they never get worked up about anything. I needed to hear it from someone else."

"He should be back in a couple of days. Why don't you go home, Dolly, it's late."

Dolly walked back and fetched her purse from her desk drawer. "Jean Luc told me how you saved Misha's life. If you were a man, I'd kiss you and tell you what a big pair you have."

I laughed. "Thanks, Dolly."

I walked around the reception area toward the back office with Dalton in tow. Jean Luc was nowhere to be found. The coffee pot was frantically calling my name. It was hard to believe Misha had been shot just this morning. It felt like a week had passed.

I held up the pot. The remaining dregs had turned to sludge. I dumped out the burnt offerings and filled the carafe at the sink, opened the cupboard and reached for a filter. An image flashed in front of me. It was a bracelet with heart-shaped charms dangling from my wrist. I stared at it for a second and then blinked. My wrist was bare.

"Kyle, are you okay?" Dalton asked.

Dalton and Jean Luc were standing next to me. I wasn't sure when they had gotten there, or how long I had been standing and staring at the cupboard, for that matter. I lowered my arm to hide the trembling. "I'm fine. I think I just need something to eat."

"When you called and told me you were coming back to the office, I ordered food from the Thai restaurant you like so much," Jean Luc volunteered.

"Thanks. I haven't eaten anything all day. While we're waiting, why don't you tell us about the supes on our list."

Jean Luc flashed away and, within seconds, flashed back with his laptop, which he set on the table.

"I have taken the liberty of adding the names to the white board with notes under each."

"We've already talked to Boris. He came to visit Misha." I added.

Jean Luc asked cautiously, "What did he have to say?"

"You smug little vamp. I know Misha is Boris's son."

Jean Luc's smiled. "I am glad you know the truth. Who told you?"

"Misha. He declared me his *sestra*."

"Why do I always miss the excitement?" Jean Luc shook his head.

"It wasn't very exciting. Misha asked me to be a member of his clan and I said yes. I did tell him there would be no drinking of demon blood."

Jean Luc grimaced. "I should hope not, demon blood is bitter. When they induct you at their next clan meeting, you will only be naked for a short time before they clothe you in the sacramental robe of his people."

"What!"

Jean Luc laughed. "You are delightfully easy to upset, Kyle."

"Let's get back to the list," I snarled.

"As you know, Josiah Akers is the head of the Pavel clan and is very well connected, despite the fact the Pavels segregate themselves from the rest of society, supernatural and humans alike."

I stared at the board. "What about Griffin? Isn't he the same shifter who told the Connors not to let me help Trina?"

"Yes. Griffin is in charge of a large portion of the shifter population. I am not sure how the shifters would play into this equation, if at all."

"He still should be questioned anyway," Dalton said.

"So should Sebastian." I studied the list for a moment. "But I think Akers should be the first one we talk to."

Jean Luc answered, "Nicholas will need to pave the way for these meetings. He wanted me to call him when you were back in the office. I gave him an update on Misha and what happened today."

I glanced over at Dalton while Jean Luc placed the call. A few seconds later Nicholas appeared on the monitor.

"Kyle, it's good to see you're safe." Nicholas's eyes moved to Dalton. "You must be Joe."

Dalton nodded. "Nicholas."

"Jean Luc told me what happened this morning. Doc has forwarded me her findings on the bullet. Do we know anything about the shooter yet?"

"No...but once Misha is up and moving again, he may be able to give us a description," I said.

"Do you think the shooter works for someone on the list?"

I shook my head. "I don't think so. I think there is another player in the game right now. My gut tells me it's linked to Cowell."

Nicholas's eyebrows rose. "The dead priest? Why do you think so?"

"Because we think the shooter is human, since he was using bullets that are toxic to all supernaturals. Supes don't normally hire humans to do their dirty work."

"So the names on the list are your suspects for what?"

"They have the means to pay three mil for Hampton's head. Is there anyone else who should be added?"

Nicholas sat quietly for a moment before responding. "Are you tactfully asking me whether I should be added?" He shrugged. "If you are simply considering money and power, then I should be on your list. But the more important question is motive."

"Except we don't know what the motive is right now," I persisted. "We will need to speak to each person on the list. Jean Luc thought you could pave the way for us."

Nicholas's eyes darkened. "I am not convinced you need to speak to them. We don't want to create waves. My philosophy has always been that we handle a case before involving those in the community."

I clenched my fists. "Misha almost died today."

"We still need to be cautious."

Dalton spoke up. "I think we have moved past caution. Considering the fact there are angels and demons fighting each other in public, I'd say this is not your normal case. Sometimes philosophies need to change."

Nicholas was silent for a moment. He stared at Dalton, who met his gaze without flinching.

"I will make some calls and see what I can do. I'll follow up in the morning and let you know who you may speak with." Nicholas signed off.

I stared at Dalton with awe. That was either the bravest or most reckless statement I'd ever heard. Either way, all I wanted to do right now was kiss him and tell him what a large pair he had.

CHAPTER 18

As a rule, I've never been a bath person. I don't have the patience for it. Showers are my MO—in and out and on my way. Tonight was an exception.

I leaned back in the bathtub and let the hot water slosh over my aching shoulders. I wasn't sure whether the pain was because Dalton had shoved me out of the way in the alley, or because I tighten my shoulders when I'm tense. Today was definitely a shoulder-clenching day.

Replaying events as I rested in the tub, I hoped for an ah-hah moment, where all the puzzle pieces would fall into place. The heavens would open and a choir of angels would sing. On second thought...nix the angels, since these days they were wielding swords and lopping off heads. I giggled. Lord, now I was getting punchy. Maybe it was because I'd inhaled the pint of spumoni ice cream Tony had sent over. Definitely an ice cream headache waiting to happen.

I thought about the flash I had earlier with the bracelet. What did it mean? I wasn't exactly the charm bracelet type, especially not heart-shaped charms. Was I cracking under the stress? And what about the freakadilic dream I had where I was trapped. Was it a premonition?

I sat up in the now-tepid water and shook my head. My bed called to me. Tomorrow would be a busy day. If Nicholas actually heeded Dalton's advice and called the names on the list, we could have some interesting conversations ahead of us.

After drying myself, I slathered on moisturizer and pulled on my normal sleeping attire of boxer shorts and a tank top. Wiping the steam off the mirror, I took a gander at my forehead. Doc should be able to take the stitches out soon. I opened the bathroom door and was surprised to find Booger waiting for me. As I walked through the kitchen, I checked his food dish, and it wasn't empty. Maybe he was coming to appreciate me?

I plopped down on the couch and Booger actually jumped up and sat next to me.

My cell rang and I picked it up off the coffee table. It was Dalton.

"What's up?"

"It's been a long day. I was just calling to see if you're okay."

"Stop it!" I hissed.

"Ahh...Sorry, I shouldn't have called."

"No, wait. I didn't mean that. I wasn't speaking to you. Booger is trying to rub his chin against my phone." I pushed him away. "I'm doing better. A tub of ice cream and a hot bath did the trick."

"I'll have to keep it in mind the next time I do something to piss you off."

"You might want to buy stock in Ben & Jerry's, then."

He chuckled. "Got it. I'll see you in the morning."

"Good night, Galahad."

It was just seven o'clock when I pulled in the storage facility's back bay area. I balanced the box of cannoli and the bag of breakfast sandwiches and maneuvered my way between the shelves until I reached the morgue door. Balancing the box and bag, I typed in the key code and the door swished back. Doc stood next to a lab table scrunching her shoulders up and down as if trying to get the kinks out of them.

"Did you sleep here last night?"

"Yeah, Boris had the two guards posted overnight to guard Misha. But I stayed to make sure he was recovering."

"How is he this morning?"

"Cranky. Please tell me you brought him some food."

"Yep."

She fell into step beside me on the way to Misha's room.

"I didn't have much here to feed him this morning and he's not happy."

"But being hungry is a good sign, right?"

"It's a very good sign." Doc knocked on the door. "You have a visitor."

"Come in."

Doc opened the door. Misha sat up in bed looking almost back to normal. *Thank God.* "How are you feeling today, Mish?"

"Good." He glared at Doc. "I'm ready to get out of here."

Doc sighed before speaking directly to me. "I told him he has to stay in bed at least one more day and then we'll see how things go."

"How am I supposed to get my strength back when you're starving me to death?"

Doc rolled her eyes at me and I suppressed a chuckle. "Well, I brought you two breakfast sandwiches and a box of cannoli."

"I can always count on *you*, Kyle."

Doc grimaced. "I'll leave you two alone."

I sat down and handed him the sandwich bag first. "Eat these while they're still warm."

Misha dug into the first immediately, and the smell of eggs and ham filled the air. He groaned after the initial bite. I sat for a few minutes watching him eat and breathed a sigh of relief. He was going to be fine.

As he unwrapped the second sandwich, I spoke up. "So, Boris is your father, huh?"

"Yeah." He studied me for a second. "What did you think of him?"

Ooops. Shaky ground, here. "At first, before I knew he was your dad, I thought he was an arrogant ass."

Misha snorted slightly. "And after you knew he was my father?"

"I still thought he was a bit full of himself, but he was scared for you, which didn't seem to bring out the warm and cuddly in him."

"Father can be a bit intense when he doesn't get his way."

Which was putting it mildly. "So why the big secret about your lineage?"

"My father is a very influential man. It is not common knowledge outside the clan that he is my father. He does not want me to be used as a pawn against him."

My opinion of Boris just went up a notch. "Makes sense. But I have to ask you something about your powers."

Misha flinched slightly, then proceeded to stuff the last of the sandwich into his mouth and begin chewing. He wasn't going to put me off so easily.

"I have been working with you for ten years, Mish. How come I didn't know you were telekinetic?"

He swallowed and then crumpled the wrapper, throwing it into the bag. "Have you told anyone?"

"I mentioned it to Doc. I didn't know it was a secret. She told Dalton and me not to tell anyone about it until I spoke to you first. What's the deal?"

He sighed before continuing, "Since my father is our clan leader, the next choice to succeed him would be one of his children. I have two other brothers who are in line for leader."

"Are you the oldest?"

"Yes, but clan succession does not work that way. The one who has the strongest powers is given the role."

"And your telekinesis tips the scales in your favor."

"Yes. The last thing I want to do is lead the clan. My younger brother Aleksei is being groomed for the leadership role, and he will make a good one."

"No one will hear it from me, and I'll make sure Dalton zips it, too."

He reached for the pastry box, opened it and grinned like a kid in a candy store. "Thanks again for the food. Now it's my turn to ask you something."

"Go ahead."

"What did you talk to my father about yesterday?"

"The price on the street for Hampton's head has gone up to three mil. Doyle gave us a list of supes who have the resources to pay that kind of money."

"My father was on the list." It was a statement, not a question.

"Yes."

Misha reached for a cannoli and powdered sugar sprinkled onto the sheets. Doc was going to kill me.

"He does have the money. What did he say when you questioned him?"

"That he's not involved, and that he would have the elders work on those drawings you gave him." I waited for a response, but none was forthcoming. "I have to get going. Will you behave today for Doc?"

"Only if you bring me a treat later."

"Fine. Since, you're feeling better, let me ask you another one. Did you get a good look at the guy who shot you?"

"Good enough."

"Why don't you call Jean Luc today and describe the guy to him so he can start a trace?"

Misha's eyes lit up. "I'll have Jean Luc bring me a computer so I can build something in the facial recognition program. Maybe we can find the bastard before he hurts anyone else."

Back in the lab, I found Doc sitting at the desk drinking a giant mug of coffee. "I think I've calmed him down for a while."

"Thanks."

"Are you up to checking my forehead?"

She set the mug down and stood. "Yep, is something wrong?"

"No, I just wondered when you would take the stitches out."

Doc pushed back my bangs and stared at my head. "You're looking good. But you still need to wait a few more days. Scalp wounds can be tricky and I want to minimize any scarring."

"Thanks. I'll be back later with more food for Misha. He promised to be good today if I bring him another treat."

"I owe you one."

I pointed to my forehead. "I think we're even. I better get to work."

"Before you go, tell me how things are going with Joe."

"Fine," I answered automatically.

Doc chuckled. "That sounds convincing. Misha told me you're pissed because you think Joe tricked you."

I bristled. "Yeah, what of it?"

"After almost losing Misha yesterday, I shouldn't have to remind you life is short and you better smell the roses and grab onto a decent man when you find one."

"Thanks, Dear Abby, I'll keep it in mind."

"Fine, I'll cut the crap and get to the point. You can't compare every man to Jack."

My stomach clenched. "I knew I should never have agreed to truth or dare after a whole bottle of wine. You can't throw drunken confessions back in my face."

"Jack was a user. You were twenty years old, Kyle. Trying to find your way in the world, and he manipulated you. Would you have honestly thought of scamming casinos out of money on your own?"

I didn't bother answering. What was the point?

"Joe is good for you. I've never seen you so engaged with someone before. Let him through the wall you've built around yourself, or you'll spend your life wondering what could have been."

I almost fired back a glib response, until I caught sight of Doc's expression. "I'll take what you said under advisement."

"It's all I can ask."

CHAPTER 19

Jean Luc glanced up from his computer screen with bleary eyes.

"Misha would be proud," I teased as I walked into the office.

He leaned back and stretched. "I just spoke to him. He wants me to bring him a computer so he can work on a facial recognition image of the man who shot him."

"My fault, sorry. I told him to call you today and give you a description, but Misha being Misha..."

"Saw it as an opportunity to play with his gadgets. I was planning to go over and relieve Doc today anyway."

"Make sure you take him some food by lunchtime. He should be done with the cannoli well before then."

"Lunch will depend on how long our meeting with Josiah Akers takes."

I took a step forward. "He's agreed to see us?"

"Yes. Nicholas talked to him last night, and he has agreed to meet with us at his offices in Tower City."

"Great."

Dalton's voice chimed in behind me. "What's great?"

I faced him. "We're going to pay a visit to Josiah Akers today."

"When?"

Jean Luc stood. "Now."

As we headed down Superior, Jean Luc negotiated morning rush hour traffic while filling us in on Akers' background.

"He runs a number of business chains throughout the Midwest. Laundromats, automatic car washes, and storage units."

"That's an interesting combination," Dalton interjected.

"Not really," Jean Luc replied as he drove into the garage and took the parking ticket. "Pavels do not like dealing with humans, so it makes sense they would invest in self-service businesses."

Jean Luc always amazed me with his insights. "What about Akers himself? What do we know about him?"

"He is older than I am, although I do not know how old, since they are very secretive. He has been in charge of the clan for more than one hundred and fifty years."

"Anyone in line to succeed him?"

Jean Luc pulled into a parking space. "Succession in the Pavel clan is not through lineage. It is through power and determination, with a little blood lust thrown in for good measure. Rumor has it the previous leader was Josiah's uncle. He was killed by a rogue demon. Josiah stepped up and assumed command shortly thereafter."

I nodded. "Anything else we need to know before we go in?"

"Pavels' disdain for humans is pretty strong. So I should be the one to interrogate him. Try to stay calm, Kyle. If you make him angry, we will not get anything out of him, and then we will have to deal with Nicholas afterwards."

I smiled at Jean Luc. He was so cute when he was being all preachy. "Got it. I will be the poster child of diplomacy."

Jean Luc rolled his eyes. He wasn't so cute after all.

We took an elevator to Akers' offices on the upper floors. No side trips to peruse the stores on the lower levels or grab a burger at the Hard Rock. When the doors opened with a ding on the fifteenth floor, I immediately knew we were in demon territory.

There were several large-ass males standing at the far end of the hallway outside a closed door. "Does he rent this entire floor?"

"Yes, so behave, or we will not make it back to the elevator in one piece," Jean Luc murmured.

We walked down the hall, and within seconds a man who seemed to be lacking a neck greeted us. On second glance, he did have a neck, but it was short and thick and dwarfed by his massive head. I hoped they didn't all look like this one. The image of a low-budget alien movie invaded my thoughts. Laughing in Akers' face was not going to win points or influence anyone, demon or not.

"Josiah is available to speak with you now. Follow me."

The demon spoke directly to Jean Luc, barely acknowledging Dalton's or my presence. I could see how this was going to play out already, and I didn't like it much. Dalton must have sensed my irritation, since he shook his head slightly at me. I took a deep, calming breath.

At the end of the hallway, I was relieved to see the guards standing outside the doorway did, indeed, have necks. Maybe I could avoid an interspecies incident after all. Before we could go through the door, one of the guards held up a wand metal detector. Was he serious? I stood there glaring at him while he ran the wand over my body. There would be no strip searches today. He did the same with Jean Luc, who wore a bemused expression.

When they got to Dalton, I bit my lip to keep from laughing at the ridiculousness of it all. Dalton was wearing his gun holstered to his belt. He pulled out his wallet and showed them his badge, shaking his head when the guard motioned for him to give him the gun. Before the guard could protest, a voice came through the door.

"He can keep the gun. They are no threat. Let them in."

My eyes widened. How did he know what was going on outside the door? Was he the great and powerful Oz?

The guard stepped back and we were herded into the room. The man behind the desk, who I assumed was Josiah Akers, stood slowly. He was tall and thin, but not lacking in muscle. His tailored suit fit him perfectly and I'm sure cost him a pretty penny. His black hair was slicked back, and his brown eyes were small relative to the rest of his face. I took an immediate, irrational dislike to him.

He of course addressed Jean Luc first. "You must be Jean Luc. Nicholas mentioned you would be coming to talk to me today." He then glanced at Dalton and me. "And are these your...*colleagues*?"

How he could make the word colleagues sound like pond scum was beyond me, but he did. I smiled at him anyway. What was the saying, attract more bees with honey? "Kyle McKinley," I said. "And this is Joe Dalton from the police department."

He motioned to the chairs across from his desk. "Please, have a seat."

I took a quick gander at his office. The view was nice. Windows overlooked the city behind him. His desk was mammoth but practically bare, except for a monitor perched there with a view of the hallway. So, like Oz in the movie, he was not all-powerful. The rest of the office was understated, but elegant, done in silver and blues. I wondered if it clashed with his purple skin when he changed to his demon form.

He turned to Jean Luc again. "What can I do for you?"

God, I was so sick of the games. Forget sweet, why would I want to attract bees anyway? They sting. "Didn't Nicholas tell you why we wanted to meet with you?"

His small eyes flicked toward me. "He mentioned you would like to talk to me about the incident at the Erie Bar. But I am not sure how I can help you with that."

My internal voice screamed "pompous ass", but my external voice calmly stated, "A Pavel demon was seen at the Erie Bar that night, and identified by multiple witnesses. Since you are the Pavel clan leader, we hoped you could provide us with some insight."

He leaned forward, resting his forearms on his pristine desk. "How can you be sure a Pavel was involved?"

"Witnesses saw a man with purple skin and yellow eyes."

"Can you produce these witnesses?"

I shook my head. "You are aware of standard procedure in these cases. The humans' minds were scrubbed."

"Since you have no *credible* witnesses, then you have no proof a Pavel was involved."

"We had a shifter witness who also corroborated the human accounts. He was sure it was a Pavel," I countered.

"And where is he now?"

"Dead."

"Then you have nothing but hearsay."

I stared at him for a moment before responding. "Actually, what we have now are two murders. This gives us an even bigger reason to find out more about the Pavel at the bar, since he is the number one suspect for the shifter's murder."

Akers snorted. "Why would this alleged Pavel go after the shifter?"

"Because he would have assumed the shifter's memories were not scrubbed, so he would go to him for answers."

"And what answers would those be?"

"Where Hampton's head is, of course."

He tapped his fingers on his desk. "Well, your argument doesn't hold water. The head is still missing. Word on the street is someone is offering a large amount of money for it. I strongly doubt if a Pavel had, indeed, gone after this shifter, he would have come away without the information." He smiled in triumph.

"Not when I had already swept the shifter's memory."

Akers' eyes widened for just a second before he blinked and reverted to feigned indifference.

Dalton spoke up next to me. "Mr. Akers, we are not here to argue *ad nauseum* about whether or not a Pavel demon was in the bar. We know it's true. What we *are* doing is trying to protect the supernatural community from exposure. I assume you want the same thing?"

Akers' lips tightened into a thin line. "Of course."

"Do you know who might have been in the bar that night and why?" Dalton persisted.

"No, I do not."

"Then we have a common goal. To find this rogue demon and stop him from causing more damage."

"If one of my clan is involved, I will find out and deal with the situation internally."

Jean Luc spoke then. "Unfortunately, when Hampton and the shifter were killed, it became more than a clan matter, sir. Now other factions are involved."

Akers grimaced. "Sebastian does not scare me."

"Can you think of any reason why a Pavel demon would be working with Hampton?" Dalton continued.

"No. Vampires and demons normally do not work well together. No offense, Jean Luc."

Jean Luc inclined his head. "None taken."

Akers stood, signaling the end of our meeting. "I will conduct an internal investigation of this matter, although I am not convinced a Pavel is involved."

"Can you think of anyone with the means to offer large amounts of money for the head?" I asked.

Akers had the nerve to smirk at me. "Well, I have the available capital, as do several others in the supernatural community. I assume you will be speaking to them as well."

I smirked right back. "Of course."

"I will be in touch if I learn anything more." He ushered us to the door and opened it. Two of his goons stood just outside.

"If I may, I have one more question."

He gave me a look much like a parent would give a disobedient child. "Yes?"

"Would a Pavel hire a human to help retrieve the head?"

"Absolutely not. We do not work with humans."

Condescending, much? "And yet it's humans who have provided you with the money to live like a king in your mini-fiefdom, right?"

Akers pupils darkened for one second before he regained his composure. "You know your way out."

We walked to the elevator, Jean Luc and Dalton flanking me. They seemed a bit anxious. I was just pissed. I had thought Boris was arrogant. He was a cute, wiggly puppy compared to this barracuda.

We rode the elevator in silence and then walked through the parking garage to the van before speaking. I had calmed down considerably by then. I couldn't say the same for Dalton and Jean Luc.

Dalton slammed the door so hard the van rocked. "Jesus, Kyle, did you have to goad him?"

I scowled. "I behaved until the end. He was giving us the bum's rush. I just wanted to see if I could get a reaction."

"What if his reaction had been to have his guards come in and take care of us?"

"He's too smart to do that. Nicholas knew we were there. How would he have explained it?"

Jean Luc put the van in reverse and backed out of the space. "I thought we agreed I would interview him. You really should watch your temper, Kyle. We may need Akers' help."

I shook my head. "Akers isn't going to help us at all. He's lying. I think he knows very well who was at the bar. The question is, was he the one who sent him?"

Jean Luc nodded. "I listened to his heart beat to see if he was lying, but he regulated it most of the time."

"Of course he did," I added, "he knew exactly what we were going to ask."

Jean Luc paid the parking fee and pulled out onto West Sixth. "He did get agitated when you mentioned you had swept the shifter's brain."

I smiled. "You noticed it too? He definitely didn't know that, which means either he isn't in control of the Pavel or it wasn't a Pavel who killed the shifter. My vote is on the latter. Especially since Byron was not killed in a typical Pavel manner."

"Akers was also lying when he said Sebastian did not scare him. His heartbeat accelerated then."

"I don't blame him for that one. Now, what are our next steps?" I glanced first at Dalton and then Jean Luc.

Dalton jumped in. "I think we need to talk to the shifter leader. It's interesting Akers only mentioned Sebastian and did not refer to Griffin as a threat. Maybe he isn't going to be a major player in this."

"Or maybe," Jean Luc added, "Akers is underestimating him."

CHAPTER 20

I fiddled with the pepperoni on my pizza, pulling it off and stacking the pieces one on top of the other, the smell of the spicy meat making my mouth water. Out of the corner of my eye I saw Dalton's right eyebrow rise questioningly. I picked up the pizza and went to town, the steamy mozzarella nearly taking off the roof of my mouth. Pizza paradise.

"I'm glad to see you enjoy food."

I shrugged. "Why wouldn't I?"

"I don't know. Most of the time women either pick at their food or insist on having only salads."

"It's not because they don't like food. It's because they're trying to impress you. They don't want you to think they eat a lot. Heaven help you imagine them gaining weight. When they get home after the date they probably pack away a half gallon of Rocky Road."

"That's ridiculous."

"I agree. Most men don't think that far ahead. They aren't thinking any further than 'will I get lucky tonight?'"

Dalton chuckled. "Wow, talk about harsh...and more than a bit sexist."

"No, just honest. I believe both women and men are messed up in their thinking." I took another large bite.

"Good to know you aren't trying to impress me right now."

"Nope. And you aren't thinking about how to get me into bed, right?"

Smirking, Dalton reached for another slice of pizza. "I have to know. What are you going to do with the stack of pepperoni on your plate?"

"When I get down to the crust, I like to lay the pepperoni across the bread and eat it like a sandwich."

"I'll have to try it some time."

"Thanks for having lunch with me. Jean Luc would have come, but it's a bit disconcerting to have him just sit and watch me eat. Besides, he wanted to go check on Misha."

"Misha's doing better?"

"Yeah. He's big-time cranky, which means he's feeling much better. Jean Luc is going to relieve Doc so she can get out of there for a while."

"It's nice to see how much you care for each other."

"They're my family," I answered automatically. I sat back for a second, stunned. I hadn't ever said it out loud.

Dalton took a sip of water and stared at me for a moment, as if wanting to choose his next words carefully.

"Spit it out, Dalton. I can smell the wood burning."

"Do you mind me asking about your biological family?"

My chest tightened. We were not heading into happy territory, but I reminded myself normal people talked about this kind of thing all the time. "I never knew my father. My mom got pregnant when she was a teenager. I ended up having to take care of both of us while I grew up, and by the time I hit eighteen I was on my own." I patted myself on the back. In four sentences I had succinctly answered his question.

He gazed a little too long at me. "Sorry to hear that."

I squirmed a bit under his turquoise scrutiny. "It is what it is. What about you?"

"My maternal grandmother raised me. My parents were killed when I was six."

"That's awful. I'm really sorry."

He wiped his mouth with a napkin. "We were talking about you. What about your friends? What do you do when you're not working?"

I pushed the plate with the half-eaten slice away. I wasn't hungry anymore. "What's with the twenty questions?"

"I'm just curious about you."

"Misha, Jean Luc and Sabrina are my friends...and I don't have any hobbies, if that's what you mean." He frowned slightly and I plowed on. "I know, all work and no play makes Kyle a dull girl."

He shook his head. "I would never say you're dull." He paused. "So, no human friends, huh?"

"No, what's wrong with that?"

"Nothing. I was just noting it." He grinned. "I'd like you to consider me a friend. Now that we've called a truce and all, I was hoping a treaty would be next on the agenda."

I chuckled. "You are a slick operator. I need to remember that."

My phone rang, interrupting any response from Dalton. "It's Nicholas. I'm going to take this outside." I walked out of the restaurant and hit the button. "Hello."

"Hello, Kyle. I was calling to see how the discussion with Josiah Akers went."

Right. "I'm sure you've already spoken to Jean Luc and Akers, so can I just hit the highlights?"

He paused for a moment and I held my breath. Not being able to see his face was a bit nerve-wracking. I wasn't sure if he was amused or pissed. After a second, he chuckled. I let out my breath.

"I will say I'm surprised you waited as long as you did before insulting Josiah. He can be a little..."

"Pompous, arrogant, bigoted...would you like me to continue?"

Nicholas ignored my comment. "What was your take on his responses?"

"He knows more than he's letting on. He tried to argue we have no proof a Pavel was involved, but it was all subterfuge. He knows a Pavel was working with Hampton. I'm just not sure whether Akers was the one calling the shots or not."

"And the money?"

"If I was a betting woman, I would say he is the one offering the money."

"Why do you think so?"

"Rumor is the vamps may already have the head. Since the Pavels are also interested in Hampton, I would say they are the front runners."

"Thanks for the recap."

"Before you go, have you been able to speak to Griffin yet? Is he back in the states?"

"How did you know he was traveling?"

"I have my sources."

"Griffin arrived last night, but his assistant said he had some important matters to handle today, and he has not returned my call yet. I will let you know when I can set up a meeting. Griffin has been told about the bartender's death. I understand you let the cat out of the bag with Josiah about Byron being dead."

"I don't think he was all that shocked to hear it."

By the time I hung up and walked back into the restaurant, Dalton had finished eating.

"How did it go with Nicholas?"

I quickly relayed the conversation.

"So, we are on hold for today, until Nicholas can hook us up with Griffin?"

"Yep, looks that way."

Dalton motioned for the check. "I'm going to go into the station this afternoon and take care of some things, then. Okay with you?"

"Sure."

We were only a few blocks from my office, so I decided to hoof it back so Dalton could go directly to the station. Dolly was still at lunch, so I unlocked the door and walked into the back room. The white board called my name. I added notes under Akers and then paced in front of it. What was the next step?

I really wanted to talk to Griffin. Maybe I could track him down. Nicholas had mentioned he was dealing with important matters when he returned. Maybe one of those matters was how Trina Connor was doing after her abduction. If not, I could find out if Tim or Stephanie would be willing to hook me up with him sooner rather than later.

I took off for the suburbs. While I drove, I clicked on my sync, trying to call Dalton. His cell rang but never went to voicemail, which was strange. I called the police department next.

"Cleveland Police Department."

"Yes, can I be connected to Lieutenant Joe Dalton?"

"Hold please." Muzak filled my ears while I waited. "I'm sorry but the lieutenant is not in today."

"I spoke with him this morning, and he said he would be working there this afternoon."

"Sorry, ma'am. He's not here. Can I take a message or direct you to someone else?"

"No, thank you."

I hung up, and checked my watch. He hadn't left very long ago. Maybe he got sidetracked.

It didn't take me long to reach the Connors' house. I pulled next to the curb and parked when I spotted a black Audi sedan in the driveway. Maybe my hunch had paid off.

Stephanie answered my knock. She looked a lot better than the last time I saw her.

"Kyle. What a surprise."

"Hello, Stephanie. I'm sorry to drop in unannounced, but I wanted to see how Trina is doing. Is this a bad time?" Just a small white lie. I did want to know how Trina was—I wasn't heartless, after all—but it would be an added benefit if I ran into Griffin in the process.

She hesitated for a second and then beckoned me in. "Trina's in the back yard. Griffin is back in town. He's with Tim in his office."

I stepped over the threshold. "Tim isn't in trouble because I helped Trina, is he? I can speak to Griffin if you want."

"I don't think that will be necessary."

We walked toward the back of the house. Tim's office door was shut. *Damn.*

"I was just going to get some lemonade and cookies for Trina, would you like some?"

"Sure."

"Go on out back, Trina is playing."

I opened the screen door and walked out into the fenced-in back yard. It was a kid's dream. A wooden swing set and jungle gym sat to one side. In the middle of the yard was a large tree with a tree house. And it was not one of those houses with a simple floor and stairs made of wooden planks nailed into the trunk. It was a mini replica of the main house. How awesome was that? I stared up for a second longer and noticed small legs dangling from the side.

Walking over to the tree, I hollered, "Permission to come up?"

Trina's head popped over the balcony. "Hi. Yeah, come on up."

I climbed the ladder and plopped down next to her. My legs kept time with hers as they swung back and forth and we peered out over the yard.

"This is a great tree house."

"Thanks. My dad made it for me and my sister. You're Mommy's friend."

"Yep. I'm Kyle. Are you feeling better, Trina?"

"Yeah, much better." She reached for my hand and grinned. "You're still wearing the nail polish."

"Of course. It's an awesome color. I told you I might dye my hair purple to match it."

She giggled. "Really?"

"Yeah. I've had it black for a while now. I think it's time for a change."

"Has it been other colors?"

"Yes. Let's see...it's been red, blue, green, orange, um...pink, and burgundy."

Her eyes got bigger. "What was your favorite?"

"Blue. My least favorite was green. It made me look like a reject from a St. Patrick's Day float."

"I bet you look pretty with any hair color," she said.

A deep male voice chimed in from below. "I would have to agree."

CHAPTER 21

I gaped down at the man who stood at the foot of the tree. He was tan, as if he worked outside all day, but his tailored pants and button-down shirt squashed that notion. His brown, wavy hair was pulled back at the nape of his neck and his large green eyes twinkled with amusement. My stomach lurched slightly. Shit, he was the shifter version of Jean Luc.

"Uncle Griffin!" Trina squealed, jumping up and leaning over the balcony.

"Trina, be careful," I cautioned, but she scrambled part-way down the ladder and then leaped into his arms.

He smiled and twirled her around. "Hello, pet, how are you feeling?"

"Much better now. Kyle is here to visit me, too."

"So I see. Should we ask her if she needs any help getting down?"

"I'll be fine, thanks."

I walked over to the ladder and turned, knowing full well my ass was going to be the main attraction while I climbed down. When I reached the ground, I expected to find Griffin standing behind me. Instead, he and Trina were already halfway to the picnic table, where Stephanie was in the process of setting out lemonade and cookies.

Stephanie handed me a glass when I walked up. "Would you like an oatmeal cookie? They're fresh from the oven."

My mouth watered. "I never say no to warm cookies." I helped myself and took a bite, the cinnamon bursting in my mouth. "These are amazing. I have a friend who would kill for these cookies."

"I'll send some home with you, then."

"Mommy, Kyle is going to color her hair purple."

"Is she, now?"

"Yeah. Can I see it when you do?" Trina asked.

"Sure," I nodded. "You'll be the first person I show."

We sat for a few minutes, listening to Trina chatter away. It was hard to believe she was the same girl I had spent time with less than a week ago. When I finished my second cookie—I couldn't help myself—I turned to find Griffin watching me. I stared right back at him until he had the nerve to wink at me before addressing Trina.

"Trina, do you mind if I borrow Kyle for a few minutes? We have something to discuss."

"No problem. Are you going to come back and tell me about your trip, Uncle Griffin?"

"Yes, I have new adventures to share with you."

We walked toward the house. Griffin opened the screen door and ushered me inside, then led the way down the hall and into Tim's office, shutting the door behind him. I guess it was time to get down to business. If he thought I was going to apologize for helping Trina, he was mistaken.

"I want to thank you for what you did."

I stared at him in confusion. "So you aren't angry with the Connors for asking me to help her?"

"No, I'm angry with myself." He gestured for me to take a seat. Instead of sitting in Tim's chair, he surprised me by sitting down in the other guest chair next to mine. "I wasn't here when Trina was taken. When the pack retrieved her, I instructed them to keep a low profile. I didn't realize how traumatized she was until later."

"I'm glad you didn't punish them."

His eyes widened and then his mouth curved up slightly. "I don't punish people, Ms. McKinley."

"I've worked with the supernatural community long enough to know there are established hierarchies you do not ignore."

"True. In my case, pack rules are established to protect our anonymity."

"It's also the aim of the BSR."

"Yes, Nicholas works hard to hide our community."

His tone when speaking Nicholas's name was not one of admiration. "I take it you're not a fan of his?"

His eyes held mine for a second, as if gauging how honest he could be. "Nicholas has done more than most in our community to protect us. However, I am not always sure of his true agenda."

"He can be *ambiguous* at times"—I shrugged—"but he's my boss."

"And yet I have a feeling he doesn't have much control over you. Correct?"

I decided it was best not to answer, so I played to his vanity instead. "So what's it like, being responsible for half the U.S. shifter population?"

He paused, as if seriously considering his response. "Not to sound cliché, but it can be a blessing and a curse. My people are thriving, and when I look at Trina, I see our future, and I'm humbled to be leading them. But with power comes responsibility. I have to make decisions not everyone supports."

I wondered if those decisions included offering big bucks for a vamp's head? But it was probably not the best question to ask at this point. "Do you know Dolly Thompson?"

"Yes. She works with you as well."

"Yep. She helps with identifying the supe clients and convincing humans to find another agency to do their detective work."

"I find it interesting you refer to humans as if you aren't one of them."

Had he and Dalton been comparing notes? "I guess it comes from working almost exclusively with the supernatural community. Most of my friends are supes."

He leaned closer to me. "And male."

"*Excuse me?*"

He held up his hands. "Oh, I mean no disrespect. I can smell them. A vampire and a Shamat...which isn't too difficult to guess, since I know about Jean Luc and Misha from Dolly." He paused. "But right now, the stronger smell surrounding you is a human male and, if I'm not mistaken, he is very interested in you."

I sat up straighter. "I think you're off base."

"Did you know shifters have been accused of being able to smell emotions? In truth, we smell hormones, and the chemicals which are released when we are angry, scared, sad...or aroused."

"What is this, a shifter version of eHarmony?"

He laughed. "I'm sorry if I have made you uncomfortable. I forget how repressed humans are about their emotions. Shifters aren't shy about voicing our interest in someone else. Now, let's get down to the reason you're here today. My assistant told me Nicholas called."

I started to protest, but he interrupted me. "I have seen you with Trina and know you have her best interests at heart.

But you are also a woman of action, and I suspect if you saw the opportunity to kill two birds with one stone, as it were, you would take advantage of it."

I didn't bother with denials. His lie-detector nose would probably pick up on my deceit anyway.

"We are investigating the vampire murder at the Erie Bar, as well as Byron's murder."

His eyes narrowed. "I am assuming they're related."

"Yes, we believe Byron was killed because he was the only supernatural witness at the bar."

"I was not given the specifics of what happened to Byron. Would you please explain?"

"He was tortured and then murdered."

Griffin's jaw tensed and he stared at me for a second before responding. "Do we know by whom?"

"Not yet."

"Where is Byron's body?"

"At our storage facility."

"I would like him returned to us as soon as possible."

I nodded. "I'll speak to Nicholas. I don't see any reason we couldn't release him to you."

"And what can I do to help find Byron's killer?"

"Right now someone is offering three million for Charles Hampton's missing head. He was the vampire decapitated at the bar. There are only a few members of the community who would be able to produce this type of cash."

He frowned. "And now you're telling me I'm a suspect?"

"I'm asking you if you know why a vampire's head would be worth that kind of money."

He shrugged. "I have no idea. Once a vampire loses his head, there's no coming back. Why someone would pay for the head is a mystery to me."

I moved on to another tack. "Can you tell me more about Byron?"

Griffin picked up a paperweight from the desk. "Byron was relatively young and had not figured out what he wanted to do with his life. He was a bit of a wanderer."

He bounced the glass ball in his hands, tossing it back and forth. I realized in shock it contained some fierce-looking canines. A shifter's version of baby teeth? I refocused on Griffin's face.

"Ah, has he ever been in any trouble?"

"Minor scrapes as a youth. I thought you said his death was related to the dead vampire, so what would Byron's past have to do with it?"

"I need to rule everything out. I don't want to make an assumption which might lead us down the wrong path."

"And what does Nicholas think this is about?"

"I don't know if he has a specific theory. He's working with us to find out who did this and stop them from hurting anyone else."

He put the paperweight back down and stood. "Byron died days ago, and yet you have very few answers. I'll be forming a group of my own people to open an investigation into what happened."

Lord, the last thing we needed was a group of pissed-off shifters. "I know how frustrating this is for you. But we're all trying to accomplish the same thing here, to stop humans from finding out the truth."

"Actually, my goal is to find out who killed Byron. His death will not be swept under the rug."

"You're right. But if we have another event like the Erie Bar, I don't know whether we'll be able to cover it up. And then what? Humans far outnumber supes, and if our past shows us anything, it's that they will lash out. Scared humans means deadly humans. I'm just asking for your cooperation."

He shook his head. "Instead of being here with me, why aren't you questioning Sebastian? I refuse to believe he's innocent of what's going on here."

"We'll be talking to him as well. Please give us some more time before you guys come out with guns blazing. The last thing we need is a supernatural civil war."

Griffin's eyes bored into mine. "You might think shifters are mindless animals. Rest assured I *will* control my pack. Tell Nicholas I'll be in touch concerning Byron's remains. Now if you'll excuse me, I promised Trina I would tell her about my trip."

He opened the door and I watched his retreating back. I'm not sure how things had deteriorated so much in a matter of minutes. It was now official. I had pissed off the entire supernatural community.

Yay, me!

Chapter 22

I remember watching cartoons when I was little where the character's face turned red and steam came out of his ears when he was mad. I had always thought it was the funniest thing, until I got a good look at Dalton's face when he found out I had met with Griffin on my own.

"What the hell were you thinking?" he growled.

I plopped down on the office sofa. "I was thinking we need information. You were the one who said we should meet with Griffin next."

"I didn't mean for you to go off half-cocked. Are you trying to get yourself killed?"

"Now you're being melodramatic. I wasn't in any danger. I met with him at a family's home in the suburbs, for God's sake. We had cookies and lemonade."

"And what did you find out from him?"

"He denied having anything to do with the events at the bar."

"What about the head?"

"I don't think he's looking for it," I responded.

"So he isn't going to cause any trouble?"

I hesitated. "I wouldn't say that. He wants to know who killed Byron. Shifters are big into revenge."

"Great, so now we have a pissed-off shifter leader thrown into the mix. I think you should interview for a job at the UN, Kyle."

"All right, I get it. I'm sorry. I tried to call you to see if you could go with me and the guys at the station told me you weren't there."

"Why didn't you try my cell?"

"I couldn't get through. It wouldn't even let me leave a voice mail."

He shrugged. "Maybe I was in a dead zone. Please, don't go see these guys by yourself again. Take Jean Luc or Misha with you if I'm not around."

"Fine. So did you get your work done at the station?"

"Not the work I was planning to do, no. We got a hit on the FBI database on the Father Cowell murder."

"What does that mean?"

"When a murder occurs, police enter relevant data about the death in a centralized FBI database. Cause of death, crime scene, etc. Our detectives loaded the details into the database and it matched another recent case. A body was found a month ago in Chicago with the same figure eight mark on the back of his neck. Because of this second body, the FBI will begin profiling in the event it might be a serial case."

"The last thing we need is FBI involvement," I sputtered.

"I agree, especially since the odds are Hampton killed the guy when he was still in Chicago."

"Have they determined who the victim was?"

"Yeah, they have a positive ID. We should be able to compare the Chicago information with what we have shortly. It's coming through my secure email."

I nodded and checked the clock on the office wall. "I wonder where Jean Luc is?"

A voice sounded behind me. "He had to come pick me up."

"Misha!" Spinning around, I ran over and threw my arms around him. A little girly, but I couldn't help myself. He picked me up and hugged me back. I always forgot about his extraordinary strength until he tossed me around like a rag doll.

"Are you feeling good enough to be at work?"

"Little one, I *need* to be back at work. It's good to be out of Doc Miller's clutches. She is a beautiful female, but a tyrant."

I laughed. "I'm sure you were the model patient, causing her no grief."

"Humph," Jean Luc muttered.

Misha's eyes widened.

I laughed even harder. "Jean Luc just harrumphed you."

Misha scowled. "If you have something to say, Jean Luc, spit it out."

"My dear friend, you are a terrible patient. Doc should have given you a sedative just to stop the whining."

Before Misha could respond, I played peacemaker. "All right you two, enough with the squabbling. Dalton and I need to fill you in on a few things."

I told them about my meeting with Griffin. If I thought Dalton had reacted badly to my going there alone, Misha almost turned purple. But Jean Luc was the worst. Instead of getting mad, he gave me his disappointed face. I hated when he did that to me. Disappointment was a preemptive strike against any and all sarcastic comebacks.

Luckily Dalton distracted them with his info regarding the body in Chicago. "Misha, I'm glad you're here. I'm going to check my email and then we can start going over the case notes."

Misha sat down at the table, flipping open the waiting laptop and powering it up. "I've been working on something as well. I have a composite of the man who shot me and tried to mow you down. I'm going to run it through a facial recognition program and see if we get a hit."

I leaned forward. "Let me see him."

Misha inserted a flash drive into the USB port and pulled up a file. The man was Caucasian, with close-cut brown hair, blue eyes and a hawk nose. I had never seen him before. Dalton leaned in as well and shook his head.

He checked his phone. "I got the file from Chicago PD."

"Send it to my email address and we'll open it on the laptop." Misha volunteered. After a second, he clicked the file and grimaced. "The picture of the corpse is the top file, and it's not pretty. There is a closeup of the back of his neck, and it looks like the same mark we saw on Cowell." He clicked on the next page.

"The victim's name is Jonathan Brubaker. Age twenty-five, single. He was a lawyer by trade. He worked in contract law for Smith & Turner, a large law firm in Chicago. His body was found in an abandoned warehouse set for demolition. According to the contract foreman, the crew always does a preliminary sweep to chase out vagrants before they tear the buildings down, and they found him hanging from one of the rafters."

I grimaced. "It sounds like something from a bad gangster movie."

Misha continued. "According to the report, the police didn't find anyone with a motive. Even though he was a lawyer, he worked more behind the scenes. He was not trying criminal cases. He had no jealous exes, or anyone else they could find who might have had a reason to do this to him."

Dalton spoke up. "I'm going to go through the case notes thoroughly. Now that we know who this guy is, can you research his background to see if he was connected in any way to our first victim, David Cowell?"

"Yes." Misha's fingers flew across the keyboard.

Dalton turned to Jean Luc. "Have we heard from Nicholas about a meeting with Sebastian?"

"He has not been able to reach him to discuss a time or place yet."

"What about the translation from Cowell's book?"

"Misha provided me with a translation software program, but so far we have not been able to even figure out what language it is. I will work on it some more now."

I waited for an assignment and when none came—thank God—I decided to take advantage of the situation to escape for a while. "Guys, I'm going to go run some errands while you work on the case."

They nodded in tandem as they bent over the computer screen and I headed for the door before one of them thought of something for me to do.

Dolly sat out front reading *Popular Mechanics*.

"I'm heading out for a while. Do you need anything?"

"Dark chocolate and string cheese."

"I'll bring some back."

Since it was midmorning, the parking garage was quiet when I exited the elevator and walked toward my car.

"Ms. McKinley?"

The hairs on the back of my neck stood up when that smooth voice called out. I turned. Sebastian stood a few feet away from me. This was *so* not good. He was the last supe I wanted to be alone with.

"Sebastian."

"I understand you're looking for me?"

I peered around the garage surreptitiously. Were his goons nearby? "Our *team* wants to speak with you concerning Hampton's death."

He took a step toward me, a self-satisfied grin on his face. "Since we're both here now, you may ask me your questions."

"Actually, I have an appointment. We'll need to do this another time." My external voice stayed relatively calm, but my internal voice shrieked, "Don't listen to my heartbeat, don't listen to my heartbeat!"

He disappeared. Where was he? In the next second, his warm breath landed on the back of my neck. *Holy shit.*

"I can't believe your other appointment cannot be rescheduled," he whispered.

I swallowed. "Fine, let's go upstairs to the office, then." I spun around and took a jerky step back from him.

His dead green eyes stared at me. "You amuse me, Ms. McKinley, trying to appear calm, but we both know the truth."

That was it. Enough with the intimidation tactics. If he wanted to kill me, he would have done it already, right? "Actually, the truth is what we're looking for. I'm not sure you know what truth is."

His perfect façade slipped as his green eyes darkened and he had the nerve to flash his fangs. "You may be able to talk to Jean Luc in such an insolent manner, but I will not tolerate it."

He advanced on me slowly while I backed away, toying with me like a cat with a mouse. There was no point in running. He could be on me in a split-second. I took another step and twisted my ankle, my arms spinning like a helicopter in an attempt to right myself. As I started to fall, hands clutched me from behind and I landed against a strong chest.

I couldn't breathe and didn't want to turn around to see who had me. It had to be one of Sebastian's guards. But as the seconds ticked by, he did not hand me over to Sebastian. For that matter, I wasn't sure why Sebastian was standing in front of me frowning.

"It will be okay, *ma petite*."

I sucked in a breath when Jean Luc's comforting voice filled my ears. Once again he had saved my ass. Misha and Dalton walked up next to us. Jean Luc handed me off to Dalton like a sack of potatoes, and I did not complain in the slightest. Dalton carried me a short distance from the impending brouhaha. I sucked in a shaky breath.

From out of nowhere, two of Sebastian's guards joined the fun.

Misha stepped up closer to Jean Luc and grinned. "It's been a while, Sebastian."

"Misha, Jean Luc. As I was just saying to Kyle, I understand you wish to speak with me."

Jean Luc did a little fang-flashing of his own. "You know the rules. Do not come here again. You were not invited. This is my territory."

"Really? I would argue everyone here is fair game. You have not tasted either of the humans."

"They come to me of their own free will. I do not have to resort to compelling a human for sexual favors."

Sebastian growled deep in his throat. "Remember who you are addressing."

"I have not forgotten your status as a Founding Vampire, nor the respect normally due one who holds the title," Jean Luc answered in a low voice. "However, the moment you threatened one of mine, you forfeited the right of respect."

"I will be speaking to Nicholas."

"And I will be speaking to the vampire council," Jean Luc countered.

Sebastian and his minions marched away, their steps echoing loudly in the parking garage.

CHAPTER 23

I let out a hiss when Dalton placed the bag of ice on my ankle and a chill shot up my leg.

"Sorry, did I hurt you?"

"No, it's cold, that's all. My ankle doesn't even hurt. I'm fine, guys, honest." Misha handed me a mug of coffee. "Thanks. How did you know I was in trouble?"

Jean Luc stared at me for a moment, his pupils almost entirely black. "I sensed Sebastian in the building. Tell me exactly what happened."

I relayed the story, watching all three of them tense, testosterone thickening the air. It was sweet, really, but a bit claustrophobic. "What was the deal with the whole territory thing you spouted at Sebastian?"

"Vampires have established territories," Jean Luc explained. "As a courtesy, you do not go into another's territory without asking permission first. And you definitely do not threaten someone under a vampire's protection. Sebastian broke the rules."

"What about when we went to Hampton's?" I pushed back.

"He was already dead and we were investigating a case. There was no infraction on my part."

"I can't take the blame for this one, guys. He found me."

"Will he come after her again?" Dalton asked.

"Probably." Jean Luc nodded. "I need to decide how best to protect her. Sebastian seems to be obsessed with her for some reason."

"Ahhh, guys? I'm in the room here. Maybe he's taken with my sparkling personality?"

"No, that is not it. I think he wants to exploit your gift. Sebastian is a user."

"I appreciate your concern and all, but I need to be part of the decision-making process here, okay?" The three of them went silent, staring at me as if I had announced the world was flat. "What?"

Misha was the first to recover. "You didn't have a fit about us wanting to protect you."

"What's the point? You're just trying to keep me safe. When are you going to talk to the vampire council, Jean Luc?"

"I have not yet decided if it will cause more harm than good. I will let him sweat tonight and decide in the morning. In the meantime, you should not stay at your place tonight."

I stared at him incredulously. "You really believe he would come after me?"

"I do not know what he is thinking right now. I am shocked he came here today and threatened you. He seems to think he is untouchable."

"She can stay at my house tonight," Dalton volunteered.

"Wait a minute," I announced rather loudly. "I don't need a babysitter."

Misha sighed. "You were doing so well with your temper, Kyle, don't blow it now."

"He doesn't know my name, so she should be safe with me tonight," Dalton insisted.

I swallowed my frustration. "Fine, just for tonight. Jean Luc, please come up with a solution by tomorrow. I want to be home in my own bed. And besides, Booger needs me."

"Let me sleep on it."

I huffed. "Says the vamp who never sleeps."

Dalton drove us to the storage facility, since we were meeting Doc there before going to his house. I was fine, but Dalton had insisted on having my ankle checked. I was sure Doc would end up clucking over me.

We stepped into the lab. Doc stood next to a gurney zipping up a body bag.

"Byron?" I asked.

"Yes. Nicholas called. We're releasing the body to the pack, and they're on their way to pick him up. Let me wash up while you tell me what you did to yourself this time."

"You need to work on your bedside manner."

"Whatever. Tell me what happened."

I spilled the ridiculous events as Doc washed and then examined my ankle. She wrapped it in an ace bandage.

"Is she okay?" Dalton asked.

"Her ankle will be fine, but we'll wrap it for tonight, just in case. Now let's have a look at your stitches." She pushed back my bangs and stared for a moment. "These can come out. Do you want me to do it now?"

"Sure."

Doc walked over to a cabinet along the wall and pulled out some instruments.

I grimaced. "Are those the same instruments you use for autopsies?"

"Yes, but I sterilize them. Are you going to get all squeamish on me? "

"Just do it."

Doc snipped the first stitch and pulled it out lightly. As she snipped the second one, the buzzer to the back door sounded. Doc and I looked up at the monitor on the wall. A dark van sat in the back bay area.

"It's the pack to pick up Byron. Joe, would you let them in?"

Dalton nodded and left. Doc kept snipping away. Within a couple of minutes, Dalton came back through the door, followed by Griffin and two other men. I was surprised to see him. This was going to be a bit awkward.

Doc set down the scissors. "Griffin, it's been a long time. I'm sorry it's under these circumstances."

"Sabrina." He turned to me, his eyes moving from my forehead to my wrapped ankle. "Don't let me stop you from helping Ms. McKinley."

"She's fine. Let me get you a copy of the autopsy report." Doc walked to the other side of the room and Griffin continued to stare at me. "Are you all right?"

"Yes. Doc is just taking out some stitches."

"And your ankle?"

"I'm fine. No big deal." Dalton watched our exchange closely. "Griffin, this is Lieutenant Joe Dalton from the Cleveland Police Department."

"The lieutenant was kind enough to introduce himself when he let us in. I didn't realize you had a human on the team."

"Besides me you mean?"

"Of course, besides you, but I should have guessed as much."

He had the nerve to smirk at me. What the hell was that supposed to mean? Was he going to tell Dalton he could smell him on me? Not good. I needed to change the subject quickly.

"I apologize for getting off on the wrong foot yesterday. I meant no offense."

He shrugged. "I'm used to people making assumptions about shifters. You might want to spend some time with us to gain a broader perspective."

Smug bastard. "I'll make sure to schedule some time after this investigation."

Doc returned and handed Griffin an envelope. "It's all in here. If you have any questions, feel free to contact me. Would you like to spend some time alone with Byron before you move him?"

Griffin's smugness disappeared immediately. "I would like to see him."

Doc moved to the gurney, unzipped the bag and flipped back the top to show Byron's head. Griffin walked over, his jaw muscles rippling as he stared down. After a second, he placed his hand on Byron's forehead and whispered a few words, then backed away. Doc zipped up the bag and the two other shifters pushed the gurney out of the room.

"Thank you, Sabrina. I'll review the information and will contact you with any questions. We'll also conduct a full investigation of this murder." He smirked at me. "Don't worry, I'll keep the pack in check as long as I feel confident a true investigation is underway, one whose goal is to find and bring Byron's killer to justice. Lieutenant, Ms. McKinley." With a nod, he walked out of the lab.

"I'm surprised he didn't make us kiss his ring," I mumbled.

Doc chuckled. "I don't know how you manage to piss off everyone you come into contact with, Kyle."

"He's overly sensitive for a guy. Strikes me as a pouter."

"He strikes me as someone who knows what he wants and goes after it," Dalton said. "I'll go bring back the gurney for them."

"I've got a few more stitches to remove." Doc walked over to the sink and washed up again before picking up the instruments. "So what is the deal with you and Griffin, anyway?"

"I met him the other day, and he spouted a bunch of crap about smelling Dalton on me, and then I proceeded to piss him off."

"I'm not surprised he can smell Dalton. His pheromones are off the charts when he's around you."

"Why does everyone keep sniffing me? For the love of God, cut it out!"

"I'm a succubus. I can sense sexual frustration across a football field. Yours *and* his."

"Well, I'm just sick of fighting with Dalton and Griffin."

"Sweetie, you're not fighting. It's your version of foreplay. And for the record, Dalton isn't the only one releasing pheromones around you."

"What the hell are you talking about?"

"Our shifter-king is also interested."

"Dear God, give me strength."

"Give you strength for what?" Dalton asked as he pushed the gurney back into the room.

I froze like a deer in the headlights and Doc saved me. "I was just telling her I'm going to start charging for all these medical services. Come check out my handiwork."

Dalton walked over and leaned in close. "Looks good."

I stared up at him. His eyes weren't on my forehead, but latched onto mine. Heat raced through me. If I didn't watch myself, I was going to end up like a heroine from one of those novels I hid under my bed.

It was time to make a decision about Dalton. I just didn't know if I was ready to sign the treaty yet.

CHAPTER 24

Dalton's house was a craftsman-style bungalow with dark green shingles and a large front porch. Not what I was expecting.

"This is a nice house."

"For a cop's salary, you mean."

"I wasn't going to say that," I protested.

"No problem. When I first bought it, it was in bad shape. I've been working on it for a couple of years now. It's finally looking good."

"Ohhhhh, so you are one of *those*."

"One of what?"

"One of those annoying people who can fix things."

"Yep. I even sanded my own floors."

I rolled my eyes. "Now you're just bragging."

He laughed and opened his front door for me. The inside was...beautiful, in a guy kind of way. The living room had a fireplace with finished, but empty, bookcases on either side. There was very little furniture, just a well-worn brown leather couch, a wooden coffee table and a TV.

"A little stark, Dalton."

"Yeah. I haven't had much time to do anything with the inside, except the kitchen. The furniture is left over from my last apartment, and it's seen better days."

"I see you had enough time to go out and buy a huge flat screen."

He grinned. "A guy has to have a vice or two."

I walked over to the fireplace. There were two pictures sitting on the mantel. One was of an older woman who had Dalton's nose and mouth, but her eyes were a dark brown.

"That's my Grandmother Marie, who raised me."

I reached for the other frame, hesitating until Dalton nodded and then I picked it up. A woman with long dark hair and a man with Dalton's eyes stared back at me. "How did your parents die?"

He stared at the frame and I passed it to him. "My parents were murdered. My dad was FBI, and he was working a mob case. They threatened my mom and me, but my father wouldn't back down. They broke into our house and killed my mom when my dad wasn't home to protect her. Afterwards he went after the guys who did it, but they killed him, too."

My throat tightened and I had to swallow hard before I could speak. "I am so sorry. Were you in the house?"

He shook his head and placed the frame back on the mantel. "I was spending the night with my grandmother. She definitely would have liked you."

"How can you be so sure?"

He shrugged. "I just am. Are you hungry?"

I took that as his hint to change the subject. "Yeah. Do you have good takeout around here?"

"Wow, I think you're a closet sexist, McKinley."

"Why do you say that?"

"Sounds like you assume just because I'm a guy I don't know how to cook."

I shrugged. "I don't cook very well, so my phone is stuffed with restaurant numbers."

"Well, I thought I would make dinner, if it's okay. Do you like chicken?"

"Yep."

"If I give you a knife, can I trust you to chop up some vegetables? I'd rather not visit Doc again today."

"Very funny."

We walked into the kitchen and *now* I was impressed. It was understated and simple, but he had installed stainless appliances that gave it a sleek look. "Good job on the kitchen."

"Thanks. This was the first room I worked on when I moved in." He washed his hands and then opened the refrigerator and took out carrots, celery and lettuce. "Can you put together a salad for me?"

"Sure." I also washed my hands and he set a chopping block and knife on the counter. I chopped while he worked on the chicken at the sink. "So what's on the menu tonight?"

"Chicken Marsala."

My eyebrows shot up in shock and he laughed. "My grandmother taught me to cook. She said a man who cooks is a good catch."

"Your grandmother is a smart woman."

"Yeah, she was. She's been gone for three years now, but I still think about her a lot." He got a bottle of white wine and a container of mushrooms from the refrigerator. "Want some wine before I use the rest of it in the sauce?"

"Sounds good."

He poured me a glass and then hesitated before handing it to me. "Chop up the veggies before you have too much of the wine."

"Good Lord, cut me some slack."

"When you cut me some slack, I'll cut you some."

A comfortable silence followed while Dalton floured the chicken and placed it in the skillet and I finished putting together the salad. The whole scene was a bit too domestic, though, and my panicky flight mechanism kicked in. Then Dalton gazed at me with those ridiculously gorgeous turquoise eyes and I knew I was a goner. *Damn pheromones.*

When the food was ready, we sat down to eat at his kitchen table, since he didn't have any dining room furniture. Dalton waited expectantly while I took my first bite of chicken. The wine and mushroom sauce was just right. "It's delicious."

He grinned. "Don't sound so surprised."

"Sorry. You are a man of many talents."

"You have no idea."

His eyes danced, but his tone made me take a large gulp of wine. It did little to calm my nerves.

The conversation turned to more mundane things once we started eating, and I had no trouble cleaning my plate. I sopped up the last of the Marsala sauce with a piece of bread and sighed, replete.

"Do you want some more?"

"No, I'm good. It was excellent."

He stood and reached for the plates. "How about some ice cream for dessert?"

I never pass up ice cream. "What kind do you have?"

"Vanilla."

I shook my head in disgust. "Figures."

He chuckled and carried the dishes to the sink, rinsing them off and placing them in the dishwasher. "What's wrong with vanilla?"

"Nothing, other than it's boring."

"Oh, ye of little faith." He reached into the cupboard and pulled out a small pan. "Do you like strawberries?"

"Love 'em." Curious, I walked over to the counter.

He opened the refrigerator and found a container of strawberries. Making quick work of removing the stems and slicing them, he then put a small amount of water into the pan. As the water heated, he slowly added some sugar. After a couple of minutes, he dropped most of the strawberries into the pan and let the mixture simmer. The scent of berries permeated the air.

"Can you get the half-gallon out of the freezer?"

I got the ice cream while he gathered the bowls and spoons.

"This should be good to go." He scooped generous portions of ice cream in the bowls—a man after my own heart—and then poured strawberry sauce over the top and garnished it with the slices he had reserved. "Enjoy."

I took my first bite and had to close my eyes when the tart sweetness burst in my mouth. It was better than I could have imagined. After I swallowed, I opened my eyes and found him watching me intently.

"I love the way you savor food, Kyle."

"Food is a big part of life."

Living up to my mantra, I practically inhaled my dessert. Dalton offered me the rest of his when I finished the last bite. But I declined.

I rinsed my bowl and put it in the dishwasher, but when I started to clean up, Dalton shook his head. "I'll get it later. You're a guest."

I didn't have any energy to argue, so I watched him finish his dessert.

"Why did you become a cop? Because of your dad?"

"No," he answered much too quickly. There were definitely some unresolved daddy issues for Dalton, but the frown on his face said now was not the time to delve into them.

He took a deep breath and continued. "My grandmother worried about me not having what she called a 'positive male influence' in my life. She signed me up for a police department program where a kid was paired up with a cop and they spent time together. Kind of like a Big Brother program."

I nodded for him to continue.

"I was assigned to Sergeant Manny Wilcox, a burly, middle-aged guy who epitomized every cop stereotype. Loved to eat and throw back a couple of drinks at the end of each shift. But there was something honorable and amazing about Manny. He didn't believe much in God, he had seen people do too many bad things over the years. I would say his religion was taking care of the people on his beat."

"So he was like a father figure to you?" I stifled a yawn that snuck up on me.

"More like an uncle. But after spending time with him, I knew being a cop was what I wanted to do."

I yawned again.

He smirked. "Am I boring you?"

"Sorry, no. The day is just catching up with me." I smiled apologetically.

He reached over the counter and ran his thumb along my lower lip. "Your lips are red from the strawberries."

My eyes bugged and I struggled between leaning toward him and backing away. He must have sensed my hesitation.

"Don't worry, Kyle. I'm not going to rush you. But, trust me, this is going to happen at some point. I've known since the day we met, when we argued, that we would end up together."

I stood there speechless for maybe the first time in my life. All right—Jean Luc and Misha would definitely say it was the first time.

"Go sit on the couch, I'll just be a couple of minutes cleaning up. Turn on the TV if you want."

I walked into the living room and sat down on the couch, TV the furthest thing from my mind.

I should jump him. Hell, normally I was the pursuer. But there was something different this time. My warning bells kept clanging in the back of my head for some reason. I yawned yet again. I was slowly slipping into a food coma. I closed my eyes. I would rest them for a little while until he came in. Then we would talk or something.

I screamed. Hands gripped my shoulders and I screamed louder.

"Kyle! Wake up! You're safe."

My eyes shot open. Dalton was holding me. I took a deep breath. I was in Dalton's living room, not the dark room I couldn't escape. It was that dream again. Dalton reached over and pulled a blanket from the back of the couch to cover me. I was going to protest until I realized I was shaking uncontrollably.

"Do you want to talk about it?" he asked softly.

My gut reaction was no, but I didn't want to handle this alone, and confiding in him felt scary but right somehow. "I've been having a recurring dream where I'm held captive in a dark place. I can't see much of anything, except a light streaming through a slit in the wall. In the background I hear noises, and I know he's coming for me." My shaking increased and Dalton tucked the blanket up around my shoulders.

"Do you know who he is?"

"No. I just know he's going to hurt me. The whole thing is extremely detailed. It feels like a real event instead of a dream."

He sat quietly for a minute reviewing what I said. "Are you afraid you're seeing the future?"

"Yes," I whispered, as if saying it too loudly would make it come true.

"I'm not going to let anything happen to you." He hugged me to his chest and my heart started pumping hard for other reasons.

He took a deep breath. "Woman, you're going to be the death of me."

"What did I do?"

He stared down at me, but didn't say a word.

"Well?"

"Shut up, Kyle."

"Wha—"

Before I was able to issue a brilliant comeback, his mouth covered mine. His lips were as yummy as I remembered and his tongue was begging for entrance.

I was in deep trouble.

CHAPTER 25

I opened my lips eagerly as his tongue slipped in and played with the roof of my mouth. I sank further into him. He moved the blanket and ran his hands down my arms, which for some ridiculous reason had suddenly turned into erogenous zones. I would probably self-combust when he touched my girly parts.

I moaned and threw my tongue into the mix, jousting with his. After a few more inspired tongue-tangling moments, he pulled back.

"What are you doing?" I whined.

"We need to stop now if you don't want this to go further."

"Don't stop."

He cupped my face with his hands and his gaze bore into mine. "Are you sure?"

"Oh, for God's sake, Galahad, you're not deflowering me. Let's get it on."

He laughed and hugged me tight. For a second my chest expanded and ached. But I wouldn't think about that right now. I wanted sex and I was going to get sex.

He stood, holding out his hand, and I clasped it, no hesitation. He led me around the couch and down the hallway. At the second door, he pulled me inside and kissed me like a fiend. I returned the favor, and after a couple of seconds, pushed back and laughed.

"Dalton, I didn't think you had it in you."

He smiled wickedly. "You ain't seen nothing yet."

"Really? And what did you have in mind?"

He stepped toward me and I retreated. His eyes took on a predatory glint as he stalked me around the bed. Within seconds—okay, I wasn't trying very hard to escape—he grabbed me around the waist and tossed me on the bed.

"You're a brute!"

"Brute?" His one eyebrow rose. "Where did that come from?"

"I don't know."

He stared at me for a second. "You're lying."

"No, I'm not." But my voice cracked as I denied it.

"Kyle..."

"Fine. I read it in a book."

He chuckled. "Was there sex in this book?"

"Yes."

"Do you want to describe it to me?"

"Why...can't you think up things on your own?"

"Yes, but if you want to act anything out, I'm your man."

"You're talking me to death, here, Lieutenant."

He crawled onto the bed and straddled me. "Talk time is over." He buried his face in my neck and kissed me, following up with a playful nip.

I moaned. Couldn't help myself. I felt him smile against my neck, and then he kissed up along my jawline and ended back on my lips. As he distracted me with kisses, he worked his hands underneath my shirt. Not to be outdone, I unbuttoned his shirt, pushing it back and running my hands along his hard chest. I had been fantasizing about touching him since the day he stood shirtless in the alley.

His kisses grew hungrier, and when I squeezed his nipple, it was his turn to moan. Lifting up, he tried to pull off my shirt. I sat up and helped him. Once it was off, he ran his beautiful eyes over my body, his stare piercing me.

I couldn't get over the intense gleam in his eyes, especially since I was wearing my boring white bra. Why I had not started wearing my slutty undies the minute I laid eyes on him was beyond me.

"You are gorgeous." He reached around and unhooked my bra, sliding the straps down my arms and exposing my breasts.

I wanted to respond, but all words left me when he palmed my breasts. The roughness of his fingers against my skin set off a tidal wave of electrical currents, and I arched closer. He kissed me again, his tongue dueling with mine for the briefest moment. And then he was gone, his lips traveling down to kiss the top swell of my breasts.

God, yes! I trembled and took choppy breaths, anticipating where he was going next, and was rewarded when his tongue teased my left nipple. Sensation raced through me, electrifying my skin, and when his lips finally enveloped it, I cried out.

He looked up at me, lips still surrounding my nipple, and his eyes danced. After another moment, he released me and grinned, apparently feeling quite proud of himself. Not to be outdone, I reached for his pants and fought with the button, then rasped his zipper down. But he moved quickly out of my reach.

"I want to touch you," I whined. Wow, he had me whining *again*.

"Not yet. We're going to take this slow."

When he slid off my pants I thanked God it was summertime and I shaved more frequently. But as soon as his lips touched my inner thigh, all inane hairy leg thoughts vanished and I was left with *oh, oh, ohhhh!*

Blazing a slow trail of kisses up my leg, he finally made it to the Promised Land. I squirmed immediately and he held my hips down, torturing me. Crying out, I was on the brink, ready to fall off the cliff, when he stopped.

"Don't stop!"

"Trust me, we're not done." He stood up and finished undressing, and my eyes were glued to him the whole time. He was as lean as I imagined, but muscular in all the right places. Reaching for the bedside stand, he opened the drawer and pulled out a condom. *Good boy.*

"I hope you have more than one of those," I purred.

He shook his head. "Yep, you're going to be the death of me."

"Just being honest, Dalton. Please tell me you're up for the challenge."

"With you, always."

His turquoise eyes darkened as he ripped open the package and sheathed himself. I crooked my fingers at him and he joined me on the bed. I reached down and ran my palm over his length and he growled. It was the sexiest sound I had ever heard. While I was playing, he started his own game with his fingers and we were both sweating within seconds. I had challenged him earlier, and if I'd had the strength I would have held out, but I was beyond that point.

"Dalton, now!"

He thrust inside me and then froze for a moment, watching my face with concern. I gazed into his eyes and lost myself for the briefest of seconds. Then I took a deep breath and relaxed, nodding. He sighed and started to move again. Within seconds, tremors threatened my control, and my vision went hazy. Our bodies found a slow rhythm. It didn't take long before the pace ramped up and was in sync with my thudding heart.

I screamed when colored lights flashed behind my eyes and I toppled over the edge. Dalton groaned and followed me. Once we stopped moving, he lay next to me, wrapping his arms around me. "You okay?"

"I'm more than okay. You didn't figure it out from the screaming?"

He smiled. "I just wanted to make sure."

"Give me a few minutes to recuperate and then I get to be in charge this time."

He buried his head in my shoulder and mumbled something.

"What did you say?"

"I said, do you know CPR?"

I laughed. "Don't worry, I got you covered."

I lay next to Dalton and closed my eyes. His even breathing for the past few minutes meant he was probably asleep, which was fine with me, since I wasn't much of an after-sex talker. For me, sex good, talking bad. Sometimes I wondered if I had been a man in a past life.

I moved slightly and cringed when Dalton rolled over to face me and wrapped his arm around my waist.

He opened his eyes and smiled sleepily. "Hey."

"Sorry I woke you."

"No problem. Sorry I fell asleep on you. I'm not being a very good host, am I?"

"If this is how you take care of all your guests, I'd say you're a damn fine host."

He chuckled. "Only very special guests get this type of treatment."

I ran my hand lightly over his chest. "I don't know how I landed on your special list, but I thank you."

"If you need me to spell it out for you, I can." He rubbed my back lightly. "But there's no doubt in my mind."

"Right...girl who can erase memories."

"I don't mean your power, I mean you." He frowned. "Someone did a number on you, some jackass man, right?"

"A jackass by the name of Jack, actually."

"Let me guess, your friend in Vegas?"

I nodded. "Your powers of deduction astound me."

"Hasn't anyone ever told you you're special...like your mom?"

I tried to laugh but wasn't able to pull it off. "Hardly."

He pulled me closer to him. "Didn't you have anyone else you could talk to growing up?"

"Not unless you count her string of boyfriends, but most of them ignored me." He gazed at me with sympathetic turquoise eyes and suddenly I felt more exposed than when he first saw me naked. "Stop looking at me like that."

"I can look at you any way I want."

I ran my hand along his jaw. "I can think of other things we could be doing. Shut up and kiss me, already."

His eyes narrowed on me. "You're trying to distract me."

"Is it working?" I asked.

"For the moment." He pulled me closer and ran his lips lightly over my face.

My phone rang, jarring me awake. *What ungodly hour was it?* The clock on the bed stand said six a.m.

Where was my phone? In my jeans. *Where were my jeans?* Then, I realized I was naked, and lying in Dalton's bed alone.

My phone rang again, and I jerked back the sheets. Searching around the floor, I found my jeans in the corner of the room and pulled my phone out of the pocket. It was Jean Luc.

"What?"

"Good morning, Kyle. Your tone tells me you did not have an enjoyable evening with Joe."

"It was fine. What's going on?"

"We have a development. Where is Joe?"

Wasn't that the question of the century? "It's six a.m., he's probably still sleeping."

Misha's voice chimed in. "You sound upset. Turn on the video conferencing on your phone so I can see you."

"Not gonna happen, Misha."

"Come on, I got you this cell phone so you could use all the cool features. Why not?"

"*It's six a.m.*, I'm not dressed yet." Apparently they were not getting my subtle hints about how ridiculously early it was.

"Oh, right. Well, we ran the composite I made of the guy who shot me and we have a hit."

"Who is he?"

"Jason Watson. Thirty-two. Ex-military. He served in the army for ten years before receiving an honorable discharge. According to his tax records he's been working as a free-lance security specialist."

"What does that mean?"

"It can mean anything from a bodyguard to a mercenary," Misha answered.

"Also," Jean Luc added, "his fingerprints are a seventy percent match to the print I took from Byron's apartment."

"So, not only did he shoot Misha, he knocked me over the head and may have played a part in Byron's death. Do we know how to locate him?" I flipped the phone to speaker and threw it on the bed, so I could gather up the rest of my clothes.

"His current address is false. Misha and I checked it out and found an abandoned building."

"Let me get dressed and then I'll find Dalton and we'll come in." While I was pulling my shirt on over my head, the door opened. By the time I wrestled it over my face, Dalton was in the room carrying a tray.

"Here's breakfast. I thought we could eat in bed. After last night, you have to be starving."

I stared at Dalton for a second and then back down at the phone. My look of panic must have clued him in to the situation. His face turned an interesting shade of magenta. I had become the lead in a comedy of errors.

Silence reigned for several long seconds until laughter burst from the phone.

CHAPTER 26

The last thing I wanted to do was face Jean Luc and Misha. God only knew what either of them would have to say about what happened this morning. But Dalton and I were on the way into the office anyway. I wasn't sure what last night really meant, and after the phone call fiasco this morning we hadn't talked too much about it. Was it a one night stand? I couldn't afford to assume anything else. Luckily, Dalton's phone rang, interrupting my nervous reverie.

"Dalton here...Yes, Father Brown, we can stop to see you. Actually, Miss Smith is with me now...okay, we'll see you in fifteen to twenty minutes."

"What's up?"

"Father found some old letters and thinks it might help with the investigation of Cowell's murder."

Great, so I had avoided the two fussbudgets at the office for a while in exchange for spending time with a priest. A priest who would probably take one look at the two of us and know we'd been fooling around. Would Dalton crumble under his scrutiny and feel the need to go to confession?

We were at the university in less than twenty, and parked next to the administrative offices. A different student manned the front desk and sent us back to Father Brown's office. We entered and he gestured to the guest chairs across from his desk where he sat with a stack of letters piled in front of him.

"Lieutenant, Miss Smith, thank you for coming on such short notice."

"Father." Dalton nodded. "You said you might have some information that would help the case?"

"Yes. After you left the other day, I tried to remember all of the places David had visited while on sabbatical. And then I remembered his letters." He picked up the stack in front of him and handed them to me. "I know it may seem strange we corresponded via letter, instead of email, but I collect stamps. David and I had a deal. Whenever we traveled, we would write letters and send them from all over the world. I was hoping they might help you now."

I flipped through the envelopes. There were stamps from at least a half dozen different countries. "Did you find anything in particular when you reread them?"

"It gives you a good timeline of when he was in each country. Italy, France, Switzerland, Monaco, Turkey. When I read the letters this time, I noticed his tone changed. He went from the David I knew to one who seemed more withdrawn. At the time, I think I chalked it up to him being tired, but in hindsight, I wonder if this was the start of his delusion."

"When did you notice the change?" Dalton interjected.

"He was in Turkey working on a dig. I had forgotten all about it."

"Why would he be involved with an archeological dig?" I asked.

"Apparently there was speculation they might find religious artifacts, and so they asked David to stay and examine them."

"Did he mention if they ever found the artifacts?" I persisted.

"Nothing in particular. Maybe you will notice something more telling than I was able to find. I only hope it helps find David's killer."

I held up the envelopes. "Can we take these with us? I'll return them."

"Please. Let me know if they help in any way."

Dalton pulled out of the university parking lot and I opened the first letter. The postage was from Rome.

"Can you read in the car without getting sick?"

"Don't worry, I won't mess up your leather seats."

The letter was the first Cowell had sent to Father Brown while on sabbatical.

"What does it say?" Dalton asked.

"Sorry, there isn't much in it. Cowell arrived in Rome and met the priest he stayed with. He was excited about being at the Vatican. I'll open another one."

"How many are there?" Dalton asked.

"A dozen or so."

"When you get to the good stuff, read it to me."

"Okay, Mr. Impatient, give me a couple of minutes." I skimmed the letters while Dalton drove. The next six were the same as the first, just general info about his travels. In the eighth letter he had arrived in Turkey. "All right, here is the info Father Brown referred to. Let me read you part of it.

"*I met some young U.S. students working an archeological dig. When I told them I was a priest and a religious historian, they asked me to visit their site. Apparently, there is some indication there may be religious artifacts they are close to unearthing. They would like my opinion on the relics.*" I read the rest of the letter to Dalton, but there was nothing out of the ordinary. The ninth letter had more specifics on the site.

"'*I have been at the dig site for the last two days. There have been some interesting artifacts unearthed, but none hold any real religious significance. Today, they hope to work in the area where they speculate several are located. I must admit, I am as excited as these young people. Their enthusiasm is contagious.*'" I read down through the rest of the letter, but there was nothing else of real interest.

As I was folding the letter and placing it back in the envelope, we pulled into the office parking garage. "These others can wait until we get upstairs. It may help distract Misha and Jean Luc from going on and on about what happened this morning."

Dalton cringed. "What do you think we're up against?"

I shrugged. "It could go either way. They might act like clucking grandmothers, which means you'll be safe and they'll suffocate me. Or they may act like overprotective big brothers—"

Dalton interrupted. "Which means I'm in trouble."

"Yep." We got out of the car, and when the elevator doors opened, we stepped in and I hit the button for the third floor. The moment the doors closed, Dalton yanked me into his arms. My mouth opened in shock and he took full advantage. I leaned in, and he wrapped his large hands around my waist, pulling me closer. Thank God the elevator was as slow as a Sigmut slug demon. My heart pounded, and we accomplished some decent tongue Olympics before the trip was over.

The bell dinged and we reluctantly broke apart. "What was that for?" I gasped.

"A thank you for last night. No matter what happens with Misha and Jean Luc, you are amazing."

A surge of heat rushed up my neck onto my face, an honest-to-goodness full-face blush. *Damn.* "Don't get all mushy on me, Dalton."

We walked down the hall and opened the office door. Dolly was sitting at the front desk and, from the wicked grin on her face, it was obvious she knew what had happened. I wouldn't have been surprised to find out she'd been listening in on the call this morning.

"Good morning, you two. Sleep well?"

I smiled wickedly. "Like the dead. I always sleep well after strenuous exercise."

Dolly chuckled. Dalton shook his head and kept walking. After he made it through the door into the back office, Dolly held up her hand in a high-five gesture. I smacked it. "I'm proud of you, Kyle. He's fine for a human. Next time don't wait so long, or I might have to step in."

"I'll remember that." I headed toward the back, but Dolly stopped me.

"I know humans are all uptight about discussing sex, so I won't ask the specifics, but at least tell me if it was good."

"My toes haven't uncurled yet." She was still laughing when I walked through the door. Apparently a little office sex and I was Dolly's new best friend. Who knew that was all it would take?

I peered around the back office cautiously, not knowing what to expect. Dalton was at the coffee pot. Jean Luc and Misha were nowhere to be seen. Dalton handed me a mug of coffee and I raised my eyebrows in a silent question. He shrugged. It was too quiet.

We both jumped when Misha walked into the room. He smiled and grabbed me, somehow avoiding spilling my coffee. He then kissed me on both cheeks. "I am so happy for you both."

So Misha was going to play my gushing grandmother in this scenario. Dalton let out a relieved sigh, until Misha grabbed him, too, and planted kisses on both his cheeks. I stifled a laugh when Dalton's mouth fell open and his eyes bugged out.

Misha plowed ahead. "You must tell me about last night. I'm curious about human sexual practices."

Dear God in heaven. He went there. I glared at him. "Misha! *So* not appropriate. Where's Jean Luc?"

He had the nerve to grin. "He'll be here in a minute. We've been trying to track down Jason Watson, but haven't had any luck so far. He appears to have gone underground."

"Have you been able to access his military record?" I asked.

Dalton's eyes widened. "Don't tell me you have access to military computers too?"

Misha preened. "We have supes in the military who help us when we need it."

I nodded. "And to think, 'don't ask, don't tell' was the only thing the military used to worry about. I think they were asking the wrong questions."

Before I could get a rise out of Dalton, Jean Luc came into the room. His manner was not as exuberant as Misha's. I stared at him cautiously. Dalton was doing the same.

Misha jumped in, oblivious. "I was just updating Kyle and Joe."

Dalton filled them in on our visit with Father Brown. In the meantime, I set the letters on the table, opened letter ten and scanned it. I did the same for the next. When the rattling of the letters became the loudest sound in the room, I realized they had stopped talking. I looked up into three expectant faces.

"Not much here in the first letter. He mentions that the project benefactors were going to visit the site in the next few days, but he doesn't say anything about examining religious artifacts. The second letter is much more interesting, listen to this:

"'*There was some excitement today. An intact clay vase was unearthed. We believe from the markings that it was used as a religious vessel. The expedition sponsors arrived today, just in time to see the vase. It couldn't have been timed more perfectly. Two of the men were ecstatic. But the third man was more reserved. I asked one of the students about him later, and he said they knew little about him. His name is Joseph Small. He is not affiliated with the university, but appears to be funding the dig. From the look on his face, I'd say he expected to find more than a religious vase.*'"

I stopped for a second and skimmed the rest of the letter. "Here's something else. '*I spoke with the mysterious Mr. Small. He did not seem very receptive until I introduced myself and he realized I was a priest. He asked me several pointed questions about God and my faith. At first I thought he might be an atheist, but he did not seem to doubt the existence of God, rather he was not impressed by it, if that makes any sense. To be honest, the conversation unsettled me a bit, but I am used to speaking with men of science who do not have room for God in their lives. I will sign off now. I am staying late at the site tonight. They are going to dig overnight while the benefactors are here.*'"

I reached for another letter and opened it. Right away, I could tell the tone had changed. "The letter is only a short paragraph, listen to this. '*Father, I have decided to move on from Turkey. I was not of much help to the dig, and I have other places I would like to see before I return home. I will write again once I have settled in a new spot.*'" I set the letter down. "That's a change. He was so excited to be at the dig and now he leaves with no mention of what else was found."

Dalton piped up. "How many more letters are there?"

"Two." I opened one and handed him the other. I scanned the letter. "This one is only a few lines as well. No more mention of the site. Actually, there is not much mention of anything at all. Just that he arrived in Switzerland and would be touring the Alps before returning home."

Dalton spoke up. "The last letter is only a couple of lines, too. Talks about cutting his trip short and returning to the states. Misha, can you research the dig and this Joseph Small he mentioned?"

"I'll start now."

I turned to Jean Luc. "Have you come up with anything to keep Sebastian from coming after me?"

He scowled. "I have some ideas, but nothing I want to share yet."

"I have to go home some time."

"Since you and Joe appear to be getting along quite well, why not stay with him until we can rectify this?"

"And when will that be?"

Jean Luc studied me for a second. "I do not know."

Dalton jumped in. "I think we need to go to Chicago and find out more about Hampton's first victim, Jonathan Brubaker. The case notes have some basic information about him, but the cops in Chicago would not have known what questions to ask. We can fly there today and stay overnight. It will give Jean Luc more time to figure out what to do."

At least we were doing something. "Fine. Misha, can you book us two tickets to Chicago and a hotel?"

"Already on it."

"And can you go to my apartment tonight and feed Booger?"

Misha frowned. "That cat doesn't like me."

"Please?"

"Fine," he grumbled.

Jean Luc nodded and headed toward his office. I followed him into the room. "What's up with you?"

He sat down. "What do you mean?"

"Why are you being so quiet? Are you pissed about Dalton and me? You were the one who threw us into a closet, for God's sake!"

"I am pleased for you both. I did not want to embarrass you in front of Dalton by talking about it, but I have never seen you look happier."

My face began to burn again. "Stop."

He smiled. "I will never understand humans' reluctance to show emotions."

I laughed. "This from the vamp who never lets anything get to him."

"I wish that were the case all the time."

"Sebastian has you worried for real, doesn't he?"

His smile vanished. "Yes. I am unsure of his plans. I will not let him get to you, Kyle."

"I know."

"Perhaps your trip will provide us with helpful information regarding this case. Try to have some fun, too."

"I'm sure I'll figure out something fun to do..."

CHAPTER 27

It was a good thing I didn't have Stanley with me. The honking car behind us was getting on my nerves, and I was entertaining myself with a fantasy of taking out the headlights in two clean shots. We were inching along the Kennedy. I had wisely suggested Dalton drive when we landed in Chicago. Even though I loved visiting the city, I hated driving in it. Low patience threshold and ridiculous rush hour traffic did not mix.

The car honked again. Where did he think we were going to go? We weren't in a flippin' hover car.

"Where to first?" I muttered.

"I'm going to get off at the next exit and take the back way to Brubaker's apartment. His roommate is home from classes today. He's a graduate student at Loyola. Depending on time, we'll either hit Brubaker's law office today or tomorrow morning."

"You seem to know your way around Chicago."

"I used to come here a lot a few years ago."

"For work?"

"My girlfriend at the time moved here."

"Oh."

He glanced at me. "Don't worry, it's been over for a while."

"I'm not worried." At least my outside voice sounded calm. My inside warning bells were clanging loudly.

We arrived at the apartment building thirty minutes later. When we reached the third floor, Dalton knocked on 3A. After a minute, the door opened and a tall, gangly man in a T-shirt and jogging pants greeted us.

"Carl?" Dalton asked.

"Yes."

"I spoke to you on the phone. I'm Lieutenant Joe Dalton from the Cleveland Police Department, and this is my colleague Ms. Smith, may we come in?"

Carl stepped back and held open the door. The apartment was bigger than I expected. A table piled high with books sat next to a large, open window overlooking the park across the street.

"This is nice," I said.

"Thanks. Jonathan picked it out."

"I'm sorry about Jonathan."

He flinched slightly. "Thank you."

Dalton stepped up and took over. "Do you mind if I ask you a few questions?"

"If it will help find Jonathan's killer." He motioned us toward the living room.

Dalton and Carl sat on the couch, but I walked over to the fireplace to check out the photographs. From the case notes, I recognized Jonathan in some of the photos. He was a large man with an infectious smile. What a waste.

Dalton started his questioning. "How long have you known Jonathan?"

"We were paired up as roommates our freshman year, and we hit it off. We lived together until he died."

"Can you tell me about the last time you saw him?"

"It was five weeks ago now. I had a night class and Jonathan was going to a meeting."

"What type of meeting?"

"CLG, Chicago Lawyer's Group. He joined it a few years ago to help advance his career. He made a lot of connections through them."

I continued to look at the photos as Dalton spoke. "The detectives questioned several group members, and they all said Jonathan wasn't at the meeting. The secretary of the event actually said Jonathan had declined the meeting invite."

Carl shrugged. "I don't know what to tell you. Jonathan told me he was going to the CLG meeting. Maybe he changed his mind and planned on attending but was grabbed before he could get there?"

I zoned in on a picture of Jonathan standing in the middle of a desert. Behind him were people bending over, digging in small squares cordoned off by markers.

I held up the photo. "Carl, where and when was this picture taken?"

"Um, I think it was about four years ago. Jonathan minored in archeology. He went on digs during the summer between classes. He was in Egypt."

"What other digs did he go on?"

"He went to Venezuela one year and Turkey the next."

"When was he in Turkey?"

"Two years ago. It was the summer before he took his bar exam. He called it his last chance at adventure before becoming a lawyer." Carl frowned.

"What is it?" I asked.

"He was always so pumped when he came back from a dig. He would go on and on with all his stories. How they would spend days digging in a small square space and come up with nothing. But when he came back from Turkey, he really didn't talk much about it at all."

"Did you ask him why?"

"Yeah. He just told me he had to buckle down and study for the bar exam. I knew he was under a lot of stress, so I didn't push it."

"Do you know if Jonathan would have any other pictures of the digs he worked on?"

"Probably, he was a camera fanatic. I can go through his DVDs and find them for you. Why are you so interested in this?"

I hesitated, choosing my words carefully. "If we can't find a connection between Jonathan's professional life and the killer, then we have to examine other aspects of his life. If you find any pictures of other groups he was involved with, please send me some of those as well."

He nodded. It was a flimsy story, but at this point Carl would probably do anything to help. His haunted eyes stared at me for a moment, begging me to discover the reason why his friend had been murdered.

We spent another thirty minutes with him, Dalton asking him a bunch of questions about Jonathan and his friends and coworkers. When we finished, Dalton gave him his card and asked him to email any of the pictures he found.

As we walked out of the building, I almost started to skip, but restrained myself. Once we were in the security of our car, I called Misha immediately and flipped on the speaker so both Dalton and I could participate.

"Hello."

"Mish, we got a lead. We think Brubaker was a student working the Turkey dig when Cowell was there. Do you have anything on the dig yet?"

"There isn't too much information. The dig was sponsored by private investors and no major discoveries were announced."

"Can you find out who else worked the site?" Dalton asked.

"I can access the student listings, but if they hired workers in Turkey, I don't know if I will be able to get those names as well."

"Did you find out anything about Joseph Small?" I interjected.

"I don't think he exists."

"You can't find anyone named Joseph Small?"

"Yes, I found several men with that name, but none of them fit the profile. They are either dead, or wouldn't have had the money to fund an archeological dig in Turkey. I'm still looking into it. I'll get back to you."

Dalton checked his watch. "By the time we drive downtown, the law office will be closed. We can go there tomorrow, unless Misha comes back with something for us."

"Sounds like a plan."

Dalton hesitated before starting the car.

"What's up?"

"I think I know someone who might be able to give us more information."

"Who?"

"My ex-girlfriend, Lauren."

"Why would she be able to help?" *Damn, damn, damn.*

"She works for the DA's office here in Chicago. She actually moved here three years ago to take the job. We tried to make the long distance thing work, since I had just taken the job in Cleveland, but it got old."

"She isn't working this case, is she?" I couldn't help myself, the jealous beast had busted out to wreak havoc.

"No, an attorney wouldn't be assigned from the District Attorney's office until they actually had someone to charge for the crime. There are no suspects for this murder right now."

"How can she help?"

"She may be able to shed some light on the case for us. When we were dating, she was a member of the CLG. I don't know if she still belongs, but if she does, she could tell us more about the group. It seems strange that Jonathan told Carl he was going to the meeting, when he'd told the secretary he wasn't."

"If she can help with the case, you should call her." I could be an adult about this.

Dalton pulled out his phone and flipped through his contacts and hit send. When he got her voice mail, he left a message.

I took a couple shallow breaths. Wow, should I be so upset to learn he still had her in his contact list? I mean, just because I deleted my exes from my phone nanoseconds after the breakup, didn't mean Dalton had to do the same...right?

CHAPTER 28

I gaped at the hotel suite Misha had booked for us. It was top of the line with—no big surprise—one king-sized bed. I checked out the bathroom and found a two-person bathtub and his and her bags of toiletries. Two plush robes hung in the closet.

Dalton whistled softly. "This is really nice."

Typical Misha. "I'm starving. Do you want to get a burger somewhere? I'm afraid to look at the prices on the room service menu."

"Sure."

Before we even collected our stuff, there was a knock on the door. I walked over. "Who is it?"

"Room service."

Dalton stepped up beside me and said, "We didn't order anything."

"Your food was preordered by a Mr. Misha."

I rolled my eyes and opened the door. A waiter pushed the dinner cart into the room rolling it over next to the table. "Would you like me to set this on the table for you?"

"Yes, please. What are we having?"

"Cheese and crackers, oysters, chocolate-covered straw-berries and champagne."

I stifled the laugh threatening to erupt and waited until the waiter had left to say anything. "Did you see the look on his face when he told me the menu? Good grief, all we need is a heart-shaped bed and we'd have our own porn movie."

Dalton laughed. "At least it isn't low-budget."

"No, Misha would never do low-budget."

Dalton's eyebrows rose. "I can't imagine Nicholas approves of spending company money on these types of things."

"Oh, no, this is all Misha. He's loaded."

Dalton walked over to the table. "Family money?"

"No, he's a self-made demon. Stock market. It doesn't hurt he has a photographic memory and a head for numbers. He spots trends and plays the market very successfully."

"You work with an interesting group."

"A little too interesting at times."

"Well, I plan to enjoy the food." Dalton lifted the bottle of champagne from the bucket. "What about you?"

"I'm game."

It didn't take long to polish off the oysters. The cheese plate came next. Dalton poured the last of the champagne into my glass and I sipped the sweet-tart liquid, savoring the bubbles.

We finally moved to the chocolate-covered strawberries. Dalton selected one and held it up to my mouth. I smiled and took a large bite, juice running down my chin. He reached out and caught it with his thumb, bringing it to his mouth and licking the juice off. *Woo-hoo.* I finished the strawberry and before he could reach for another one, his cell phone rang.

"It's Lauren."

Of course it was. I nodded and he stood, answering the phone.

"Hello...Yes, it's good to hear your voice too... Well, I need your help. I need some information on the CLG, are you still a member? Good, yeah, we're here in Chicago." He glanced at me. "I'm with a colleague. No, you don't have to meet us. We can do this over the phone. But... I'm at the Chicago Historian Hotel. Fine, we'll see you then."

His guilty expression would have been amusing if I hadn't been trying to figure out what the word *colleague* was supposed to mean.

"Ah, Lauren wants to meet us for a drink downstairs in an hour. She's close by."

He was incredibly cute when he was nervous. I really didn't have any hold on him, I mean, we weren't exclusive or even dating, for that matter. I wasn't sure what we were, but I wasn't going to let insecurity get in the way. Honest, I wasn't.

I shrugged innocently. "Whatever will we do for a whole hour?"

He grinned. "We have strawberries to finish."

I picked up the silver tray and sauntered to the bed. "Yes we do."

Between finishing our dessert and dressing, we barely made it to the bar in time. I thought it might make Lauren more open to talk to Dalton if I wasn't sitting at the same table scowling at her. I had explained my reasoning to Dalton, minus the scowling part. I would sit at a small table close by and eavesdrop. He agreed reluctantly.

I sat down and ordered a drink. He took the table beside me, fiddling with the menu. Lord, the man would never be good at working undercover, he was too jittery. After a few more minutes, he stood up and smiled, and I forced myself not to gawk at the vision walking toward him. Lauren was beautiful, with long, gorgeous, light brown hair straight out of a shampoo commercial, big blue eyes, and pouty lips. She beamed at him and kissed him on the cheek before sitting down. My waiter came by, and when he finally finished giving Lauren the once-over, I ordered another drink.

"It's so good to see you, Joe. You look great."

He bobbed his head slightly. "So do you."

"It's been too long. How's Cleveland?"

"Good."

I downed the last of my drink just as the second one arrived. I really did not want to head down memory lane with them. I asked for a food menu, just to have something to do.

I read every item on the menu twice while they reminisced, finally ordering some chips and salsa so the waiter would stop hovering. Not long after that Dalton got to the good stuff.

"I'm sorry to call you on such short notice, but I could use your help."

She leaned forward slightly. "You mentioned CLG on the phone. What do you want to know?"

"Did you know Jonathan Brubaker? He was in your group."

Her eyes narrowed on him. "Yes. Is this official business, Joe?"

"I'm not sure if the DA office knows this yet, but there was a hit in the FBI database. We recently had a murder in Cleveland where the vic had a figure eight-shaped mark on his neck like Brubaker's."

Lauren shut her eyes for a second. "Damn. A serial case?"

"I don't know. I thought I would look into it while I was here."

"So what does the CLG have to do with this?"

"The night Brubaker went missing, according to his room-mate, he was supposed to be going to a CLG meeting. But when we asked the group's secretary, she said Brubaker had declined the event."

"Interesting, but not too strange. Maybe he just changed his mind."

"Or maybe he was going somewhere else and lied to his roommate?"

"It's a possibility."

"What was Brubaker like?"

"Smart, young, full of enthusiasm. Kind of like we were when we first started dating, remember?"

Whoa, Nelly, was she *hitting* on him? I grabbed a chip and stuffed it in my mouth.

Dalton smiled. "Did he attend the meetings regularly?"

"Somewhat. I would say probably every other one."

"That's not what his roommate said. Said Brubaker was religious about going to the sessions."

"Maybe he was stepping out on him. Jonathan never said anything outright, but I got the impression he was gay. Maybe he was cheating on his roommate?"

"Maybe."

An awkward silence followed for a second, which Lauren filled. "It's really good to see you, Joe." She laid her hand on top of his. "Sometimes I wish I had accepted your proposal and moved with you to Cleveland."

Holy shit. My heart clenched. I took a large sip of my drink and choked, coughing like a maniac. They both turned to me and, once I was able to breathe again, I smiled and made a never-mind gesture at them. I threw some money on the table and walked out, swearing under my breath. Wow, that had been beyond smooth.

Once back in the room, I stripped and jumped in the shower. I needed to wash away my doubts and the strawberry juice from earlier. Ten minutes later, I walked into the room to find Dalton waiting on the couch.

"You beat a hasty retreat."

"I thought you two might have some private things to discuss."

He stood. "Not really."

"Are you sorry you aren't with her anymore?" Blunt question, but I couldn't erase the doubt threatening to take over.

He reached for the ties on my robe. He hadn't even touched me yet, but heat shot from my stomach through the rest of my body.

"The only thing I'm sorry about is I didn't get here in time to wash your back."

I woke up and stared at the bright red numbers on the clock. Three a.m. I turned over and Dalton was gone. Sitting up, I glanced around the room. He wasn't there. I got out of bed and walked to the bathroom. The door was open and the bathroom was empty. Where the hell was he?

I picked up my phone and tried his number. The call didn't connect, though. What was going on? I reached for my clothes and then stopped. Where exactly was I going to go at three in the morning in Chicago to look for him? He was a grown man. He would come back.

I got back into bed and lay there wide awake. Should I confront him when he got back? Did I really want to know what was going on? Maybe he just went for a walk. Hell, who was I kidding? He could have decided to take Lauren up on her offer. They could get married and have perfect babies and live happily ever after. I sighed. It was official, I had reached pathetic stage.

I took a deep breath, going through the case notes in my head to distract me. The dig was the key. Hopefully Misha would have more information in the morning. The clock now said three thirty. Closing my eyes, I tried counting sheep, but I couldn't relax. It didn't help that my irritation level had spiked. At three forty-five, the hotel door opened. I lay still for a moment. *Decision time.*

I didn't move, trying to regulate my breathing as he undressed. A few seconds later, he slid back into the bed and wrapped his arm over my shoulder slowly. Up until then, I had been telling myself I was not going to make a scene. I had no right. But when he laid his head on the pillow and I caught the smell of flowery perfume, anger surged through me like a tidal wave.

"You might want to shower the perfume off next time."

He tensed.

"Although there won't be a next time with me." I pushed his arm off my shoulder and sat up, flipping on the bedside lamp.

He blinked at the light. "It's not what you think."

"Really?"

"I wasn't with Lauren."

My stomach twisted. "Then you were what? Picking up strange women in the bar downstairs?"

He opened his mouth and then shut it again. *Smart man.*

I got out of bed and pulled on my jeans. "You know what? I have no hold over you. We aren't in a monogamous relationship. Hell, I don't even know if you could call what we have a relationship. But I have enough self-respect to not tolerate a man leaving, meeting another woman, and then crawling back into bed with me for a snuggle."

I snatched the rest of my clothes and my phone and stalked into the bathroom, closing the door. Plopping down on the toilet seat, I rested my head in my hands. Why was I so shocked? This was typical. I couldn't count on humans, they let me down every time. He wasn't any different, no matter how much I wanted him to be.

I dressed and then changed my flight once my hands stopped shaking. Thank God Misha had gotten me the stupid smart phone. I stepped out of the bathroom. Dalton was dressed and sitting in a chair.

"Don't leave, Kyle."

"That's the best you've got? What was this whole thing for you? Sleep with the freak show?"

Dalton surged from his seat. "No. That's bullshit, and you know it."

"I don't know anything right now. Tell me who you were with tonight."

"I wasn't with anyone."

Picking up my bag, I opened the hotel door. "I'm going to catch an earlier flight home. Stay. Go to the law offices. Do what and who you need to. I don't care."

He reached for me, but I backed away. "It's not safe for you to be alone."

I shook my head. "Alone is the only way I am safe."

I walked out the door.

Chapter 29

The cab driver pulled up in front of my apartment building, and I almost choked when he told me the fare. When my plane had landed, I hadn't been able to bring myself to call Jean Luc or Misha, so it was my own damn fault. Once inside my apartment, I took a quick shower and then changed into boxers and a tank before falling into bed. Needless to say, I was a bit tired.

I tossed and turned, unable to shut my brain off as thoughts of Dalton invaded my cerebellum and wouldn't let me sleep. Why had I let my guard down with him? Finally I settled down and was drifting to sleep when a noise came from the vicinity of my living room. I lay still, holding my breath. Maybe I had imagined it. But after a couple of seconds, I realized the squeak was my living room window opening.

I reached behind my headboard and eased Stanley out quietly, flipping off the safety. Sliding out of bed, I walked silently out of my bedroom. Breathing shallowly, I paused in the hall, listening. Nothing. I held my automatic in a two-handed grip to steady my shaking hands while I peeked around the corner, catching movement near the window.

"Don't move," I hissed.

"Don't shoot me!" he hollered back.

Okay, I almost shot him. The guy was crouched on the floor. When he stood up, he was tall and lanky, with yellow eyes. He was also stark naked.

I continued to point my gun at him, amazed my arms were holding steady. I was proud of my composure until I tried to talk and my voice cracked. "What are you doing here?"

"Wait, Kyle, let me explain."

My hands tensed. "How do you know my name?"

"I was given a profile on you when I was assigned to watch you."

The answer threw me. "Who the hell are you?"

"My name is Matthew Johnson."

"And why are you watching me, exactly?"

"I was contacted several months ago. There was a concern that you were in danger," he answered.

"Not possible, I would have noticed you before now."

He shook his head. "You wouldn't have known what to look for."

"Why in the hell are you naked?"

"I just shifted, I can't exactly wear clothes when I'm in my cat form."

Cat form? I stared at his familiar yellow eyes for a moment longer and my stomach sank. *Jesus.*

"Booger?"

"Yeah, it's me."

The room started to spin, and I focused on a picture on the wall to maintain my balance. This was way too much. All these months, and I'd had a shifter living in my house. I had been feeding and taking care of him. I snorted to myself. The one thing in my life I thought didn't have an ulterior motive just morphed into a frickin' male with an agenda. *Perfect.*

Adrenaline fueled my anger and I seriously considered going postal. "You son of a bitch." I glared at him. "You've been living here with me! What about my right to privacy?"

"Don't worry, Kyle. I didn't see any of your naughty parts. You might want to stop singing those show tunes in the shower, though."

My mouth fell open, but I recovered quickly. "Do you think you should be making jokes right now? I have a clear shot at all of *your* naughty parts."

He gulped and backed up.

"I want to know who sent you."

He shrugged. "I don't know."

I scowled and pointed the gun lower.

He held up his hands. "I swear! I don't know. I was given the assignment through a third party."

"Explain."

"I was given a file on you with instructions to watch over you and report if anything mysterious happened."

"How do you report in?"

"I have a prepaid phone I use to call an answering machine and leave my reports."

"And you didn't question this setup?"

"They wanted me to protect you, not kill you, so I didn't see the harm in it."

"Well, I won't be needing your services any longer. Tell that to your boss."

Surprisingly, he shook his head. "Nope."

"What?"

"You're in trouble. In the last few days, there have been a lot of vamps scoping out this place."

I didn't have to ask who they were working for. "Well, you're not staying here."

"No problem, but I'll be around if you need me."

I motioned with my gun toward the door.

"Ahhh, I have some clothes stashed in your trunk. Can I put them on before you throw me out?"

I nodded and he pulled out a pair of jeans, T-shirt and tennis shoes, putting them on quickly. He opened the door and smiled. "See you later, Kyle."

I closed the door and threw the bolt lock in place, then slammed the window shut and latched it. Flipping the safety on, I set the gun down on the coffee table, not wanting it too far away from me at the moment. I sat down on the couch and ran my fingers through my hair, yanking at the tangles. Who would have sent him to watch me? It wouldn't have been Jean Luc. He was worried about me, but Booger had been here for months. Griffin? Matthew was a shifter, so it made sense he would work for him, but I had just met Griffin. Why would he be watching out for me?

There was only one way to find out. I called Griffin's office and his assistant answered. After I identified myself, she explained Griffin was tied up all day. The clan was burying Byron. I thanked her and went to my bedroom to dress in funeral attire. I had never been to a shifter funeral, so I wasn't sure if black was appropriate, but I put on a black suit and shoes, erring for once on the side of caution.

The funeral was held at a small hall on the west side. The parking lot overflowed, and by the time I found a space the service had already begun. It was standing room only, so I stayed in the vestibule, scanning the crowd. I was shocked to see Jean Luc and Misha standing to the side. They were doing the same thing I was, watching the crowd. Maybe they were hoping to see someone who stuck out like a sore thumb—the killer maybe?

I looked toward the front of the hall. Griffin sat facing the crowd. He stared directly at me. I nodded slightly and then resumed scanning faces.

When the service ended, I stood over to the side and watched everyone file out toward the parking lot. Griffin held the elbow of a female shifter who was probably Byron's mother. He escorted her past me and continued to the black SUV waiting at the entrance, helping her into the vehicle. He then shut the door and tapped on the car lightly, signaling for the driver to go. After they pulled away, he walked over to me.

"Thank you for coming."

"The service was nice."

"We're having another ceremony for just the pack tonight. Did you see anyone suspicious in the crowd?"

He was ridiculously observant. "No, unfortunately, I didn't." I paused, not sure how to proceed.

"Is there something else you needed?"

"I just found out a shifter has been hired to guard me, and I was wondering if you know anything about it."

His eyes narrowed slightly. "No, I do not. Who is it?"

"Matthew Johnson."

"I know Matthew. He's very good at what he does."

"And what does he do, exactly?"

"Matthew is one of the rare shifters who can almost completely mask his scent. Which means he can be in a room full of supernaturals in his shifted form and they would not know what he is. And you say he has been watching you?"

I cleared my throat. "Actually, he has been living with me in his cat form for several months."

Griffin grabbed my arm and practically growled. "If he has done anything inappropriate to you..."

"No, it's not that. He actually was a perfect gentleman, uh...cat. Whatever. I'm trying to figure out who hired him."

"I can speak to him if you'd like."

"He says he doesn't know who hired him, but if you can find out anything more for me, I'd appreciate it."

"Of course. Are you okay otherwise?"

"Why do you ask?"

He stared intently at me for a moment, like he was trying to read my mind. "I can smell the lieutenant strongly on you now. I can tell your relationship with him has progressed, but I also smell the sharp tang of pain or anger as well."

I shrugged away from his hand on my arm. "I'm fine."

"I will let you go, then. Your team is waiting for you."

I glanced over my shoulder. Jean Luc and Misha stood across the parking lot staring at me. "Thanks for your help."

"If you need anything, Kyle, please know you can contact me at any time." He handed me his business card, then turned and walked toward his black Audi.

I turned and walked toward an irritated vampire and a pissed-off demon.

CHAPTER 30

I had to hand it to both Misha and Jean Luc. They settled down quickly after leaving the funeral. I told them I had come back early and Dalton stayed to follow up on the investigation, so they didn't push me too much. What I didn't tell them was what had happened between us, but they knew it was bad. Jean Luc berated me slightly for not calling one of them to pick me up from the airport, but he finally let it drop. Their calm demeanor, however, changed when I told them about Booger.

Misha paced the office floor. "I never trusted that shifty-eyed cat. And to think I made a special trip over there last night to feed him. If I get my hands on him..."

"Calm down, Mish, he was there to protect me."

"So he says. And it's pretty flimsy to claim he doesn't know who hired him. Come on!"

"Well, he gave me some information today. He said vamps have been all over Little Italy the past few days."

Jean Luc's jaw tightened. "Sebastian is after you now and is not hiding it."

"So what do we do?"

"Give me a couple of minutes in my office, I will be back shortly." He flashed from the room.

I huffed and picked up my empty mug from the table, and Misha poured a fresh cup for me. I was facing away from the door when it opened, but Misha's tense expression told me who it was. I turned. Dalton stood in the doorway.

Misha's voice dropped an octave. "I don't know what happened, but do not hurt her again or you will answer to me." Then he looked questioningly at me and I nodded. Misha backed away toward the front office. "I'm going out for a while, but Jean Luc is in the back." He stared pointedly at Dalton before closing the door.

I sat down at the table with my cup and took a large swallow, burning my tongue in the process.

"Kyle..."

Shaking my head, I examined my cuticles. "I don't want to talk about it."

"Please, let me explain."

I stared at him blankly although my insides were tumbling. "Did you find anything else to help with the case? That's all I want to hear about right now."

"We can't leave it like this."

"If you say one more word about it, I am out the door. Do you have any news about the case?"

He blew out a hard breath. "The law office was a bust. But Carl sent me an email with some of Jonathan's pictures this morning. I emailed it to you since it's hard to make them out on my phone."

I brought my email up on the laptop on the table and clicked open the attachment. Dalton sat down next to me and I tensed for a second before turning the screen so we could both see it. It was a zipped file, and when I opened it there were hundreds of photos.

I saved the zip file on our main server and pointed to another laptop. "You start at the bottom, I'll start at the top. With us both going through the pictures, it might go faster."

Dalton scooted over into the other chair and opened the file. We sat in silence, clicking through the pictures. It wasn't long before I found some pictures from Turkey. In the first one Jonathan was standing on a hill of dirt. The next photo showed a trio of students outside a tent. They were smiling and sunburned, with Jonathan standing in the middle. The third picture was a larger group photo. I zoomed in on the faces and reviewed them.

"Bingo!"

Dalton moved over. "What did you find?"

I pointed to a face in the back row. "Cowell."

"This is definitely the connection."

"Yeah, but to what?"

"Did Misha find anything?" Dalton asked.

"Not much. He said the dig was almost a nonevent. He's having trouble even tracking down who was involved."

"Well this picture might help."

I stared at the faces on the screen. "Something must have happened to them at the site. Did they see something they shouldn't have? What did Hampton think they knew to make him torture them with straends?"

"Maybe something was discovered at the site. Something important enough Hampton was willing to kill for it."

"It might explain why Cowell and Jonathan were so close-mouthed about the dig." I started to click on the next picture when Dalton laid his hand over mine and I jerked away from him.

"Sorry. Zoom in on the right hand corner." He pointed. "There. I think it's a U.S. soldier. Sometimes, if a dig is in a volatile area, soldiers are sent in to protect the site."

I clicked on the intercom. "Jean Luc."

"Yes."

"Did Misha get any info back from our military contacts on Jason Watson?"

"Yes, it is on the server under his name."

"Thanks."

I did a quick search and pulled up the army record. I paged back two years and couldn't believe it. Watson had been stationed in Europe. He had been assigned protection duty for a dig in Turkey. The stars were aligning.

"So Watson was part of this too. Now he's trying to kill supes, and Cowell had a book about demons. What if somehow supes were exposed during this dig and these guys formed some sort of supernatural hit squad to take them out?"

"It's a possibility."

Jean Luc came into the room. "What did I miss?"

We filled him in.

"We are getting closer to the truth," Jean Luc murmured.

"But not close enough to get Sebastian off my back."

Dalton tensed. "Has something else happened?"

"Apparently, Sebastian has his minions out looking for me."

"Damn. What's the plan, Jean Luc?" Dalton asked.

I stared at Jean Luc. "What aren't you telling me?"

"Sebastian wants to control you. Your ability would be a powerful tool for him."

"Well, I won't agree to that."

Jean Luc paused for a second before responding. "You do not have to agree to anything. He can compel you to help him."

Dalton grabbed my hand, and I was too upset to yank it away this time. "What the hell do you mean he can compel her?"

"It is not like the movies. Vampires cannot look into your eyes and command you to do their bidding."

I released the breath I had been holding. "Then I'm safe."

"Let me finish. They cannot compel you unless they have tasted you."

"There is no way I would let him bite me."

"He will not ask. He could bite you at any time."

My voice ratcheted higher. "Wait a minute. Isn't it the number one vampire commandment? That you can't bite a human unless they agree to it?"

Jean Luc shook his head. "Sebastian thinks of humans as cattle. Do you honestly believe he thinks you have the right to free will?"

"Great. So what do we do now?"

"He cannot touch you if you belong to another vampire."

"Excuse me?"

"Once another vampire has tasted your blood, it cannot be overridden. You would be safe."

I stared into Jean Luc's sorrowful eyes. Dalton's hand tensed over mine and he leaned forward. "You're not suggesting *you* bite her, are you?"

"She would be safe. Sebastian could not touch her then, unless she wanted him to."

Dalton pushed his chair back with a loud scrape and stood.

Jean Luc's eyes never left my face. "What do you think, Kyle?"

I knew in my soul Jean Luc would never hurt me intentionally. "What would happen if you drank my blood?"

"Jesus!" Dalton started to pace.

"I would have to take enough blood that another vampire would sense you belonged to me."

"You would have to bite me."

"Yes, but just once, Kyle."

Dalton interrupted. "What if you turn her into a vampire?"

"It does not work that way."

I tried to swallow down the lump forming in my throat. "Would you be able to control me?"

He exhaled sharply. "Since I would only be taking your blood one time, I would not be able to fully control you. At the most, I might be able to plant some suggestions you might accept. But I would not do that to you, Kyle. Just like you would never use your power to make me forget."

I nodded. "I need to think about it."

Jean Luc stood. "I will leave you two alone."

"Wait," I exclaimed, turning my back on Dalton and walking over to Jean Luc. "Why are you leaving me alone with him?"

"This is a momentous decision, Kyle. You need to talk to someone besides me about it. Put whatever is going on between you and Dalton aside for the moment and discuss this."

Before I could protest, he flashed out of the room. Dalton walked into my line of sight, glowering at me. But I wouldn't be intimidated. "You don't have a say in this matter."

"Fine. Throw me out of the equation, since you've already written me off, but think about this. You are one of the most independent people I have ever met. Are you going to be able to handle someone having any type of control over you? Even the littlest bit?"

I bit the inside of my cheek to stop from laughing, crying, I don't know what. He had no idea how much control he had over me now. Jean Luc didn't scare me. Hell, Sebastian didn't even scare me as much as my feelings for this man in front of me. What a mess.

I answered him as calmly as I could. "The alternative is worse. If Sebastian gets hold of me, he could make me use my power to hurt people. That's something I could never live with."

His eyes softened and he stepped toward me. "Just make sure to think this through. There will be no going back."

"I know. Can I have a few minutes to myself?"

He nodded and walked down the hall to Jean Luc's office. I didn't want to know if he was going to pump him for more information on this whole blood-drinking thing or what. I paced and mentally list the pros and cons of having Jean Luc bite me. Within a few minutes, I had made a decision.

I walked down the hall and found both of them in Jean Luc's office. Dalton took one look at my face and tensed. It was scary, how well he was starting to know me.

I swallowed hard. "Will it hurt?"

Jean Luc paused before answering. "Biting is actually pleasurable. It often releases pheromones, making the whole episode quite enjoyable."

"What the hell!" Dalton barked and leaned forward.

"Kyle is like a daughter to me. I would never take advantage of her in such a way. Which is why you will stay to help her throughout the exchange."

"No," I blurted.

Jean Luc shook his head. "He stays or I do not bite you. It is standard protocol in blood exchanges between non-mated partners for a third party to remain in the room."

Great, like having Dalton there was going to relax me. I wondered what else they had talked about while I was out of the room. "Where do you want to do this?"

"The couch in the outer office." Jean Luc flashed out of the room.

Dalton stood. "Are you scared?"

"A little bit."

"I'll stay with you. I told him, vampire or not, if he hurts you, I'll find a way to kill him."

Sir Galahad on his white steed. "*Jean Luc* would never hurt me."

He paused. "Then you have no reason to be scared." He smiled tightly as we walked down the hall.

We arrived in the main office too soon for my comfort. I took a deep breath and went over to the couch, sitting down on it gingerly. Jean Luc came through the door from the front office and shut it, clicking the lock in place. My heart pumped faster.

Jean Luc stood in front of me. "Do you still wish to do this?"

"Yes, I need to do this. I don't want to be Sebastian's mindless robot."

"I am going to tell you exactly what will happen, but you need to try and relax, Kyle. Your heartbeat is erratic."

Dalton spoke up. "What about her power? Could your bite stop her ability?"

My mouth dropped open. I had never thought of that. "What do you think?"

Jean Luc pursed his lips for a few seconds before responding. "I do not believe her power would be affected. Vampires have bitten other supernaturals and their powers were not negatively impacted."

I took a deep breath. "Let's do this."

Jean Luc sat down next to me on the couch and I gulped. He motioned to Dalton. "Sit on the other side of her. Kyle, I want you to watch Joe through the whole thing."

My voice squeaked. "Where are you going to bite me?"

"Your wrist." He picked up my hand and I jumped. He ran his thumb over the pulse point. "Easy, Kyle. I will not do anything until you are ready."

I nodded, staring into Dalton's concerned eyes. How could he look at me like that one second and cheat on me the next? How did I always end up in such crappy relationships? Jean Luc interrupted my pity party.

"Kyle, I need you to listen to me. Take some deep breaths and think about something pleasant."

Something pleasant. Headless vamps, sword-wielding angels, carved-up shifters, cheating boyfriends. I got nothing. Man, my life had been peachy lately. So I thought about Trina. How she was back to normal. A beautiful little girl sitting up in her tree house with her legs dangling over the side, and after a while my muscles relaxed.

"Much better." Jean Luc's thumb rubbed over my wrist languorously. He lifted my arm and I felt a pinch. I flinched slightly.

Dalton framed my face with his hands and held me steady. "Stay with me. It'll be over soon."

This really wasn't so bad. I wasn't sure what I had been so worried about. But when Jean Luc pulled on my arm, everything swirled around me. Warmth ran along my wrist, wrapped up my arm and shot through my chest. I moaned and closed my eyes, but as soon as I did, images of Dalton and me in bed flooded in. My skin tingled and I opened my eyes and stared at his lips, licking my own in the process. I leaned in to kiss him, desperately needing some sort of contact, but he held me still, shaking his head slightly.

After a few more seconds, Jean Luc stopped and lightly lapped my wrist with his tongue. Jean Luc's voice sounded deeper when he spoke. "This should heal quickly."

I tried to turn to him, but Dalton held me firm.

Jean Luc spoke again. "I have to leave for a while, Kyle. You should be fine with Dalton. Sebastian cannot hurt you now."

"Thank..." But the air moved around me and I knew he had flashed out of the room.

Dalton released my face. "Are you all right?"

"Yes, I don't feel any different. Just a little sleepy."

"Jean Luc said it might happen. Why don't you lie down for a while and rest? I'll stay here until Misha gets back."

I propped my head on the arm of the couch and closed my eyes. I didn't have the energy to tell him I was better off alone.

CHAPTER 31

Misha was clicking away on his laptop when I woke up on the couch. I sat up slowly. He came over and sat next to me.

"How are you feeling?"

"Fine. I actually feel good after the nap. Where is everybody?"

"I sent Dolly home early and Dalton left shortly after I got back."

"Jean Luc?"

Misha's normally open face closed down. "We probably won't see him until tomorrow."

"What aren't you telling me?" I asked nervously, "Is something wrong with him?"

"No, nothing like that." He hesitated. "He just needs a break."

"You mean he needs to feed?"

He sighed. "Yes. He only took a little bit from you. It whetted his appetite, so he'll need more now." Misha pulled me into his embrace. "Don't worry. I was going to order Thai, are you hungry?"

"Yes. I have a lot to tell you."

While we ate our dinner, I filled Misha in on the pictures and how we had found what linked Cowell, Brubaker and Watson. Misha was ecstatic.

"I'm going to try to track Watson's whereabouts over the last few years. It sounds like he's fighting supes for a reason. If Hampton was after people at this dig, we need to find out who the others were and determine if they're safe."

"The pictures might help. If we could find one person, they might be able to identify the others."

We cleaned up and I volunteered to help with the research. To be honest, I wasn't too keen on going home anyway.

Misha searched on Watson while I decided to do a little investigative work on my own. I clicked through Jonathan's pictures again, paying particular attention to the one of Jonathan and the two other college students. The picture title read Tiff and Rich. I scanned the other pictures and found both Tiff and Rich in several photos from other digs, as well as general college pictures. I then called the number Carl had given us when we were in Chicago. I got his voice mail.

"Carl, this is Jill Smith. I was with Lieutenant Dalton when we spoke to you yesterday. Thank you for sending these pictures. I have a question. In several photos there are references to a Tiff and Rich. Do you have more information on these two people, possibly their full names and where I can reach them? Any help would be appreciated. You can either call, text or email me the information. Thanks." When I hung up, Misha was clearly waiting to get my attention. "What can I help you with?"

"Watson is a slippery devil. His address is phony. I can't find any credit cards on file for us to track, either."

"What do we know about him?"

"His military record is pretty straightforward. He worked special forces for a little over ten years in the Army."

"Did he have a specialty?"

Misha grimaced. "Ammunition."

"Sorry I asked."

"Wait, that gives me an idea." Misha clicked away on his computer.

"Are you going to fill me in or what?"

"Ammo. Bullets are normally made out of lead with a copper casing. Watson can't go into his local gun shop and buy silver bullets filled with iron and salt. He has to be making them himself."

"So what are you looking for?"

"I'm going to find out if any equipment has been purchased recently for casting bullets, and search for iron and silver purchases."

"Seems like a bit of a stretch, Mish."

He smiled. "Let the master work, grasshopper."

Two hours later, Misha slapped his hands on the table. "I think I have something."

I closed my Sudoku puzzle book. "What?"

"Most of the deliveries I've been tracking have gone to businesses. But there have been some deliveries to a Simon Williams on the west side.

"Could be an alias." I sighed, because I knew exactly what was coming out of Misha's mouth next.

His eyes filled with glee. "I think we need to stake him out."

I did an internal eye roll. Misha loved stakeouts. Hours of eating junk food and reciting TV shows was his idea of heaven and my idea of purgatory. "Let me change out of this suit. I have some extra clothes in my car."

I trudged down to the parking garage, retrieved my bag of clothes, and trudged back upstairs. I changed in my office and came back into the main room to find Dalton sitting there with Misha.

"I understand we're going on a stakeout."

Great, purgatory had just turned into hell.

When we arrived at Simon Williams' address, we drove by slowly and checked the place out. The area was pretty run down. The small, ranch-style home had seen better days, and there were no lights on in the house. There was also a large metal outbuilding to the side with a padlock on the front door.

Dalton spoke first. "It doesn't look like anyone's home right now."

Misha continued driving. "I'm going to park the van down the street so we have a clear line of sight."

We parked and Misha grinned at Dalton. I had insisted they both sit in the front seat, hoping Misha's ramblings would be directed at him.

"This whole thing reminds me of an episode of *Magnum, P.I.*"

I shut my eyes and leaned back. The fun had officially begun. After a couple of minutes, Misha's voice faded.

The next thing I knew, I was skipping along the sidewalk humming. I moved my arm and metal jingled. Smiling, I held my arm out in front of me. The heart-shaped charms on my bracelet danced along my wrist, the sun catching the silver, making it shine even brighter. But a shadow blocked out the sun behind me. Before I could see what it was, an arm grasped me from behind. I tried to scream, but a white cloth slammed over my face and I couldn't breathe. Within seconds, everything went dark.

"Kyle!"

I jerked awake. Dalton's concerned face filled my view.

"Are you okay?"

I rubbed my hand over my eyes. "Yeah, just a bad dream."

Before he could ask me what it was about, Misha interrupted. "We have company."

We watched a beater truck coming down the street. It was the same one that had tried to run us down in the alley. The truck pulled up next to the outbuilding and parked. Watson stepped out of the car.

"I think we have our winner," I announced.

"Except he's not alone." Misha motioned to the car following him. It screeched up along the curb. Watson made a grab for a gun in the cab of his truck, but they were on him in a millisecond.

Misha growled. "Vamps."

He jumped out of the car and ran toward the house. Dalton pulled his gun and yanked open the passenger door.

"Wait. Bullets won't kill them, but it will slow them down. Aim for the heart." He nodded and jumped out as well.

I moved to the driver's seat and whipped the van around. By the time I drove back down the street, Misha had one of the vamps in a headlock. Dalton shot at the other vamp until he let go of Watson, who dropped to the ground.

The vamp took a step toward Dalton and my heart sped up. Before the vamp could even think of attacking, I slammed my foot on the accelerator and plowed into the bastard. He skidded up over the hood and smashed into the windshield, cracking it with a sickening thud. I swallowed back the bile in my throat, put the van in reverse and jammed down the pedal, launching him off of the van onto the ground.

Misha threw the other vamp down, but he jumped back up immediately. Dalton shot him in the chest. This time he staggered and fell to his knees. In the meantime, Misha scooped Watson up and threw him in the back of our van.

Dalton jumped into the front seat and I took off, craning my head to see around the cracks in the window.

I gripped the steering wheel tightly to keep my hands from shaking. When I looked over my shoulder I saw neither vamp had pursued us. Turning my attention to what was going on inside the van, I watched in the rear view mirror as Misha ripped off Watson's shirt and used it to staunch the blood pouring from his stomach and arm.

Misha barked, "Get the first aid kit in the back."

Dalton retrieved it and they worked on him.

"How bad is it, Mish?" I asked.

"They ripped him with their claws, and I think his shoulder is dislocated."

"Did they bite him?"

"I can't tell right now. Get Doc on the phone and see if she can meet us at the facility."

"Do we really want to take him there?"

"How are we going to explain his injuries at a hospital?"

"Good point." I called Doc. She was just getting off her shift and could get there in a half hour. It would probably take us that long to get there ourselves. I hung up and my phone rang. It was Jean Luc.

"What happened, Kyle?"

"We have Watson, but two vamps attacked him, and we're on the way to meet Doc at the facility."

"I will meet you there."

He hung up before I had the chance to ask him how he knew we were in trouble.

CHAPTER 32

Doc and Jean Luc had been patching up Watson for forty-five minutes. Misha, Dalton and I waited in Doc's office, not wanting to crowd them. After another ten minutes, both Doc and Jean Luc came into the room.

We stood up, Misha speaking first. "How is he?"

"I put a lot of stitches in him. Luckily, the gashes were not too deep, so no organs were affected," Doc replied.

"Can we speak to him?" I asked.

Doc shook her head. "Not right now. I knocked him out while we were stitching him up. It would have been too painful otherwise."

"But he's going to be okay?" I persisted.

"Should be. He needs some blood. I have some O-neg in the back which I'll use until I can type him."

"He is A negative," Jean Luc said.

My mouth dropped open. "You can tell just by the smell?"

Jean Luc grinned at me. "I am good, Kyle, but not that good. I noticed it in his military records."

Leave it to a vamp to notice and remember blood types. I wondered if blood types tasted different, depending on availability. Did O-positive taste like cheap wine and AB-negative like Château Lafite? It was a question for another day. Doc and Jean Luc left to check on Watson. Misha went to the van to bring in some of the snacks he had stashed in there for the stakeout, which left Dalton and me alone.

I stood and he reached an arm out to stop me. "Wait. Are you okay?"

"Why wouldn't I be?"

"Back in the van, you were having another nightmare."

I shrugged. "I'm fine."

"Tell me about it."

Before I could protest, he held up his hands to stop me. "If it really is a vision of the future, you should tell us about it so we have an idea where to look if it happens."

"I'll tell Misha and Jean Luc about it later."

Before he could comment, Jean Luc poked his head into the room. "Watson is awake."

"I'm going to check on our patient to see if he's ready to talk." I walked down the hall, Dalton following me. I was fine with that. He could give Watson the scary cop face while I asked questions.

We walked into the room. Watson leaned back against a pillow while Doc checked his stomach. His eyes were glassy. I wasn't sure if it was because of the drugs or Doc being so close to him. He was male, after all.

He looked up at us and tensed slightly. Doc placed a calming hand on his shoulder. I pulled a chair over next to the bed so I could be at eye level while I spoke to him.

"How are you doing?"

"Better. Where am I?"

"In a safe place for the moment. We need to ask you some questions. But first, let me make some introductions. If you don't recognize me and my colleague here, we're the two you tried to run down with your truck in the alley a few days ago."

His eyes narrowed. "I don't know what you're talking about."

"Do we need to face away from you? Maybe the backs of our heads will jog your memory. After all, we were running away from you at the time."

"What do you want?"

"We want to know why you're trying to kill supernaturals."

"Is that what you call yourselves instead of monsters?"

I smiled tightly. "Actually, I'm human, and so is he."

He stammered, "Human...but why would you be helping them?"

"Doc, why would we be helping you?"

"Because of our sparkling personalities?"

Watson cringed under her touch. "You're..."

"A demon who just spent an hour saving your life." She winked at him before placing the bandage back on his stomach.

"Why are you helping me?"

The door opened and Misha walked in. "Because we are not the mindless demons you think we are." Watson took one look at him and jerked upright, moaning. Misha walked around the bed pushing him gently back down on the pillows. "Hold still or you will hurt yourself again."

I continued. "I see you remember Misha, here. He almost died from your bullet. He's also the one who fought the vamps earlier and saved your ass."

Watson's confused eyes stared up at Misha. "Why didn't you just let them kill me?"

"Because I am not evil. I protect supernaturals and people. Like humans, there are both good and bad demons and vampires walking the earth. I think you have only met the bad ones, yes?"

Watson let out a harsh breath.

I jumped back in. "We need to know what's going on and why you're gunning for supes. Believe it or not, we're on the same team. Not the 'shoot first and ask questions later' team, but the 'stop the rogue supernaturals from destroying the earth' team. So spill what you know."

He hesitated, and I could almost hear the wheels turning as he weighed his options. Were we really trying to help him, or were we just acting nice while we pumped him for information? I couldn't blame him.

I acquiesced. "Let's do it this way. We'll tell you what we've learned so far, and you can fill us in on the rest. A week ago a vampire named Charles Hampton was decapitated in the Erie Bar. By the time we arrived on the scene, Hampton's head was missing."

Watson interrupted. "How did you get the people in the bar to keep quiet? Did you kill them?"

I sighed. "No, we erased their memories of the event. As Misha told you, our job is to protect. This means we sometimes make people forget what they saw. Do you have Hampton's head?"

"No."

I hadn't thought he did, but I wanted to be sure. "How did you end up at the bar?"

Watson stared at me for a moment before responding. "I had been following Hampton."

"Because he killed Father Cowell and Brubaker?" I asked.

His eyes widened. "Yeah, the bastard tortured them to death."

I continued. "You followed Byron home to ask him about Hampton's head?"

"I thought since he worked as the bartender and was a mons...I mean a supernatural, he might know where the head was."

"And you tortured him."

"No." He shook his head and cringed at the movement. "I went to his place and found him dead. Then I heard a noise at the front door so I hid." He stared at me. "When you came into the apartment, I thought you were a supernatural, so I hit you over the head and ran."

"Why were you looking for Hampton's head?" Misha interrupted.

"I was afraid he had learned too much from Father Cowell and Jonathan. I didn't know if those memories could be extracted or not. Hell, I wasn't sure if he was really dead. For all I know, vampires are like worms and can grow body parts back when they're cut off."

A soft chuckle came from the doorway. "That would be wonderful, but unfortunately, we cannot grow back appendages."

Watson's eyes widened and Jean Luc held up his hands. "Please do not try to run. Doc and I spent too much time sewing you up earlier. I do not want to have to start over again."

Dalton interrupted. I was actually surprised he had waited this long to ask questions. "Why did Hampton kill Cowell and Brubaker? Was it related to the dig in Turkey?"

"Yeah. Two years ago I was stationed in Turkey protecting the dig site. There had been some threats of violence from the locals, who felt their land was being desecrated, so we were called in. I met Father Cowell and Jonathan on the site. At first, everything was fine, uneventful really."

"What happened to change that?" I asked.

"The dig overall seemed to be a bust. There were no major finds. When the dig sponsors arrived, everyone was scrambling around making a big deal out of nothing. But Hampton was not impressed."

I leaned forward in my chair. "Hampton was there?"

"He was going by the name of Joseph Small at the time."

Several eyebrows raised.

"What happened then?"

"Since the boss men were there, the dig coordinators decided to work overnight. Jonathan and Father Cowell were working in a remote area and thought they had come across something. But when the rest of the group got to them, they said it was a false alarm. After that, they both started acting strange, withdrawn. I watched them, thinking maybe they had found a relic and were trying to steal it or something." He paused. "I'm sorry, can I have some water?"

I waited impatiently, biting my bottom lip, while Doc handed him a cup and he took a sip before continuing. "The next night, everyone left early to get some sleep. I got the short straw and had to stand night duty. While I was walking the perimeter lights, Father Cowell and Jonathan came back to the site and entered a tent. I hung back to see what they were up to and after a couple of minutes I saw Hampton enter the tent as well. By the time I got closer, I could hear yelling. Hampton was demanding they give him the key and they told him they didn't have a key. When Jonathan started screaming, I ran into the tent. Hampton's nails had turned into claws and he had freaking fangs. I pointed my rifle and capped him where he stood."

Unfortunately, I knew where this was going. "And he didn't go down."

Watson nodded. "He staggered, and looked down at his bloody chest then back up at me and took a step toward me. I shot him again. Father Cowell grabbed a small bag and screamed for Jonathan to run. Before they made it out of the tent, a Pavel materialized. At the time, I didn't know what the hell it was, other than I thought the world was coming to an end."

"How did you get away?" Misha asked.

"Father Cowell threw the bag he was carrying at the demon and spouted something in Latin, and then he shoved us both out of the tent while the vamp and demon fought over the bag."

"What did you do then?" Misha persisted. His eyes were dancing. He was enjoying this story as much as his TV shows.

"I seriously thought about going AWOL until Father convinced us we were safe. He said the angels had given him a prayer that he had spoken to make them forget about us. All they really cared about was the key anyway."

"And where is this key?" I asked.

Watson answered, "I don't know. All Father would tell me was the vampire and demon did not have the real key. No one could ever actually possess it."

Dalton took a step closer to the bed. "Father Cowell was keeping a journal with information about demons. There is an excerpt in the front which was partially translated. Is that information about the key?"

"Yeah, he said it referenced the key. But he had more than one journal. I have his other book stashed."

"Where is it?" Dalton asked.

"It's at the train terminal in a locker. The key is in my pants."

Doc interrupted. "Okay. Enough, he needs some rest."

"But we're not done," I grumbled.

"He isn't going anywhere right now."

Watson looked around the room, and when he saw we weren't going to do anything to him, let out a deep breath. I grinned and patted his arm. "Don't worry, we aren't going to kill you. We're the good guys."

CHAPTER 33

"Are you ready for a field trip to the train station?" I asked.

Dalton grinned. "Yep."

I grinned back. Boys and their trains. I picked up my phone, noticing I had a new email message. I clicked it. "Carl emailed me."

"About what?"

"I totally forgot I had asked him about two of the students in the pictures he sent. He gave me the names, but he isn't sure where they are at this point. Jonathan hadn't kept in touch with them after graduation." I scanned the names. "Let me forward this to Misha and get him to start digging into their whereabouts."

Dalton and I walked out of Doc's office into the hallway. Watson was hobbling along slowly with Doc clucking like a mother hen behind him.

I called out to him, "You're not trying to be an overachiever are you?"

He shook his head. "The faster I start moving around, the faster I can be on my way."

Jean Luc entered the hallway through the morgue door. "I would not be in any rush."

"What do you mean?" Watson asked.

"Misha just called. When he left here a few minutes ago, he was followed. He planned to lead them away and call us to evacuate, but after a couple of minutes the car turned around and headed back in this direction. I think whoever was following him realized you were not with Misha, so they came back here."

I had to ask, but I was pretty sure I already knew the answer. "How did they know he wasn't with Misha?"

"They could tell there were no humans in the car by scent. Plus, if they are the vampires who attacked Jason, they will be able to identify him by his blood."

"Great." Watson stepped into the morgue area and sat down heavily in the chair I offered him. "What's to stop them from coming in here?"

Doc answered him. "This facility is like a supernatural version of an embassy. They don't dare come in here. It would cause an incident that would be, at the very least, viewed unfavorably by most of the supernatural community."

"But once I leave here?"

"All bets are off," I said.

Watson glanced around at us. "Now what do we do?"

I smiled. "We'll give them what they're looking for. Dalton, are you up for a little bait and switch?"

Jean Luc drove us to the train station. Dalton sat in the back seat wearing a hooded zip-up jacket. Stuffed in his pocket were several pieces of Watson's bloody shirt.

Jean Luc peered in the rear view mirror. "They are still following us."

"Like damn blood hounds." I peered sheepishly at Jean Luc. "Sorry."

"No offense taken."

"Do we know the plan?" I prodded.

Dalton nodded. "Jean Luc will get me on a train, and hopefully our two vampire friends will follow me."

"Right, and in the meantime, I'll get the journal out of the locker. And while we're gone, Misha will move Watson and Doc to a safer place."

Jean Luc parked and the three of us entered the station. I separated from the guys and took a roundabout route to the lockers. Plenty of people were milling around the terminal area, but no one seemed to be following me. I slipped into the women's restroom, and after a couple of minutes came back out again. No one lurked outside waiting for me.

Weaving through the lockers, I found number 321 and opened the door. It appeared empty, but I didn't panic. Instead, I reached up and found the plastic bag taped to the inside top of the locker as Watson had instructed. I ripped it down, took the small book out of the bag and slipped it into a new plastic bag to mask any scents, stuffed the book in my bag, and walked toward the exit. Pulling a sanitizing wipe from one of the containers strategically located throughout the station, I cleaned my hands quickly, and chucked it into the garbage.

With a relieved breath, I went out to the car and jumped in. My whole adventure had taken a whopping twelve minutes. I started the car and pulled up closer to the station doors. My phone beeped. It was a text message from Misha. He had successfully moved Doc and Watson.

After another five minutes, my nerves jangled, especially since I had to circle the parking lot once when a cop motioned me to move on. When I came around and parked the second time, Dalton walked out the door and got into the back of the van.

"Go. Jean Luc is going to meet us around back."

I pushed lightly on the accelerator when what I really wanted to do was slam my foot to the floor in a rubber-burning getaway. Then I maneuvered around to the back of the building, as close to the door as I could. Within a minute, Jean Luc came out and climbed into the car, as calm as could be.

I pulled out of the parking lot. "Did it work?"

"Yes. Joe did a wonderful job. They followed him onto the train."

Dalton chimed in, "I waited until the train was almost ready to leave. Then I threw pieces of bloody shirt in several garbage containers, ditched the sweatshirt and the last bloody shirt piece in the garbage in one of the lavatories, and jumped off when the train started moving."

"Once Joe disembarked, I watched, but they did not follow him. They must have been confused by the smell of blood scattered throughout the train."

"I got a text from Misha while I was waiting. He's moved Doc and Watson out of the facility."

Jean Luc preened and then gave me a quick pat. "You could be a criminal mastermind if you let yourself, Kyle."

"I'll stick with the job I have for the time being. In my bag is the book, Jean Luc. Why don't you check it out while I get us to the safe house."

The safe house was a place Misha's demon clan used in times of crisis. According to Misha, it could not be linked to anyone in the clan, but was always kept available. I was pretty sure when Misha had asked Boris if he could use the place, he neglected to tell his father the person they were protecting was the one who'd shot his son. Misha was a forgiving demon, but Boris did not strike me as having the same inclinations.

The house was a nondescript two-story in a middle-class neighborhood. When we turned into the driveway, the garage door opened and I drove inside. We got out and went through the door into a large kitchen, where Misha waited for us. "I saw you coming. Everything went okay?"

"Yep, the vamps are on their way to Columbus," I said. "Where's Doc?"

"She left. Don't worry, they won't find her. If a succubus doesn't want to be found, she won't be."

I walked over and sat down next to Watson. "How're you doing?"

"Good, I guess."

Jean Luc placed the book on the table in front of Watson. "This book contains descriptions of the five demon clans missing from the first book. There is also information in here about vampires and shifters."

"How did Cowell find out about them?" I asked Watson.

He shrugged. "I guess once you know demons exist, you are more open to seeing the supernatural things around you. Ever since the Turkey dig, Father Cowell, Jonathan, and I have kept in touch. Father spent the last few years researching demons. He felt if we knew more about them, it would help us deal with them. Jonathan and I took a more pragmatic approach. I wanted to know how to kill them, so he helped me with that part of the research. After shooting Hampton in the chest and then watching him walk away, I knew we had to find a better way to defend ourselves."

"What about the writing in the beginning?" Jean Luc asked. "This is the same as in the other book, and I cannot translate it."

Watson shook his head. "You wouldn't be able to translate it, anyway. Father worked on it himself for years. He said only a man of God could translate it. That the angels protected it. He always said he wished he could have Father Brown work on it."

"Why?" Dalton asked.

"Brown is a linguist. Father Cowell said if anyone could figure it out, he could."

I rubbed my temples with my fingertips, trying to stop the headache threatening to pounce. "I still don't understand why Hampton decided to go after Cowell and Jonathan now."

Misha sat down at the table next to an open laptop. "I think I found the answer. The two names you sent me—the students who had been on the dig?—are both dead. They died under mysterious circumstances in the past year. One in Pennsylvania and the other in Milwaukee."

"But they weren't part of this!" Watson protested.

Misha continued. "Hear me out. I don't think Hampton knew which of the people on the dig were involved. You told us Cowell said a prayer to make Hampton and the Pavel demon forget you were in the tent. But it doesn't mean they forgot why they were there in the first place—to get this key.

"If the artifact Hampton and the Pavel got from Cowell was not the real key, they would need to start over. They might have recently come to the conclusion someone at the dig took the real key. I don't think Hampton zeroed in on Cowell and Jonathan specifically. I think he was systematically going through the list of dig participants to find out who had taken the key."

Watson scowled. "Shit. Now what?"

"We stop this any way we can," I said.

"Do you have a plan, Kyle?" Dalton asked.

"I think it's time for me to go to church."

CHAPTER 34

I looked cautiously up at the painted ceiling filled with cherubs. I had been inside the church for a while now and had not been smote yet...or was the word smited? Or smitten? Dalton and I waited in the back vestibule while parishioners filed past Father Brown on their way out.

When the crowd dispersed, he motioned for us to follow him into the back. "Do you have news regarding David?"

"We found something David was working on which needs translation. I understand you are a linguist and might be able to help us with it."

"Yes. Do you have it with you?"

I handed him the copy Jean Luc had made of both the excerpt and Cowell's translations.

"Is this related to his murder?"

"We believe so, yes. But we've been unable to interpret it. David translated some of it, so we thought it might be a type of ancient religious dialect."

"I'll see what I can do."

"Thank you. And Father, would you please keep this to yourself for the time being?"

He nodded. I could tell he wanted to ask more, but resisted. I hoped to spare him from the truth if I could.

We drove to the office, since Misha didn't want us coming to the safe house any more than necessary, in case we picked up another tail. Dalton dropped me off out front and went to park. Since it was Sunday, the office was officially closed, but Jean Luc was in the back room working on his laptop when I unlocked the door.

"How did it go?" he asked.

"Father Brown is going to work on the translation for us."

"Did you tell him the truth?"

"No, I'll tell him only if necessary. For all he knows, he's translating some type of apocalyptic religious text."

Jean Luc closed his laptop. "That makes sense."

I stood for a second, trying to decide how to broach the question which had been bugging me since yesterday.

Before I said anything, he quirked his head to the side and looked at me quizzically. "Is something wrong?"

I sat down across from him. "Nothing. With everything that's happened with Watson, we haven't had time to talk."

"What do you want to talk about?"

"Last night, how did you know we were in trouble?"

Jean Luc hesitated, as if choosing his words carefully. "When a vampire bites a human, there are sometimes different outcomes. We often will form a connection with the human we bite. With you, I could feel you were in trouble."

Wow. First Tony feeding me based on my moods, and now this. "Will you always be able to sense me?"

"To some extent, but it will probably fade over time. Last night was extremely powerful, but I had just fed from you."

"Anything else I should be worried about?"

"I do not think so. We are fine, *ma petite*?"

I grasped his hand. "Don't worry, I'm not regretting it. Have we heard from Misha?"

Jean Luc chuckled. "Yes, apparently Jason is a TV junkie."

I shuddered in mock fear. "Dear God, no."

"Yes. Misha is in heaven. They talked about *The A-Team* until midnight."

"I'm speechless."

"Just be happy we were spared."

I checked my phone. It had been fifteen minutes since Dalton had dropped me off. "I wonder where Dalton is?"

"Maybe he went to get some food for you both?"

"Maybe." I called his number, but the call didn't connect. That was the third time it had happened. For some reason, this time I wasn't going to ignore it. "I'll be back in a couple of minutes."

I ran down the stairwell, and stopped at the level leading out to the parking garage. Dalton's car was parked outside the door, but I didn't see him anywhere. I opened the door and could hear low voices. Walking slowly across the concrete floor, I tried not to make a sound, since the garage was relatively empty.

When I got closer, I could tell the lower voice was Dalton's, but there was also a feminine voice I could barely make out. Jesus, was he talking to Lauren on his speakerphone?

I came around the corner. Dalton was alone and he wasn't speaking into his cell or any type of earpiece. He jerked as he noticed me walking toward him. I paused when I smelled the slightly sweet scent of flowery perfume—roses—in the air.

I whipped my head from side to side. "What the hell is going on? Who else is out here?"

"No one is here."

"Bull. I just heard you talking to someone."

"I'm alone, Kyle."

I closed my fist to stop myself from slapping his lying face. "I can smell that perfume again."

"You're imagining things."

"Don't insult my intelligence. Damn it! Tell me now."

He blew out a heavy breath. "It was my grandmother."

I couldn't have heard him right. "Your grandmother? I thought your grandmother is dead."

"She is."

I tried to count to ten before I spoke to calm myself down, but the numbers jumbled in my head. "What the hell is going on, Dalton?"

"My grandmother has been visiting me."

I blinked in confusion. "Explain."

"The night before I first met you, an angel came to me and said I was being called upon to fight evil. I thought the whole thing was a dream until you started telling me about angels cutting off vampire's heads. Then it didn't seem like a dream anymore."

My heart slowed down and seemed to stop. "Why didn't you say anything?"

"At first I didn't know what to say. You weren't exactly welcoming me with open arms at the time, so I wasn't about to confess angels were talking to me. I doubted it myself."

I was still having trouble following him. "How does your grandmother fit into all this?"

"After that first visit, she came to me and told me she had been sent by the angels. She asked me how the case was going."

"When was this?"

"The first time was the afternoon you went to see Griffin."

"When I couldn't reach you on your phone?" What the hell? Was she blocking his calls or something?

"Yes."

"And she came to you the night in Chicago?"

"Yes."

My heart jump-started itself. "Okay. Again, why didn't you tell me?"

"She said if I told anyone what was happening I would put them in danger. I wasn't going to risk your safety."

I stared at him in shock. "So you would rather I think you were a cheating SOB?"

"If it keeps you safe, yes."

Lord, *if* he was telling the truth, he was a selfless fool. "And just now?"

"She wanted to know what we'd learned from Watson."

I threw my arms up in the air. "Why do they need to ask? Don't they already know what is happening? They *are* angels."

"They don't know everything at all times."

"Says your dead grandmother. How do you know she is really who she says she is? She could be a shape-shifting demon, for all we know, working for Sebastian or the Pavels. You may have given information to our enemies."

He shook his head emphatically. "No, she knows things only my grandmother would know. I questioned her thoroughly when she first came to me."

"Well, if she has a direct line with the angels, then why aren't they helping us? They could translate the mystery writings for us. Hell, they could be putting the hammer down on Sebastian."

"I asked the same question. They aren't supposed to interfere."

"Interfere?" I rolled my eyes. "Interfere?!? They chopped off Hampton's head. How is that not interfering?"

"They can't help us directly with fighting Sebastian or the Pavels."

"It's official. We're living in Hypocrite Land."

Dalton took a step toward me. "I'm sorry, Kyle. Please believe me."

"I do believe you, because the story is too outrageous not to believe." But I didn't feel any better. Pressure built behind my eyes.

"I had no choice," he argued.

"No, actually, you could have told me the truth."

"Not if it risked your safety."

And just like that, I realized what family drama I had fallen into. "You are not your father, Dalton. And I am not your mother."

He jerked back a step as if I had slapped him. "I didn't want to hurt you," he answered, his voice coming out low and rough.

"But you did, Galahad. So I'm going to need some time to digest it all."

Jean Luc's voice sounded behind me. "Kyle, are you okay?"

Great. Another overprotective male. I was practically tripping over them. "I'm fine, Jean Luc. Dalton was telling me about the conversation he just had with his dead grandmother. Let him fill you in. I'm going to the hotel down the street for a drink."

I walked a block before crossing the street to enter the hotel. I marched into the bar and sat. Before the bartender could place a menu in front of me, I ordered a Great Lakes Dortmunder and started slugging it. Several other people were drinking their lunch as well. I slowed down the imbibing. I wanted to relax, not pass out.

I ordered a second beer and a burger and fries. By the time I was dunking my last fry in ketchup, Jean Luc stood next to me.

"Are you feeling better?"

I scowled at him.

"I came to drive you home."

"Thanks." I gestured for him to take a seat. "So did Dalton tell you everything?"

"Yes. It puts an interesting twist on things."

"You think? I thought he was cheating on me. Instead, he's been having secret rendezvous with his dead grandmother."

"He feels bad about the whole thing. He wanted to come over and talk to you, but decided you needed some time."

"He's right."

"You really care about him."

"I don't need all these complications in my life," I grumbled.

"*Mon Dieu*. It is not complicated. You are falling in love. There is nothing more simple."

"How can you say that?"

"I have seen all types of love matches over my rather long life."

"But have you ever been in love?"

"Several times. Now, have you finished drowning your frustrations in alcohol and fried food so I can drive you home?"

"Only if you tell me about someone you loved."

Jean Luc paused for a moment. "Her name was Talia."

CHAPTER 35

Monday morning. New week, new attitude. Or so I hoped.

The night before I had eaten a bowl of wedding soup for dinner, compliments of Tony. He called it brain food, and he was right. As soon as I'd sopped up the last morsel, I reviewed every event from the past couple of weeks, picturing the white board in my head. Too many people and supes had been hurt or killed, and for what? This mysterious key Hampton was looking for?

It had to stop. I went to bed with an action plan. Today I just needed to get the others on board.

Jean Luc, Dalton, and I pulled up to the safe house. It took twice as long to get there, since Jean Luc took a circuitous route in case we were being followed. I had brought a dozen glazed donuts for Misha and a coffee cake for the rest of us.

We gathered at the large kitchen table. Misha beamed at me when he saw the boxes, poking Watson with his elbow. "I told you she would bring us something to eat. Thanks, Kyle."

"No problem. Please tell me you have coffee ready."

"Yes. Let me get plates for everyone."

I smiled as Misha played host. Once everyone was settled and eating, I opened the conversation. "Okay guys, we need to brainstorm. Last night I went over all of the events leading up to this point. Watson, here, gave us some important information about the key Hampton and the Pavel are after. Can you tell us anything more about it?"

"Only if you stop calling me Watson, I feel like I'm in a Sherlock Holmes movie."

Misha laughed and winked at him. Good Lord, they were becoming BFFs.

"All right, *Jason*, what can you tell us about the key?"

"Father Cowell was pretty closemouthed about it. Jonathan had unearthed a small box, and he called out to the group to come look at it. But when Father saw its markings, he realized it should not be given to anyone. Those markings warned of death and destruction in the wrong person's hands."

"What was in the box?" I prompted.

"I don't think anything was in the box. At least, Father Cowell said it was empty."

"Is that what the key was *supposed* to be in?" Jean Luc asked.

"Yeah. Father threw the box at Hampton when we ran out of the tent."

I patted Misha's arm. "Can you do some research on this key?"

"I have already begun. I haven't found much yet, since what we have is pretty vague, but I'll keep searching."

I nodded. "Maybe we can get some help elsewhere. Dalton, can you summon your grandmother or the angels?"

"I've never tried before. The angel came to me, and then my grandmother started her visits. I don't have a way to contact them."

"I think you should try to contact them later. And if the angels do come see you again, would you ask them why they chopped Hampton's head off? I mean, if they are so big into this not interfering thing, then why was it okay to chop off his head? And ask them about the key...it doesn't hurt to try, anyway."

I turned to Jason again. "You said you were following Hampton. Where did he go?"

"All over Cleveland. His apartment and warehouse were the two main places."

Misha leaned forward and clicked on the laptop sitting in front of him. "The one on Superior in the warehouse district?"

Jason shook his head. "It's the address in his books, but it's not where he went to meet with other supernaturals. That warehouse is on St. Claire."

"Do you know who he was meeting?" Dalton asked.

"I didn't recognize most of them."

"Misha, show Jason pictures of Sebastian and Akers," I said.

A few clicks of the mouse later and Misha turned the screen toward the group. Akers' face was smiling smugly back at us. Jason stared at him for a second. "Nope, I don't remember him."

Misha clicked a couple more times and Sebastian appeared on the screen. "I remember him. He met with Hampton a couple of times. Is he a vampire?"

"Yeah, and a royal pain in the ass," I answered. "Did you ever get a look inside the warehouse?"

"No, I never wanted to risk it by myself. I wouldn't have seen a vampire coming, and they were constantly hovering around. I came back to check it out after Hampton died, but the place was still crawling with them."

"Do you think the box from the dig may be there?" I persisted.

"If Hampton still had it, I would say it would be the most likely place to find it."

I clasped my hands together. "Who's ready to go on another field trip?"

Jean Luc spoke up, "Let me watch the warehouse for a time before we go in."

"Are you even allowed near it, since it isn't your territory?" I countered.

"I should be okay. Normally, you must claim your territory. This warehouse is not listed as an 'official' holding for Sebastian, so I would not violate any treaties."

I rolled my eyes. "You have the most convoluted system of rules."

"We have had centuries to develop them."

Jean Luc, Dalton and I piled into the car, and Jean Luc dropped us back at work before he went to the warehouse. I didn't like that he was going alone, but he insisted he would be fine and would contact us later.

Once in the office, we sat down and Dalton tried to summon the angels. He concentrated, said a prayer, paced, and concentrated again, but nothing happened.

"Maybe I need to try this alone. Let me go into the parking garage for a few minutes and see if it helps."

"Fine, I'll wait here for you."

I went back to my office to go through some paperwork, or at least that was what I'd planned until I was interrupted. I pulled the first file up on my computer and moaned when the blue screen of death appeared. And Misha wasn't there to bail me out. When the lights flickered, nerves fluttered up my spine. And when the overheads went off completely and the smell of roses hit my nose, I braced myself for a ghostly visit.

"Hello?" I walked out of my dark office into the hallway, the hairs on the back of my neck standing at attention. The window at the end of the hall provided much-needed light to soothe my nerves. There would be no grabbing me in the dark. I headed toward the front office, but didn't make it. A female voice came from behind me.

"Kyle."

I jumped. Couldn't help myself. I was in the middle of my very own scary ghost story. Spinning around, I came face-to-face with Dalton's grandmother. She had on the same yellow sundress she wore in the picture on Dalton's mantel. She smiled at me and I smiled back. *What else was I supposed to do?*

"Don't be afraid, child. I won't hurt you."

"Dalton's been calling for you," I blurted in a tight voice.

"I know. But I think it is more important to spend time with you right now."

"Why?"

"Because I am counting on you to protect Joe."

My heart sped up. "From what?"

"I don't know exactly. What I do know is Joe has been chosen to protect something vital to heaven."

"How vital? Is it the key?"

"I don't know about any key, but it's important enough an angel felt it necessary to come to earth and kill Hampton because of it."

"Doesn't it go against the *no interfering rule* they seem so keen about?"

She chuckled. "Yes, I think there were some feathers ruffled on that one."

"So how am I supposed to protect him if I don't know what to look for?"

"I have confidence in you. You are resourceful, and as beautiful as Joe told me you were."

A lump lodged in my throat. "He told you about me?"

"Yes. You are definitely keeping him on his toes. I always knew he would end up with a strong woman. Promise me you will watch out for him."

"Of course." She started to fade and I had not asked nearly enough questions. "Wait! Before you go, why did the angels send you to Dalton instead of talking to him themselves?"

She frowned. "I wanted to see him again, and they owe me."

"What does that mean?"

"I'm sorry, dear. I have already said too much."

She faded right in front of me and I stared openmouthed at the empty spot where she had been seconds before.

Dalton's voice echoed in the hall. "Kyle, where are you?"

"Right here."

The lights flicked on as Dalton walked down the hallway toward me.

"Are you okay?"

"Yeah."

"What happened?"

For a second I contemplated not telling him, but then I had made him promise not to keep things from me, right? Right? I took a deep breath. "I just met your grandmother."

CHAPTER 36

Dalton's eyes darkened as I spun the tale of his ghostly grandmother's visit. His hands tightened on his coffee mug. His tight-lipped look told me he would have liked something stronger than coffee.

He set his cup down and ran his fingers through his hair. "This is getting stranger by the minute. What the hell..." He cringed at his word choice, glancing guiltily toward the ceiling, "What do they want me to protect?"

I shrugged. "I don't know. And what about your grand-mother's comment 'they owe me'? What in the world could she be holding over angels' heads?"

It was Dalton's turn to shrug. "You got me. She was never especially religious that I saw, other than going to Mass each week."

"Another puzzle to solve. Hopefully she'll come back and tell us more. In the meantime, let's get out of here for a while. I feel claustrophobic."

On our way out of the building, I jerked to a stop in the hall as the world spun out of control. I righted myself, but then the hall in front of me faded, replaced by the dark room from my dreams. Light cascaded through the slit, shining along the floor, and I knelt in this light, digging frantically with my hands until I had made a small hole. I unhooked my heart bracelet and buried it, tamping down the earth. I had to hide it before he came back. Strong male hands wrapped around my arms and I screamed until Dalton's voice broke through the vision.

"Kyle, what's going on?"

I shook my head to clear the fog and took a deep breath. "I just had a flash of something. I think it's related to the dream I've been having."

Dalton held my elbow firmly. "Do you want me to take you home?"

"No, but will you go with me somewhere else?"

"Does it have to do with your premonitions?"

"That's the thing. I don't think it's a premonition anymore, but I have to find out for sure."

I directed Dalton to the burbs, and within twenty-five minutes we parked in the Connors' driveway. I hadn't planned anything, since I wasn't sure I even knew what to ask. I convinced Dalton to wait in the car, so we didn't upset the Connors any more than necessary. When I rang the doorbell, Stephanie answered.

She smiled. "Kyle! It's great to see you. What brings you here?"

"Sorry to disturb you, I just need a minute of your time. I have to ask you a couple of questions to close out the case. Do you mind?"

"No, come in. Trina's at a play date today, so we can talk inside if you'd like."

"I'm sorry to bring this up again, but I want to make sure all the loose ends are tied up. Some of the questions might appear strange, but please bear with me."

Stephanie motioned me to the couch. "What do you need to know?"

"The day Trina was abducted, do you know exactly how the man grabbed her?"

Stephanie closed her eyes for a second before answering, "When we first brought her home, she was filthy. After the doctor's exam, I tried to wash her up a bit. When I put the washcloth up to Trina's face she started screaming. Once I was finally able to calm her down, she told me the man had put a cloth over her face and then everything went black."

"What was Trina wearing—clothes, shoes, jewelry?"

"I'll never forget it. She had on a pair of pink shorts, a flower top and yellow sandals. And her new bracelet."

"What type of bracelet?" I tried to ask calmly, even though my nerves were rioting.

"We had gotten her a silver heart charm bracelet for her birthday. She was so excited about it." She frowned. "She wasn't wearing it when they found her."

I stood. "Thank you. I'm sorry I had to bring it all up again. The last thing I need to know is the address where the pack found Trina."

Stephanie walked me to the door, giving me the address.

"How's Trina doing?" I asked.

Stephanie smiled. "She's great. Back to her old self again. Thank you!"

"You know, if you want me to help you forget what happened, I could try."

"No, I don't want to forget. I will never take anything for granted again. I'm blessed, and I know that now more than ever." She hugged me and I promised to come visit Trina again soon.

I climbed into the car and Dalton stared at me for a second before speaking. "Where to next?"

I gave him the address I'd gotten from Stephanie, then closed by eyes and leaned my head against the headrest. I was almost certain what I would find, but I had to confirm it for my own sanity.

To Dalton's credit, he didn't press me, so we traveled in silence. After a few minutes he stopped the car. I opened my eyes and studied the house. It didn't look sinister from the front, just your normal-looking suburban home. Of course, evil didn't have to stand out, did it?

Dalton interrupted my thoughts. "Do you want me to come with you?"

I nodded and got out, walking slowly around the back, with Dalton right behind me.

I saw the dead tree first. Empty branches waved slightly in the breeze. A jingling sound caught my attention. It was a homemade wind chime, its music made by metal and sea glass.

The metal shed loomed in front of me, and I walked toward it, my chest tightening with each step. It wasn't my own fear I was experiencing, but that didn't make it less powerful. The door hung on its hinges, claw marks scored down the length of it. I imagined Tim trying to get to his daughter. I stepped into the room and the smell of dry grass and earth almost brought me to my knees. Dalton braced me again. He had been keeping me from hitting the ground a lot lately.

"Kyle, tell me what's going on, right now!"

"This is where Trina was held. I haven't been having premonitions of the future. I've been seeing memories of the past. Trina's past."

Dalton brows furrowed in confusion. "Wouldn't you know about some of this from what the Connors' described to you?"

"No, we didn't talk about the specifics of the shed. Only Trina knew about them. When I erased her memories, somehow I absorbed the events, and now they're part of *my* memories."

"That has never happened before?"

"Never. I don't see inside someone's mind, I place new thoughts there to replace others."

"So your power is evolving?"

"I guess so." I scanned the ground, and after a couple of seconds, found a small mound of dirt sitting just a bit higher than the rest of the earth floor. Kneeling, I dug with my fingers until I touched cool metal. I pulled out the bracelet, brushing the dirt away from the small hearts. I hadn't realized until this moment that each heart had a letter engraved on it. Holding the bracelet so each charm lined up, I read the letters spelling out one word: TRINA.

Dalton helped me up, pulling me into his embrace. I took deep breaths and inhaled his musky scent, allowing his strong arms to hold me steady. After a couple of seconds, he led me out of the shed into the sunshine.

CHAPTER 37

What a mess. At least I knew I wasn't losing it, but it didn't alleviate the anxiety over what my power might have in store for me in the future. I had finally calmed down just about the time Dalton parked fairly close to my apartment and walked me to my building. I unlocked the door and he leaned over and kissed me on the cheek. "Are you sure you're okay?"

"Yeah, I'm good."

"I'll see you later, then."

I held up my hand. "Whoa. Where are you going?"

"I was going to go back to work."

I shook my head. "No you're not. Come upstairs, Galahad."

"Okay, if you're up to talking, let's get everything out in the open."

It wasn't my plan, but I nodded to get him moving.

We jogged up the stairs. I opened my door and threw my keys and phone on the table. Before he could get a word out, I was in his arms. His eyes widened, but when I stood on tiptoes and initiated the first kiss, he didn't protest. A couple more kisses, and we stumbled toward the couch. After a few seconds, Dalton broke the kiss and glanced around.

"What are you looking for?" I asked, exasperated.

"Do I need to worry about Booger attacking me?"

I laughed. "No, Booger and I have parted ways."

"What happened?"

"It's a long story, and I can think of better uses for my mouth right now."

He grinned. "Are we going to have makeup sex?"

"Yep. You've got a lot to make up for."

He grimaced. "You are not a freak show to me, Kyle. I'm sorry about before. I never wanted to hurt you."

"I know, but next time? Just tell me the truth."

"You mean the next time I talk to angels or dead relatives?"

"If you talk to them, or Santa Claus, or the Easter Bunny, just tell me. Now start kissing me again."

"Yes, ma'am."

He followed directions well and began kissing me in earnest. Our tongues started a wonderful game of tag-you're-it. He ran his hands down my back and picked me up. I wrapped my legs around his waist and we both moaned at the contact.

God almighty, I was in heaven. We progressed to the couch, where I straddled his lap so I could unbutton his shirt and run my hands under the fabric, playing with his nipples. When I followed the same path with my lips, he jerked, almost knocking me off the couch. I laughed and he grabbed me around the middle. His eyes danced as he carried me into my bedroom and flung me on the bed before crawling over me.

He pulled the shirt over my head and unhooked my bra, settling on top of me. And the world faded. Dead vampires and torture and mysterious keys were replaced by kisses and tongue, and bare skin sliding over bare skin. Warning bells sounded in my head, just as they had the first time we were together. But this time I realized what they meant. It wasn't because we were wrong for each other. It was because I was scared to let him get close to me. He could be THE one.

I wasn't so cynical that I didn't believe in love. Hell, I loved Jean Luc and Misha. But I wasn't *in* love with them. And, while this strait-laced, ridiculously noble cop, of all people, crawled down my body and ran his tongue around the rim of my belly button, I knew it was too late. I had fallen hard.

My ridiculous reverie was interrupted when he unbuttoned my pants and pulled the rest of my clothes off. As his exploration headed further south, I heard Barry White's Biggest Hits playing in my head. When the Hallelujah Chorus chimed in a short time later, I pulled on his hair and he moved back up my body.

He sat up and yanked off his clothes while I reached into the drawer by the bed to get a condom. I might be in love with him, but I wasn't reckless. I opened the packet and knelt in front of him, helping him roll it on. He growled at me, an honest-to-goodness growl, and I gaped in surprise.

He smirked. "Are you going to call me a brute again?"

"Shut up. No time for talk," I mumbled as I pushed him onto his back and crawled on top. My turn to be in charge for a while. I sank down onto him and his turquoise eyes ran over my body as he reached up and caressed my breasts. After a couple of seconds, a rhythm started and my eyeballs crossed. He pulled me down to him and we kissed again. My chest burned like it was going to explode right before I fell over the cliff into one of the best orgasms of my life. Dalton shouted and followed me over soon afterward.

For a few seconds, I gasped for air and was unable to speak...or form a coherent thought, for that matter. I flopped down on his chest like a wet noodle, my bones having disintegrated. He rubbed his hands in circles over my back.

"You okay, McKinley?"

"Yeah. You?"

"More than."

I lay in Dalton's arms, my face resting against his chest, listening to his heartbeat. I could easily get used to this.

When he spoke, the low rumble of his voice vibrated through his chest. "Are you ready to talk more about what happened earlier in the shed?"

"Not much to talk about. All of those visions were really memories from a scared little girl."

"But when you're experiencing them, it feels like it's happening to you?"

"Yeah. It's a bit of a pain. I'm not separated from the emotions, it's like they are actually mine."

"What do you think it means for your powers?"

"I don't know. I'll just have to play it by ear. This has never happened before. Maybe it's because I had to erase so much with her, versus a quick memory erase. I'll just have to see if it happens again."

"Is your mother still alive?"

Where had that question come from? "Yes, she's alive, but I haven't seen her in years. Why?"

"Hear me out before you shut my idea down. Does your mother know about your powers?"

I hesitated before answering, my chest tightening. "No."

"I've been thinking about your power and what's been happening to you. I think you should tell your mother. Maybe she knows something about it. Maybe she has some type of power herself."

I clenched the fist resting on Dalton's chest. "She doesn't have a power. She would have told me."

Dalton lifted my chin so he could see my face. "Kyle, you're not making any sense. You said your mother doesn't know about your power, so why do you assume she would have told you if she has one?"

I expelled a hard breath. "She doesn't know about my power *now*. I erased her memory."

His eyes widened. "Why?"

"When I first realized I had powers, I was so scared. I didn't know what to do. I didn't tell anyone. But after several months I felt like the secret was burning a hole in my chest, so I finally told her."

I stopped for a moment and he nodded.

"I thought for sure she wouldn't believe me, but she did. I was so excited that someone knew my secret and hadn't thrown me out. Two nights later, she came home with Doug, her boyfriend at the time, and they were arguing. Apparently Mom had been flirting with another guy at a bar and Doug had caught her. When Doug went to bed, Mom ordered me to erase his memory of the evening. She didn't want him to leave her.

"I told her no and she slapped me. Said after all she had done for me, I owed her and if she had to have a freak for a daughter, at least she could get something out of it."

Dalton ran his thumbs across my cheeks to wipe away my tears. I wasn't even sure when I had started crying. I cleared my throat and continued. "I erased Doug's memory, and that evening, when my mother went to bed, I erased hers as well. No way was I going to let her use me again."

I laid my head on his chest and Dalton pulled me tighter to him. "I'm so sorry, babe. No wonder you don't tell a lot of people about your gift."

I nodded, his chest hair tickling my cheek. "That's why I don't have human friends. When I tell them the truth, they either try to use me or run away."

He kissed the top of my head. "If you stopped using your power today, I'd be fine with it, and I'm not going anywhere."

I turned on my side and Dalton spooned against my back, wrapping his arms around me in a protective cocoon. I drifted to sleep. After a while, my grumbling stomach woke me up. Dalton chuckled behind me. "Somebody's hungry."

I flipped on my back and smiled. "Yep."

He caressed my face with his fingers, running them along my lips. "Are you feeling better?"

"Yes, much." And I was. Telling him about my past was the catharsis I needed. No wonder people paid shrinks so much money.

"I have a question for you."

I sighed. "Another one? I think I've had enough emotional breakthroughs for one evening, don't you?"

"Sorry, but I have to ask you one more."

"Fine. Shoot."

"Do you forgive me for lying about talking to my dead grandmother?"

"Maybe."

He stared at me. "Maybe?"

I rubbed my hand on his stomach. "I think you have some more work to do before you are totally forgiven."

"Work, huh?"

"Yep. You need to persuade me."

He grinned and rolled us over so he was on top. *Oh goody.* We started kissing, and it wasn't long before we were getting quite frisky. That's when my phone rang out in the living room. Before we could untangle ourselves, it stopped. We kissed again, but this time Dalton's cell phone interrupted us.

Dalton pulled his pants off the floor and fumbled for his phone in his pocket.

"Dalton, here...yeah, Jean Luc, hold on." He held up the phone to me. "It's for you."

I groaned in frustration before responding. "Hello?"

"I am sorry to interrupt you two."

"Interrupt? Jesus, Jean Luc, are you sensing my emotions right now?"

"Yes. Nothing specific, but it does not require a rocket scientist to figure it out."

I shook my head. "What's up?"

"I have been watching the warehouse for several hours, and it is finally empty. The last vampire left fifteen minutes ago, and no one else has arrived. I think this would be a good time to go in."

"We'll be there in twenty." I handed Dalton the phone. "Remember where we were when we were so rudely interrupted, because right now we need to meet Jean Luc at the warehouse for a little B&E."

He kissed me on the nose and sat up. "Don't forget you're talking to a cop right now."

"You can arrest me later. I like role-playing with handcuffs."

It was his turn to groan in frustration.

CHAPTER 38

Call me silly, but it occurred to me breaking into a vamp warehouse was probably not a good idea.

Dalton and I parked a block away and walked through a back alley to the set of scarred bay doors where Jean Luc waited for us. It didn't take long for him to get the door unlocked, and we slipped inside. The inside was spacious, but relatively empty, with the exception of packing peanuts scattered all over the floor. Up toward the front of the building was a set of offices. We headed there and split up, each through separate doors.

I ended up in the main office area. In the middle of the room sat a chair with arm and leg manacles. Where did you even find a chair like that? Dungeons R' Us? I stepped closer. Rust-colored stains spotted the seat and arms. Even without Jean Luc's nose, I knew it was blood.

The sight made me sick. Had Father Cowell died here? I skirted around the chair through a door on the right that opened into a storage space with shelves and a half dozen boxes. I opened the first box and found newspaper and some metal statues. They didn't look valuable, just stuff you would sell in a tourist trap. The second and third boxes held much the same junk.

There were two boxes on a separate shelf. I picked up the first and opened it. Nothing important. The next box was heavier. I picked it up carefully. As I pulled back the flaps, Jean Luc walked into the room and said "no," but it was too late.

I stared down into the face of one Charles Hampton, vampire.

I dropped the box—who wouldn't have?—and it landed on its side. The head fell out and rolled until his nose touched the floor. Hampton's head rolled back the way it came and settled, continuing to rock slightly back and forth as if he was shaking his head.

What. The. Hell.

I held my breath to keep from gagging. "Why would they keep his head in the closet?" I asked. It was a ridiculous question, but it fit the ridiculous situation.

Before Jean Luc could answer, Dalton's voice called out. "Jean Luc, I could use some help in here."

"Bring the head, Kyle." Jean Luc flashed out of the room.

Come on! I was not getting paid enough money for this, really I wasn't.

I snatched some newspaper out of another box, using it as a barrier between my hands and the head, then picked it up and wrapped the paper around it. Stuffing the head back into the box, I carried it in the direction of Dalton's voice. I hurried down a hallway and found him and Jean Luc standing in front of a safe.

Before I could say a word, Jean Luc held up his hand to shush me. He leaned close to the safe, turning the dial and listening to the tumblers. I set down the cardboard box. It was amazing how heavy a head could be. A minute later the latch clicked and Jean Luc pushed down the handle, opening the safe.

A stack of papers and a small wooden box sat inside. "I think we have the key." Jean Luc examined the box and frowned. "This box is solid. I thought Jason said Father Cowell had opened it."

I thought back to the conversation with Jason. "No, he said that Cowell said it was empty. He didn't say that he actually opened it."

He handed it to me and reached back into the safe to pull out the papers. I examined the box as well. It had markings on it, but there was no seam along the box. "You're right, I don't see anything either." I handed the box to Dalton. "Let's get out of here, before someone comes back."

I walked over to pick up Hampton's head, but Dalton interrupted me. "Hey, this does come open, but there's nothing in it."

I looked back at him. He stood with two box halves in his hands. "How the hell did you do that?"

"I don't know. It just came open."

I caught the puzzled expression on Jean Luc's face, but we really couldn't take the time to ponder it now. "Bring it along so we can examine it later."

Lifting Hampton's head as we moved out of the room, my eyes were drawn upwards. That's when I noticed the camera in the upper right-hand corner of the room. *Not good.*

Back in the car, Dalton drove and Jean Luc sat in the passenger seat paging through the documents.

"What have you got?" I asked.

"A list of names. I think they were participants from the dig in Turkey. The other pages are notes about where most of them live and work."

I shuddered. "I wonder how many people he killed."

"We will know more once I give this to Misha. We should go back to the office and switch cars before we go to the safe house."

We finally arrived at the safe house an hour later. I guess I had been hanging around with Misha too long, since the *Mission Impossible* theme kept running through my head while we drove.

There was an unfamiliar car parked in the safe house driveway. Jean Luc flashed out of our car and we followed quickly.

As Dalton and I walked into the house, raised voices met us. In the living room, Misha and his father were having a face off. Boris's bodyguards shifted warily while Jean Luc observed with a bemused expression.

"Father, keep it down. Jason is sleeping," Misha hissed.

"You need to explain to me what is going on here. You are using the clan house to hide a human? Why would someone be after him?"

"He's part of our investigation. Vampires are after him."

"Vampires are too arrogant to even consider humans a threat. Why should they care so much?"

Misha rolled his eyes. "Now you're insulting Jean Luc."

Jean Luc shrugged. "I agree with his assessment. Normally most vampires are arrogant. But if a human threatens them, their arrogance will not tolerate it. Or if the human has information they may need, he does become a priority."

Boris continued. "So, which is it?"

Jason's voice answered from behind me. "Right now, they're after me because I'm a thorn in their side. A gnat buzzing around them."

Boris studied Jason as he walked further into the room. "And why are you buzzing around them? They will swat you down sooner or later."

"I know, but they killed two friends of mine. Someone needs to make them pay."

I wasn't sure if I imagined it or not, but I could have sworn Boris's face took on a look of respect. "A warrior's code."

"Yes."

"And how did you meet Misha and his teammates?"

Misha stepped forward. "That's not relevant. It's part of an ongoing investigation."

Jason shook his head. "Don't, Misha. Your father deserves to know the truth. We met when I shot your son."

Boris growled deep in his throat. The hairs on the back of my neck—hell, on every part of my body—stood at attention. In a blink of an eye, Boris's veneer slipped. The polished leader and businessman morphed into a seething father, his eyes glowing right before they turned black as pitch. Everyone tensed. The bodyguards stepped forward to flank Jason as Boris stalked into his face. He towered over Jason a good five inches, but Jason stood his ground.

"Tell me why I shouldn't eviscerate you right now." Boris's voice had dropped an octave, as if he hadn't been scary enough already.

"If I were in your place, I would ask the same question. I have no excuse. The first demon and vampire I met tried to kill me. When I saw Misha use his powers, I struck first before he could get me. I was wrong. And on top of that, your son saved my life, knowing I was the one who almost killed him."

After a second, Misha stepped next to Jason. Boris's gaze moved to his son's face. "I've forgiven him, Father. You cannot claim right of aggression here. That would be my choice to make, and I have chosen otherwise."

Boris nodded tightly and stepped back. After a few seconds, his eyes returned to their usual blue. The entire group heaved a collective breath.

I cleared my throat and jumped into the fray, speaking directly to Boris. "If you have time, we could sure use your help."

We sat at the kitchen table, passing around the two halves of the small wooden box and the safe papers so that everyone could examine them. Now that Dalton had opened the box, anyone could open and close it. Hampton's head remained on the floor in its cardboard container. I refused to let it join us at the table.

Boris picked up the small box pieces and turned them over in his hand. "I have not heard of this key before. The writings on the box are not familiar to me either."

"Well, Hampton, and now Sebastian, found it important enough to systematically locate and murder everyone associated with the dig where this box was discovered," Dalton explained.

Misha chimed in, "And there was nothing else at the warehouse besides the papers, this box, and Hampton's head?"

I shook my head. "No. Maybe they cleaned out the place after Hampton died. But there were security cameras."

Misha's eyes lit up. "If the cameras are wireless, we may have gotten lucky."

"How?" I asked.

"I can hack into the system and we can watch any recorded feeds. Give me a few minutes."

True to his word, Misha called us back into the room in twenty minutes. "I think we got something. There is no sound, but we have picture. Let me hook it up to the TV so we can all watch."

We waited another minute until the TV screen filled with an image of the warehouse. Misha rewound the film. "The nice thing about these cameras is they are motion-sensitive, so we don't have to wade through hours of footage with no one in the room. There are several cameras, so let me figure out which one has something interesting to watch."

"Here's something." We watched the screen and saw Dalton, Jean Luc and me go through the offices and end up in the room with the safe. I watched as Jean Luc and I tried to open the box, and then Dalton opened it with ease.

Misha went through a few more minutes of footage until he came to a demon standing in one of the rooms, bent over something on a desk. He was blue with black stripes. Sebastian stood in the corner watching the demon with fascination.

"What kind of demon is that?" I asked.

Misha grimaced. "It is similar to one of the pictures in Cowell's journal we didn't recognize."

Boris leaned forward. "One of our ancients recognized that picture from her childhood. She heard stories of a powerful demon banned from earth called the Majock."

The demon continued to block the camera's view.

"What the hell is he doing?" I blurted.

As if in answer to my question, he backed up, and we could see Hampton's head propped up on the table. Electrodes were attached to his face and the other ends to a machine. The demon flipped a switch and the head actually shimmied across the table.

The demon on the screen closed his eyes and concentrated. After a few minutes, he opened them and shook his head.

Sebastian stepped forward and started talking agitatedly. The demon responded, at which point Sebastian backhanded him and left the room. The demon flicked the switch again and closed his eyes. After a few minutes, he shut off the machine, and walked out of the room. Misha stopped the replay.

Jason spoke up. "What was that about?"

Boris answered him, "I think in order for the demon to attempt reading Hampton's memory, he needed electrical impulses. Since Hampton is dead, they had to provide the impulses to bring him back to life."

I gasped. "Good Lord, he's trying to create a Vampenstein."

Jason chuckled. "Or a Frankenpire."

Misha's eyes twinkled. "But it didn't work."

"Or it worked and Hampton didn't have the information they wanted," Dalton said. "Either way, Sebastian has to be stopped."

CHAPTER 39

What a change of pace, waking up in a man's arms. After we left the safe house, Dalton took me home and we ended up in bed again. I guess my handcuff and role-playing comments had inspired him.

I rolled over to face him. He was frowning.

"What's wrong?"

"Nothing, I had some really wild dreams last night, and then I woke up with a headache."

I sat up. "Let me try something." I placed my hands on his temples and rubbed my fingers in tiny circles. "I can probably stop those pain receptors from firing by planting a suggestion in your head if you want."

He hesitated for a second.

"Trust me. I won't make you cluck like a chicken or anything like that."

"Okay."

I concentrated and pushed a feeling of warmth and calm into his brain and he relaxed in a matter of seconds. "Thanks, I feel much better."

I snuggled up against him. "You're welcome."

"How did I get so lucky?"

"I don't know. I've been asking myself the same question about you."

He watched me skeptically as if waiting for the punch line but his features changed to surprise when he realized I was serious. "And when exactly did you start feeling lucky about me?"

I thought for a moment. "In the office, the day I erased Trina's memory."

His mouth dropped open. "You almost took my head off that day."

"You pissed me off because you were trying to tell me what to do, but you told me to stop using my power if it hurt me. You're one of the only people who sees me, not my power." I twined my fingers with his and kissed him lightly on the lips.

An hour later, Dalton went home to clean up and change before going into the office and I was on my way to work. As I drove up Murray Hill, my phone rang. It was Father Brown.

"Hello, Father."

"Ms. Smith."

I cringed slightly. I needed to tell him the truth about my name sooner rather than later. "Have you had any luck with the translation?"

"A little bit. I was wondering if we could get together to discuss it?"

"Sure. Let me get in touch with Dalton and we'll meet you later."

"Actually I called Lieutenant Dalton first but got his voice mail, so I tried you. I'm downtown. I just finished a breakfast meeting and wondered if we could meet now."

"Sure. Where are you?"

"I'm at the Hyatt Regency."

"I'll be there in fifteen minutes."

I hung up and tried to call Dalton, but got his voice mail as well. I left him a message to meet us at the hotel, or call me if he couldn't get there in time. When I arrived at the hotel, I was lucky enough to find a spot on the street. I shoved a couple of quarters in the meter and entered through the door. Father Brown stood in the lobby.

"Thank you for meeting me."

"No problem." I looked around the busy lobby, trying to find a spot for us to sit.

"Don't worry, there's a small conference room that's unoccupied at the moment. We can talk in there." Once in the room, Father Brown sat at the head of the table and I sat beside him. He pulled a folded piece of paper out of his pocket and opened it, placing it in front of me.

"I see you've made some progress."

"A few lines yes, but not all of it yet."

I read the first stanza.

Evil thrives amongst us
Angels descend, preparing for battle
Weapon of knowledge in hand
With it the tides turn
And light will triumph

Father interjected. "I have started on the second stanza, but am not having much luck."

"Is there any reference to a key in the stanzas? If so, does it say what it is?" I asked.

"It's interesting you brought that up. In the third line, I struggled with the word weapon. I wasn't sure if it was right. The other word I thought it might be was key."

"So the key of knowledge can defeat evil?"

"If you interpret it that way, yes."

"Then what is the key?"

"I don't believe it is a *what*. I think it is a *who*."

"I don't understand."

"The key isn't a tangible object. It is the knowledge imparted to a person. A protector of secrets, if you will."

My stomach twisted. "How would this be given to the person? Could it be held in some type of container, like a box?"

Father hesitated for a second before answering. "If I thought this was an actual prophesy and not one of David's delusions, I would say this knowledge would need to be delivered by some type of holy receptacle."

I pulled out my phone and opened a picture of the small engraved box. "Like this?"

Father's eyes focused on the box and then up at me. "Yes. Those markings are warnings against evil."

"So how would this box deliver the knowledge?"

"I don't know exactly. But if it really contained the knowledge that is referenced in the prophecy, it would be protected so only the right person could access it."

"Thanks, Father. I've got to go." I stood.

"Aren't you going to tell me what's going on?"

"I'll tell you everything when I can," I promised.

"Including your real name?"

I nodded. "Including my real name."

I ran toward my car, goose bumps shooting down my arms. I tried Dalton's number again, and when he didn't pick up, I left him an urgent voicemail, praying there was some silly, everyday reason he wasn't answering, and not what I feared. I called the police station and left a message there as well.

I called Jean Luc and had him conference Misha and Jason into the call, filling them in on my conversation with Father Brown.

"I don't want to sound like an emotional female, but I think something's wrong. If Dalton has somehow absorbed this key, Sebastian will be after him."

Misha spoke up. "I'll see if I can triangulate Dalton's cell phone."

"Jean Luc, where do you think Sebastian might take him?"

"He will not take him back to the warehouse or Hampton's loft, since he is aware that we know about both places. Let me talk to a few people and see if they have some ideas. Where are you now?"

"I'm getting on the highway to go check Dalton's house."

"Call again once you arrive. Misha and I will work on finding him in the meantime."

As I drove toward his house I prayed to Dalton's grand-mother, the angels, God, anyone who chose to listen, but got squat. I drove faster.

After twenty minutes, I pulled into Dalton's driveway. Nothing looked out of the ordinary, but something wrong and heavy hung in the air. I yanked the baseball bat from under my front seat and walked around to the back of the house. The door to the kitchen was ajar. I held the bat tighter and pushed the door open slowly.

I took one step into the house and a voice called out to me, "I'm glad you were able to join us, Kyle."

I would know Sebastian's slimy voice anywhere. I walked into the living room. Sebastian sat in an armchair next to the fireplace. One of his vamp flunkies stepped toward me and I took a swing at him with the bat. He grabbed it out of my hands and pushed me roughly in front of Sebastian.

I turned my head and barely stopped myself from scream-ing. Dalton sat slumped and handcuffed to a chair. Blood ran down the side of his neck onto his chest. I rushed to him. There were no bite marks, though. The blood was coming from straends attached to the back of his neck.

"What the hell are you doing to him?"

"Trying to get answers."

"To what?"

"I want the key. I saw the security feed. He was able to open the box."

"And you couldn't?"

He frowned. "No, we had given up on the box. We assumed it was some sort of talisman. It appeared to be made of solid wood."

"What is so important about this damn key?"

"With it I can defeat the angels."

"Really? And who told you that? Hampton?"

"When Charles first spoke of it, I dismissed it as a myth. Then one day an angel came down from heaven and lopped off his head. That's when I decided he might be on to something. So I enlisted my own help."

"The Majock demon."

Sebastian's eyes flared slightly. "You continue to surprise me."

"How did you break him out of the demon realm?"

"I have my methods." He smiled smugly.

"Why would you even want to be in control of earth? You think humans are useless. Jesus, don't you have enough power now? You've lived for centuries and you're *still* an idiot."

Dalton gasped. "Kyle, don't."

Sebastian smirked. "Oh, I already know what she is doing, Lieutenant. She's trying to distract me from my dealings with you." He stood and strutted over to me like a proud peacock. It made me want to kick him in the balls.

He circled me. After a couple of seconds, his eyes flared and he hissed, the sound skittering along my nerve endings.

"You stupid child." He snatched me by the arm and held up the wrist Jean Luc had bitten. "You are ruined!"

"I don't think so."

He threw me to the ground. "You have no right to think. You are nothing."

"If I'm nothing, then why are you after me?"

"For the power that has been wasted on you."

"Yeah, well, deal with it." Not the smartest of statements on my part, since he yanked me up from the floor by my hair, and pain lanced across my scalp.

He shook me in front of Dalton like a rag doll. "If you don't give me the key now, I will kill her."

Dalton tried to lunge out of the chair, but the handcuffs held him in place. "I don't have the key. The box was empty when I opened it."

"You lie!" Sebastian leaned forward, spittle forming on his lips.

"No he doesn't. Think about it. The straends should cause him excruciating pain if he's lying, right? He didn't even flinch just now."

"Then where is the key?"

I jumped in with both lying feet. "I have it."

CHAPTER 40

After I dropped that bombshell, Sebastian let me go and I nearly lost my footing. "You couldn't open the box. How do you have the key?"

"Dalton was the one who found the key," I said.

Sebastian frowned. "But he doesn't know where it is."

"He doesn't know where it is *now*. I changed his memory."

Dalton shook his head adamantly. "Don't listen to her, she's lying."

"No, I'm not. If this key is as powerful as you say it is, the supernatural community will not allow humans to control it. So I made him forget."

Dalton's eyes met mine. "When did you erase my memory?"

"This morning when you had your headache. I changed it then."

Up to that point, Dalton hadn't believed me, but I saw the first tinge of doubt in his eyes and it was the equivalent of being sucker-punched.

Sebastian smirked. "A lover's quarrel. Is this your first? I will never understand humans. Do you want to know when the straends punished him for lying?"

I didn't answer, figuring he was going to tell me regardless. "He reeks of you and yet when I asked him if he cared for you, he said no. He almost passed out from the pain.

I believe he was trying to protect you. And in return, you played him for a fool. Maybe you are not as pathetic as I thought."

The bile rose in my throat, but I ignored it. "I don't need your approval to do my job."

"Where is the key?"

"My apartment."

His lips tightened into a thin line. "Why would you leave it there?"

"Because I don't want Jean Luc or Misha to get their hands on it, either. Nicholas's instructions were to give the key directly to him."

Sebastian chuckled. "I'm sure they were." He motioned to the guard I'd tried to brain with my bat. "Go with her to the apartment and bring me back the key."

My mind reeled. "What are you going to do with Dalton?"

"Kill him."

Stay calm. "Don't do that. The police and FBI are already looking for a serial killer. If you kill a high-profile cop, you're just asking for trouble. I can erase his memory later. I was planning on doing it anyway."

"Kyle, no!" Dalton blurted.

Sebastian stared at me for a moment before replying. "I will wait here with the lieutenant. I want to believe you, but if you're deceiving me, you will both pay."

The drive to Little Italy went way too fast. I just hoped it was enough time for Jean Luc and Misha to get concerned when they hadn't heard from me. By this time they should be on their way to Dalton's house, and would be able rescue him. I didn't have much time to figure out what my next steps with the vamp guard would be, but I wasn't going to give up without a fight.

We pulled up to my building and were able to find a parking space right outside my door. *Really?* I mean, any other time it would take me ten minutes circling the block to find a space, and evil vampire henchman parks immediately. I was so screwed.

We headed upstairs, and I opened my apartment door. The vamp plowed in first, making sure no one else was in the apartment. As he looked around, his lip curled in disgust. "This place is a hole."

"Thanks, that's what I was going for."

He backhanded me and I staggered, pain piercing my jaw.

"Enough of your insolence. Where is it?"

I touched my cheek gingerly. Clearly we were done with the pleasantries. Before I could answer, a horrific screeching interrupted me. Booger was outside the window mewling at the top of his lungs and scratching to get in.

"What the hell is that?"

"My cat. If I don't let him in, the neighbors will call the cops on me again."

"Fine, let him in."

I opened the window and he leapt through it. With his tail high in the air, he walked into the center of the room and stared at me. I wasn't exactly sure what he was going to do in his cat form, but for some reason a sense of calm came over me. Then he opened his mouth and caterwauled again.

"Either shut him up or I will wring his neck."

"Stanley, stop it right now! Stanley, go into the bedroom. Go on now."

Booger stopped screaming and ran out of the room. I stared at his retreating form, hoping he remembered what Stanley was, and that it was strapped behind my headboard.

"I'm done playing games now. Where is the key?"

I walked away from the bedroom, hoping to distract the vamp from Booger/Matthew. I opened the trunk to dig around in it. I only had a few seconds to figure out something before he got suspicious.

I peered up in time to see Matthew slink down the hallway, naked as a jaybird. He aimed and shot the guard twice in the heart. The vamp went down on his knees. Matthew walked over and shot him again. The vamp fell face-first onto the floor.

I gripped the sides of the trunk and pushed myself up on shaky legs. "Thank you."

Matthew nodded. "No problem. You better get going before he starts healing."

"Cover him while I find his keys." I reached down and pulled them out of his pocket. Luckily he didn't move. I stood up. "Are you going to be okay here?"

"Yeah. Here, take Stanley. I have backup on the way. I'm good."

"I owe you one."

He smiled. "I'll remember that."

I ran to the car and took off, calling Jean Luc.

"Kyle, where are you?"

"I'm driving back from my apartment to Dalton's house. Sebastian's holding him hostage there."

"I am at Dalton's house now. No one is here."

"That doesn't make any sense. Why did he leave? I was supposed to come back with the key."

"Maybe he sensed something went wrong," Jean Luc added.

Damn. "Would he sense if one of his guards had been shot?"

"Yes, there would be a strong enough link for him to feel something."

"Where would he take Dalton?" I asked.

"I am not sure. Come back to the safe house so we can figure out what to do next."

I took a deep breath, unable to speak for a second.

"Kyle, if he had wanted Dalton dead, he would have killed him at the house. He is using him as a bargaining chip."

"I know." But it didn't make me feel better.

I stopped pacing long enough to glare at Misha. "What's taking so long?"

Misha glanced up from the computer screen. "Sebastian owns multiple properties, little one. I'm sorting through them to see where he might take Dalton."

I turned to Jean Luc. "Have you reached Doc?"

"Yes, she is available when we need her. She is doing research on the straends right now so that she can treat Dalton when we find him."

"Why hasn't Sebastian contacted me? He knows Dalton doesn't have the key."

Jean Luc stood up and put his arm around me. "He is regrouping. Dalton's house was not his territory, and when he felt something go wrong with the guard, he ran for safer ground."

"What is it with vamps and marking territory?"

Before Jean Luc could answer, my phone rang. I yanked it out of my pocket. It was an unlisted number. "Hello."

"I warned you not to play me for a fool," Sebastian hissed.

"I didn't play you, your guard did."

"What are you talking about?"

"Your guard double-crossed you. When he saw the key, he tried to kill me. Unless you ordered him to do that, I'm pretty sure he was planning to make a run for it."

"You lie. He would not have the ability to betray me, I am his sire."

"Who knows what possessing the key might do? Maybe he thought it would break your hold over him." I waited, holding my breath to see if he bought it.

"How did you get away from him?"

"I had a gun hidden in my apartment and I shot him."

"I think you are playing me yet again."

I scrambled quickly for the next words. "Has your guard called you yet or come back to you?" Silence. So I pushed the envelope a little more. "I think your puppy has run off so he doesn't have to face your wrath."

He ignored my dig. "You have the key?"

I stared at the box with the strange markings sitting on the table. "Yes."

"Bring it to the following address. And if I see Jean Luc or Misha, I will kill Dalton immediately."

I scribbled down the address. "I already told you, they're not involved in this."

"Good. And I would hurry, Kyle. Your lieutenant is not doing very well."

CHAPTER 41

I drove up to yet another warehouse, and, ignoring my internal warning bells, parked smack dab in front of it. Knowing Sebastian, there were probably cameras recording my arrival. Taking a deep breath, I rehearsed what I was going to say while I climbed out of the car. I stopped myself from checking on Stanley, tucked safely into my waistband, and prayed the unbuttoned shirt I was wearing over my tank covered the gun. Grabbing the key box, I ran to the door. It was unlocked. I rushed inside.

There were a few large cardboard boxes stacked in the corner, but otherwise it was pretty barren. Vamps must just be square footage junkies. I took a few steps into the warehouse.

Sebastian's disjointed voice echoed toward me. "Why are you scared?"

I gulped. "I think Jean Luc is after me."

"I told you not to bring him here," he hissed.

"I didn't bring him here, he's following me!"

"Why?"

"I called him earlier and told him I wouldn't be at work. I think he's suspicious, since Dalton opened the box yesterday. I don't want to be anywhere near him right now. If he knew I had the key, he would compel me to give it to him."

"Let me see the key."

I held the box up in front of me.

"Open it so I can see the inside."

I pulled open the box and showed him both pieces, as well as the key I had placed inside. I shut the box again with a resounding click.

"Show me Dalton," I demanded.

Sebastian walked from behind the boxes, holding Dalton by the arm. He was in a stupor. I locked my knees to stop myself from running toward him. He was pale and bleeding, and the straend was still in his neck.

"Give me the key."

I started toward them when Sebastian tensed, looking around quickly. "There's a vampire close by."

"Damn. Here, take the key and give me Dalton. We need to get out of here."

The air moved around us and Jean Luc appeared. He seized my arms and shook me hard. "You dare betray me!"

"No, no...I would never betray you."

"Why are you here, then?" he growled.

"Sebastian kidnapped Dalton, I was trying to get him back for you. I know he's your favorite."

Jean Luc sniffed me and scoffed. "You stink of lies."

Sebastian chuckled maniacally. "I told you centuries ago not to trust humans. They are greedy bugs. This little ant was bringing me the key."

Jean Luc yanked the box from my hand and slapped me. I fell to the ground. The action brought Dalton out of his stupor and he growled, wrenching his arm away from Sebastian. He took a menacing step toward Jean Luc.

"Do not even think about it." Jean Luc's tone was one of an irritated father speaking to a petulant child.

I stood up and grabbed Dalton's arm. He trembled slightly, and I longed to gather him in my arms and tell him everything would be all right. He leaned against me heavily as we slowly backed toward the door.

Jean Luc opened the box and fished out the key. "This is what all the fuss is about?"

Sebastian nodded. "Yes, we can rule the world with it."

"How does it work?"

"I don't know the specifics. Father Cowell shared his translations with Hampton. This key is called *custos arcanorum*." At the sound of the name, Dalton flinched and then stopped his retreat. I pulled hard on his arms, but he refused to move toward the door.

My heart pounded even louder in my chest as I eased Stanley out of my waistband. But Sebastian didn't seem to notice and kept blathering on. "If we, rather than the angels, are in possession of the key, the balance tips in our favor. Those smug bastards won't be able to stop us. So what do you think, Jean Luc? We can rule together."

Jean Luc grinned and wrapped his fingers around the key, forming a fist. When he reopened his hand, the key was bent in half.

Sebastian backed away. "What have you done?"

"You will never have the key," Jean Luc declared.

Sebastian scowled and flashed. A split-second later, Jean Luc flashed as well. The air whooshed around me and Dalton, the sounds of grunts and fists pounding flesh echoing through the empty space. Jean Luc reappeared first, with blood running from his mouth. Sebastian came into view next, across the room. He surged toward me and I fired Stanley, hitting him twice in the chest. He barely flinched, flashing again.

At the sound of gunshots, Jason rushed in from the back door and raced across the warehouse. In the next instant Sebastian stood in front of Jason and threw him across the room like he weighed nothing. I gasped, waiting for Jason to slam into the concrete. Instead, he stopped mid-flight. Misha stood at the back of the warehouse, arms in the air. He lowered Jason to the ground with his telekinesis.

Sebastian's eyes widened in surprise, but quickly recovered. "Did you honestly think bullets can stop me?"

Jason shook his head. "Those aren't normal bullets, asshole. You should be feeling the sting shortly."

Sebastian's cocky veneer slipped. Gazing down at his shirt, he seemed puzzled to see that blood continued to flow from his bullet wounds. Misha reached behind his head and pulled a sword from a sheath tied to his back. I gaped at him. I was in a *Highlander* episode.

I reached for Dalton, making another futile effort to pull him out of the way. I heard a warning yell, and then a rush of motion surrounded me. Sebastian wrenched me from Dalton's side and Stanley slipped from my hands and clattered on the ground. He carried me on a wave of speed toward the back of the warehouse. He kicked open the door, and we emerged on a concrete landing overlooking a loading dock. Slamming the door shut, he bent the handle down with his bare hands to jam the door.

I tried to stop my head and stomach from spinning. Sebastian's fingers tightened on my left arm. His fingernails lengthened and I screamed when they punctured my skin. While he hauled me down the stairs, Misha and Jason ran around the back of the building toward us. Jason was carrying Stanley, but Misha's sword was gone.

The back bay door went up and Dalton stood in the opening. He was mumbling something to himself as he stared down at Sebastian. Surrounded, Sebastian's last vestige of humanity left him and he became a beast, fangs extending as his face distorted into a feral caricature of its normal self.

Dalton spoke calmly. "Let her go. Take me instead."

"Why would I want you?" Sebastian scoffed.

"Because I know where the key is."

"Dalton, no!" I yelled.

"Where is it?"

"I am the key." And then he started speaking what sounded like Latin. Sebastian released me and flashed for a second before reappearing and stumbling a step. Were the bullets getting to him? But then he leapt onto the truck dock, and lunged for Dalton. Jean Luc appeared, brandishing the missing sword.

Jean Luc swung the blade so fast I barely registered the motion. Sebastian still had a look of wide-eyed surprise on his face as his head tipped forward and fell to the concrete, rolling off the dock onto the ground below with a resounding thud.

I gazed up in astonishment at Dalton, who smiled at me just before he clutched his head in agony and collapsed.

CHAPTER 42

"What aren't you telling me?" I glared at Doc, Jean Luc and Misha as we stood in the hallway outside of Dalton's room.

Doc hesitated as if choosing the right words. "Even though I was able to remove the straend, his neural pathways are damaged."

"Damaged how?"

"Every time he thinks about what happened, he relives the pain. It is similar to the phantom pain patients experience when they lose a limb."

I stared at the three somber faces in front of me. "So, how do we make it better?"

"I don't know if we can make it better," Doc said.

I shook my head. "Bull. There has to be something we can do. Misha, contact Boris and have him ask the elders what to do."

"The Full Council has been called. Demon, vampire and shifter council leaders are on their way here right now to discuss what happened and what can be done for Joe."

"Well then, by all means let's go greet them."

Jean Luc grabbed my arm. "Kyle, you need to calm down and let the councils meet first."

Soothing warmth flowed up my arm into my shoulder. I glared at him. "Stop trying to compel me, Jean Luc."

He dropped his hand from my arm. "I was not doing it purposely. I am worried about you."

I closed my eyes for a moment and took a deep breath. "I know. I promise to behave. I won't do anything to keep the councils from helping Dalton. But I can't just sit around here and wait. I have to do something."

Jean Luc nodded. "Misha and I will go with you. We can watch the arrivals from the back dock area."

We stood to the side watching as the various supes entered the warehouse. Between the actual leaders and their guards, a large gathering was expected, and I didn't recognize a lot of them. Misha's father arrived with his two guards and acknowledged us briefly before he walked into the throng.

Minutes later, shifter guards brought in a vamp in chains. It was the one Matthew had shot in my apartment. Griffin walked in behind them. Instead of joining the council members, he came over to us.

His eyes rested on my bandaged arm where Sebastian had clawed me. "Are you okay?"

"I'm fine."

"Can we speak alone for a moment?"

I glanced at Jean Luc and Misha and they walked away without a protest.

Griffin began. "Matthew told me what happened at your apartment."

"I owe him my life. Please thank him again for helping me."

"The vampire has not said much to us, but I don't believe he will be so closemouthed with the vampire council leaders."

I grimaced. "The vamps need to save face after what Sebastian did. This meeting should be interesting."

Griffin leaned closer to me and spoke in a hushed tone. "I asked Matthew if he had any idea who hired him to protect you, and he said he doesn't know. I believe him."

"Thank you for trying."

"I'm sorry I could not be more help. Matthew did say he has been protecting you for months. Whoever is watching over you believes you have been in danger for some time now."

In danger from what? I wanted to ask, but kept it to myself. Had they known Sebastian would be coming after me? Was it something else entirely? I stopped myself from dwelling on it for too long. I didn't need to add paranoid delusions to my list of neuroses.

Griffin interrupted my thoughts. "I'm sorry about your lieutenant. If there is anything I can do, please let me know."

I nodded, throat tightening. "Just please think of something to help him. Someone on the council should know a way to reverse the effects of a straend."

Before Griffin could answer, Nicholas joined us. Griffin's demeanor changed almost immediately, and he slipped on his leader hat and greeted Nicholas formally. I ignored the posturing. Every muscle in my body tensed when Josiah Akers sauntered into the room. He smirked at me as he walked over to the cluster of demon leaders.

"Why is he here?" I hissed when what I wanted to do was scream.

Nicholas answered. "He is the leader of the Pavels and one of the Council of Twelve." Before I could protest, he continued. "We have no proof he was involved in this, Kyle. We don't know who in his clan was at the bar with Hampton, and we probably never will."

"I know he was part of this."

"I can't stand up in front of the Full Council and tell them he should be punished because of a hunch you have. If you will excuse us, I believe everyone is here and we can begin the meeting."

Ninety minutes later I was still pacing the hallway outside Dalton's room. Misha, in turn, was hovering over me. I stopped when Jean Luc came toward us.

"Misha, they want to speak with you next."

"What the hell is happening in there?" I demanded as I watched Misha walk down the hall.

"There is a lot of evidence to be reviewed." Jean Luc tried to reason with me. "Sebastian's fledglings have not said anything helpful. They have stated Sebastian was in charge and, as their sire, was able to force them to do his bidding."

"That's convenient. What about Akers?"

"Akers testified he did not know what was going on. He is conducting an internal investigation to see *if* a Pavel was involved."

"If! The smug bastard."

"We have little evidence to support the Pavel story. Byron is dead, and the only others who can corroborate the story are a vagrant human and a demon who live in a back alley. Do you really want to bring them in to testify before this Council?"

I started pacing again. "What about the Majock demon we saw in the security feed?"

"Which is why Misha is with them now. They want to see the footage."

"Have they said anything about Dalton? What can we do to help him?"

Jean Luc shook his head. "They did not talk about it while I was in the session."

Fifteen minutes later, Misha walked back down the hall-way.

"Well?" I blurted.

"They had me go through all of the case notes with them."

"And?"

"And then they excused me and said they would be out shortly."

"They don't want to hear my side of the story?"

Misha shrugged. "I don't think so."

Before I could launch a verbal response to the ridicu-lousness of them not wanting to speak to me, steps echoed behind us and I whipped around. Nicholas stepped up to me and placed his hands on my shoulders. I shrugged out of his paternalistic grip.

"How can we help Dalton?"

"Let's talk alone, Kyle."

Before I could argue, Misha and Jean Luc disappeared into the morgue, leaving us alone in the hallway.

"What did the Council come up with to help Dalton?"

"Straends were not designed with humans in mind. They were made to interrogate demons, whose neural pathways are much more resilient. Joe had the straend attached for hours, and Doc was lucky she was able to remove it at all."

I was having trouble absorbing what he was saying. "An-swer my question, damn it!"

"The only possibility we could come up with to help Joe is in your hands."

"What do you mean?"

"His only hope is if his memories can be erased. That should allow his pathways to repair themselves."

Relief surged through me. "Fine, I'll go scrub his memories of Sebastian's torture right now."

"It would not be enough. It isn't just the memories of the torture that are causing the damage. The pain is also attached to particular questions Sebastian asked Joe. Any questions he asked and the memories associated with them would cause him pain."

I took a shaky breath. Sebastian had asked him about me.

"You need to erase his memories of this case entirely. He cannot remember anything about us."

"No! There has to be another way."

Nicholas shook his head. "I'm sorry, but there is not."

I backed up and glared at him. "Is it really the only solution, or is this the Council's way of protecting themselves from Dalton? The fact that he's the key might put a crimp in supernatural activities, right?"

Nicholas snagged my arm and dragged me into an empty room, shutting the door. "The Council has not been told of Dalton's possible merger with the key."

"What? Why didn't you tell them?"

"Because if I had, he would be in danger for the rest of his life."

I started to protest, but Nicholas plowed over my objections. "Think about it. Look how many dead bodies Hampton and Sebastian left behind on their quest for the key. We know Pavels are involved. If the community were to find out Joe might have this key inside him, what do you think they would do then? At the very least, they would try to control him, or they might try to remove it by force."

"This is insane."

"It's the world we live in. Joe needs to stay out of our world. He can't afford to have any suspicion attached to him. And the best way to accomplish that is to make him forget. If there was any other way to guarantee both his recovery and his safety, I would recommend that instead."

I glared at him. "I don't trust you."

"Let me lay it out for you in simple terms." He lifted his hand, ticking off points on his fingers. "By erasing Joe's memories of the events you will, one, hopefully reverse the effects of the straends and save his life. Two, stop others in the community from coming after him. And three, give us more time to figure out what this key is all about." He took a deep breath. "I'm also trying to protect you, Kyle. It's what I have been doing all along."

And like that the light bulb went on. "It's you. Matthew worked for you."

He smirked half-heartedly. "You always have been a smart one."

"Why did you do it?

He looked at me incredulously. "You have to ask, after what's happened over the last few weeks?"

"But Matthew has been protecting me for *months*. How did you know this was going to happen?"

His face shut down. "I had been warned you were in danger."

"By who? Some fortune teller?"

"I can't tell you."

"Bullshit."

"I'm not the enemy here. In your heart you know what I'm telling you is correct. You have to let him go, Kyle."

"Screw you." I jerked open the door and ran into Dalton's room. Doc was leaning over him checking his IV. He opened his eyes and they brightened when he caught sight of me. But a moment later he grimaced and writhed on the bed. Doc yelled and Jean Luc appeared in a heartbeat, holding him down while Doc gave him a sedative. I backed out of the room and stumbled down the hallway.

CHAPTER 43

The heart rate monitor traveled in a slow and steady rhythm across the screen. Pain pulsed through me in much the same pattern, and the longer I stayed in the room, the more erratic my breathing became. I had been sitting in this dark room watching Dalton sleep for several hours now, and I couldn't put it off any longer.

He had been mine for only a moment in time. Now I had to make the decision to save him. For a second a small part of me toyed again with the idea of erasing only his memories of the torture and running with him. But it was a fleeting thought. Where would we go? Would Dalton want to leave everything behind just to be with me? It was not my place to make the decision for him.

I would have given anything to see those turquoise eyes one more time, but I couldn't bear to cause him any more pain.

The group had devised a plan. Dalton would be the hero who stopped a serial killer from killing again. Jean Luc and Misha were handling the details. I had my own part to play.

I leaned forward in the chair and removed the memories, unraveling them all piece by piece. I blocked out chunks of time or replaced them with memories of Dalton working on the serial killer case by himself, sitting behind his computer and trying to piece together the clues I planted in his head.

I took away the pain of his torture, and replaced it with resolve to bring the killer to justice. The doctors would say his loss of memory was due to the trauma he suffered at the killer's hands before Dalton was able to escape and kill him instead. As the last memory transferred to his brain, I savored our mental connection, caressing his thought patterns before I reluctantly severed our connection.

"Goodbye, Galahad," I whispered.

I stared at him for a moment, memorizing his face, his body, his smell, and then I turned away.

I walked out into the empty hallway. He would be safe now. That was all that mattered. I rushed through the storage area and out the rear door, running to my car.

As I started my car, I caught sight of myself in the rearview mirror. Blood streamed from my nose. I sopped it up with napkins I found in my glove compartment and jammed the car into reverse. I would not cry.

My phone rang while I was driving home. It was Nicholas. I pushed the button on my sync.

"What."

"Has it been taken care of?"

"Yes."

"What about Captain Morrison's memories of the case?"

"I scrubbed him hours ago. He doesn't remember sending Dalton to work with us. He thinks he assigned Dalton to work on the serial killer case."

"Are you okay?"

"You don't get to ask me that."

I hung up.

Once in my apartment, I stripped and threw myself into the shower. Standing under the pounding spray, I tried to wash away my own memories, but there was no relief. After the hot water ran out, I dressed in my terry cloth robe and stood staring at my reflection in the mirror. Roses perfumed the air.

"He'll be okay now," I whispered and closed my eyes. A delicate hand rested on my cheek for a moment. The doorbell rang and I opened my eyes as Dalton's grandmother faded away with the steam in the bathroom.

I walked out to the living room and peeked through the peephole. Tony stood on the other side. Opening the door, I shook my head and backed away from it.

"I'm not hungry, Tony."

"I know, dear. Food will not make this better." And he held his arms out to me, wrapping me in his embrace.

My throat tightened and the tears began—endless, wracking sobs. Standing in the doorway in my bathrobe, holding on for dear life to the restaurant guy from down the street, I sobbed until my chest hurt and I had no moisture left in my body.

When I finally stopped crying, he settled me on the couch, covering me with a blanket. Sitting down in the chair next to me, he sang Italian lullabies until I fell asleep.

CHAPTER 44

I finally got up from the couch the following day at dawn. I had two things on my list for the day. First I called Father Brown. I wasn't surprised he was an early riser, and he agreed to meet me in the chapel on campus. I arrived at the JCU campus early, hoping to avoid the summer students.

He was kneeling in prayer when I arrived, so I bowed my head and waited for him to finish. He stood and motioned me to join him in the front row. I sat down next to him and handed him Father Cowell's letters.

"My name is Kyle McKinley."

"I saw the newspaper this morning. Lieutenant Dalton is a hero."

"Yes he is."

"Are you here to tell me the truth, Kyle?"

I clasped my hands and started at the beginning. He said very little, letting me weave the story as I saw fit. When I finished, I waited for him to tell me I need therapy. But he didn't.

"I'm sorry to think David must have felt I had abandoned him in the end."

"You have to admit, the whole thing does sound insane."

"Is David's killer really dead?"

"Yes."

He stared at me for a moment. "What has changed to make you trust me now to keep your secret?"

I took a deep breath. No more lying. "I promised I would tell you the truth. But I can't let you remember it. For your own safety, I'm going to make you forget what happened. You will not remember me, you'll only remember meeting with Dalton about the serial killer case."

"Before you erase my memory, I have another part of the translation for you. The first few sentences in the second stanza."

"What is it?"

He pulled a paper out of his pocket and unfolded it, reading the newest excerpt aloud.

"'*The war will be long*
And fraught with treachery
The path will be riddled with fallen
And the key will change hands'"

He refolded the paper and handed it to me, clasping my hands. "I'm sorry you feel you have to go through this alone."

I nodded and smiled, tears blurring my vision. I concentrated and created new memories that I pushed toward him. The warmth cascaded over my senses and my energy flowed silkily around his brain waves.

After a couple of minutes I stood and he touched my wrist to stop me. "I thought you were going to erase my memories?"

I stared at him in disbelief and plunked back down in the seat. After two more tries, I realized it was useless. I couldn't make him forget. I had only encountered a couple of humans over the years whose memories I couldn't change, and apparently the Fates had decided Father Brown would be another. *Crap.* Maybe the angels were messing with me. I told him what his story needed to be and he promised to follow it to the letter.

He also promised to continue to work on the translation for me. But we could not be seen together in public, since he was not supposed to remember me. He pushed a small volume into my hand.

"Take this, you may find it of some comfort. God has given you your gift for a reason, Kyle, don't forget that."

He left me alone in the chapel, and I sat for a while. I wasn't sure what I should do with my life. I hadn't decided yet if I could ever work for Nicholas again.

I ran my thumb over the textured cover of the small book I still clutched in my hand, then opened the cover and paged through what turned out to be the Psalms. I continued to flip the pages until I came to an excerpt in Latin. I stared at it for a moment and the words changed before my eyes.

I could read them.

I dropped the book on the chair with a hard smack which echoed through the chapel. How could I understand Latin? I vacillated between running like a scared rabbit and picking up the book again. Maybe I was hallucinating? I opened the book again before I could chicken out, flipping through some more pages. I found a Latin verse and stared at it like it was a Rorschach test. After a couple of seconds, I breathed a sigh of relief. I could not read the passage. My imagination must have been in overdrive.

I took one more tentative look at the page and gasped when the words shifted to English so I could read them. And it hit me like a bulldozer. Dalton had been spouting Latin at the time Sebastian was beheaded. Had I absorbed his memories the way I had Trina's? But if I'd just absorbed his memories, why could I read the passage in front of me?

Knowledge. If Dalton was the key of knowledge, had I absorbed the same knowledge? Was I the new keeper that Father Brown's translation referred to? I shook my head. No jumping to conclusions. This would have to wait. I had another promise to keep today. I stuffed the book into my bag and walked out onto the quad, dodging the students who were just beginning their days.

Two hours later, after a trip to the drug store and a ruined T-shirt speckled with dye, my jet-black hair was no more. I stood on the Connors' front porch ringing the bell. Stephanie opened the door, her eyes widening before she smiled.

"Hello, Kyle."

"Stephanie. Is Trina home?"

"She's in the back yard in the tree house. She'll be excited to see the new you."

I opened the back door and walked across the yard. Unlike the last time, gangly legs were not dangling down from the tree house ledge, so I hollered up to her.

"Trina, it's Kyle. Can I come up?"

"Yeah."

I climbed up the ladder and Trina came out the door and dove into my arms.

"You did it. Purple. It's awesome!"

I smiled at her, running a hand through my hair. "Thanks. I wanted to show you first."

"It looks like Purple Passion."

I held up my hands and waved my ratty fingernails. "My nails could use a touch-up. Are you game?"

"Sure. Let's go into the house."

"Before we go, I found something of yours in the yard." I pulled the heart bracelet out of my pocket and handed it to her. "Here."

Her eyes widened and I held my breath praying I had made the right decision. "Wow! Thanks, I didn't know where I had lost it. I can't wait to tell Mom. Come on, let's go in the house. Are you hungry?"

And I found I was hungry, for the first time in two days. "Do you think your mom can make some of her famous cinnamon toast?"

CHAPTER 45

It was exactly eleven days, five hours and twenty-three minutes since I had erased Dalton's memory. And in the next thirty seconds, I was going to bludgeon an annoying customer to death with a menu. Not the lunch menu, which was too flimsy to cause any real damage, but the dinner menu, which had enough heft to achieve my goal.

Every August, Little Italy celebrated the Feast of the Assumption. Throngs of people invaded the small neighborhood, eating, shopping and generally celebrating the end of summer.

Normally, I avoided the Feast like the mall on Black Friday. Too hot, too many people, too much aggravation. But this year it beat being alone, something I had grown anxious to avoid.

It didn't help that I had taken a leave of absence from work. Actually, I had quit, but Nicholas had insisted it was a leave and I had insisted he could go to hell. We were at a bit of an impasse. So I had volunteered to help Tony at his restaurant for the week. It was the least I could do for him. Although why he thought I could be hostess material was beyond me.

"How much longer are we going to have to wait?" a voice whined.

I looked up into the face of a tall man whose lips were pressed into a thin line. The petite woman next to him wore a short dress designed for a woman half her age. Tony *so* owed me for this.

When I didn't answer him, he spoke in a louder voice. "Why is this taking so long?"

I took a deep breath, counting to ten in my head. "Sir, there are thousands of people in town today for the Feast, so nothing is going to move quickly."

The woman with him had the nerve to roll her eyes at me. I looked beneath the podium for my weapon. The dinner menus were made out of a heavy cardboard and covered in a thick vinyl which was sure to sting. Perfect.

Just in time, Tony came bustling up to the hostess stand carrying a tray of meatballs and sporting a huge grin. "Thank you all for your patience. While you wait, I thought you might like to try some appetizers."

Tony then relieved me of my hostess duties, and tucked me away in the corner making cappuccinos. It was the best place for me. I didn't have to deal directly with customers and it allowed me to work with my first love—java.

Tony walked up and I held up the iced cappuccino he had requested. "What table gets this one?"

"It's for you. Take a break." He motioned to a small table. "You've earned a couple minutes off your feet."

I looked up into Tony's sweaty, red face. "I'll take a break if you do."

He dismissed my comment with a wave of his hand. "Everything's good." But he sat down next to me anyway. "How are you doing?"

"Fine," I answered automatically.

"Right," he answered, but since he was reading my emotions, we both knew I was lying. He stared hard at me for a second. "Well, I'm on the lookout for you."

Little alarm bells sounded in my head. "What do you mean?"

"I've decided to expand my horizons. Besides matching people with their favorite foods, I'm going to do a little actual people-matching on the side."

I shook my head a bit too emphatically. "No, thanks. Besides, I can't imagine there are too many people out there who would take to my 'forceful' personality."

"Oh, you'll be a challenge, for sure. But I'm tenacious." He stood and pushed in the chair. "I've already got some ideas."

Before I could protest some more, he ambled away. Good Lord, that's all I needed. Knowing Tony, he would have men serenading me outside my apartment window. The neighborhood already thought me strange; this would tip it over the top.

Plus, I definitely was not ready. No jumping right back up on the horse for me. I was just fine with brooding. I was an expert at it, as a matter of fact. I took a large swallow of the coffee and turned to watch as the crowd outside surged and ebbed along the sidewalk.

After a couple of minutes, I stared down at the dregs of iced cappuccino puddled in the bottom of my glass and closed my eyes. I had not been sleeping well. My dreams were peppered with Dalton's memories. Fearful I would relive his suffering at the hands of Sebastian, I fought REM sleep at every opportunity.

"Where have you been all my life?" a voice asked softly.

I was going to kill Tony. He had to have set a land speed record setting me up with someone. "Are you kidding...?" I lost my power of speech when I looked up into a set of luminous turquoise eyes. Only one person had those eyes. My stomach twisted. I had to be imagining him. I blinked back the moisture threatening to erupt as he sat down across from me.

It was official. I had lost it. Now I had graduated to having visions of Dalton when I was awake.

He leaned in close. "Did you think erasing my memory would get rid of me so easily?"

"You're not real." I pushed the chair back and stood. He reached his hand out and I sucked in a breath when his warm, callused fingers circled my wrist.

"It's me, Kyle. I'm real."

"I don't understand," I mumbled, sinking back down. "How..."

"I've been having nightmares for days now, images of people and events which didn't make any sense. When I would wake up, my head felt like it was going to split open. The doctors chalked it up to the trauma. But I couldn't let it go, not after I saw you in my dreams. I couldn't let *you* go."

I took a deep breath. "What about the pain?"

He grinned. "My grandmother started talking to me in my dreams. I thought I was really losing it then. When I finally spoke back to her, she asked me what I wanted, and I told her I had to know the truth about you. She must have called in her marker with the angels, because the next thing I knew, I had a divine visitor who helped me fill in what happened and the pain simply went away."

I gaped at him. "Those damn angels are getting pretty loose with the whole not interfering thing."

"Are you really going to complain?"

"Hell, no."

"Can I get your friend something to eat?" Tony asked as he walked up to the table.

"You can see him?" I muttered.

Tony stared at me for a second before grinning. "Yes, dear, I can. Let me get you both some tiramisu. On the house." He walked away.

Dalton chuckled. "I'm holding your hand and you still thought I was a figment of your imagination?"

"It's been a long couple of weeks."

The humor left his face. "For me, too. I'm sorry."

"For what?"

"For putting you in that position. I know the last thing you wanted to do was mind sweep me."

"I did it to save your life." My heart picked up speed and I tried to pull my hand from his grip. "Wait! You can't be seen with me. What if the supernatural community comes after you again?"

"I'm not afraid, Kyle."

"You almost died. You need to forget about me."

He shook his head. "Already happened once, and it won't be happening again if I have anything to say about it."

My head was spinning. There were a dozen reasons why he needed to walk away and not look back, but now that I stared into his eyes, I couldn't bear the thought of losing him again. I opened my mouth and he placed his fingers over my lips to silence me.

"Listen to me. There's a reason why I have my memories back. We have to figure out what the key is all about and where it is now. It's not in me anymore."

I nodded, and when he moved his hand away from my mouth, I spoke in a whisper. "We need to talk about the key."

"Let's make a deal. We talk about saving the world tomorrow. Tonight, I simply want to be alone with you. Just the two of us. Do we have a deal?"

I smiled. "Yep. But I have to finish my shift here."

"No you don't." Tony held up a bag. "I packed your dessert to go. You're fired."

I laughed as Dalton took the bag and pulled me up from my seat.

"You, sir, are a prince among men," I called over my shoulder to Tony as we headed toward the door.

We snaked our way through the crowd, Dalton holding tight to my hand as we crossed the street to my apartment building. I unlocked the door and we stepped into the cool lobby.

Dalton handed me the dessert. "Hang on to this."

"What..." Before I could get my question out, Dalton lifted me and carried me up the stairs.

"Dalton, put me down!"

"Not on your life." Once inside my apartment, he refused to set me down until we reached my bedroom. His eyes took on that predatory glint I recognized all too well. I backed away from him.

"I almost didn't recognize you with your new hair color. What do you call it?"

"Purple Passion."

He cocked his head and stared at me for a moment. My skin tingled under his scrutiny. "The name fits," he responded.

I smiled and stood on tiptoe to kiss him soundly. He growled and pulled me up against him. "Soooo...do you want to eat dessert before or after?" he asked in a low voice.

I backed away again and held the bag up, dangling it in front of him. Turning, I glanced over my shoulder.

"During."

His eyes darkened and he made a grab for me. I laughed and ran to the other side of my bed.

It didn't take him long to catch me.

Thanks!

Thank you for taking the time to read *Mind Sweeper*. The next book in this series is *The Fledgling*. Some of you may have thought I was being a bit of a tease when Kyle asked Jean Luc if he had ever been in love and he simply answered, "Her name was Talia." Well... there was a method to my madness. Jean Luc and Talia's story unfolds in the next book, a story about how they first met and fell in love while hunting down a supernatural serial killer. *Shifter Wars* continues Kyle's story.

I hope you enjoyed the first book in the Mind Sweeper Series. Please consider telling your friends about it or posting a short review. Word of mouth is an author's best friend, and much appreciated. Thank you! – AE

If you would like to know when my next books will be released, please join my newsletter at aejonesauthor.com

Please turn the page to find a list of my other books and to learn more about *The Fledgling*.

EXCERPT: THE FLEDGING

Sometime in the mid 1980's

The smell of blood no longer excited him. Whether that was a good thing was debatable. However, in this particular instance it worked to his advantage. The stale, tinny odor engulfing the room had already sent several men out the door to lose their most recent meal.

"Jean Luc?"

Mon Dieu. He turned toward the voice and stifled a groan. Three hundred and seventy-five year old vampires did not groan in the face of overzealous human females. And one such female sashayed toward him.

Well, sashayed was perhaps an overstatement, since she wore paper slippers over her shoes and studiously tried to avoid the human detritus littering the floor. The extraordinarily large shoulder pads in her suit made her look like a small child playing dress-up in her father's clothes.

"It *is* you! Hi, how have you been?"

"Good evening, Muriel."

She smiled and her eyes assessed him quickly, the way a shifter would peruse a fresh piece of meat. "You still look the same. I'm trying to remember the last time I saw you..."

Was she really flirting with him, here? Jean Luc took a calming breath. "We met over the previous dead body."

Muriel giggled. "Of course. Well...I guess I should get to work, then." She snapped on her rubber gloves and squatted down next to the corpse.

And within a matter of seconds, the flirtatious woman disappeared, replaced by a focused, professional Medical Examiner who barked orders. "Harper, did you get pictures on both sides of the body?"

When no one responded, Muriel's head jerked up in irritation. "Harper!"

"Is he the redheaded technician with the camera?"

"Yes."

Jean Luc nodded toward the door, and the muted sounds of retching. "He is a bit indisposed."

Muriel sighed, "He's new. I hope he sticks around longer than the last tech. They all think this job is going to be like that TV show, *Quincy*." She stood and scanned the room, homing in on an older officer. "Simmons, would you go get the camera from Harper and make sure all angles are captured."

When Simmons returned, she stepped out of his way and motioned for Jean Luc to follow her into the garage.

Peeling off her gloves, she said, "I thought I had seen it all before, but this? His throat was ripped out. If I didn't know better, I'd say he was attacked by a bear or a wolf."

"Indeed."

"Except we're in a split-level in the Indianapolis suburbs."

Jean Luc shrugged. "There is that."

"Come on, Jean Luc, the department didn't just hire you for your pretty face. Give me *something* to work with."

The department had not actually hired him at all, but the misconception helped him with his real job. The police commissioner contacted the Bureau of Supernatural Relations whenever something "irregular" occurred, so Jean Luc could help cover it up. But there would be no concealing this type of death. The killer might as well have posted it on a billboard. And claw marks did not narrow the field of potential supernatural killers. It could mean vampire, demon, or shifter.

He paused for a moment, debating how much to say. Unfortunately, he had seen this type of kill before. "The viciousness of these murders is increasing. He either knew the victim or is beginning to enjoy the savagery of the act."

Muriel nodded. "I see no evidence of hesitation this time."

He opened his mouth to respond, but something light as a gossamer thread brushed his consciousness, and he looked out the open garage door, casing the yard. Several uniformed police officers stood outside, but none were paying attention to his discussion with Muriel.

A supernatural was nearby.

"Jean Luc?"

He turned back to the Medical Examiner. "What do we know about the victim, Muriel?"

"Not too much yet. But they should have found out something by now. Charlie!"

After a few seconds, a heavyset man in a worn corduroy suit lumbered into the garage. "You bellowed, Muriel?"

She chuckled. "You're the only one who isn't scared of me. Why is that?"

"Unlike some of these cave men, I think you actually know what you're doing, even if you don't have a penis."

Muriel grinned. "You always say the nicest things. What have you got for us on the vic?"

Charlie pulled out a small notebook and flipped it open. "Guy's name is Peter Peters."

Muriel rolled her eyes. "Cut the crap, Charlie."

His mouth quirked up a bit. "Honest, I'm not making it up. His parents need to be smacked upside the head a couple times. According to the neighbors, he's been living here for two years. He was, and I quote 'quiet and kept to himself.' Why am I not surprised?"

"Do we know if he had any recent altercations?" Jean Luc asked.

"Nada. I've radioed into the station, and they're checking the files, but nothing came up so far. No domestics. The neighbors don't remember seeing any steady girlfriends, either."

"Did he have a steady job?"

Charlie turned the page of his notebook. "That's where it gets interesting. He was an *accountant* for Manny Edwards."

Muriel frowned slightly. "You don't think it's legit?"

"Oh, he probably did work with numbers, but I'm pretty sure it wasn't on the up-and-up. We've never been able to catch him, but I'd bet my shield Manny's restaurant is a front for a bookie joint."

Manny was also a shifter who dealt with many of the supernaturals in the city, but they did not need to know that.

"We've tried to place several cops under cover in his operation, but no one has ever lasted for long."

Which was no surprise. Shifters were incredibly skillful at sniffing out emotions, walking supernatural versions of a lie-detector. They would see right through a cop's cover. "Will you be interviewing Manny?"

Charlie smiled. "Oh, yeah. He's top on my list."

Once Charlie had finished with his interrogation, Jean Luc would visit himself to find out the truth. After all, Charlie had no inkling of what to ask.

Jean Luc watched a very irritated police detective peel away from Manny's establishment. He would wait a few more minutes before approaching the restaurant.

He rested his head against the car seat and closed his eyes. He was tired, as much as a vampire could be tired, and he longed for a moment of quiet. However, instead of silence, he was being serenaded by his partner, who, if he was not mistaken was whistling the theme song from one of the multitude of television shows he regularly devoured, memorized and then trotted out to fill every quiet moment.

"Misha, may I have a moment of peace, *s'il vous plait?*"

The whistling stopped.

Jean Luc took several deep breaths. Why did he continue doing this work? Another dead body. Another case of a supernatural risking exposure to humans. Another lie he must fabricate to conceal the truth. A century of the same issues, of moving back and forth across the country, unable to build a sense of permanence. Misha and he had only been living in Indianapolis for a couple of months. Nicholas had reassigned them to Indiana a week before the killings started. Which was a very significant coincidence, and Jean Luc didn't believe in coincidence. But until they found the killer, he would table the list of questions he had for his boss.

"What is wrong, my friend?" Misha asked, his deep Russian accent rumbling in the close quarters of the car.

"Nothing. We should go see Manny now."

Misha shook his head slightly. "You may be older than I am, vampire, but it does not mean you're a good liar."

Jean Luc turned to issue a retort, but instead quirked a brow at his teammate. He had not paid attention to the demon's outfit earlier. He was wearing a white suit with a turquoise t-shirt and shoes with no socks. Did he dare ask him why he was dressed this way? No, ignorance was truly bliss when it came to Misha's peculiarities. And he was glaring at him as only a stubborn Russian could.

Jean Luc blew out a breath in defeat. "These murders worry me. I have not seen this kind of blatant disregard for exposure of our kind in centuries." Not since The Wars, and that was not a subject Jean Luc wished to discuss.

"Do you have a theory yet?"

"No. And I have arrived at the crime scenes too long after the killer left to sense any residual energy which might reveal what type of supernatural we are pursuing." He reached for the door handle. "Shall we go in?"

They climbed out of the car and were greeted at the restaurant door by Manny's version of a host. He loomed as tall as Misha, who stood six feet six inches, and his neck was as big around as Jean Luc's waist.

"Welcome to Manuelo's."

Jean Luc glanced around the restaurant. "We would like to speak with Manny."

The behemoth crossed his arms over his broad chest. "Sorry, he's not available right now."

A door behind the host's counter opened and a short, portly man appeared. "It's okay, Jacob, I'll take it from here." He gestured them to a corner booth.

Once they were seated, he smiled and said, "I'm Manny, and you must be the new team Nicholas assigned to the city."

"How did you know?" asked Misha.

He shrugged. "Vampires and demons don't normally mix, so I put two and two together."

"Then you also know we are here to discuss Peter's murder," Jean Luc said.

Manny frowned. "I can't believe Peter's dead. The cops wouldn't tell me what happened."

"Peter was killed by a supernatural."

"Damn."

"What can you tell us?" Misha interjected.

"Same things I told the cops. I don't know who would want to kill him. He was a good employee and got along with everyone."

Jean Luc tuned into the flow of Manny's blood, listening to his heartbeat, which remained slow and steady. "What about one of your clients who might hold a grudge?"

Manny's eyes narrowed for a moment, as if he was trying to decide how much to say. "Peter didn't deal directly with my *customers*. He worked in the back room and balanced the books."

"Did he know about supernaturals? That you are a shifter?"

"Nope. We're careful here. Our human employees don't have a clue."

Jean Luc opened the restaurant door. Dusk cast a light orange hue over the street as the sun sank beneath the skyline.

Misha walked around him toward the car. "Well, that was a bust. It reminds me of a recent episode of *Magnum, P.I.* Magnum questioned this guy who had stolen..."

The tingling started again, traveling lightly up Jean Luc's spine, and Misha's voice faded away. He would swear he sensed a fledgling, but it was not possible. Vampires were required to register with them when entering their jurisdiction. And there were no new vampires under the age of fifty currently living in the city.

He looked across the street, studying the area illuminated by the neon sign advertising the Gentleman's Club. But unlike the refined gentleman's clubs Jean Luc had frequented centuries ago, the name now represented something seedy, sordid.

He surveyed the immediate area. No one stood outside the club, and the windows were covered with thick curtains. The street appeared to be empty.

But someone was watching.

AUTHOR'S NOTE

This story takes place in Cleveland and while I tried to stay as accurate to the city as possible, I did bend the truth slightly in order for the story to work. For example, there is a scene in the story that takes place in the locker area of the city's train station. In real life, there is no locker area in the Cleveland train station. And the office building that the team works in and the warehouses that they frequent throughout the story do not actually exist. Please forgive this author for taking creative license with this and some of the other items concerning the wonderful city of Cleveland.

ACKNOWLEDGMENTS

Wow, where to begin? The writing and publication of this book has been such a rollercoaster ride for me. And I have countless people to thank.

Let me start off with my town's small but mighty writers' group that I joined several years ago. I remember the first time I went to a meeting. My hands shook and I started to sweat profusely as I read my story out loud for the first time. Thank you for your suggestions and encouragement as you read my books chapter by revised chapter.

Thanks to my friends and beta readers, Audrey, Helen, Jayne, Karen, Lara, Ruth and Trish. You have been my support system throughout this and I could not have gotten here without you.

To my local writer's chapter, NEORWA, what a wonderful group you are. I have learned so much and found new friends who are not afraid to announce that they hear voices in their heads like I do.

To my friend and critique partner, Becky Lower, thank you for everything and for allowing me to follow in your published writer footsteps. Your late night calls have made all the difference!

To my editor, Faith, who has made this process as painless as editing can hope to be. I am so relieved that you get my humor and patiently answer my numerous questions!

To my cover artist, Melissa. Thank you for taking on the task of redoing this cover. You knocked it out of the ballpark on the first try with this one—this is Kyle to a T!

Finally, to my family who didn't think I was silly at all when I announced I wanted to be a writer. Instead they argued over having characters named after them in my stories (You got your wish, Dad!). Thanks for never doubting that I could do this even when I doubted it myself.

ABOUT THE AUTHOR

Growing up a TV junkie, AE Jones oftentimes rewrote endings of episodes in her head when she didn't like the outcome. She immersed herself in sci-fi and soap operas. But when *Buffy* hit the little screen, she knew her true love was paranormal. Now she spends her nights weaving stories about all variations of supernatural—their angst and their humor. After all, life is about both...whether you sport fangs or not.

AE won the prestigious Golden Heart® Award for her paranormal manuscript, Mind Sweeper, which also was a RITA® finalist for both First Book and Paranormal Romance. AE is also a recipient of the Booksellers' Best Award and is a National Readers' Choice Award Finalist, Holt Award of Merit Finalist and a Daphne du Maurier Finalist.

AE lives in Ohio surrounded by her eclectic family and friends who in no way resemble any characters in her books. *Honest.* Now her two cats are another story altogether.

Learn more about AE and her books on her website ae-jonesauthor.com

58361337R00202